Seventh Crossing

JULIANA ANDREW

Inquiries and Book Orders should be addressed to:

Great Writers Media
Email: info@greatwritersmedia.com
Phone: 877-600-5469

ISBN: 978-1-960605-29-0 (sc)
ISBN: 978-1-960605-28-3 (ebk)

With love to
My Sister Shirley
And
In remembrance of
My Father Bert Hebert
My Mother Isabel
My sister Myra
Brother Vern
Brother Dale
And my Beloved Husband Roy

Also by Juliana
Vienna
The Curse of the Infinity Bracelets
The Ladies of Avanloch
The Arcadia Project
Beyond the Yellow Doors
November Queen

Author Photograph
Karren Almstrom-Dixon

CONTENTS

CHAPTER 1

Kings Crossing
Revelation

Marsha turned off the kitchen light and collected her purse and briefcase and called to me that she was leaving for the McMann's. "If Hilary or Vivian phone tell them they can reach me on my cell. See you later; don't stay up all night reading that brief."

I sighed and reached for the folder that had been couriered to me. I decided to refresh my drink before scanning what was bound to be a mind-numbing read and went to the refrigerator for ice. The wall phone squawked. I let the answering machine get it.

"Hey Jess, Sam Blier here; sorry I missed you. I was hoping to touch base with you…"

I cursed as the ice machine jammed and then spewed chunks everywhere but in the glass. I reached for the phone. "You got me Sam. Sorry, I was just having a disagreement with the refrigerator. God, it's good to hear from you. I hope you're calling to say that you and CC are coming for a visit?"

"Wish it was Jess. Truth of the matter is, I was hoping for a little legal advice."

"You haven't gotten yourself into trouble have you Buddy?"

"It's not for me Jess, but an old friend. She may just require a good lawyer, and we're pretty sure that she won't get an unbiased one in this part of the country."

"Why's that Sam?"

"It's a high profile case; family has ties to the town that go back more than a century. No one is going to want to step into this, so I thought if worst comes to worst you may be able to steer us in the right direction of a good criminal attorney."

"I must have heard of this prominent family, right? What's the nature of the crime?"

"Murder…sorry Jess, the girls just drove up so gotta go. I'll see what transpires before I bother you anymore."

"Murder, Jeeze Sam, and it's no bother." I realized that I was talking to a dead line. I placed the receiver back in its cradle and went into my office and opened the computer. I typed in Kings Crossing B.C. wondering if anything would even show up. Something did. I scanned down the page that popped up. It was impossible to miss the name Lacey King.

I took some deep breaths until my heart rhythm returned to a tolerable level before reading the headline:

Murder in Kings Crossing

Former resident Arthur King, playwright and entrepreneur, was found dead in his mother's home on Wednesday, May 18. He had returned from New York to attend to his mother Hilda King's affairs as she was in poor health. However, she passed away before he arrived. Lacey King, the former Lacey Monroe of Kings Crossing and wife of Arthur King, is reported to have discovered the body. The R.C.M.P is not commenting on the nature of the death, but they are not ruling out foul play. An inquest is underway and a forensic unit and criminologist have been called in.

I closed the computer. Wasn't that the way things always happened? Just when everything was running like clockwork a wrench entered the picture and screwed everything up. Only in my case there was nothing to screw up because my life was already at a crossroads. I was bored silly with my law practice. One could only handle so many personal injury cases before they became predictable. I had no personal life beside the usual neighbourhood block parties and obligatory office socials. The girls were in Victoria attending university so that left me and Marsha alone in an empty house. It should be the best times of our lives; no financial worries and no health problems. We should be out travelling the world, but she had her wedding planning business and had no desire to give it up. I didn't blame her as she had been the long suffering woman who had supported me through all the ups and downs of my career. We never said "I love you" anymore, and there certainly wasn't any passion in the boudoir. I had already moved into the spare bedroom. Hell, I was bored…bored with a capitol B!

Lacey Monroe…how long had it been? I didn't even have to close my eyes to picture her. She was fifteen when we first met; I was sixteen. We had lived in the same town all our lives, but she lived across town and we had attended different grade schools so we had never met. My sister Chloe had invited six girls over for a sleep-over to celebrate their first year of high school and Lacey was one of them. I remember almost colliding with her in the hallway as she had come running out of Chloe's room en route to the one and only upstairs bathroom. She brushed by me as if being chased by the devil. I could have left to use the facility downstairs but chose not to as I could hear her gagging. I had knocked on my sister's door and asked her if she had been practising being bartender again. I told her that she was going to poison someone someday. She had snarled and told me to mind my own business, but when Lacey came out of the bathroom white as a ghost, she realized that her initiation concoction had been anything but harmless. Chloe had apologized profusely. Lacey had accepted her apology but begged out of the sleepover. I offered to give her a ride home, and that was the beginning of our three year relationship. There was no one else for either of us.

It had all fallen apart the summer of 1975. Rumours were circulating like wildfire when I had returned from Vancouver. I had been searching for an apartment for Lacey and me as I had every intention that she would come and live with me while I attended university, but it never came to pass. I had listened to the gossip that she had been cheating on me. She denied it all, but I chose not to believe her and committed the ultimate sin by consoling myself with Lacey's best friend Mavis. By the time I realized the error of my ways and wanted Lacey back, it was too late… she could not forgive me. Nothing had happened, but Mavis would not deny it. I never knew if she was punishing me for the way I had treated Lacey or if she wanted me for herself. It didn't matter because the girl I thought I would grow old with ran off and married the town's rich boy, Arthur King.

Now, twenty four years later we would both be back in Kings Crossing. It didn't seem right that Arthur's death would reunite us. I trembled thinking she might still hate me.

I picked up the phone and called Marsha. She was more than a little surprised to be hearing that I was leaving town for a few days. It wasn't like me to just up and leave on a moment's notice. She said that she hadn't even heard me mention Sam Blier's name in years. I told her I would call her when I knew what was happening. She told me to drive safely and hung up.

I pulled an overnight bag down from the top shelf and tossed it on the bed. Thinking that I might need more than one change of clothes, I opted for a suitcase instead. I had told Marsha that I planned on being on the road by 5:30 a.m. the next morning. I was pretty sure that I would have a restless sleep, but in fact it was just the opposite and I slept peacefully awaking before the alarm went off.

I checked the weather report for the Cariboo area and found that it was going to be a sunny warm day just as it should be for May 21st. I was glad to put the rain behind me as I turned off at the junction for the Cariboo Hiway. Kings Crossing had once been known simply as Cross Roads. Richard King arrived from England in 1859 to look the country over. He liked what he saw and there were rumours of gold in the hills to the north. He purchased a large parcel of land that was off the worn wagon trail that bordered on a small tributary to the Fraser and Thompson Rivers. It was on high ground and he hoped that someday it would host a township. He had the finances and the fortitude to turn a desolate property into something grand. Labourers flocked to Cross Roads hoping to be hired on by the man that was rumoured to be paying triple what every other employer was. While a three room cabin was being built for him, he had a small stage coach stop erected. Soon barns and a roadhouse were constructed to accommodate overnighters that included prospectors, fur traders, settlers and travellers on their way further north. Two years later at the height of the Cariboo Gold Rush, a store, church, post office and telegraph station were fully operational. Land was offered for sale at $2.00 an acre and families arrived to start farming and ranching. A one room schoolhouse was raised to accommodate the growing number of children. Cross Roads was one of a number of roadhouses that sprang up along the Cariboo Wagon Road. Many had names such as 70 Mile House, 100 Mile house, 125 Mile House; the mileage denoting the distance they were from Lillooet. Many roadhouses went under or changed ownership continuously, but Richard King's endeavours endured the hardships of an uncertain future. In 1872 he enticed Elizabeth Love, a woman from a prominent Victoria family to marry him. She bore him three sons before she packed her bags and left taking the youngest child, Mitchell with her. Years later Mitchell returned to his father's fold with a degree in economics and it was he who changed the name of the settlement from Cross Roads to Kings Crossing. There had not been a time when there wasn't a King involved one way or the other in the town's politics. I thought that might not be the case anymore as it appeared as though the Kings were a dying breed and there was no one left to take up the reigns of the dynasty. I was forgetting someone though and that was Lacey, and hadn't Sam told me once that she and Arthur had a child?

Five hours later I pulled up alongside the curb at the Blier residence. "Hell," I said out loud. "I don't even know if they still live here." Then I saw the license plate 'Can Can' on the little orange Volkswagen and I laughed. That was Candida Canary Blier's personal plate. She could never live down the jokes about her name and so she made the most of it. Everyone just called her CC. I heard laughter and music emanating from the back yard. I assumed that CC was engaged in one of her dance classes. I was wrong.

I rounded the corner and was met with a scene that I hadn't seen since the second grade. There was a tall green stake in the middle of the yard with colourful ribbons streaming down from it. A dozen or more children and one adult were holding hands and bobbing up and down with the rhythm of the music as they danced around the pole. I stepped back into the shadows realizing the elder sprite was Lacey. I was captivated by their joyfulness and was mesmerized by Lacey's grace. I watched the merriment for several minutes until Lacey suddenly stopped and her followers crashed into one another, some falling to the ground. I realized that she had spotted me. She gathered the children and sent them over to a picnic table covered with papers and told them to finish their drawings. She walked over to where I was standing; she did not seem pleased to see me. Before she could utter a word I applauded.

"Bravo! Hello Lace, I didn't know they had resurrected the May Pole, but I must say that I'm glad to see it has made a comeback." I hoped she would appreciate my enthusiasm, but I could see by the look on her face that she was not happy.

"What are you doing here Jesse?" She demanded.

Well, she still called me Jesse and not Jess… that was a good sign, wasn't it? "Just stopped by to visit with old friends… is that all right with you?"

"I don't think that is the reason you are here at all. If you came to see how I was handling the situation you can see I am doing just fine so you can turn around and go back to where you came from. I'm going to kill Sam for calling you; the courts may as well have a two-for-one trial!" She fumed.

"I may as well confess, but as usual, you have the facts all wrong. Sam called me for some legal advice; he never mentioned your name. I had to get the story from the internet. Now, do you want to stand here and rant, or will you let me help you?"

"I have the facts wrong…well, that's a good one coming from the man who wouldn't know the truth if it bit him in the ass! I don't need your help Jesse; I haven't even been accused yet. It's not in your best interest to be here. It won't do you or your career any good to be involved in what will probably turn into a three ring circus."

"How about you let me be the judge of that? I didn't come as a curiosity seeker, but as a concerned friend. I would do the same for anyone." I realized what I had said and apologized.

"I didn't mean it that way Lace. Hell, I've only been here two minutes and I have already alienated you. Can we sit, and will you tell me all that has happened?"

"I mean it Jess, I don't want you involved. You should say hello to Sam and CC and leave."

"I think I will pay my respects as here they are, but I'll be around for a while…just saying."

CC almost dropped her pitcher of Kool-Aid when she saw me standing beside Lacey. "Did you call him Sam?" She said to her husband through clenched teeth as they walked down the steps to the yard.

Sam ignored her and placed the treats and paper cups in front of the kids. He walked over to me and shook my hand. "What a surprise! To what do we owe the pleasure old man?"

Lacey lashed out at him. "Are you really going to play the dumb card Sam? You had no business calling Jess! He has nothing to do with any of this!"

Sam smiled at the tongue lashing. Before he could exonerate himself CC stepped in. She gave me a big hug and said that under any other circumstances she would be glad to see me, but it was obvious that Lacey didn't want me here and perhaps I should leave.

"Nonsense CC, we will make ourselves scarce and you and Lacey can continue on with the children. I don't know about you Jess, but I could sure use a drink." Sam suggested.

"Go on with you two then. Lacey and I will finish up here." CC said not too happily.

I started to follow Sam but decided to say something first. "Don't be angry with Sam, Lacey; it really was my own doing… coming here. For what it's worth, I am sorry about the death of your husband."

She snapped at me. "He was not my husband! Perhaps it's time you enlightened your friend Sam as you seem to know what is best for me!"

She walked away towards the children and CC shot daggers at her husband. "Yes, perhaps you should Sam! Have your little drink and then vacate the premises. See what you have left me to deal with now? We've just got her calmed down and now this…" She shook her head and shot daggers at me.

"CC, there is no reason to be angry with Sam…"

"Leave her be Jess, she'll come around later. Now, how about that drink…"

I followed Sam up the steps to the back door glancing down at Lacey. She did not lift her head in my direction. Sam grabbed a pitcher of what appeared to be ice tea from the refrigerator and directed me to the living room. We sat across from each other in a private nook at the far corner of the room. Sam passed a glass of amber liquid to me. I took one sip and grinned.

"I see that CC still likes a little tea in her gin."

"Yeah, nothing has changed there. It's been a long time Jess; I don't even know where to start."

"At the beginning Sam, start at the beginning. I have a feeling that we are going back some twenty four years…am I right?"

"That we are my friend. I've let sleeping dogs lie as both of you appeared to be reasonably happy, but no one was more shocked when you and Lacey called it quits, but the real shocker was when she ran off with Arthur King. What I am about to tell you doesn't leave this room unless it has some bearing on exonerating Lacey…are you all right with that?"

"It's my job as a lawyer to keep confidences and if it involves Lacey, you can be sure I will. She is the reason I am here after all."

"I never thought the day would come when I would be telling you this, but who the hell would have ever dreamt that Arthur would be murdered in his own home; well, technically it was his mother's home, or that dear sweet Lacey would be the one to find him?" It was more a statement than a question. "Anyhow, back to square one. There are only a handful of people who know this; CC and me, Lacey, James, and of course Richie, and now you. That's not to say that half the population of New York doesn't know, but they could care less and are not at all involved in this mess."

"I have no idea who James and Richie are. Do they have any bearing on the story? Come on man, spit it out."

"Sorry; okay, James is Lacey's son and Richie is …was Arthur's partner, and I do mean partner…not only in business, but in life. We all had doubts about Arthur's sexuality and I suppose he was the brunt of our stupid jokes, but he was a good friend to all, and the girls loved him. Well, that theory was awash when he and Lacey went off and eloped…or so we thought. Truth of the matter is that they made a pact; she would marry him to hide his secret that he was gay, and he would marry her to give her baby a name and give his mother a grandchild." Sam stopped talking to let me process what he had just told me.

I put my drink down on the table. "Are you saying what I think you are Sam? Are you telling me that Lacey was pregnant when we broke up? If Arthur isn't the father then who is? Is it me Sam? Am I Lacey's son's father?"

"First of all, Lacey has never said that you are James's father… never. After we found out the truth about Arthur she kind of let us believe without saying so that she didn't know who the father was, and you had accused her of cheating on you, so…Anyhow, we didn't find out about Arthur until James was about ten. He talked too much about Uncle Richie and all the things the three of them did together, and so we discussed it with Lacey. She confessed that Arthur was and always had been gay and he certainly was not James's biological father."

"You know James…Christ, she named him James; didn't that set off any alarms?"

"Yeah, sure it did, but maybe she just liked the name and maybe it's just a coincidence that your middle name is James and your last name is Jameson. As far as ole lady King knew, James was her grandson and she doted on him as any grandmother would and she adored Lacey. Now and then she would make the trip out to the east coast until about seven years ago when her health went downhill. Arthur and Lacey lived separately so I have no idea how that worked."

"Really, just a coincidence Sam? Why didn't she divorce him and remarry? Why didn't she tell me she was pregnant?"

"You'll have to ask her that yourself Jess."

"You saw her hostility towards me and so I doubt if I will be having that conversation with her. Just out of curiosity, does James look anything like me?"

"I think I see a little of you in him, but maybe that is just wishful thinking."

"Why would you wish that Sam?"

"Maybe because I think everyone has the right to know their biological parents."

"So you do believe that I am James's father, and you want me to come right out and ask her... is that what you are saying Sam? Well, she hates me and so she is going to laugh in my face and ask me what I've been smoking."

Sam laughed. "Yeah, I think you may be right about that, but it's obvious that she wanted you to know or else why would she tell me to enlighten you?"

"I don't know Sam. I won't lie to you, I have thought about her from time to time and from the moment I saw her name in the Crossing headline I felt a rush that I haven't felt for a very long time. Then I saw her dancing with the children and my heart skipped a beat. That shouldn't be happening, not after so many years. I am not sure what to do about it. Maybe I should just take her advice and go home."

CC knocked on the open door. "You're in charge of Haney, Sam. The rest of the kids have gone home. I'm taking Lacey to the police station as she wants to see if she is allowed to go to Tudor House now."

I jumped up. "Let me take her CC; I can see that her rights are protected."

"Oh no Jess, that is not a good idea."

"Is she waiting in your car? Throw me the keys please."

"Sam, help me here…"

"Jess is right Honey, he knows about procedure. Give him the keys and we'll deal with the consequences later."

CC surrendered her car keys. "I have a bad feeling about this but I will trust you to handle her with kid gloves. If it goes well with her, I want the two of you back here for dinner. Call us and let us know what happens." She gave me a hug and said her fingers were crossed.

Lacey did not notice me taking the driver's seat as she was engrossed in reading the latest edition of the Crossing's newspaper. As soon as I started to adjust the seat, she turned and seeing me lashed out again. "What the hell do you think you're doing?"

"Accompanying you to the police station my dear; give me a dollar and we'll make it legal."

"I will not and I am not your dear! If you think you can intimidate me with your legal mumbo jumbo you are sadly mistaken. Now get out; I'll drive myself."

I smiled at her. "That's my job…intimidating people and I am pretty damn good at it. Now, about that dollar…"

"Screw you Jesse Jameson!"

Her hand was on the door handle. I put my hand on her shoulder. "Think about it Lace; I know my way around and I can procure information while protecting your rights…up to you, and I will even waive the dollar fee."

She took her hand off the door while brushing my hand off with the other. She reached into her purse. "Here's your damn dollar, but just for today. If I need a lawyer it's not going to be you!"

Neither of us spoke again until I signalled to turn the corner at 12th and Vine.

"Where are you going?" She asked belligerently.

"To the cop shop of course; have you changed your mind about going there?"

"You really have been gone a long time haven't you? They built a new R.C.M.P headquarters on Piccadilly Drive years ago. It's one block up from Londonderry Bridge."

"Well, I'll be damned; the city fathers finally went along with naming the town and everything in it after their sister city in England did they? You're right though, I haven't been back for a long time. It would appear that everything has changed…except you. You are still the same… except a little more cantankerous."

"Thank-you, I will take that as a compliment because I was too wishy-washy before." Lacey turned her face to the window and I was pretty sure she was smiling.

I pulled the car into the visitor's parking lot and before I could even engage the parking gear Lacey was out and heading up the steps. I had to run to catch up to her.

"Are you going to let me do the talking?"

"You may not need to." She said hello to the officer behind the desk.

"Good afternoon Ms. King. How are you today, and how can I assist you?" He was a young man of about thirty and I was sure he'd be calling his superior for instructions.

"Despite the circumstances, I am well Constable Jones; thank-you for asking. My son and his family and Mr. King's business partner will be arriving soon, and so I would like to prepare the Tudor House for their arrival. Your constabulary has confiscated my keys to the house. I would like to have them returned. I believe they have had ample time to inspect the house and can see no reason why I cannot take up residence there. Is there any problem with that?" I was impressed with Lacey's calm but authoritative voice.

"We have been expecting that you would be dropping by. I am pleased to inform you that you are free to take up residence at the Tudor House. It has been affirmed that it is not part of the investigation, at least for the time being. Canterbury House is still cordoned off and entrance is denied until after the forensic team has completed their investigation. We do want to advise you however that the team may want to do their own search of the Tudor House, so they may be contacting you. Constable Jones opened a drawer and handed Lacey a large envelope. "Is there anything else I can help you with today Ma'am?"

Lacey thanked him and left. I smiled at the young constable and handed him my business card. "Any further meetings with Ms. King can be made through me. I can be reached at this number day or night. Have a nice day."

I heard Constable Jones say in a hushed voice to the officer sitting next to him just before I walked out. "I see Ms. King has hired herself a lawyer. It would seem as though she expects to be charged in her husband's death. How do you think a personal injury lawyer is going to be of any help to her?"

"I guess time will tell." Jones answered.

I wondered how he knew that personal injury was my field.

In the car, Lacey asked me for her dollar back.

"Not so fast young lady, we need to talk." I put the car in reverse and started to back up.

"We have nothing to discuss Jesse."

"I am now officially your attorney whether you like it or not, so I need to know the facts starting with the moment you discovered Arthur's body."

"And whether you like it or not, if I am charged, I do not need to keep you as my lawyer. I fail to see how you could defend me anyhow, not that it will ever come to that, because you do not practice criminal law." Lacey stated affirmatively.

I stopped the car and put it in drive and pulled up to the curb again. I wanted to be able to see Lacey's reaction when I asked the next question. "Do you know for a fact that I have never defended someone accused of murder before?"

She didn't answer me.

"Well, for your information, I have, and quite successfully too, I might add. Now, are we going to talk or not?"

"I was under the impression that Sam told you everything?"

"We only discussed your 'non marriage.' And, while we are on that subject, I want you to tell me who the father of your son is."

Lacey was out the door before the last word was out of my mouth. "We are done here." She uttered in an incensed voice. She slammed the door and stormed off down the road.

"Yup, I've got a live one on my hands." I smiled as I watched my former sweetheart strut down the sidewalk. I waited until she was out of sight and drove off in the opposite direction. I figured it would take her about fifteen minutes to get to the King residence…well, maybe ten at the pace she was walking. I decided to familiarize myself with the layout of the town I had called home for the first nineteen years of my life. Nothing much had changed except the names of the streets. I drove by the old neighbourhood and was pleased to see my old family home still standing and children playing in the front yard. Next I went by the high school which had been enlarged and then Lacey's sister's house where we had first become lovers. I shouldn't be thinking of such things, but how does one turn off a memory? I wondered if her sister Connie still lived there.

I passed Lacey as I drove down Knight Street. I put the car in low range as I reached the short hill that marked the entrance to Tudor House. I parked in the circular drive at the front of the stately home. If I remembered correctly, the house had been built to resemble an English mansion from centuries ago. It was the house Arthur's great grandfather had constructed himself. He was also the King that changed the town's name. The outside was still in immaculate condition and the inside probably was too. The lawns needed tending to and perhaps I could see to that later. I laughed and asked myself if I really thought I'd still be here in a few hours. I leaned up against the car and waited for a breathless Lacey to arrive. She ignored me and walked haughtily past me. I wasn't going to be put off by her impudence and followed her around to the back yard and found her trying to unlock the door. Her hands were shaking and she was cursing under her breath. I put my hand on top of hers. Together, we turned the key and entered the kitchen. The house was cold and Lacey shivered. She went immediately to the thermostat and turned it up and threw the keys and her purse on the counter.

"Do you want to warm up before we start?" I asked her.

"What do you mean… start?" She asked gruffly.

"Inspecting the house of course; what's down here?" I pointed to a locked door.

"Just the furnace and storage rooms. The police already searched the house so there is no need to do it again." She started to walk away.

"Suit yourself, but I want to check it out for myself."

I had only been in the house half a dozen times and when you are young, you don't pay much attention to the layout of the house, but I remembered being impressed. Now, I fully appreciated the grandeur of the highly ornate interior. Where there was no carpeting, the floors shone as if they had just been buffed. The main floor consisted of the oversized kitchen which had a small dining area and a separate laundry room and pantry, a large formal dining room, a family room, a den with a library and a spacious living room which overlooked the town of Kings

Crossing. All of the doors were opened except one at the end of the long hallway that separated the living room from the rest of the house. I asked Lacey, who had followed me silently from room to room, what was behind the door. She reached around me and opened it.

"It used to be the maids' room or butlers', who knows. It was Hilda's companion's room, but when Hilda could no longer manoeuvre the stairs they exchanged quarters. I thought you were a lawyer, but you're acting more like a detective?"

I smiled at her and after checking the closets, I proceeded up the main stairs. There were six bedrooms, each with their own bathrooms, two linen closets and French doors that opened unto a veranda that overlooked the neglected gardens and mountains to the southeast and the town to the west. Satisfied, I started down the back stairs that came out in the kitchen.

"See, I told you everything was okay; you can go now." Lacey said coolly.

I turned around and smiled again. "I'll collect your luggage; which room is yours?"

"You don't need to know that. Just leave it at the door on your way out."

"You're persistent, I'll give you that, but if you think being petulant will get rid of me, you have another thing coming. When I get back, you are going to reiterate the events of Tuesday so you may as well make yourself comfortable." I shut the door before she could respond. When I returned with her luggage she was still standing in the same spot.

She stormed off to the family room and plopped down on an oversized armchair gathering her legs under her. I followed her and pulled up a chair opposite her.

"Why you want to know the gruesome details is beyond me… unless that's how you get your kicks. You didn't believe me twenty four years ago, so I doubt you'll believe me now."

Before I had a chance for rebuttal, she jumped up.

"How rude of me, I haven't even offered you a drink."

"Honey, you have been nothing but rude to me from the moment you first laid eyes on me, but as you can see, I am not easily insulted."

"What's your poison; there is whiskey, bourbon and everything else under the sun?"

"I'll have whatever you are having. I guess we won't need any ice though will we?"

Without saying another word she picked up the crystal ice bowl and stormed into the kitchen. She returned to the living room and carried on as if she had never left, told me that she was having club soda and if I hadn't had enough ice, she had more.

"I'll have the same as you, thank-you. I can take a little ice, but don't overdo it."

She handed me my glass and our hands brushed ever so slightly. I waited until she was seated cross-legged again. "Lacey, I know you will never be able to forgive me for my actions and accusations years ago…I was wrong, and I tried to make it up to you, but you wanted nothing more to do with me, and I don't blame you for that. However, in my own defense, I was not unfaithful to you with Mavis. She was your best friend; I never cared for her in any way what so ever. I was a lot of things, but I would never have done that to you. It was probably her that started all the ugly gossip that made me doubt you and it is high time that she comes clean about the whole mess. There was nothing in it for her and there certainly isn't now. Do you have any idea where she is?"

"As far as I know, she is pushing up daisies somewhere in hell, so if you are looking for a confession, one will not be forthcoming."

"So that is that then, and you will go on condemning me forever… is that right?"

"Jesse, it makes no difference to me one way or the other. I really just don't care. The past is dead and gone and what happened then has no bearing on today."

She did not look at me when she talked and I was pretty sure that she was still harbouring feelings of betrayal. I'd have to let it go for now. Winning her trust today was the only concern right now. She was putting on a brave front, but I could see she was worried.

"Perhaps and perhaps not, but we will put that aside for now. Do I need a tape recorder?"

"This is not a long story. I arrived at the airport at 4:15 on Tuesday, May the 18th. My connecting flight from Kamloops was early and so I called a cab as Arthur was not answering his cell phone. I tried the numbers at both Tudor and Canterbury Houses. The driver offered to take my bags into the house but I told him that I didn't know where I was staying yet so he could just leave them in the driveway…big mistake on my part. I noticed the front door was slightly open…"

I interrupted her. "Sorry Lace; but you knew that Arthur might be at Canterbury?"

"Yes, he was staying there as he was looking for a copy of Hilda's will and it wasn't in the safe at the big house, so he was hoping it was somewhere in the carriage house."

"How much was the door open?"

"It was only slightly ajar."

"Thanks; go on."

"I called out to Arthur as I took my shoes off and placed them on the rubber mat on the entrance rug… no, that's not right; the mats weren't there, so I just left them in the corner. Arthur didn't answer me. I could hear music coming from down the hall and I called out again as I went in the direction of it. I had only gone a few steps when I realized that my feet were soaking wet. I thought that Arthur must have just had the carpet cleaned. I could feel what I thought was the residue of soap oozing out of my stockings. I picked one foot up and was startled to see red beads dripping off it. A few more steps and I was at the den door. At first I didn't see Arthur as an overturned chair was blocking my vision, and his body was partly concealed by the desk. The carpet in the hall is dark brown and so I hadn't realized that the substance my feet had been absorbing was not dirty water but something else entirely. It was quite obvious when I looked down at the floor and seen that the mushroom coloured carpet of the den had patches of red. Arthur was lying face down on the now scarlet rug. My first impulse was that he may still be alive and I turned him over and saw the knife protruding from his abdomen..." Lacey quit talking; she was reliving the scene over again and was understandably distraught.

I reached out to her but she did not acknowledge the gesture. "Jesus, I am sorry Lace. Do you want to take a break? How about I fix you something stronger to drink?"

"No, I want to finish." She uncoiled herself and placed her feet on the floor and then quickly withdrew them and placed them under her again. I wondered if she was having visions of blood bubbling through her toes again. She continued. "I guess I stepped back, and I honestly don't know if I screamed or not. If I did, it was silent because I didn't hear a thing… only that unnerving music. And then, as I bent down to see if Arthur was still breathing I put my hand on the knife and I heard a voice yelling at me from the hall. "Don't touch it Lacey!" But, it was too late, and I pulled the knife out and flung it away from his body."

I was hoping I had misunderstood her. "Tell me I heard you wrong Lacey…tell me you didn't put your hands on the knife? Tell me that your fingerprints are not all over it?"

"They are, all ten of them, and when they put them into their data base they will find that they match the ones already on record for when I was busted for possession of marijuana."

I thought she was trying to make light of a most alarming revelation. "I'm glad you can joke about it Lace, but really, do you expect me to believe you were arrested for carrying weed?"

"Doesn't much matter what you believe does it Jess? But, it's true; I bought it for my daughter-in-law, and I would do it again in a heartbeat."

She got up and said that she was going to take a bath and I could do whatever I fancied.

"Christ All Mighty Lace, what's the matter with you? You could be facing life threatening charges and you pass it off as it was an everyday occurrence. I saw how traumatized you were as you were reliving the murder scene so I know you have the sense to be scared." I grabbed her arm. "Now sit down and tell me why you bought marijuana for your daughter-in-law?"

To my surprise she answered instead of telling me to mind my own business. "Blythe has fibromyalgia and smoking pot seemed to alleviate her pain for a little while. Before she found a doctor who would prescribe it James and I would procure it for her. However, she has since been diagnosed with rheumatoid arthritis and her and James and the children are in Virginia Beach where she is taking part in a clinical study. They are testing new drugs for their effectiveness in treating the disorder. The drugs seem to be working, but I wouldn't expect you to know anything about the debilitating effects of the disease. Now, I am going to take a bath."

I couldn't help myself. "So, I have grandchildren?"

Lacey sighed and shook her head. "Are you at it again? I thought we had reached an understanding? There is no 'you' in the picture."

"We haven't even come close to reaching an understanding, and the sooner you come clean the sooner we can move forward. Go have your bath and I will see what I can find to make us to eat. We have only begun to scratch the surface of the events of Tuesday, so enjoy your soak because we are going to be right back at it until I am satisfied you have told me everything I need to know. And, by the way, I know a lot about all kinds of arthritis. I have helped half a dozen people receive disability benefits; "personal injury" doesn't just refer to accidents."

Her tone was condescending but I was used to it. "Imagine… a big shot lawyer who knows medicine and can also cook! Well, you won't find anything to eat in **this** house and we are not allowed in the carriage house, so good luck with that. Oh, and by the way, you wouldn't know the truth if Mother Theresa handed it to you in a box neatly tied up with a big red ribbon!"

I watched her walk away. I didn't need a ton of bricks to fall on my head; she had pretty much said in her round-about way that James was my son if I was to believe that she had never fooled around on me twenty four years ago…and I did, but I needed her to come right out and say: "Yes, Jesse, James **is** your son." I needed something stronger than soda and poured myself a generous portion of bourbon. I didn't think there was enough liquor in the house to get me through a weekend with her. So, why was I still here? She had told me to go enough times hadn't she? If I was completely honest with myself I'd have to admit that it wasn't just about me representing her. Never would I let a client berate me the way she did, so why was I putting up with it? She was a challenge, and I was enjoying my every exchange with her. I hadn't once thought about Marsha and home. I found himself whistling as I rummaged through the cupboards. Lace was right; they were empty. The phone rang just as I was about to go upstairs. I answered it.

"Jess Jameson here."

Sam was on the other end. "What's happening over there ole man? I thought she'd have thrown you out by now."

I laughed. "It's not for lack of trying, but I actually think we're making a little progress…you know, one step forward, two back."

"Yeah, I get your drift. Look, the real reason I am calling is that our son had a bit of an accident at the mill and he is at the hospital getting stitched up. CC is more upset than anyone else and she wants to know if we can postpone dinner until tomorrow night?"

"To tell you the truth Sam, I forgot all about it. No problem and tell CC not to worry. Hope your son will be all right; promise to call you later." I hung up and proceeded up the stairs. I saw a light coming from under one of the doors and surmised that it was Lacey's room. The door was open a crack and I thought I heard humming. I tapped on the door lightly and called out to her. "Lace, you were right; the cupboards are bare. I'm going to order in."

The humming ceased. "I can't hear you; I'm in the bath… come in, the door is open."

Was she inviting me into her bedroom? I stepped inside. The bathroom door was slightly ajar. "I said that you were right; I'm going to order in. What do you feel like, pizza, burgers or Chinese, or something else?"

"Shanghai Zoos has the best Chinese food. Who was on the phone?"

"Okay, Chinese it is. What should I order? Sam called; I'll tell you about it when you get out."

"You know what I like Jesse. My wallet is in my purse." The humming resumed.

Yeah, like I was going to take money from her wallet and how would I know what she liked? Did we ever even have Chinese food together, and what was with these mood swings of hers?

My daughters would call it "p.m essing" or something like that. I wondered how long it would be before Godzilla would show up again.

Back in the kitchen I found the number for the restaurant. I ordered one of everything on the menu… just to be safe. The person at the other end of the line asked me how many were in my party. I said two. She informed me that I had ordered enough food for twenty people. I replied that we would have leftovers then wouldn't we? She asked me for the address which I didn't know, only that it was the King residence on Knight Street figuring that everyone knew the house. I instructed the delivery to be sent to the back entrance. I then unlocked the door to the basement hoping to find a wine vault. I wasn't mistaken, but it was pretty much depleted except for half a dozen bottles. I assumed that Hilda must have liked her wine. I picked out the best of the lot, opened it, and left it to breathe on the kitchen counter along with the wine glasses. I heard the squeaking of a step and looked up to see Lacey descending the stairs. I wondered if she had been watching me putter around the kitchen. She had dressed in a red lounging gown. Red was her favourite color. I told myself that I shouldn't be remembering that. The years had been good to her. She was a little rounder, but it looked good on her. She wore her chestnut hair the same way I remembered it, short and wavy. She smiled at me when she reached the bottom of the stairs and for the first time today I saw a twinkle in her lavender eyes.

"I see you found the wine cellar…did you have a look around while you were down there?

"I did, and it is locked up tighter than Fort Knox."

She laughed at the reference and said that she was starving. I poured her a glass of wine and she took it from me making sure she touched my hand and I knew I was in trouble. I wanted to look away from her smiling eyes, but couldn't. The chiming of the doorbell saved me from saying something stupid. I paid the delivery boy and retrieved the two boxes from him and carried them into the dining room where I had set the table and turned on the electric fireplace. Lacey followed me bringing the wine and glasses.

"I didn't know we were expecting company." She said with an amused grin.

"We're not, but I wanted to make sure all my bases were covered."

"You always were the cautious one weren't you Jesse?"

"Obviously, not cautious enough." The words were out of my mouth before I realized what I was saying and of course, she took them to mean something.

"Is there a hidden meaning there somewhere?"

Yup, I had done it…her tone indicated that I had stepped in it again. "No, not at all; I just meant that I have made many blunders and that I don't always consider the consequences before I've weighed all the facts."

She started opening up the containers. "Do you want me to continue where I left off this afternoon?"

"I think not, let's just enjoy our dinner. After I get back from exchanging cars will be time enough. Before I forget, CC's and Sam's son had a little mishap at the mill today…I take it that means sawmill. Anyhow, that is why Sam called. He wanted to know if we could postpone our dinner with them until tomorrow night. I told him that was not a problem and that you would call CC later."

"How badly was Gary hurt and what dinner are you talking about?"

"Gary, I had forgotten his name, was getting stitches; it didn't sound like it was too serious. I'm sorry I forgot to mention that CC wanted us over for dinner. I was just going to see how things went because at the time I didn't think you would want to have dinner with me. Do you want chopsticks?"

"You know I can't make those things work, and I am too hungry to even try. Sorry, of course you wouldn't know that. Sometimes I forget that we haven't seen each other for two decades.

Shall we do as you said and see how things go before we except any invitations before I change back into Godzilla again…are you all right?"

I almost choked on the broccoli. How the hell had she known what I had been thinking earlier? I regained composure and said I was sorry I had interrupted her. She made light of it.

"I don't like broccoli either. I was just saying that I know I have been bitchy and I will apologize ahead of time for any further outbursts. Thank-you for the dinner and the wine and turning on the fire… there are a few things missing though like candles, music and flowers."

"You're not the only one who was hungry and there is no need to thank me." I decided not to comment any further. "Let's make a list and I will make a grocery run on my way back from Sam's to return CC's car. I know we need coffee."

"Okay, but do you have to take the car back to-night?"

"Probably not, but I need a change of clothes, and I need my computer and it's in my car. I think you should come with me."

"Why?"

"Because I don't want to leave you alone."

"I have been looking after myself for a very long time Jesse, and if I can in the big city, I assure you I can definitely manage here."

"Yes, I am sure you can, but at this point we don't know who is responsible for Arthur's demise, or if you are safe from that unidentified person or persons? It's easier to be cautious now than sorry later."

"I will secure the doors behind you and we have already checked all the windows so I will be perfectly fine. Does this mean that you think I am innocent?"

I was a little startled by her question. "Of course I think you are innocent! The thought never crossed my mind that you weren't."

"Why is that Jesse? You don't know me or Arthur, or anything about the lives we have been living, so you shouldn't be so sure of yourself."

"In the dream land that teenagers live in I once knew this girl who went by the name of Lacey Leigh Monroe. That girl used to pick caterpillars up off the road so they wouldn't get run over. She is sitting across from me all grown up now, and I know the only way she could commit such a crime would be to protect a loved one. No, Lacey Leigh, you did not kill Arthur."

"No, I didn't and thank-you for believing in me." We finished our meal in silence.

Lacey handed me fifty dollars for groceries as I was leaving for Sam's and the store.

"I'm not taking your money, but you can give me the house keys because I don't trust that you won't lock me out."

She knew I was trying to humour her and I had succeeded. "I can always put the deadbolt on you know?"

"Yes, I know, but then I would have to break a window and you would have to report an intruder and I would get locked up... so you see we would just be defeating the purpose of me being here." I refused her offer of money again.

"But Jesse, you're my guest."

"Is that what we are calling me now? Are you sure you won't come with me?"

She shook her head 'no' and locked the door behind me but not before she said, "Hurry back."

I looked back at the house before I climbed in behind the wheel. "What the hell am I doing?" I asked myself. "I should go home and pretend that I ever knew anyone by the name of Lacey Monroe, and perhaps I will when she sends me packing. But, what's there for me to go back to?" I drove to the Blier's reiterating in my head Lacey's account of finding Arthur's body. I asked Sam how his son was and was told that his blood pressure had plummeted and so he was spending the night in the hospital for observation. He and CC were over-nighting the kids. I declined the invitation for a drink saying that I had to make a grocery run and didn't want to leave Lacey alone for any longer than necessary. Sam asked if I was worried for her safety.

"I don't know the full story yet Sam, so I can't answer that. We only got to the part where she pulled the knife out of Arthur… I have a lot of questions and I hope she will be honest with me."

"Why do you think she did it Jess; pull the knife out I mean?"

"I don't know her reason, or why others have picked up the murder weapon. Some say they didn't remember doing so, and others say they were compelled to. You wouldn't believe the stories people concoct."

"Since when have you been in the practice of defending people accused of murder? You don't have any doubts about Lacey's innocence do you?"

"I have to think that she is innocent and by the end of the night, I hope that my assumptions will be validated. I've only defended two people accused of murder. They both started out as routine injury claims against the employer but escalated into homicides. I'll fill you in on the details sometime. Right now I need to get back to Lacey. It would be beneficial to have your input Sam, so hopefully you and CC can drop by tomorrow."

"We'll be there Buddy. Take it easy."

I rapped three times on the back door knocker of Tudor House and the devil in me made me say, "Honey, I'm home."

She opened the door with a big grin and relieved me of one of the grocery bags.

"Be right back." I said as I went back to the car for more.

"How long are you planning on staying Jesse?" She asked.

"As long as it takes." I pulled a bouquet of flowers out of one of the bags and passed it to her. "I thought these might brighten the place up a little." I didn't want her to think I had bought them especially for her.

"Yes, they will and I have the perfect vase for them."

She pulled up a chair and climbed up on it so that she could reach the top shelf.

"What do you think you're doing?" I asked even though it was quite obvious.

"You are not very perceptive for a lawyer are you?"

She found what she was looking for and handed it down to me. I took her elbow and helped her down scolding her for not using a proper step stool. She shrugged her shoulders and proceeded to cut off a piece of each flower stem under running water with large scissors before placing it in the vase. I had never paid it any mind when Marsha did it.

She was aware that I was watching her. "Have you never seen anybody do this before?"

"Sorry, I didn't mean to stare. I have a feeling it is going to be a very long night so I think I will put a pot of coffee on and I bought a blueberry pie…do you still like sweets?"

"I do, sometimes." She leaned over and peeked into the grocery bag and smiled when she saw that I had indeed bought her favourite ice cream. She said she'd pass on the coffee though as she already had a difficult time falling asleep. I told her I would make decaffeinated if she liked. We finished putting the remainder of the supplies in the fridge and cupboards. I told her to go and get comfortable in the family room and I would join her as soon as the coffee was ready. She said she would wait for me and asked what Sam had said about Gary. I filled her in while I cut the pie and she scooped generous amounts of French vanilla ice cream on top.

"Is you're wife a good cook Jesse?"

I was surprised by her question. "She doesn't have much time for it anymore, but yeah, she's a good cook."

"What does she do? Does she have a demanding job?"

I didn't want to talk about Marsha, but said bluntly. "She's a wedding coordinator."

"I've never met a wedding planner before…are they in great demand?"

"Well, she is the only one I know and she is very busy, so yes, I guess they are." I poured two cups of coffee and automatically added a dab of hazelnut cream to hers.

She put the dessert dishes on a tray and followed me into the family room.

I immediately noticed that she had started a fire. "Did you go outside for the wood Lacey?"

"No, I borrowed it from the fireplace upstairs. But, so what if I did?"

"I thought we were going to be cautious for a while?"

"I never said anything of the sort! Now quit bullying me and eat your pie and tell me about your family." She sat down on a hassock next to the fire flashing her perfectly white teeth at me and flaunting her impish dimples.

"You can only delay the inevitable so long you know Lacey, so what say we get started?" I had no desire to discuss my family with her…there was no need.

"Can I finish eating first Sir; I don't like blood and guts with my blueberries."

I picked up my coffee cup. "Thanks for the graphic image, and what's with this sir thing?"

"You kind of remind me of ole man Murray from history class."

I laughed. "Thanks for the comparison Little Miss Muffet… wasn't that his nickname for you?" I pulled a notebook out of my pocket.

"I thought you didn't need to write anything down?" Lacey laid her plate on the coffee table.

"While you were in the bathtub I jotted a few things down that I wanted to ask you. Now I believe we had just pulled the dagger out of Arthur and someone yelled at you from the hallway…"

"There **is** no **we!** The voice belonged to Hank Bernard; you remember him don't you?"

"I can't say that I do; the name doesn't sound familiar."

"Oh, of course it doesn't because you know him as Bernard Hanks!" Lacey exclaimed.

"You don't mean 'weird Bernie', do you, and what's with the name change, and why was he at the carriage house?"

"Which question do you want answered first; I already feel like I'm on the witness stand."

"Good." I picked up my cup and asked her if she wanted more. She shook her head 'no.'

I returned with a steaming cup of coffee and a bottle of Irish liqueur which I added to it. "You sure you won't change your mind?" Again she shook her head. "I'm sorry if you feel that I am bombarding you with questions, but the truth is that I haven't even started yet. This isn't easy for me either you know."

"What do you mean by that?"

"This isn't any ordinary run-of-the-mill case Lacey."

"I haven't even been charged yet, so there may very well be NO case."

"And, if you are charged, I am going to defend you. I have never had a client or a victim that I have known personally before…do you get my drift?"

"Sort of, are you saying that you might have difficulty because you once knew us?"

"YOU Lacey, not just anyone, but YOU!" I could not emphasize the 'you' enough. "I didn't **just** know you…you were my girlfriend, my first everything, and I loved you."

Lacey appeared to be moved by my confession and I could see she was fighting to hold back tears. She turned away from me. I was sure she wasn't ready for me see to see just how vulnerable she was.

"Maybe you should reconsider representing me then." She said indifferently.

I was wounded, but I wasn't a quitter. "You've been trying to get rid of me ever since I got here, and perhaps after I hear the rest of the account, I will choose not to take your case, but I hardly doubt that is going to happen. Shall we get on with it?"

Lacey asked me point blank if I ever thought of her.

I looked her straight in the eyes and said. "No Lace, I never thought about you. I left King's Crossing and I never looked back." I was lying and I was pretty sure she knew it.

She wouldn't let me see the hurt in her eyes so she looked down and continued on with the sequence of events as if she had never been interrupted. "First of all, the reason Bernard changed his name was so he wouldn't be confused with someone who shared his name and was a known felon…at least that is what I heard. He is still weird and still lives with his mother over on Railroad Street. He was riding by on his bike and yes, that is still his only mode of transportation. He saw the taxi drop me off and wanted to say hello and so he came on up. So, there I was about to extract the knife from Arthur's chest and

Hank was yelling at me not to. I already had my hand on it so I just pulled it out. Then…"

"Sorry Lacey, earlier you said all ten of your prints would be on the knife, so think, did you use one or both hands?"

"I am quite sure I had both hands on the knife. I pulled it out and threw it on the floor and turned the eerie music off and told Hank to call the police. He started to come into the study, but I yelled at him to use the hall phone. His shoes would have already been covered in blood so why did it matter? I sat next to Arthur and took my pantyhose off and wiped my hands on them."

"That's it?" I was disturbed by the image she had created of herself sitting with blood on her hands beside Arthur's body. I told myself to remain objective.

"Yup, that's it. I have no idea how much time elapsed before the R.C.M.P. showed up. I think that Hank was talking to me but I cannot recall anything he may have said. I just kept wondering where all the blood came from. How could there be so much blood Jesse? One body can't possibly hold that much blood… and it was so red."

I got up and sat on the table in front of her and took her hands. I was a little worried because she seemed so calm, but she was trembling. "You were in shock Honey, and I can assure you that our bodies hold gallons of fluid. Arthur would have bled out, and I am assuming that he was killed not very long before you arrived. Can you tell me what happened once the police arrived…take your time."

Our knees were touching and I wanted to hold her, but she let go of my hands, got up and went over and stood by the fireplace. "Of course I can tell you what happened. Two officers came in and one said. "Holy Mother of Jesus!" and crossed himself. They identified themselves to me and Hank and asked who we were. We told them and they asked why we were there and who had discovered the body. One at a time we related what had happened and they asked us to both come with them so that we could be processed and away we went."

"Think carefully Lacey; what were they wearing on their feet?"

"Boots of course."

"They didn't have protective coverings over their boots then?"

"I'm pretty sure they didn't…you can ask Hank. Why would it matter?"

"Don't worry; I fully intend to have a long talk with Hank. Do you recall the names of the officers and did they at any time read you your rights or ask if you wanted a lawyer?"

"No. Are their names important?"

"Their names and everything they said or did is important. They never read you your rights?"

"No. Constable Jones was one of the officers. I don't remember the other's name. There were also two more outside."

"Not to worry, it will all be in the report. How did they get you out of the house?"

"I don't know what you mean."

"Did you all retrace your steps, or did they take you out another way?"

"There is only one entrance into the study and we all went out the same way we came in."

"In other words, the murder scene was compromised. Did you see them remove any evidence like your hose or the knife?"

"I don't think they did, but as we were leaving I saw the other officers enter the house. They put us in separate vehicles and drove us to the station. We gave them our statements and then they let me call Sam and CC to come and get me."

"Let me get this straight…they only took your statement?"

"They never questioned us, just took our statements. That was legal wasn't it?"

"You didn't volunteer that you had any contact with the assumed murder weapon did you?"

"No, I'm not stupid Jesse."

"I didn't mean to imply that you were Lace. What about Hank? Did he volunteer any info?"

"I don't know what he told them in his statement, but at the house he told them that it didn't matter what it looked like, because I didn't do it."

"Have you had any contact with him since?"

"He phoned me the next day at Sam's and asked me how I was and that he was really sorry about Arthur, that's all. It's been a long day, I'm going to bed." Lacey placed our cups and plates on the tray and walked out of the room before I could question her anymore.

I followed her into the kitchen and watched her load the dishwasher. "Your fortune cookie is on the table…you may want to heed its warning."

I opened it and read: This is not the time to be venturing into untamed seas.

"How do you know this is mine and not yours?"

"Because I read mine first and it doesn't apply to you."

"What does it say?"

"It said that I shouldn't put my trust in a stranger's hand."

"I'm hardly a stranger Lacey."

"Just as a matter of curiosity, your wife is a blonde isn't she? You always liked blondes." She didn't wait for an answer and started up the stairs. "I turned your bed down for you. Your room is the second one on the right. I am very glad that you are here Jesse, and unlike you, I have thought about you many times over the years. Goodnight and pleasant dreams."

I stood dumbfounded as to how she could change from one topic to another so quickly. Against my better judgement I called after her. "And, I lied when I said I never thought about you."

She turned at the top of the stairs and looked at me and said. "I'm sorry Jess."

I didn't know what she meant, and I didn't miss that she had called me Jess.

I checked the doors and windows again and grabbed my computer and headed upstairs. I heard the sound of faint music coming from Lacey's room and reminded myself to ask her about the eerie song that she had referred to at the manor house. I thought I heard crying and put my ear to the door. I wanted to ask her if she was all right but talked myself out of it. I crossed over to the room she had assigned to me. I had planned on doing some research on the internet, but my mind kept wandering to the exasperating girl across the hall.

CHAPTER 2

Awakenings

Lacey

I awoke with a start. What was that noise? I glanced at the clock; it read 12:45. Lordy, I had only been asleep for a short while…there it was again…what was it? I climbed out of bed and threw a housecoat on over my flimsy nightgown. I tip-toed to the door and listened; someone was in the hall. I grabbed the baseball bat from the closet and opened the door and saw Jesse at the top of the stairs. He heard me and put his fingers to his lips to caution me to be quiet. I approached him and in a whisper asked him if he had heard something too. He nodded and took the bat from me and told me to go back to my room.

"I'm coming with you." I murmured.

He knew I wasn't going to do as he had asked so told me to stay behind him. When we reached the first floor landing I tapped him on his shoulder and in a hushed voice asked him if he felt a draft. He nodded again.

"I think it is coming from the back bedroom." I said.

Jess agreed and we proceeded stealthily down the hallway. The door to Hilda's bedroom was partly open.

"I thought we closed it last night?"

"We did, and I checked all the doors again before I went to bed."

With bat in the air, Jess pushed the door wide open and flipped on the light switch. We were met with a gust of wind wafting through what used to be a window. There were shards of glass everywhere, the mattress and bedding were lying in a heap on the floor, and the contents of the dresser drawers were thrown about the room. I said I wondered if they had got what they were looking for.

"So Hilda's valuable were still here?"

"I doubt it, but if there is any, they would most assuredly be in the safe. Shall we check it out?"

"Yes, but first I am going to call the R.C.M.P. and report the break-in."

"Oh Jesse, do we have to? I've had enough of cops."

"Sorry Honey, but it could have something to do with Arthur's death."

"Do you really think so? I'm hoping it was just someone looking for Hilda's stash."

"Stash…stash of what…cash?"

"Come on Jesse, you know what a stash is…Mary Jane, of course!"

"Are you telling me that Hilda smoked pot?"

"Yes, everyone in town knows she did. She has a prescription for it for her glaucoma."

Jesse followed me into the den where I pulled back a wall hanging and opened the safe.

"Do you know where she kept her supply? Do you know the number at the station?"

"I wish you would quit asking me half a dozen questions at a time. I never went to college you know, so I can only focus on one thing at a time."

Jesse seemed amused by my assessment of myself and peered into the vault with me.

"Can you tell if anything is missing? How much knowledge do you have of the family's worth?" He was ribbing me and I hit his arm.

"I thought you were going to call the police. No, I don't know the number; can't you just call 911? The King assets are not as great as one might think and no, I have no idea if anything is missing. I suppose the accountant or lawyer would know about that. Yes, I know where Hilda kept her stash and it certainly wasn't in her bedroom. Whew, any more questions Sir?" I pretended to wipe my brow all the while smirking as I led the way to the kitchen.

"I think that just about does it. I won't call 911 because I think the emergency is over. We didn't catch anyone in the act, and I don't think we want a police battalion and fire trucks on the premises. I will explain the situation and I am sure one or two officers will suffice."

I passed him the phone book and pointed out the number. He dialled it and said that an officer by the name of Mike Pattroni answered and told him that someone would be over immediately.

"You can handle things Jess; I'm going back to bed."

He took hold of my arm. "I don't think so my dear. I want you right here with me."

I looked at him and a tear escaped from my eye. He let go of me.

"I don't want to play this game anymore Jesse."

He seemed perplexed and said in a soft tone. "What game Lace?"

"This cat and mouse game; each one of us baiting the other; you calling me honey and Lace, and me pretending that I don't want you here and calling you Jesse. Neither of us wants to make the first move because we are afraid the other won't reciprocate and..."

He interrupted me. "Is that what you think is going on here? You think it's a game and that we are testing each other? Perhaps we have been, but I for one have enjoyed the banter."

"You would because you have nothing to lose."

"What do you mean by that?"

"You have a wife to go home to. I have no one waiting for me. You can have your fling and then find some excuse to kick me out of your life…well, no thanks… I have been there and done that and I don't care to do it again! We can't just take up again as if August 1975 never happened."

This time Jess corralled me with both arms. "Uh uh, you don't get to run away from me again! You are going to stay and fight fair." He sat me down in a chair. "Do you think you are the only one who remembers what happened back then? Do you think I haven't played the events over a thousand times in my head? We both chose to listen to idle gossip instead of trusting our love for each other. Who knows if we would still be together if those events never happened, but they did, and it's time you stopped blaming me for the whole freaking thing and took a little blame yourself. And, for your information, I may have a wife at home, but we are more like roommates then husband and wife. When I decided to come here to Kings Crossing I didn't know what to expect, but I sure as hell didn't think that I would take one look at you and old memories and feelings would come rushing back. I'll be the first to say it out loud; I still have feelings for you and God help me, I want you, and I'm not just fooling around"

He took my face in his hands and looked deeply into my eyes. "What do you say to that?"

I didn't cry though I wanted to. "I'm scared Jesse. I've never been able to give my heart to anyone again and it's all because I never got over my love for you. I should have been able to because I was only eighteen and I had a lifetime ahead of me. I never forgot you and I compared everyone else to you and no one ever came close. I guess there is much to be said about first loves. You can't imagine the emotions I was fighting when I first saw you at Sam's. I wanted to run right into your arms, but in the minute it took me to cross the yard I came to my senses and realized that it was 1999 and not 1975. I thought if I gave you the cold shoulder you would go away but you didn't…why did you stay and endure my insults Jesse?"

"Because you needed me; you just couldn't admit it. You have been slightly belligerent and perhaps I should have taken offense, but the truth of the matter is I've enjoyed every minute. You've aroused feelings in me that I thought I laid to rest many years ago. I knew I was doomed from the moment I looked into your mesmerising eyes."

"That's the nicest thing anyone has ever said to me. I want to…damn it, the police are here."

"I'll let them in, don't go anywhere."

"I won't…and Jesse… I still have feelings for you too."

He turned, and the way he looked at me made my heart skip a beat.

Corporal Timothy Newman took his hat off as he crossed the floor. He took my hands in his and said. "I am so sorry Lacey. I just got home and heard the horrendous news when I reported for duty a few hours ago. Is there anything I can do for you? My parents send their condolences and Mother wants to know if you are up to visitors? We were all at my niece's wedding in Victoria. God, I can't believe that you were the one who found Arthur's body."

"Thank-you Timothy, but I am all right. Tell your mother I would love to see her and perhaps your dad will come too because an old friend of his has come to help me in case I should require a lawyer. Let me introduce you to Jess Jameson; we all went to high school together. Jess this is Tim and Laura's son, Timothy Newman."

"It's a pleasure to meet you Sir. I have heard your name a time or two."

Jess extended his hand. "The pleasure is all mine Timothy. How are your parents? I look forward to seeing them."

Timothy shook his hand. "I'm sure they'll be anxious to see you also. I've heard the talk at the station Lacey, so I'm aware of the gory details. I can see why you want to be prepared and hired a lawyer, but I am hoping it won't come to that. Is James in route?"

"Yes, he and Blythe and the kids will be here Tuesday or Wednesday." I turned to Jess and told him that Timothy and James have been good friends ever since they were six years old.

"I'm glad that we may have one copper on our side. Now how about I take you down to the bedroom so you can survey the latest crime scene? I'm just glad that I accepted Lacey's kind offer of a bed and she wasn't alone when it happened." Jess winked at me. "Come on Lacey."

Timothy didn't want to enter the ransacked room. He said the forensic team was arriving later in the morning and he didn't want to compromise the scene, and would we be comfortable with the open window for a while longer. Jess assured him that we would be, and he didn't think that the ruffian wouldn't be so bold as to return tonight. Timothy looked a little puzzled.

"Sorry, I should explain myself. Lacey thinks he was looking for Hilda's supply of weed. She is sure that it is common knowledge that she was a user of it for her glaucoma."

Timothy agreed that it was a possibility, but we shouldn't make any assumptions as it could very well be connected to Arthur's death. He asked me if there was a key for the lock. I told him that I didn't know where it would be. We walked him to the back door. I said I had understood that the forensic team wasn't coming until Monday to process the carriage house, so why earlier.

"Head office deemed it was a priority as well they should have, and ordered a team be sent immediately. The longer a scene is left unprocessed, the more room for corruption. That shouldn't be a problem for I have been told that the house has been secured and that it is under guard 24 hours a day. Have you noticed an officer making his rounds around the perimeter?"

I said I hadn't, but then it was not easy to see the carriage house through the trees and I hadn't been here all that long.. Timothy said he would go by and check it out. We said our good-byes and Jess locked up.

"Is this night ever going to end? Now, where were we?"

"I don't know where you were Jesse, but I was on my way to bed…" I started up the stairs.

"Not without me you're not! Let me check the doors one more time."

I waited outside the bedroom door for him.

"Before we go through this door Jesse, I need to say a few things."

"I'm listening."

"I was wrong when I said that I would be alone when you were done with me. I will always have James and Blythe and Harry and Leah… they will never abandon me; no matter what."

"Do you honestly think that I'm going to kick you to the curb after this charade is all over and done with and I've had my way with you?"

"Can I finish? Right now you say that you still have feelings for me, but you don't know me anymore Jesse. Twenty-four years is a long time and I am not the same girl you used to know. It's no one's fault but mine that I have not been able to make a commitment to anyone. I never let my guard down. I have never had a relationship that lasted more than three months. I have never invited anyone to move in with me, and I have never accepted any kind of a proposal. I have met dozens of kind and caring men, but I could never return their affections.

Three years ago I decided that enough was enough and I made a pact with myself to quit trying to find someone to share my life with. It was time that I stopped trying to find another Jesse James Jameson, but here you are in the flesh, and you say you still have feelings for me, and I want that to be true, but…"

"You're not the only one who has changed Lace. Do you honestly think that I haven't? Your right, twenty four years is a long time and I'm not the same insensitive jerk that I was back then. I've gained a pound or ten and my hair's getting greyer by the minute."

"Up until that ill-fated day you were always kind and caring Jesse. I'm heavier too and I have to colour my hair to keep the white from showing and I am only forty two, but I'm talking about what's in the inside. I'm bitter and cold, and it is quite possible that not even you can defrost the ice queen."

He tried not to laugh and put his arms around me. "I think you are underestimating me. I look into your eyes and I see fire and yearning and I want to bring love back into both our lives."

"You have aroused feelings in me that I thought were lost forever and perhaps we will ignite the passion, but are you willing to deal with what it may cost you?"

"Are you referring to my law practice or something else?"

"Well, of course there is your marriage, but it won't be the first time that a man has cheated on his wife, but it will be a first for me…at least as far as I know. I have never wanted to be the other woman. Would I just be your mistress Jesse? Would I be the one who turned you into a liar and a cheat or have you done this before…are you an old hand at deception?"

"God, you ask a lot of questions. I thought we could have this discussion another day."

"Another day…are you kidding? Are you forgetting that there is a ninety five percent chance that I may be incarcerated any day now? That is the only reason I am willing to risk being hurt again as this may be the last night I will ever have with you again."

"Lacey, that is not going to happen."

"You can't say that with any certainty Jesse. The evidence points right to me. Who was found standing over the body with the smoking gun, or in my case, the bloody knife?"

"Honey, you are getting way ahead of yourself and don't underestimate my proficiency as a lawyer. No charges have been brought against you and if they are, where is the motive and opportunity? Let's not speculate until we hear the coroner's report okay? Now, if I don't get to hold you and kiss you in the next minute I am going to go downstairs and get plastered."

"Just one more thing…it's you I am worried about. Suppose if all the bad things happen and you can't save me…what then Jesse? Would you go on blaming yourself for the rest of your life? I need you to think long and hard about this."

"I don't need to think. I'm in this for the long haul and nothing you can say or do is going to make me desert you. Hold on…okay, worst case scenario…the chips are stacked against you and we have played our last card…what do we do then? Simple, we flee the country!"

"Simple; how do we do that?"

"I have many friends in high places and even more in low places. Don't worry, I'm your man. You should quit talking now Lace." He started to kiss me.

"Just one more thing; I don't think I remember how to kiss, it's…"

"I mean it Lace…you should really stop talking."

I think I had a normal childhood. I lived in Kings Crossing from the time I was two years old. My parents and my sister Constance, who was four years older than me, had come to the south Cariboo in 1959 from a small town in Washington State.

My mother always said that her family roots went back to the dawn of civilization as they were Native Americans. My father's ancestors had migrated from Scotland to Ohio in the early eighteen hundreds and his grandfather had settled in Novia Scotia. His father had traveled west and bought a homestead in B.C. My dad was born in a small town near the Washington State border. He and my mother met at a cross border youth rally in the early nineteen fifties. They were married a year later and chose to live in the Okanogan area of Washington where they worked in the fruit orchards residing in a small camp trailer. That winter they were both hired on at a dairy farm which led to employment at a large farm and nursery which supplied plants and produce to the local outlets. In the next few years Dad managed to get a degree in horticulture and worked for the state for several years until coming to Kings Crossing to start up an experimental agricultural farm. I don't know how he managed to accomplish so much in such a short time and still have time for his family. My mother was a petite dark skinned woman with long black hair which she always wore braided and pinned up. When Connie and I got older we fought over whose turn it was to comb and braid our mother's hair. I resembled mother in coloring, but my hair was chestnut brown, wavy and shoulder length. I was heavier and several inches taller than her. I had dimples which I hated and a few unusual freckles on my cheeks. Connie favoured my father and had lighter brown hair and skin and she was three inches taller than me. Father was almost six feet tall. I remember going to the farm with mother every morning after we dropped Connie off at kindergarten. I had my own little work bench where I used to play at potting plants. Mother had to sit me on a big black plastic garbage bag in the car because I was always so dirty. I missed my days at the farm once I started school, but soon found other things to take its' place. Mother worked full days alongside father, but she was always waiting for us when we got home from school. After my tenth birthday I was entrusted into Connie's care after school. I was usually left to fend for myself as Connie was off doing teen things. I lied a lot for her back then, but kind of feared for my life if I didn't. She got married when she was nineteen to a really nice fellow, Joe Dempsey. They are still married today and have two grown children and one grandchild. I haven't seen my sister in five years as they gave up their cushy lives to become missionaries and are always off in some poor country administering to the sick and needy. I wish she was here. Our parents moved to Nova Scotia when I went off and married Arthur which brings me back to the subject of me and Jesse.

I had a few run of the mill boyfriends before Jesse, but nothing serious. Our first meeting was not such a pretty one as I was extremely sick having drank one of his sister's potent cocktails. It had been my first experience with alcohol and it didn't go well. I had run into Jesse in the hallway at his family home as I was making a mad dash for the bathroom. At the time, I didn't know that he was on the other side of the door listening to me puke my guts out. I didn't see him again until Thursday at assembly. My girlfriend Mavis pointed him out to me.

"Isn't he just the dreamiest guy you have ever seen?" She crooned.

I asked her who she meant and she pointed to him. "Chloe's big brother of course."

"I guess so." I said.

There was a commotion at the back of the auditorium and everyone turned to see what the noise was all about. Jess, who was sitting two rows ahead of me, had to look directly in my direction when he turned around. He smiled, but at the time, I didn't know that he was smiling at me. Mavis asked me if I thought he was looking at us.

After the lecture we were told, as usual, to leave in an orderly manner starting with the back row first. Jess somehow managed to hop over two rows of seats and plopped himself down directly in front of me. I think Mavis probably peed her pants. He said he hadn't seen me around and thought that his sister had really poisoned me. I assured him that I had only had a headache the next day. He asked me if I was going to the basketball game on Friday. I already knew that he was a center for the senior team which was called Kings' Knights. I told him that I hadn't given it any thought and he said that he hoped I would and that I would go with him after the game to a party at Sam Blier's house. I was too stunned to say anything. I think he realized that and he said he would call me tomorrow. He winked at me and re-joined his friends. Mavis asked me how the heck I knew him and why didn't I introduce him to her. I told her that I was too surprised and explained about the disastrous sleep-over.

Jess waited for me after school that same day and offered me a ride home. I was all alone as Mavis was mad at me. I had a pile of books in my arms that were about to topple. He jumped out of the car and put my books in the back seat. I felt that I had better go with him if I wanted to see them again. We stopped at the local drive through and he bought us cokes and asked me if I had ever been up to Seventh Crossing Ridge. I hadn't, but knew that it was a local teen make-out spot. I really didn't want to go, but I said nothing. When we reached the top of the hill Jess pointed out a worn road that led to the spot where everyone partied. However, he kept driving until the so called road came to an end. He asked me if I would like to go for a walk. Again I wanted to say no, but I didn't. We walked side by side down what I assumed was a deer trail. We came to a sudden stop at a rock cliff that looked down on a covered train bridge. I knew there were many train bridges in the area but I had never seen this covered one before. Jess told me that it was called Seventh

Crossing because it was seven miles from Kings Crossing. I asked why it was covered and he said it was to help protect the tracks from falling debris from the hillside. I told him that it was a very picturesque view of the river and I thought that it must be something to see when the train cars rolled by. His eyes sparkled as he looked at me. He said that if I thought so then I was in for a treat. He took my hand and led me to a big flat rock and asked me to sit with him. I did. A few minutes later we heard the train as it rounded the corner.

Jess had looked at his watch. "Right on time."

He told me it was 4:10. The train blew its whistle. He took my hand again and told me to listen.

The train entered the tunnel and blew its' whistle again. I knew what it was, and yet it was different. It was this constant wave of sound that seemed to echo off everything around us. It was perhaps the most peaceful sound I had ever heard, and yet I shivered as it was haunting also. He watched me for my reaction.

"Does everyone know about this and can one hear it all along the ridge? It gave me goose-bumps."

"Nowhere does it resonate like it does here…must be the rocks. I don't know who else knows about this place because I have always thought of it as my own."

"Why did you bring me here then; you don't even know me?"

"I don't know, I can't explain it…I just wanted to. I have never brought anyone else here."

I thanked him and told him that I would not tell anyone about it neither and maybe he could bring me here again some other time. He held my hand as we walked back to his car. He opened the door for me and asked if he could kiss me. I don't know if I said yes or if he just kissed me. It was the first time I had ever been kissed by someone who knew what they were doing. No one, not even my sister had prepared me for the sensation that surged through my body. On the ride back he asked me if I had made up my mind about going to the party with him.

"Yes, I would like to go with you Jesse…do you mind if I call you Jesse?"

He smiled and said. "You may, but only if I can call you Lace."

And, that was the beginning of our three year relationship.

We mostly hung out with his best friend Sam and his girlfriend CC, and occasionally with his sister Chloe and her boyfriend Alex. Seventh Crossing was our secret hangout and that is where I thought we would first become lovers, but it wasn't. My birthday was on June 11th and Jesse's was June 17th. His sister held a double party for us to celebrate my seventeenth and Jesse's eighteenth. I was staying at my sister's as she and Joe were out of town and they had just gotten a new puppy so they didn't want him left alone all night. Jesse came in with me to check things out and he asked if he could stay with me. I wanted him too. We had been fighting off the desire to take that final step in our relationship for so long that it was inevitable that it would happen sooner or later. I didn't think that I could love him anymore than I already did, but I had underestimated the power of intimacy. We knew we would marry one day. Jesse graduated that year and was working full time at the family hardware store. He would be off to university the next year and his plans were for me to go with him. It all seemed so simple. We were very naïve. The year sped by. It was late August and Jesse left on a mission to find accommodations for us in Vancouver. He never called me in the week that he was gone which was very odd. The day he arrived home he phoned and said that he was too tired and would see me in the morning. I knew something was wrong, but never in a thousand years would I have dreamt that the next day he would accuse me of being unfaithful and that my world would come spiralling down.

I had waited all day for him. At noon I phoned his house and his mother said she thought he was with Scott and Mike. He finally showed up around four o'clock. I ran out of the house and jumped in the front seat. Jesse had not reached over and opened my door like he always did. I reached over and kissed him. He did not respond and reeked of alcohol. Something was wrong as he hardly ever drank, and certainly not in the middle of the day. He started the car. I thought we would be going up to Seventh Crossing, but he drove down to Dawn Lake and parked. He just sat there staring into the water. I couldn't stand the silence any longer.

"What has happened Jesse? Why won't you talk to me? Have I done something wrong?"

"Well you would know the answer better than me wouldn't you Lacey?"

He had called me Lacey. "Please enlighten me…I am in the dark here."

"How long did you think it would take me to find out about you and Jim? Does everyone know except me? Leslie has only been dead one month and you're already warming up her lover's bed. You sure made a fool out of me Lacey Monroe!"

I looked at him like he was out of his mind which at that moment I thought he was, or that he was too inebriated to know what he was saying.

"I couldn't have heard you right…did you just say that I have been unfaithful to you and with one of your best friends? What's the matter with you Jesse Jameson?"

"Oh, I am all right now…now that I know what you have been up to behind my back. You couldn't wait for me to get out of town could you? Thank heavens for friends that had the nerve to tell me all about your running around…I knew you liked sex, but I never thought…"

I had to stop him before he said anything else. "What friends are you talking about, Mike and Scott I suppose. They can't get their own girl so for some idiotic reason thought they would ruin our relationship. I can't figure out why after all this time they picked today to fabricate such a vile lie. There is and has never been anyone but you, and you know that, and yet you chose to listen to some stupid drunk gossip. Your mind was made up before you even asked me if it was true. You just went right to accusing. You have hurt me to the quick, and when you come to your senses and realize how wrong you are, it will be too late because I can never forgive you for insulting me in such a hurtful matter. Take me home and never darken my door again."

He started to say something, but I told him to shut up because I would get out and walk the five miles home before I let him insult me anymore. I stared out the window all the way to my front gate. As I was slamming the car door I heard him say, "Lace…" It was too late.

The next day Chloe phoned me and asked what had happened. I told her and she cursed and said that must be why Jess had been seen with Mavis. Thank-you; that just added salt to the wound. I told no one else and hoped that I wouldn't run into Jesse before he left town.

It's funny how life can change in a matter of minutes…but, I wasn't laughing. I had thought about confronting the lying duo of Mike and Scott, but that was Jesse's job. It was apparent that he didn't really want to know the truth. It was a very black day when Mavis came to beg me to forgive her for sleeping with Jesse.

It was 10 P.M.; three days after my life with Jesse had been terminated. I answered the doorbell and found Mavis standing there looking as if she had just lost her best friend. She had, but didn't know it yet. I didn't want my parents to hear our conversation which I knew wasn't going to be pretty, and so I stepped outside with her. It was very chilly for an August evening.

Mavis burst into tears. "It just happened Lacey…I am so sorry, it wasn't my fault. I would never do anything to hurt you. Please, please forgive me."

"I'm sure I have no idea what you are talking about and why would you need my forgiveness. Oh…is it because you have been seeing my ex. Not to worry; we're done with each other."

"Is it true then; the two of you are finished?"

I still didn't want to believe that it was, but I told her she needn't feel guilty and that Jess was free to date whoever he wanted. I said goodnight, but unfortunately, she wasn't through talking.

"We were just sitting in his car up at the Crossing and he was telling me all about your fight. Pretty soon we were kissing and then it just happened…" Mavis stopped mid-sentence.

That was too much information and yet, it wasn't enough. I had to know what she meant.

"Tell me exactly what happened Mavis."

"I let Jesse make love to me." She said it as though it was an everyday occurrence.

"Get off my porch and out of my yard! Don't you ever set one foot on this property again! And, don't you ever call him Jesse, you little bleached blond BITCH!"

I slammed the door and ran upstairs. Mother followed me. I told her to go away. I wanted to kill someone…I just didn't know who it was…Jesse or Mavis. I had accepted the fact that we were through, but the fact that he'd had sex with her the night we broke up was the final nail in the coffin. I went into the bathroom and was sick to my stomach.

The next day Chloe picked me up after my shift was over at the café where I waitressed. She told me to hurry and get in because she had just seen Jess walking towards the bridge and it was time to have it out with him. I told her I wanted no part of this, but the car was moving and I couldn't get out. She told me that Jess had been pouring his heart out to her and that he wanted me back. Sure he did and that is why he was sleeping with Mavis. They were standing on the sidewalk alongside of the bridge. He had his hands on her shoulders. Chloe slammed the car into park and ran off yelling at them. Jesse turned around and saw me and immediately removed his hands from Mavis. I fled the car dropping down a steep embankment and ran like the devil was chasing me. I don't know how many times I fell down, but by the time I snuck in the back door of the house I was bruised and blood was running down my legs. I still have a scar just below my knee on my right leg to remind me of that day. I never spoke to or saw Jesse again until yesterday when he showed up in Sam's back yard. He had tried to phone me but I would not take his calls. Shortly after he had left for Vancouver I received a letter from him. I opened it and read it not really caring what he had to say.

Dear Lace... I know you are not ready to talk to me but I need you to hear me out. I hope in time you will be able to forgive me for not trusting you. It was the worst mistake of my life when I accused you of cheating on me. Chloe read the riot act to me and with good cause. She also told me the things Mavis said to you. I would never do that to you. They are all lies Lace... everything she said is a lie. I know that I was wrong and I should never have accused you of cheating on me.

I will be home for Thanksgiving; please say you will see me then.

I do love you Lace.
Jesse

Wasn't that just peachy? Well, I wasn't going to be here when he came home. I was going to New York City with Arthur King and we were going to be married. It all happened over a period of two days. He was five years older than me. He and my sister had been friends and hung out together. Arthur was a friend to everyone and especially the girls. He left home right after graduation to make his way in the Big Apple. He was a theatre major and he hoped one day to make it big on Broadway. I hadn't seen him in years and then there he was sitting in one of the booths in the café where I worked. I recognized him immediately, but we got off on the wrong foot. He said he had just heard a sad story about me and Jess Jameson and was it true that we had broken up. I'm afraid I acted badly and slammed the menu down in front of him telling him that it was none of his business. I sent someone else over to take his order.

He was sitting in his car outside the café waiting for me when my shift ended at 6 P.M. He opened the door and asked if I would like a ride home. I told him I had my mom's car.

"How can I apologize to the most beautiful girl in town then? Won't you give me the chance Lacey?" I couldn't refuse his pouty grin.

I spent the next two days with him. We went for long drives and out to dinner and the movies. He was always polite and never made any advances towards me. We said our goodbyes as he was leaving for the big city the next day. I went home and took a pregnancy test. It was just as I feared. I thought of telling my mother or my sister, but instead I chose to confide in Arthur and ask for his advice. His mother was very pleased to see me and called to Arthur that he had a visitor. He appeared at the top of the stairs. He was just as surprised to see me as I was to be there. He was packing so he told me to come on up. I sat on the bed and told him my situation and asked him to tell me what to do. He asked me if the baby was Jess's and I said of course it was. He asked me if I was going to tell Jess and I said no because he would probably think it was Jim's and I just couldn't go through that again.

"Well, my dear, I'll tell you exactly what we are going to do. You are planning on keeping the baby aren't you?" I said I didn't know. "You are going to come to New York with me and we are going to get married. That baby is going to need a father and mother wants a grandchild."

I stood up and looked at him as if he was crazy. "Arthur, don't be ridiculous! This is my problem, and I would never saddle you with such a responsibility. Why, we hardly even know each other. Whatever are you thinking? I just came here for some advice, that's all Arthur."

"It's the perfect solution to both our dilemmas, don't you see?"

"I'm afraid I don't Arthur. Someday you will have children of your own with someone you love or your sister will. Your mother will have to wait until then. No, this is not a solution."

"Do you mean Ainsley? She could be dead for all we know; haven't heard hide nor hair of her for years. Mother and she had a parting of the ways. Mother gave her a huge sum of money, disinherited her, and sent her packing."

"What could she have done that was so horrible Arthur?"

"Never you mind that. Just so you know there will not be any heirs from my loins; you have no idea do you dear sweet Lacey? I am gay, always have been, and always will be."

It took me a few seconds to grasp what he was saying and then I was too shocked to speak. He seen my discomfort and sat me down on the bed. He put his fingers up to his lips.

"Shh…mother doesn't know. Oh, I think she has her doubts about my manhood, but would rather not confront it, and so we just play games. This can be beneficial to the both of us don't you agree?"

"I think you are out of your mind, but just say I go along with your harebrained scheme, don't you have…you know, a friend? Wouldn't he take exception to you bringing a pregnant woman home with you?"

"Sadly, there is no one in my life at the moment. I have been too busy trying to get my little theatre troupe up and running that I have had no time for romance. You could be a big asset to me you know?"

"Oh really, pray tell how?" I was becoming interested in his proposal.

"Well, my housekeeper just quit and I could use a hand with the upkeep of the apartment and I am a very poor book-keeper. Do you know how to type and file and cook?"

I laughed. "No, no, and no."

"I like this." He said smiling. "I think we will be good together. Now run along and get packed and I'll change the plane reservation to two." He kissed me on my brow.

"Arthur, are you serious about all of this?"

"Never been more serious in my life…now get a move on and get a good night's sleep. I'll pick you up at nine sharp."

"You don't even know if you can get me a seat on the same flight as you and what am I supposed to tell my parents? I can't get to the bank until ten tomorrow…"

"You're resourceful, you'll think of something, and you don't need any money; I have plenty."

I protested right until we boarded the plane in Kamloops. Then I just sat in my seat and prayed. That was twenty four years ago. I would make a life for myself in another world all thanks to Arthur. I never thought I would ever see Jesse again.

Jess

She fell asleep in my arms. She had cried just as she had the very first time we had made love so many years ago. She was only seventeen then and now she was forty two. She had told me earlier that she had never been able to give her heart to anyone after me. That was my fault and I wonder if I will be able to make it up to her, or if I will even have the chance.

If it is possible to fall in love at first sight then I did with Lacey. I was sixteen and she was just fifteen. I had taken her to my secret place in the rocky cliffs high above the Seventh Crossing train bridge which crossed over the Little Cariboo River. I told her it was an enchanted place. I had discovered this lofty perch when I was twelve years old. Everyone else was perfectly happy enjoying the view from the ridge which was half a mile away. My spot was right on top of the tunnel and I could hear the clatter of the train on the tracks as if I was standing right on them. The train would enter the covered bridge and the engineer would blow the whistle and the sound would reverberate off the walls and the tracks and the rocks. I could never quite explain the elation I experienced every time I heard that whistle blowing. Lacey said it gave her goose bumps. I guess that is the best way to explain it…ghostly, and yet spiritual. She had asked if she could call me Jesse and I said yes, and could I call her Lace?

I fell in love with her that day. I never looked at another girl for almost three years and when I did, it was the beginning of the end for me and Lace. It was the fall of 1975 and I was enrolled in university in Vancouver. I had gone to find a place for us to live as she was coming with me. I was staying with my Aunt Arla and I let myself get tangled up with a brazen bombshell that lived next door. This girl, Charise, threw me for a loop, and I began to doubt my relationship with Lace. All we did was flirt, but I wanted more.

I went home to Kings Crossing without finding an apartment for Lace and me. I let my aunt talk me into staying with her for a while. There was nothing else available and I would be saving money, so what the hell. Who was I kidding…I wanted to see more of Charise, but what was I going to do about the girl waiting back home for me?

To this day I can't explain how I could possibly have done what I did next. Perhaps the devil had taken possession of me. I called Lace and told her I was beat from the drive and just wanted to go to bed and that I would see her the next day. That gave me time to come up with an excuse as to why she couldn't come with me. I did not come up with anything that would placate her. I was still mulling over possible scenarios in my head on the way over to her place when I ran into a couple of buddies. They talked me into having a few drinks with them. I ended up spending all day with them and listening to their crude remarks about Lace. Apparently, she had been consoling another friend, Jim Clarke, while I was at the coast. "You know," Mike had said. "while the cat is away the mouse will play." They made a lot of innuendoes and I never once defended her. I left there with a belly full of beer and enough ammunition to ambush her. By the time I got to her house, I was pretty worked up. I accused her of screwing around on me even though I knew in my heart that it wasn't true. She called me an ass for listening to Scott and Mike and said that she never wanted to see me again. That's what I wanted wasn't it? My sister Chloe racked me over the coals when she found out what I had done. She told me that Lacey could no more cheat on me then I could on her. I wondered if being unfaithful in your mind counted. Anyhow, I did go to see Lace at the Whistle Stop Café where she worked. She was on a break and she was sitting with Jim Clarke and her hands were on top of his. Our eyes met and I saw something in those beautiful violet eyes that I had never seen before…disgust. I walked out without saying a word and ran into her best friend Mavis Nolan. She asked me if I was waiting for Lacey to get off shift. I told her that we'd had a fight. She said she couldn't believe that and asked me to go for a ride with her in her new car. I thought why not and she drove up to Seventh Crossing ridge and parked. I told her what I had accused Lacey of and she said she had heard the same thing. I asked her to try and get Lacey to talk to me and she promised she would. We ended up going to the movies. Lace wasn't there, but my sister was. I stayed out all night just so I didn't have to deal with the wrath of Chloe again. Of course she figured that I was with Mavis all night and so did Lace. I didn't know it at the time, but Mavis had made up some cock and bull story that she and I had made love. It didn't become clear to me that something was in the wind until Chloe and Lace found me at the city bridge talking with Mavis. We had gone for a walk and she was saying things that I didn't want to hear. I told her there wasn't going to be any us and I hoped to get Lacey back. Chloe was so furious that she drove right into a ditch. She jumped out of the car, not bothering to shut the door, and ran towards us. That was the last I saw Lace as she took off running down the bank.

I never touched that dirty bleached blonde who was supposed to be Lacey's best friend. I had always figured that she had a crush on me, but who would have thought that she would sacrifice her friendship with Lace over a lie. Anyhow, I was screwed three ways to Sunday and all because I had the 'hots' for some little vixen living next door to my aunt. I left town with my best friend Sam being thoroughly disgusted with me, my sister not talking to me, and the girl I had planned on marrying never wanting to see me again. I was some prize.

Within the first week I knew the errors of my ways. Charise disappointed me in every way. I wanted my baby back. I wrote to her and asked for her forgiveness. She never answered me. I received a phone call from my sister shortly after. Her words are still imbedded in my head.

"You dumb ass Jess Jameson; do you know what you have done? You hurt her so bad that she left town and she didn't go alone. She ran off with rich boy Arthur King and rumour is that they are getting married. I hope you are satisfied!"

She hung up and she still wasn't talking to me when I went home at Thanksgiving. At Christmas I made her listen to me. I didn't need her forgiveness; I just needed her to believe me. I told her I would regret what I had done to Lacey the rest of my life because I hadn't only hurt Lacey, but I had condemned myself to a life without her. That was that and Lacey Monroe was out of my life forever. For the next few years I lived the life every young man dreams about, wine, women and revelry. My days were filled with furthering my education and my nights were filled with self-indulgence. I had reduced my relationship with Lacey to a foolish teenage fling. My parents and Chloe had left Kings Crossing in 1976, so there was no reason for me to go back there. I didn't even attend Sam's and CC's wedding. Yup, life was pretty much going my way. I was in no hurry to settle down. I had decided on pursuing a career in the law field and that was going to keep me occupied for quite some time.

I met Marsha quite by accident. It was a cold and rainy spring day and I thought I would stay in and finish a paper I was working on. It was my first day off in months. After classes, I did grunt work for a law firm and on weekends I worked days at a hardware store. After several hours of tedious writing I decided to take a break and go for a jog despite the inclement weather.

I had the whole running circuit to myself and was nearing the end when I came upon a woman in distress. She was bent over and struggling to breathe. She complained of severe pain in her abdomen and left side. At first I thought she was just suffering from over exertion. I couldn't convince her to get up off the wet ground. I didn't know what else to do so I said I would go for help. She begged me not to leave her alone. I had a little knowledge of first aid, but managed to eliminate the breathing, blood and bone thing all the time praying someone would come by. Finally I started prodding and discovered that when I touched her right side, she had the rebound pain. I had introduced myself to her and she said her name was Marsha West.

"Well, Miss West," I said. "You may have a ruptured appendix. I am going to have to go for help or you could very well die right here." I pulled my fleece shirt off and placed it under her head. She grabbed my hand and asked me to hurry. I took a short cut across the field and flagged down the first car that came along and ran back to wait with her for the ambulance.

She did indeed have appendicitis and I think that minute in time was a turning point in my life. I stopped being the self-indulgent playboy and took stock of my life. Marsha was a kind and decent person and we became good friends before we started dating. It was a big step for me to make a commitment again. I thought that I had put Lacey's memory to rest, but it was never more evident that I hadn't then on my wedding day. I watched the tall, blonde, blue-eyed slim woman walking down the aisle and for a second she became a beautiful girl of sixteen with laughing violet eyes and cheeky dimples and a sprinkle of freckles. I filed her memory away knowing that I could pull it out anytime I wanted or needed to.

Marsha and her sister bought a boutique with an inheritance left to them by one of their grandmothers. The store was doing well financially and Marsha insisted I give up my weekend job so we would have more time together. She wanted to have children immediately and we did. Hilary and Vivian were born fourteen months apart. Marsha used to take the girls to work with her and when they were old enough they worked in the store also. I received my law degree in 1984 and have a successful practice. The years went by. We were like every other couple we knew. Our marriage and life was unadventurous, and I was disinterested in every aspect of it…I just didn't know how much.

There were no challenges; everything was routine. The girls had been gone for ten months so we didn't even have their lives to entertain us. We tried to visit them once a month and they came home for special occasions, but it had been extremely easy to get used to their absence. Marsha had a lot of evening consultations and so that left me alone on most nights. I never seemed to mind and then Sam had called me.

I fell asleep trying to rationalize what had transpired between Lacey and me. She had made it very clear that she didn't want me in Kings Crossing so why didn't I leave? I couldn't…it was as simple as that. I couldn't and I didn't want to. She aroused feelings in me that had been dormant for longer than I cared to remember. Her touch was electrifying. She was feisty and argumentative…just what I needed to breathe life back into my ho-hum being. Last night we had rekindled our love and I knew that I wanted more, and I wanted to protect her and keep her safe, and then there was the matter of James…

Lacey was not in bed next to me when I woke up about four a.m. I called for her but she didn't answer. I rolled out of bed and scrambled to find my pants; my shirt was nowhere to be found. What the hell was that smell…you got to be kidding me? I followed my nose out the bedroom door and down towards the balcony. There was no mistaking the pungent aroma of marijuana. Lace was perched atop the balustrade.

"Hi Jesse." She said cheerfully.

I held my hand out to her. "I see you found Hilda's stash? Is this a common occurrence for you…getting up in the wee hours and smoking pot?"

"This is the last of Hilda's supply and no, this is not a habit. This is only the third time I have tried it and with the same outcome…nothing."

"You do know that you need to inhale to get any benefits don't you?" She took my hand and let me help her down.

"Hilda and Bly told me the same thing, but I choke and so just blow smoke."

"Okay then. You go flush the butt down the toilet and I will see what I can find to get rid of the odour. By the way, that shirt looks better on you than it ever could on me."

She handed me an aerosol spray can and said. "Thank-you kind sir." She did a little curtsy and then danced down the hall. She made me laugh and it felt good.

Back in bed I asked her why she had felt the need to smoke pot in the wee hours and she said it was because she couldn't shut her mind off, but of course it hadn't worked.

I held her tight and asked her if the train still came into the station at 4:15 and she said it did. We listened in silence until we heard the quick shriek of the whistle. I told her that later in the day I was going to take her up to our spot above the Seventh Crossing Bridge.

"It isn't there anymore Jess. It's a park now and there is no magic there anymore."

I kissed her and said that I thought there still might be and then I said. "I love you Lace."

CHAPTER 3

Confessions

Lacey was gone again. "What the hell Lace, where are you now?"

She appeared at the bathroom door with a towel wrapped around her. "I'm right here Jesse."

"Come back to bed." I opened the covers up for her.

"It's late and the uniforms could show up at any minute. I'll put on some coffee while you shower and get dressed."

I sighed and asked her if she was sure. She didn't answer me and the next time I saw her she was sitting on the top step of the kitchen stairs.

"What are you doing there Sweetie?" I asked her.

"Well, I was on my way to see if you needed anything, but decided to sit down and have a little talk with myself instead."

I sat down beside her. "And, what did yourself say to you?"

"She said I shouldn't invade on your privacy, and that I better not put any stock in what happened between us last night."

"You mean this morning?"

"All right morning, if you want to quibble about a few hours."

"And, what do you think happened that you had to talk to yourself about?"

"You told me you loved me, and I may have told you that I loved you…"

"You did."

"It was all in the heat of the moment Jesse, and we have to be honest with each other. We can't possibly be in love. People say what they think the other one wants to hear when in the throes of passion. It was just a moment in time and we best forget it ever happened. We were just two disenchanted strangers yesterday, and maybe on my part, I was trying to rekindle the past. I was wrong and I apologize for trying to resurrect it. We can't be lovers Jesse, but we can be friends, and I will be happy with that."

"No, you won't be and neither will I! Stop assuming that you know what I want. I want you and you want me, and there is no just being 'friends'…we've already come too far for that. And, dear lady, the years did not make us strangers. I am more akin to you than anyone in my life."

"Yes, I do want you Jesse, but there is no future for us. You can't be here when James arrives."

She got up and started down the stairs. "When are you going to tell me about James, Lacey?"

"The same time you tell me about your wife…now, do you want coffee or not?"

"I thought that things were going to be better between us now?" She said over her shoulder. "Now where would the fun be in that?"

God, she was exasperating and I loved every minute of her sassiness. I followed her into the kitchen and sat down at the table where she set two cups of coffee down, both black.

"Why didn't you tell me you take yours sans cream now?"

"I can take it or leave it, no big deal. Now, what's on our agenda for today Mr. Lawyer Man?"

"You mean besides you telling me what is best for me, and that I just want you in the bedroom? Well then, after the police and crime scene analysts have departed, I plan on picking Sam's and CC's brain to see if they can shed some light on who would want Arthur dead or who would want to frame you. And then, I plan on taking you up to Seventh Crossing, talking to Hank, and then I guess I will be ready to continue quarrelling with you again. Just out of curiosity, when did you become so sceptical?"

"That would be the day you accused me of being unfaithful to you."

There was bitterness in her voice again, and I realized that she was never going to let go of the past. I could tell her the truth about that dismal day, or I could lie to her and blame it all on the liquor and make up some plausible story. What explanation did I think would benefit me the most? I put myself on the witness stand and swore to tell the truth.

"You were right all along Lace…it was my fault and I wasn't man enough to tell you the ugly truth. It all started when I went to the coast to find us an apartment…" The doorbell rang.

Lacey got up to let the crime squad in. "Saved by the Fuzz again, but you're not off the hook by any means Jesse James. Your parents were right when they named you…I guess they knew you were going to be a thief… just like your namesake. Only you don't rob banks and trains… oh no, you steal young girl's hearts instead."

She was giving me too much credit as a Romeo and I would have to set her straight on that. The virtuous maiden who I had encountered upstairs earlier opened the door. Was that it, did she have an upstairs and a downstairs persona?

"Good morning Timothy; I didn't realize that you would be on the investigating team?"

"Good morning Lacey. I am not officially on duty yet, but the Sergeant wants me to act as a liaison because I have a personal relationship with you and the King family. This is Melanie Moore from the crime lab in Kamloops. Good morning Mr. Jameson; I trust the rest of the night passed without incident?"

Lacey and I shook hands with Ms. Moore.

"Yes, I am pleased to say that nothing unexpected occurred. We did have a little trouble sleeping however." I turned and winked at Lacey; two could play in her saccharine circus. She glared at me and I knew she wanted to hit me, or worse…not talk to me.

Timothy informed us that Constable Jones and Ms. Moore's partner were examining the house from the outside and asked if we would escort him down to Hilda's bedroom again. In her sweet innocent little voice Lacey asked me if I would mind accompanying him because she had to make a phone call to the woman who had served as her mother-in-law's companion and nurse. She said she would have more insight into what was missing and she wanted the dogs returned. I wanted to say, "Of course dear", but valued my life and said that I could certainly do that.

"I wondered where those two were. It will be reassuring to have them with you." Timothy said.

I asked what kind of dogs they were as we wandered down the hall. He said they were a German-Shepherd cross and they were very loyal, obedient and excellent guard dogs and they loved Lacey. I hoped they liked lawyers.

I told Timothy and Ms. Moore that I was most anxious to view the scene of the crime and wondered when it would be possible for me to do so. Ms. Moore assured me that she and her team would be finished in two days and that we should be allowed access to the grounds and house by sometime Monday morning.

I made myself scarce and wandered back to the kitchen where I found Lacey preparing a breakfast of scrambled eggs and toast. She set a bowl of grapefruit sections on the table and told me to get started. I said I would wait for her and she said she had to watch the eggs. I wondered who I was going to be dealing with …was it Snow White or the evil queen. She placed a large serving of eggs in front of me and a stack of toast. She doled out a small portion for herself. She was up and down like a jack-in-the box. First she forgot the jam and then the coffee, and then the ketchup and sugar.

"I'm not helpless you know? Please sit down and have breakfast with me for I have a feeling it is the last meal I am going to have with you under this roof."

"I don't want to be accused of sending the condemned man away on an empty stomach."

"So, you have already sentenced me without even hearing my testament?"

"I pretty much know what it is going to be Jess, so can we just get on with the declaration?"

I pushed my half eaten breakfast aside and said. "I think not; this is neither the time nor the place. I am going outside to see how the other half of the team is coming along and then Sam and CC will be here and after they leave, it will be time. Can you be civil until then?" I didn't give her a chance to answer me but placed my dishes in the sink and walked out the door. I had a sinking feeling that she was indeed going to send me packing and I wanted to postpone it for as long as I could.

I met Corporal Jones coming around the side of Tudor House and we exchanged pleasantries. I asked him if he was at liberty to discuss any new developments in the case of Arthur's homicide. He was polite and said that most of the preliminary investigation had been conducted and they were now waiting for the forensic team to comply their report. He said that I should have access to the crime scene by Monday afternoon and a full report would be forthcoming. He also said that my client had not been ruled out as a suspect in her husband's murder. It was more information then I wanted. I did not offer any of my theories; nor did I bother to inform him that I would no longer be Mrs. Monroe's attorney after today.

A dilapidated 1950's Chevy truck pulled into the drive. Two very rambunctious dogs were scrambling to climb over the rails. The truck barely came to a stop before they were out and making a b-line for the back door of the house where Lacey was standing. One would think that they were her dogs by the way they greeted her. She was on her knees and they almost bowled her over. It was hard to tell who was happier…she or them. She called me over to meet them.

"Jesse, come and say hello to Mickey and Trixie. This one here is Mickey and this is his girlfriend Trixie. Let them smell you." She took my hand, "Scratch their chins. You want them to know you are their friend and that they can trust you." She smiled lovingly at me and it was then that I wondered if my sweet and sour Lace was bi-polar.

She introduced me to Clara Brankco, Hilda's companion. By her weathered and wrinkled face I would place her age to be somewhere in her late seventies. Her handshake was as firm as any mans. After welcoming me, she placed her arms around Lacey's shoulders and the two shuffled off to the house leaving me with two dogs sitting at my feet looking up at me as if they expected something. Lacey threw a red ball at me which I managed to catch.

"They love to play fetch Jess." Apparently, that was my new job…amusing the dogs.

By noon everyone had left the premises and I had left the dogs in the fenced back yard. They hadn't protested and went to their respective houses for a rest. I filled their water dishes and said I would see them later. They wagged their tails as if they understood what I was saying. I had taken them for a long walk up into the wooded hills above Tudor house. I had a perfect view of the town from there and I had sat down and planned my next move. I didn't want to leave Lacey, but that hour was surely just around the corner. It was perfectly clear that she wasn't going to own up to admitting that James was my son and perhaps he wasn't. I had to respect her decision and I would probably go away not any wiser. The only important thing was to exonerate her in Arthur's murder, and if that meant finding her a new lawyer, then so be it. Damn it, that's not at all what I wanted!

Sam and CC arrived and we walked together into the house where we found Lacey puttering in the kitchen. "Everything is almost ready guys; I hope leftover Chinese is all right with you. Jess, is there any decent wine left? Will you help me with these dishes CC?"

Sam followed me into the cellar. "I didn't know that Lacey was making lunch for us?"

"Sam, I don't know what that girl is doing from one second to the next. One minute she is this sweet little thing and then the next she is throwing insults around. Is it just me or is she like this all the time?"

"I've never known her to be anything but pleasant. She wasn't in a very good place after she found Arthur lying in a pool of blood with a knife sticking out of his gut, but she didn't rant or carry on. She was only worried of how it was going to affect James. She wasn't concerned that she may be charged with murder because she was innocent and she had witnesses, so no need to worry. I don't think she slept much the three nights she was with us…how was she last night?"

"I think she managed a few hours what with the break-in and all. I just can't pinpoint her moods and it could boil down to the fact that she wants to forgive me, but she just can't because I hurt her too much…half the time I think she hates me."

"And what about the other half?"

"I think she still loves me, but you know what they say about love and hate?"

"I think you need to try and meet her somewhere in the middle Jess. She's a good person and she's lived a solitude life. As far as we know she has never found her soul mate. You need to come clean with her. The only other reason besides you accusing her of cheating on you that made her run off with Arthur and claim him as James's father is that she was pregnant, and it was her way out of a difficult situation."

"She doesn't trust me enough to confide in me so I'll just bide my time until she kicks me out."

The girls were waiting for us in the dining room. I poured the wine and Sam and CC filled us in on Gary's recovery. They volunteered useless information about people that we once hung out with and what they were doing now and where they were. That was how I found out where Lacey's family was living. Towards the end of the meal, I took the bull by the horns and asked if they knew what had happened to Mavis Logan. Lacey tactfully excused herself and said she wanted to check on the dogs.

CC attacked me. "Why in tarnation would you bring that little tramps name up? How could you be so heartless?" She threw her napkin down and got up to follow Lacey.

"Hear me out CC…please. Lacey said she is dead and I just need confirmation. She played a big part in our breakup…"

CC interrupted. "No F…ING kidding! If Sam had of done that to me, I'd have killed him!

Sam asked her to calm down.

"Men, you are all the same! I suppose you are going to defend that bitch too!"

"CC, Sam has nothing to do with any of this. I was in enough hot water with Lacey already…do you really think I would stoop so low as to take up with her best friend?"

"I don't know nor do I care to know what you did with Mavis. You may as well have put a knife through Lacey's heart as accuse her of sleeping with Jim Clarke. Lord, if anyone needed comforting, it was him. What was wrong with you Jess Jameson…he'd just lost the love of his life and…it's been twenty four years and you've given no explanation for your behaviour; even Sam has no idea what made you turn on Lacey."

"You will be the first to know, right after I tell Lacey…can you give me that CC? We've only skirted around what happened, but before the day is up she will know everything and I am hoping she will come clean about a few things too. She told me Mavis was dead, but I need her to be alive. It's way past time for her to tell the truth. I never so much as kissed her let alone have relations with her. I had already pretty much sealed my coffin but it was she who hammered the final nail. She's not dead is she?"

"I told Lacey that she had died years ago in a horrible fire for that is how I thought she should perish…just as the witches did in Salem. There was a fire, but she survived, and the last I heard she was living in a commune somewhere in Montana."

I got up and hugged CC and said thank-you just as Lacey returned. She had the dogs with her who quietly nudged me and then took their place between us on the floor. It was like they knew we should be together.

"What did I miss?" She didn't bring Mavis's name up and none of us volunteered anything.

By the time CC and Sam left two hours later I was no further ahead in gaining any knowledge as to who might want Arthur dead. As far as they knew he had no enemies in town and was very well liked. They could not think of anyone who would benefit from his death. I asked if there had been any doubt that Hilda had died of natural causes and they said not that they knew. They also didn't know where Arthur's sister Ainsley was or if she was even still alive.

Lacey was not much help either but she was pretty sure that Ainsley was living somewhere in Alberta as Arthur had gone to see her years ago but he never talked about it. She said Arthur was very well liked in New York in the theatre world and no, there had not been anything to indicate that he and his partner Richie Stevens were at odds with each other. We would see as he was to arrive in a day or so. It would be a full house what with

James and his family here and Arthur's lover and me; oh wait, what was I thinking… I probably wouldn't even be here.

I needed to get my hands on the Kings' will or at least talk to the family's mouth piece. I would have to wait until Monday though. I thanked CC and Sam for their input and they said they hadn't been much help, but would remain on guard for anything suspicious. CC asked if we were up to coming for dinner.

"Actually CC, I was hoping you and Sam would come back here. I really don't want to leave the dogs alone their first night back. Would that be okay?" Lacey implored.

"But Honey, you already fed us once today; the dogs will be all right. I don't want you to have to cook; you have enough on your mind." CC affirmed.

"Actually," I said. "Lacey has a point, and I know my way around the kitchen, and I noticed one honkin barbecue out back. Does six thirty sound okay?"

"All right if you are sure, but I'm bringing dessert."

"Right you are. I'll walk you out." I called the dogs and they followed me. I told Lacey I would be right back. As I shut the car door I said to Sam. "You do know this dinner is probably never going to fly don't you?" He nodded and CC looked confused as they drove out of the drive.

I felt a breeze blowing through the house and I thought that Lacey must be out on the front porch and she was. I stood at the newly painted handrail and launched right into 1975.

"We were two teenagers in love who thought they would always be together. It was me, and me alone who brought the curtain down. I had reservations about leaving Kings Crossing and going to the big city. On one hand, I was excited and on the other, I was scared stiff. I almost changed my mind that week and thought that I should give it one more year, but hell I was already enrolled, and if I stayed out of school for another year,

I would probably never go and so I left. I am aware that I never called you while I was gone and that was because I was already feeling guilty. I gave up looking for accommodations for us after the first day because I had decided to take my aunt's offer to board with her. I didn't know how I was going to explain to you why you couldn't come and live with me." I turned away and gazed out towards the river. I took a deep breath and faced her. "I didn't give it too much thought as I was much too busy with the girl next door to my aunts'."

Lacey said nothing, but if one could hear the breaking of a heart then that is what her silence sounded like. She placed her hands in her lap and sat perfectly still waiting for the other shoe to drop. I did not keep her in suspense.

"You always said that I had a weakness for blondes, but I didn't. You were my only weakness and many nights I would lie in bed and wonder what I would do if you left me. But, you didn't."

I wanted to take Lacey's hands in mine and beg her to forgive me for what I was about to say, but I knew I shouldn't. "You never ever gave me any reason to doubt you Lace. You were always this pure sweet young girl who loved me and I wronged you. I could not take responsibility for my own depraved behaviour and so, I came home and found a reason to throw the blame at you. I knew you hadn't been unfaithful to me, but just the notion, and there was talk that you had been gave me the fuel, plus a little help from my friends and the bottle…well, you know the rest."

"No, I don't Jess. Don't stop there. I want to hear everything… everything. I want to hear how this little blonde bombshell was a better lover than me. What things did she do to you that I didn't? How did she please you in bed? Come on; don't hold back…you've already thrown me overboard so all that is left is to watch me drown. I'm ready…I know there is no lifeline."

"Lacey…" Tears stung my eyes. I had never deliberately hurt anyone in my life before except her and now I was going to make her go through that horrible time all over again. It didn't matter that more than two decades had passed, the ugly truth was here and now, and I was the one who had to face up to what I had done. I sat down opposite her.

"I came home from Vancouver in a quandary. Here was the girl I had been in love with for years, and I had just left the girl I was lusting for. I know it is little consolation, but I had not had sexual relations with her yet. Yes, I wanted to more than anything. I should have told you the truth, but I took the cowards' way out and made you the villain. So, that is what happened and I lived with it until I heard you ran off with Arthur and then I just quit blaming myself. To finish the story, I did go back and take up with the girl next door. She disappointed me in every way possible. I came to my senses, but it was too late. I lived the life of a playboy and tried hard not to look back. I eventually met Marsha and she helped me to get through law school and we married and had two daughters. I think I mistook what we had for love. I respect and care for her; she is the mother of my children and we have been together a long time. There are no surprises in our relationship; every day is the same. Yesterday I came to the Crossing and I saw you and you made me feel alive. You lit a fire in me and I fell in love with you all over again."

Lacey did not blink an eyelash. I got up and tried to smile. "I'm going to leave now Lacey. You have the dogs now and they can protect you… much better than I ever could and your family will be here soon. You told me that I had to be gone before your son arrived and even though I have been looking forward to meeting him, I won't put you through having to explain me to him. I won't leave you stranded though. I can set you up with a good criminal attorney, but I honestly don't think you are going to need one. I will leave some names with Sam. I know my words mean nothing and if I could return to 1975 and make amends, I would. Last night will live with me forever, and I know I will never love like that with anyone else. Good-bye Lace."

There was nothing left for me to do but go upstairs and gather my belongings. It took me all of five minutes. I closed the bedroom door and looked across the hall at Lacey's room and smiled. I'd had a fleeting chance at happiness again, but how ironic that the truth was my destruction.

I thought she was still outside on the porch so she wouldn't see me leaving. She wasn't. She was sitting in the middle of the main stairway. She heard me coming and without looking up she spoke, and I figured that it would be the last time that I would ever hear her sweet voice.

"I knew I was pregnant even before you went apartment hunting in Vancouver."

I left my suitcases on the landing and sat down beside her. I heard the train pull into the station and the whistle echoed long and sorrowful.

"I was going to tell you as soon as you got home. I had no idea how you would react, but I was hoping for the best and that you would still want me to move in with you. In all honesty, I was scared stiff. You had been on edge for the last few days before you left and we had both thought it was nerves, and maybe it was. Having a baby was going to put a crimp in our lifestyle, but I figured I could find a job waitressing until the baby was due and then I would come home and give birth here. I guess I had worked everything out in my mind satisfactorily and didn't think there were any holes in my plans. You didn't call me in the week that you were gone and I was beginning to worry. When you didn't come over the minute you got home I knew something was dreadfully wrong. I think I could have accepted that you had fallen out of love with me, but instead you accused me of being unfaithful and then threw it in my face when you took up with Mavis. How your feelings for me could have changed in such a short time was a mystery and I have been in the dark for two decades. You left me with very little self-esteem and I contemplated having an abortion or giving the baby away. Thankfully, Arthur came to my rescue and kept me from making the biggest mistake in my life. He offered me a solution and I apprehensively accepted it because it seemed the lesser of the two evils. He was my life-line and it is because of him that I brought James into this world. I have never regretted making the decision to keep him for he has been the shiniest star in my life. I forgave you on paper, but never in my heart, and there is still a hole within it that no one has ever been able to repair."

I said nothing and just sat staring at my feet wondering how I could undo what I had done so many years ago. I had broken her heart, and now she was breaking mine.

She took my hand and opened it and placed something in it. "Here, these are yours. This first one was taken shortly after James was born."

I looked at it for a long time and then turned it over…it read:

To Jesse April 17th 1976
I weigh 7 lbs. 2 Oz.
My mother named me James Arthur Monroe King

She passed me another one. "This is James when he was two, and this one was taken on his first day of school, and here he is in his Boy Scout uniform. This is his graduation photo, and here he is on his wedding day. This last one is of him and Blythe, and Harry and Leah…your grandbabies."

I fell to my knees in front of her and she pulled my head unto her lap and laid her head on mine. "Let it go Jesse…just let it go."

And I did. I hadn't cried since I was ten years old and my dog had died. I guess I was long overdue because I could not stop the sobs that were racking my body.

"I should have forgiven you back then, but I couldn't. I do now Jesse, and I am so very sorry."

With those words she released me from the shame and guilt that had plagued me for so long.

I pulled her into my arms and said, "Thank-you."

She flung her arms around me so forcefully that I had to grab the railing to keep from toppling over. "Honey, I think we better get off these stairs before we kill one another. I really need to hold you and to know that this is real and that you are going to let me be a part of your life."

"I do want you in my life Jesse and I want you to know James and our grandchildren, but we have a lot of obstacles to overcome and I am not sure if we are going to be able to get over them. Right now we have a dinner to go shopping for though don't we?"

"Well, it's not my first choice, but I will concede." We held hands and made it to the first floor before I kissed her and told her I loved her. Was this for real…had she truly forgiven me? God, please don't let me screw this up. Finally, I had her right where she belonged…in my arms.

"You don't need to tell me that Jesse. I like to hear it and I want to be with you, but I have to know that I will be more than just a passing fancy before I get too involved and lose myself. I don't want to be the reason you leave your wife."

I held her away from me and looked into her big beautiful lavender eyes. "Oh, you're way more than a passing fancy. I don't mind telling you that I do fancy you, and it's not just for a dalliance. I need you to know that Lace. You let me worry about what's going on between Marsha and me. There's a home, but there isn't any passion or interest there, and we are just awkward roommates. Yes, you are the reason I will be divorcing her, but together we will deal with the consequences. I want to make the rest of my life with you and I want you to trust me and let me mend that hole in your heart. What do you say… are you going to give me the chance to do so?"

"Yes, I am Jesse, but you may not have to tell Marsha a thing because in a few days you might come to your senses and realize that I am not the person you think I am."

I laughed. "Oh, I know very well who you are. You are strong willed, argumentative, temperamental, unpredictable and loyal, smart, compassionate and loving. You are beautiful and sexy. You have awakened my passion and I want you to be mine."

"There has to be more than passion Jesse; you have to like me."

I laughed again. "I like you Lace and everything about you, especially your cheekiness. It was kind of fun having you chastise me, but as you can see, I don't scare easy, and I am ever so glad that you didn't run me out of town."

"Apparently, I need you in more ways than one, but if you think that I am always going to be all sweetness and starry-eyed then you have another thing coming. Now, bring the dogs in and give them a bone while I comb my hair."

"Yes Dear; where are the dog bones?"

"They are in the bin right beside the doggie door."

"I'm sorry; I haven't seen any doggie door."

"It's in the laundry room…oh my God Jesse, I just thought of something! I think that's how the intruder got in the house… through the dog's flap. Remember, Timothy thought it was odd that there was so much glass on the outside of the window… well suppose if the so called burglar broke the window to get out and then just broke it a little more from the outside to make it look as if he had come in that way?"

"You could be right Lace; I think we should discuss your theory with Timothy." I let the dogs in and they stared at me until I gave them their bones. Lacey came in and told them to be on guard. I think they would have saluted her if they could have.

CHAPTER 4

Discoveries

Lacey

Jesse opened the car door for me. "I wonder what has caught the attention of the crows and ravens up there on Sugarloaf. I hope the coyotes haven't taken a deer down." He said he wondered the same thing earlier when he had taken the dogs for a walk but didn't want to investigate until he had them on a leash.

"I think we should go up there and see Jesse…just in case."

"Just in case what Lace?"

"In case there is a body buried up there."

"What?"

"I told you there was way too much blood for just one person. Suppose if the killer only had time to dispose of one body? Suppose if he buried him on Sugarloaf?"

"Lacey, honey…" he looked at me and could see I was serious. "All right we will investigate first thing in the morning."

I looked down the hill at the carriage house and saw that there were still three official vehicles in the driveway. "I wonder what is taking them so long especially since they don't even know what they are looking for."

Jesse asked me what I meant. "Well, they don't know about the weird music that was playing on the stereo and the missing rug and boot tray…how would they know they even existed? I sure did not tell them. I really need to get into that house."

"I don't think I want you to relive that day all over again; it could be quite traumatic Lace."

"I will deal with it, but there are things running through my head that don't make sense and I need to do some snooping to see if I can put my suspicions to rest. Do you understand?"

"Yes, I know that it is hard to make sense of things when the pieces don't fit, but we'll figure it all out I promise. I am quite sure that the Mounties have already found whatever was playing on the stereo and have it in evidence. I think you are going to have to disclose the fact that the entrance rug and boot tray are missing as it could be a crucial piece of evidence."

"First, we are going to see what has the local bird population so upset before we reveal anything. I doubt that they opened the stereo, and even if they had, they would not have found anything."

"I'm afraid to ask why." Jesse said hesitantly.

"I removed it, that's why."

He pulled the car into the Overwaitea parking lot and turned to me. "I thought you told me everything you did that day… what else haven't you told me and where did you stash the tape?"

"It wasn't deliberate Jesse. I think I thought that you would have reprimanded me for removing evidence and I wasn't entirely sure I was going to let you represent me, so I just stowed what I had done away. I have a feeling that macabre music was left by the killer for me and only me."

Jesse parked at the back of the lot and got out and came around to open my door. He pulled me up and into his arms messing my newly combed hair. "I'm sorry if you felt that you couldn't trust me and believe me, I understand. You certainly aren't the first client to keep pertinent information from their lawyer, but Honey, you are more than just any old client. You can tell me anything and if I scold you it will be for your own good for I need to know everything. Do you understand? No matter how foolish or irrelevant you might think it is, I need to know everything. Now where is that disk and more importunately, did Hank see you remove it?"

"Hank did not see me take the tape out as he was calling the police from the hall phone and he couldn't possibly have been able to see me. I just placed it in a casing and threw it in the drawer among all the other miscellaneously recordings and yes; all my faculties were working for I used the sleeve of my sweater to do so. Too bad I wasn't thinking clearly when I removed the knife." I sniffled a little.

"It's okay Babe." He turned me around. "Look, do those kids remind you of anyone?"

He had pointed to two young teenagers walking hand and hand across the parking lot. Every few feet they stopped and kissed. I sighed. "Yes, and I hope they are not in for the same heartbreak that befell us."

"I promise you it will be different this time. I will not make the same mistake twice."

"Well you can't now can you because Mavis is dead?" I walked away before he could reply.

Jesse was preparing the steaks for the barbecue when the house phone rang. I answered it and hung up almost immediately. He asked who it was.

"I don't know. They just asked if they were talking to the adulteress murderer."

"What?" He was still swearing when his cell phone buzzed. "Hello, you've got Jess Jameson." Then his voice softened. "Hi Honey, how are you?" He indicated to me that it was his daughter and held the phone so that I could hear. I shook my head, but he insisted I listen.

"We thought you were going to come over with mother for a visit but she said that you had to go out of town on some case. She said you were in King's Crossing. That's where your friend

Sam lives isn't it? Is everything all right Daddy? When do you expect to be home?"

"I'll be here for some time Leigh. I thought your mother had a wedding today?"

"You won't believe it Daddy, but they called it off at the last minute! Can you imagine all that planning and money down the drain? If I ever get married I'm going to elope. Are you and Mom at odds? She seems despondent."

"Too bad about the wedding. You know how things are between your mother and me Honey. We don't communicate much so I have no idea if something is bothering her or not."

"She said that you went to Kings Crossing to help an old friend…is it a woman Daddy?"

"Yes, it is, a very dear old friend. I have to go now Leigh, but I will call you tomorrow. Say hello to Hilary…love you both." He hung up but I could hear her say. "But Daddy…"

"Why did you hang up on her so abruptly? I thought her name was Vivian"

"It is, but I call her by her middle name. Anyhow, I had nothing more to say at the moment."

"Who named her?"

"Marsha did, but I picked out her middle name."

"How do you spell it and why did you choose it?"

"L-e-i-g-h, and maybe I just like the name." He smiled affectionately.

"It has nothing to do with me then?"

"What if it does?"

Was I to assume that he called her Leigh because that was my middle name? "They know about me Jesse; I can't do this. I will not be the one who breaks up your family. We will have today, but that is all we can ever have." I turned my back on him and collected the dog's leashes. I needed to clear my head. I heard a loud thump behind me. The dogs shot to attention.

"What was that?" The bamboo cutting board was lying at Jesse's feet. I could see that he was angry, but I asked him anyway. "Why did you do that?"

"To get your attention! Damn it Lacey, you can't keep changing your mind! One minute you say you want to be with me and then you do an about turn and say you don't. I am becoming extremely exasperated with your indecisiveness. How long are you going to keep testing me?"

"Jesse," I said through tears. "I never once said I didn't want you. I will probably take myself off to a nunnery when you leave me because you can't abandon your family, and I can't be the reason why you did. That's the only outcome here. Maybe you can leave your wife, but you can't abandon your daughters."

"Come here." He sat down and pulled me unto his lap. He dabbed at my tear stained face.

"Honey, Hilary and Leigh will always be my girls, no matter what. They can choose to accept you or not…if they don't, then it will be their loss. I am never going back to live with Marsha. I thought you were clear on that. There are no ifs, ands and buts; you are in my life to stay, and this had better be the last I hear of your threats…going to live in a convent…my ass!"

I had to smile at that. "She asked you if you were with a woman Jesse."

"I don't see how they could possibly know about you, but it doesn't matter because I would be telling them all about you myself very soon. I am not at all worried about the girls, but I am about how James is going to react to my being with you. He is going to see me as the man who abandoned his mother when she was pregnant, and he will no doubt hate me."

"That isn't going to happen Jesse because you never knew that I was pregnant. He has wanted me to find someone to share my life with for so long and even more so since he met Blythe. She has no family; her mother and father were killed in a car accident when she was fifteen. She lived with an elderly aunt for a year, but she has also passed. I am her mother and she and James both need a father and the children a grandfather…I want that to be you Jesse."

"I want that too Lace. Does this mean that you are going to quit changing your mind every time the wind blows? I'll tie you to the bed and love the doubt out of you if I have to."

"Umm, that could be very interesting. I will try my best Jesse, but as I told you before you have only known me for two days and maybe tomorrow you will wake up with a witch in your bed."

"I will take my chances, and isn't a witch just another word for enchantress?"

"I'm just warning you Jesse. I'm the valetudinarian of emotions."

"I beg your pardon…your what?"

"Have I stumped the vocabulary of the scholar?"

"You think so eh? I am well aware that you are the hypochondriac of emotions…so there!"

"Yes, I am Jesse, and I don't blame you for being frustrated with me, but I am so very vulnerable. You could promise me the moon right now and I would believe that you could deliver it. I have been imagining this day for a very long time. In reality though, I also knew that it was never going to happen, but I was unable to convince my heart to completely abandon the possibility. I played the scenario over and over in my head to what I would do if I ever came face to face with you ever again. I envisioned myself running to you and you welcoming me with open arms, and then I would do a reality check and remember that you had jilted me and wanted nothing more to do with me. How pathetic that I was not able to erase you from my memories and give myself to someone else. It doesn't say very much for my character does it Jesse? So, you see, I am still testing the waters because I am scared to death to get in over my head. I know how I feel because I have never let those feelings go, but you did, and so I can't quite believe that you are being completely honest with me, or with yourself. How can you just say goodbye to the woman you married and your life? How can you give it up for me, the girl you once walked out on? Are you not just caught up in the circumstances that brought us together?"

"And, you accuse me of asking a lot of questions! Almost everything you say is true. The way I chose to break up with you is disgraceful, but I thought we were done with that or will you never be able to truly forgive me? Evidently, I did not forget you, and it was never more evident than on the day I married Marsha. It was supposed to be the happiest day of my life, but you interfered with that…do you want to know how?"

I nodded.

"Walking down the aisle towards me was my bride to be, but she turned into my teenage sweetheart…this petite, lilac eyed beauty with the splash of freckles and dimpled cheeks. You smiled at me, but there were tears in your eyes. I almost lost my way then, but I had another vision, and it was of you with Arthur, and I realized that I had sealed both of our fates when I had sentenced you without a trial that day in 1975. If I had of known that your marriage was a sham… well, who knows? That was then and this is now, and I don't know what else I can do or say to convince you that my feelings are genuine. Tell me Lace, and I'll do it."

I kissed him long and passionately. "You just did Jesse; thank-you for telling me that. I should say I am sorry that I invaded your wedding day, but I'm not. At least you had a traditional wedding with meaningful vows and cake and dancing, and a honeymoon…albeit with the wrong woman." I laughed at that and so did he. "I only had a judge officiating over us and saying pretentious words and then going back to the apartment, downing a glass of sparkling water and going to bed alone. It was not the wedding I had once dreamt of."

"Well, we will have to see what we can do about that. I can think of nothing that I would like better than marrying you with our children standing up for us. What do you think?"

"Jesse James Jameson…do you, at long last, plan on making an honest woman out of me?"

"Eventually, but for now, I am perfectly happy having you as my erotic paramour."

"You had better get all of those explicit descriptions of me out of your mind before James gets here. He will not take kindly to you referring to me as your mistress."

"But Honey, I'm his father."

"Doesn't matter; now let me up, I have a salad to construct."

"I have a much better idea…let's cancel dinner."

The phone rang and I went to answer it, but Jesse grabbed it from me.

"Just in case it's the crank…Hello, yes, may I ask who is calling? She's right here." He covered the mouthpiece and handed me the phone. "Some guy says he's your son."

I punched him. "Darling, how are you and Blythe and my babies? He's an old friend dear and he is staying at the house until you all get here. He's also a lawyer so is…yes James, I said lawyer. Why did you say it like that? Well Dear, you don't know all my friends." I looked at Jesse and smiled. "Well, I was staying there, but I needed some time to myself. No, I haven't been charged…we'll cross that bridge when we get to it. Now, when are you coming home?"

James asked me since when did I think of Kings Crossing as home. I indicated to Jesse that James was asking too many questions. "I once lived here you know and maybe I will again. I don't know why I said that; maybe I am just tired of the big city. Now, enough about me…how is Blythe? That's wonderful;

I can hardly wait to see you all. What can we do? Are you sure? Yes, I know where it is. We will pick you up on Tuesday then… yes, okay, can't wait to see you all. Don't worry about me… why? All right, I will." I handed the phone to Jesse. "He wants to speak with you."

Jesse looked puzzled. I shrugged my shoulders indicating that I didn't know why.

"Hello James. Yes, your mother and I **are** very old friends. I won't let anything happen to her." He laughed nodding to me. "Oh yes, I am well aware of that. Don't worry Son, she is in very good hands. I'm looking forward to meeting you too. Your mother wants the final word."

"It just dawned on me that it is very early in the morning there; is everything all right? Okay, love and kisses and God speed." I hung up the receiver and asked Jesse what James had said.

"He just wanted me to know that you can be a force to reckon with…as if I didn't already know. He is curious about who I am, isn't he? I noticed you never mentioned my name."

"When he sees you will be time enough. I don't want him to have anything else to worry about. It is early morning there and he was up because Leah was crying and he had to tend to her. They will be here on Tuesday and I need to find Harry's old car seat for Leah which will mean a trip up the spiral staircase."

"Sounds intriguing. Is Harry short for Harrison?"

"Yes, it is. I'm so excited for you all to meet, but I am also apprehensive."

"I will do my best to win James over, but if he doesn't accept me and doesn't want me here, then we might just have a fight on our hands for I am not leaving you…understand?"

"Yes, and I am not giving you up. Let's not tell CC and Sam about us right now, okay?"

He laughed. "Honey, we don't have to say a thing… it's written all over our faces.

"Well then, I will have to try and look miserable and continue harassing you." I stated emphatically.

"Good luck with that. I'm going to warm the barbecue up… is it safe to leave the door open?"

"Of course it is! Jesse, will you be able to get me out on bail?"

"What nonsense is this? There will be no need to for you are not going to be charged." He ruffled my hair. "I know that answer does not satisfy you, so yes, if I had to, I could definitely arrange bail."

"I have some money and if it is not enough, I am sure Richie will borrow me the rest. I will go crazy if I have to go to jail Jesse." I clung to him and he did his best to kiss away my anxieties. I looked up at him and told him that I would be lost without him.

"Then, I had better stay close because I sure as hell don't want to lose you. Run along and wash your face like a good little girl." He winked at me and I beamed.

"Tell me it's onions that have got you crying Lacey and not Jess?"

CC had found me washing vegetables in the oversized kitchen sink. I told her it was not Jess.

"Good. Let me put this dessert in the fridge and I will help you. I made your favourite."

I looked at her curiously. "You did? I didn't even know I had a favourite."

"Mother used to call it "Pie in the Sky" or "Heavenly Hash", remember?"

I laughed. "Do you mean "Sex in a Pan"? Jesse will get a big kick out of that and I am sure he will tell you that there are a lot better places to have sex…." I thought I'd better quit talking, but I had already said too much.

"Lacey, you didn't?"

"Didn't what?"

"Look at me missy, did you sleep with Jess?"

"I wouldn't exactly call it sleeping."

"Is that what you two have been up to all afternoon?"

"No, it was early this morning…after the break-in."

"But you were so at odds earlier; have you made up?"

"He finally told me why he jilted me and I told him that James is his son."

CC hugged me. "Oh Lacey, I am so happy and yet so worried for you. You are so gullible right now and if he is taking advantage of you and filling your head with promises that he has no intentions of keeping I can't just stand by and see him hurt you again."

"You don't have a very high opinion of Jesse do you? Why? It doesn't matter because he loves me and I love him and we are going to be together!" I snapped.

"Please don't be angry with me Lacey. I hope you are right, but he has a pretty cushy life, and I can't see him giving it up. On the other hand, I can definitely see him leaving Marsha for you."

"Have you met her? What is she like?"

"Yes, several times. She is tall and leggy and is perfectly coiffured, never a hair out of place. She is very reserved and matronly mature. She is the complete opposite of you." CC opened the fridge and grabbed two bottles of beer and offered me one.

"No thanks, not right now. What do you mean by that remark?"

"Well, you are this cute, cuddly, petite pixie and she isn't… that's all."

"I am not petite! I am well-rounded and overly padded."

She laughed. "Well, it looks good on you! And, this hair, these curls," she tugged on my tresses, "and lavender eyes… who has purple eyes anyway besides Elizabeth Taylor? I've always been envious you know?"

"No you haven't Miss Beauty Queen of 1975, and I am sure lots of people have eyes this color. Their just a mixture of blues you know. I don't care what Marsha looks like; I want to know about her personality."

"She is as I said…I wouldn't say she was unfriendly, but she doesn't radiate warmth. The first time we met was when they were on their way to a wedding somewhere in Saskatchewan. The girls were maybe seven and eight. We just had a quick visit. I remember saying to Sam that she was not the kind of woman that I thought Jess would end up with. We were invited to dinner with them in Vancouver the last time we were down which was four or five years ago. I had the feeling that she couldn't wait for us to leave. I wondered if she knew about you and that I was your best friend."

"How would she, I'm sure that Jesse never mentioned me. What is their house like?"

"It is a well-kept heritage home in an affluent community. It overlooks the ocean…I think they have beach frontage. I did get the impression that it might have been her family home. To sum it up, if there was a contest, you would win in the personality and good looks department."

"Thank-you CC, I wouldn't expect you to say anything else. However, I want to know how they acted as a couple."

"Oh that, well there was never any hand holding or eyes locking and definitely no pet name calling. Is that what you want to hear?"

"Yes; Jesse calls me honey all the time."

"Of course he does. I only hope you are not his midlife crisis."

"Why are you so down on him, CC? What did he ever do to you?"

"He trashed my best friend's life."

I gave her a quick hug. "Let's go and see if it is still warm enough to eat out on the sun porch. I'll just take the potatoes out of the oven and throw the bread in first."

Jesse and Sam came in at that precise moment. Jesse handed Sam the steaks and opened the oven door for me and popped the potatoes out. Bending over he whispered to me. "You told her didn't you?"

"She didn't have to, but I have a bone to pick with you Jess." CC answered for me.

"What's going on here?" Sam asked.

CC blurted it out. "Jess has already taken her to bed…that's what's going on! You and Lacey go and set the table; I need a word with Jess!"

Jesse put his arm around me. "She's still bossy I see. Sam, how do you put up with it?"

"He's perfectly happy and you would have been happy too if you hadn't been such an asshole! Lacey may have forgiven you and succumbed to your charms, but I'm not so eager to. You're no different from any other man, or in your case, a lawyer too which only doubles the bullshit!"

Sam waylaid his wife. "CC, you are being outrageously rude! What goes on between Jess and Lacey is their business. This isn't like you…how much have you had to drink?"

Jesse grinned. "No, no, she has every right to be pissed with me. CC, whatever you want to say to me, you can say it in front of Lace because I am not keeping anything from her. I know why you are suspicious of my intentions…God, I feel as though I am talking to her father. You think we jumped right into the water before we even got our feet wet, right? Well, sometimes all it takes is just one look and that's what happened…the same as it did the first day I met her. I've never discussed what I did to Lace with you guys because I wanted to remain friends and I knew if I told you the truth, you would hate me, and apparently I was right."

CC started to cry. "I don't hate you Jess, and I am sorry, but I am only thinking of Lacey. There is so much going on with her and then you arrive on the scene and complicate matters. She is still my very best friend and I'm afraid for her. Are you her savoir Jess, or her executioner?"

Jesse took my hand and walked me over to CC. "Look at me CC. Do you not see the fire in my eyes when I look at Lacey? I'm not some stupid teenager anymore. I know what I feel for her and I can guarantee you its real. Yeah, yeah, I hear you… you're thinking that we don't even know each other anymore, right? We have been estranged for over twenty years and now after only two days we have found our way back to each other and discovered that we still have feelings for one another. I can see how you find this hard to believe, but it is true. I have told Lacey things I have never told another woman. I am not her savoir, but she is mine. She has opened up Heaven's door and shown me what real love is, and I will do whatever I have to do to keep that door open. If you give me a chance, you might come to love me a little too."

CC threw her arms around us. "Damn you Jess Jameson, you still have the silver tongue! I guess you need it being a lawyer and all."

"Thank-you both for making me cry. Sam, what say you and I get this dinner on the table and leave these two to commiserate? Oh, oh, I think I smell burning bread!" I sniffled.

"Go ahead Babe; I'll see what I can salvage. Are you sure it's safe to leave me alone with this barracuda?" Jesse joked.

I kissed him and told him the wine was chilling and to hurry because I was starving.

There was no more said of yesterday. We discussed James and how we were going to break the news to him. Sam guessed that we wouldn't have to tell him anything because he would know the second he laid eyes on Jess.

"Do you think he looks like me?" Jesse pulled out the pictures I had given him.

"Oh yes, he is very much your son." CC said. Jesse beamed at me.

We did not tell them of our plans to go up Sugarloaf Mountain or of my fears of being indicted.

We said goodnight. Jesse told me to warm up the bed and he would see to the dogs and door.

"Rats!" I untangled myself from Jesse's arms.

"What is it now Lace?"

"I forgot to set the alarm, that's all. Will it keep you awake if I put my music on really low?"

"No, I can sleep through almost anything. It's you who has to get some sleep so I am fine with the music; I can barely hear it anyhow. What's keeping you awake…is it me?"

"No, I'm just too anxious about what we may find up the mountain tomorrow. I wish I had a cigarette."

Jess raised himself up on one elbow. "You told me that was the last one last night."

"I don't mean a "funny" cig; I mean a real one. You know; the kind you buy from a store. I always used to have one with Richie."

"Well, now you have my full attention. Do you mean the same way you and I used to share one after…you know, when we were teenagers?"

"Don't be daft Jesse! Are you forgetting that Richie is gay?"

"One never knows. I'm quite sure that many men, no matter their persuasion, have succumbed to your charms…"

"Your painting me as a femme fatale, and I can assure you that I am anything but. I didn't go around enticing men into my boudoir. I told you there were very few who appealed to me.

I wasn't interested in a white picket fence, five kids, a minivan, or sex without all the bells and whistles of love. I am just a plain Jane, and I can assure you that most men never even gave me a second glance."

"Then, they must have all been blind for a plain Jane you are not! I am most grateful for their ignorance; otherwise, you would not be here with me. But, back to your story."

"Arthur was the front man. He didn't mind the press and accolades, or even the negative reviews. He was the one who addressed the paparazzi backstage after a performance and congratulated the actors and did audience participation. Richie would be gone as soon as the curtains closed. I would just hang around in case Arthur needed me, but one night, I followed Richie out the back door. I found him sitting on an old crate and smoking. At first, I was worried that it might have been "junk" because he had come to us damaged…I'll explain later, but it was just a regular menthol cigarette. I had a couple of puffs as he wanted me to know that he wasn't cheating. He would never give me something illegal. Pretty soon I would share a smoke with him until I graduated to a whole one. He bought me the most magnificent cigarette holder as he knew I didn't like the nicotine on my fingers. It was, I should say "is", because I still have it, black ebony with inlaid pearl swans. It once belonged to Bette Davis, so the story says. So, now, when I need to relax, I'll have a few drags; that's all."

"Do you inhale?" Jess asked me.

I knew he was teasing. "Not so much, I still choke."

"Good, now what did you mean when you said that Richie came to you damaged?"

"Whereas Arthur was my best friend, Richie was the brother I never had. The day we met him was indeed fortuitous. Arthur had made some investments with family monies. They had paid off substantially and were financing his lifestyle which was travelling from venue to venue with his small theatrical troupe. He was writing and producing plays, but they were inconsequential. He wanted to own his own theatre so that he could do things on a much bigger scale. He had not been successful at locating one as they were either overpriced, too rundown, or in some obscure area. It was in the autumn of 1977 and Arthur wanted me to come with him as he wanted my input on one he had found in the Soho district. I bundled James up and off we went. Arthur went off to investigate on his own and I stayed and talked with the realtor. Awhile later we heard loud voices and went down to the stage and found Arthur in a heated argument with another man.

Apparently, the realtor had screwed up and gave the same appointment to two people. I figured they would be in a bidding war before long and intervened with my two cents worth. Through much discussion we learnt that Richie already owned several theaters but had not done anything with them and had not been able to make anything work. We didn't know it at the time but it was because of his addictions. I told him that he needed a manager and that the two of them should form a partnership. Then I left them to continue arguing and took James home. Next thing I know there is a knock at the door and the two of them are standing there laughing and drunk as skunks. That's how the partnership started and because it was my idea, I was to be included. The first thing we had to do was get Richie to face up to his addictions. He had managed to free himself of hard drugs, but was not having any success with alcohol. We got him into AA and with our support he has been clean and sober for almost twenty years. Oh, there were many slips along the way, but he would right himself and start over again. Of course, finding his soul mate in Arthur helped immensely. I have talked with him every day since Arthur's death, and I am pretty sure he is handling it. He and his family are estranged as they can't handle his life choices. However, his maternal grandmother was less small-minded and left him a hefty inheritance which kept him out of the gutters…as he says. And, that is the story of how we all met. He is James's Godfather and loves us as if we were his own. He and Arthur bought me the house in suburbia and helped me to establish my four day-care centers. I am only twenty minutes by train into the city. James and Leah moved in with me when she became ill. I don't even want to think what is going to happen next."

"Why do you say that Lace?"

"I just can't think about anything at this point in time. I am going to try and be positive for you and the kids and Richie, but you know that underneath, I am scared to death of losing you all."

Jess tightened his hold on me. "You won't lose any of us Darling; I promise you. Thank you for telling me your story. I see why Richie is so important to you and I look forward to meeting him. Now, are you ready to try and close your eyes?"

"Not quite… will you indulge me a little longer and come and let me show you something?"

"You know I will follow you anywhere. Just lead me on."

I scrambled out of bed and threw my red caftan on. "You had better put your pants and a shirt on as it might be cold in there." I slipped into a pair of flats and told him that he should put his shoes on also.

"I have no idea where you are taking me Lace, but you are probably the only person that could entice me to get out of bed and follow you outside at this unholy hour."

I took his hand and pulled him down the hall. "We're not going outside Jesse, only here."

I opened the door that led into Arthur's bedroom. There was still a childhood plaque on it that read: Arthur's Kingdom.

"Have you ever been in here before Jess?"

"Oddly enough I have, twice on fact. My mother dragged Sam and Tim and I over here to visit with Arthur after his father died. We hardly knew him, but mother insisted we pay our respects. It was pretty sad as his dad was only fifty two. Did you go to the funeral?"

"No, I didn't even know Arthur then. When was the other time?"

"You are going to laugh. I don't know how you girls were initiated into high school, but we boys drew lots as to who would be our persecutors. Sam and I and several others drew Arthur. I don't know if it was the less of the evils because we didn't have to parade around town in our undies or smoke cigars and drink whiskey until we puked our guts out, or wear togas for a week. Oh no, Arthur had something entirely different for our induction. We were given pen and paper and told to write a short story or play. It was not to exceed five thousand words and must be about what we would do if we were separated from our families and whisked off to a foreign land, and how we would communicate and defend ourselves with the mystical creatures that we would encounter. He expected us to write a God damn fairy tale! Why are you laughing?"

"You told me I would laugh didn't you? What happened to your stories?"

"Damned if I know… never saw mine again. He probably had a good gut busting chuckle and then threw our agonizing four hours of work down the toilet. What else would he have done with them? I can tell you we all thought that they would pop up on the bulletin board or worse yet be read over the P.A., but nothing ever became of them."

"That's just what you think Jesse…I think I might know where they are."

"How could you?"

"First, I want to tell me what you were thinking about when you were writing your fairy tale."

"I honestly don't know, and I don't even remember one word of what I wrote. It was all very strange, but I guess it was just the showman coming out in Arthur. Do you think he thought that one of us would come up with a masterpiece and that someday he'd turn it into a play?

"Who knows? Did you get to read the other's essays?"

"Not exactly; we had to read our own out loud. It was pretty funny."

"I don't think they are funny at all and when they are all put together they make for a most interesting read." I smiled at Jess. "It never made sense to be before, but it does now. I know exactly where they are and if you are a good boy I might show you what happened to them." I took his hand. "Now, are you ready to come to Neverland with me?"

"I think you've already taken me there my dear."

"That was wonderland, silly. Was this old buckboard bench here when you were here?"

"I have no idea, why?"

"Come and sit with me." I put my arms around Jess and kissed him.

I told him that he might hear a whooshing sound and that he may feel disoriented for a second.

"Jesus Christ Lacey, what have you done to me now…just a minute…where the hell are we?"

I watched as he looked around in astonishment at his surroundings and then at me.

"I told you we were going to Neverland."

"I didn't think you actually meant Peter Pan's Neverland! Okay, a thousand questions…who built this room and when, and how in hell did they get a pirate ship in here?"

I followed Jess as he wandered around examining all the artefacts. He turned to me and said,

"Well?"

"Arthur's great grandfather, Richard King, is the one who had this house built sometime in the 1800's. He, being from England, wanted his domicile to mimic some British mansion complete with a hidden room. Of course, it did not start out like this. I'm sure it went through many changes throughout the years. Arthur's grandfather, Mitchell King, was responsible for the concept of Neverland. However, he died two years after Arthur was born. He had made specific plans for the room and the task was taken up by Arthur's father, Clive. The replica of Captain Hook's ship was assembled right here. Lots of the props like the chests, flags, and maps are authentic though I know not where they were found. Clive haunted many antique shops and old movie houses looking for the perfect specimens. He did all the painting on the walls and floor. Arthur added things like the talking parrots, fairies and alligator after his father passed away. It's all right to touch everything Jess. Come; let's walk the plank into the ship."

"I'm still back in the bedroom and this is all a dream isn't it? Really, a clandestine room that is meant to resemble Neverland… I don't think so."

"It's just a child's playroom Jesse…there is nothing sinister about it. I can hardly wait to see Harry's eyes light up when he first sees it. I think he is old enough to appreciate it now."

"I didn't say it was sinister Hon…I guess I am still half asleep. There is something missing, or maybe I should say, someone missing. Where is the forever boy, Peter Pan?"

I opened up a wooden trunk. "He's in here." I pulled out a green outfit complete with slippers and a hat. "Every size from four to twenty four is in here." I held it up to Jess. "Does the little boy in you want to be Peter? Look, there is even a Wendy costume, and my favourite…Tinkerbelle. Who would you like me to be Jesse?"

"I just want you to be you, but role playing could be fun." He teased running his fingers through my hair. "So, how many people know about this room?"

"Four now; James, Blythe, you and me."

"Arthur really kept it a secret then? What's in that tunnel-like wall over there?"

"Why the secret exit of course. What's the use of having a secret room if you don't have an escape route? There are Indians and pirates roaming around you know…" I walked over to the wall and flipped on a switch which brought the floor and ceiling to life. The painted water underneath the ship actually appeared to be flowing and the sky was alight with bright twinkling stars and colourful flying fairies. Jess shook his head in disbelief and stated that he was amazed that Arthur had managed to keep this fantasy a secret from his friends. I led him into the tunnel which was dark except for a few scattered lights hidden in the recessed walls. We turned a corner and stopped in front of a large red door. I think he was expecting me to open it.

"What's on the other side of the door?" He asked.

"There are two exits that lead from the tunnel. One goes to the root cellar and the other comes out under the pergola in the back garden. There is a big wheel-like thing at the end, sort of like a man-hole cover allowing one to enter or exit from."

"Well, what are we waiting for, let's go."

"Not tonight Jesse, it's late. I just wanted you to know about this room…I can't explain why. The door is locked and you have to know the combination to be able to open it." I opened a panel on the door. "The combination is 333-444-333; can you remember that?"

He told me that it was easy enough to remember and asked why he would ever need to know it.

"I just want you to know Jesse, that's all."

"You know Hon; it's only 2 a.m., so we can do the whole jaunt as we don't have to be up for another four hours or so."

"You know you don't have to come with me in the morning. I am perfectly capable of taking myself up the mountain." I said rather crossly.

"Aha, there she is! I wondered where your alternate-self had gotten to."

"What are you insinuating?"

"I'm not insinuating anything; I'm stating it outright Babe; you have two personalities, and the impetuous side just showed itself again."

"Well, I am taking my impetuous self to bed. You do what you want to. I gave you the combination, so have fun stumbling around in the dark!"

Jesse grabbed me laughing. "I sure know how to get your goat don't I? I'm going where you are going, so get us the hell out of here because I don't have a clue as to how we got here."

I said through clenched teeth trying not to smile. "Short attention span I see. You are not very observant for a lawyer are you?"

"All I know young lady is that you sat me down on a bench in Arthur's room and kissed me, and we magically entered Neverland."

"Sure Jesse, that's how it happened. Do you want me to kiss you again?"

"Of course I do."

"Okay, come and sit on the bench again and I will."

We were back in Arthur's room again and Jess stated that he was no more the wiser and asked me if I was going to tell him how I had manoeuvered the bench.

"You figure it out Mr. Smarty Lawyer man!"

He followed me out. "God, you're exasperating woman! You have a lot of explaining to do so don't think you're off the hook."

"Tomorrow Jesse, tomorrow. Now, who do you want to sleep with… sweet Lacey, or that impetuous woman?" I teased.

"You are going to kill me, you know that don't you?"

"Do you think that I am a hypochondriac Jesse?"

"You are the one who said you were a hypochondriac of emotions earlier, not me."

"Did I say hypochondriac? I meant nymphomaniac."

Jess pulled me into his arms laughing. "No darling, I don't think that, but come here, let's see."

Sunday, May 22nd

I slipped out of bed quietly and pulled my caftan on, collected the baseball bat from the closet and the clothes that I had laid out the night before. I stopped at the kitchen and turned the coffee pot on before getting dressed in the downstairs bathroom, gathered a few more articles that I wanted to take with us up Sugarloaf. The dogs had already been let out in their pen so I called them back in and beckoned them to follow me upstairs. I entered the bedroom and patted the bed where Jess was still sleeping peacefully. The dogs took that as an invitation and jumped up on the bed licking his face and barking loudly.

"What the hell! Lacey, call your dogs off!"

I whistled and the dogs, having accomplished their mission came running after me. I waited for Jesse on the kitchen stairs. He plunked down beside me and I handed him a steaming cup of coffee. He kissed me on the cheek. "Thanks Babe."

"What took you so long, did you forget about our mission this morning?"

"No chance of that my dear." He laughed. "Thanks for the wake-up call."

"You are welcome. You didn't have to shower you know because we are probably going to get dirty. I have everything in the jeep, and so whenever you are ready we can go."

"What do you mean by 'everything'?"

"You know, things we might need; bat, broom, gun…"

"Hold on, a gun…why?"

"It's not a real gun, just a little bee-bee gun in case the coyotes get too friendly."

"I hardly think that they will even be up at this time in the morning, but whatever…"

"I like to be prepared. Come on, let's get going." I pulled him and he followed me down the stairs. I passed the dog's leashes to him and grabbed the thermos of coffee.

"I thought we were going to have one of our heart to heart talks when I found you waiting for me on the steps; guess I was wrong." Jess said.

"Later Darling, later; now is the time to find out what lies above."

Jess tried to settle the dogs down in the back of the jeep but they were too hyper and kept barking and nipping at each other. "Do you really think we need to take them Lace?"

"They are just excited to be going on an outing; they will settle down soon." I talked soothingly to them and they did quiet somewhat. "I thought of taking the four-wheeler, but then they would have to run a long side of us and might get to the evidence first."

"There may very well be no evidence you know Honey. Where is the quad kept?"

I pointed to a large barn-like building as we drove by it. "It's kept in there."

"Well, it's not there now. I have been through every building on the property and I have not come across any quad." Jess told me.

"Arthur must have driven it over to the carriage house. We can check when we go over tomorrow. Maybe we should have taken the main road as this goat trail is pretty rough, but I wanted to come right out on top where we have seen all the activity and this is the best way."

"It's okay Hon; this is what jeeps are made for. Now, when we get there, I want you to remain in the jeep with the dogs until I can scope out the area, okay?"

"Why?"

"Will you please do as I ask Lace? I don't want you to witness anything else ugly."

I crossed my arms and pretended to pout. "I'll give you two minutes Jesse James; that's all."

At the summit we were surprized to see that only a few crows were in attendance at what looked like a fissure in the ground. The crows scattered as Jess slammed the jeep door. He surveyed the area and peered into the crevasse. He walked back to me and asked for my phone.

"I didn't bring it Jesse; what do you want it for? What did you see? Can I get out now?"

"Yes, you can get out as soon as I have contacted the police. My phone is in my jacket pocket."

I found the phone and handed it to him. I started to speak but he quietened me with a kiss. I smiled and said. "That's not going to shut me up for long you know."

"I know, hold on. Hello, who have I got? Constable Jones, Jess Jameson here; any chance that Corporal Newman is on duty today, yes thanks, I'll hold."

I was getting more impatient by the second and perturbed by Jess not letting me out the door so I climbed over the gear shift and out the other door. Jess shook his head and followed me to the newly dug hole in the ground.

"I knew it!" I exclaimed.

"Timothy, glad you're there. Lacey and I are up Sugarloaf above Tudor House and I think there is something here that you should take a look at. Yes, we came up the so called road along side of the house. Thanks Timothy. By the way, you may want to stop by the carriage house and bring the forensic team with you. Yup, to be sure, there is evidence here. Okay, see you in a bit."

I bent down to study the contents of the hole. There wasn't much to see, just a piece of dark, dirty carpet that was half buried and the remains of something unrecognizable.

"What do you think that is Jesse?"

"Don't know; if I had to guess I would say it was a carcass of a small animal like a cat."

"Well, that doesn't make any sense; why would a cat be buried with the rug?"

"Let's just wait for Timothy and the team to arrive. Let's get those wild dogs and take them for a walk. If I remember correctly there's a creek up here somewhere isn't there?"

"Yes, it is over the next knoll. I guess we could take them down to get a drink."

"We don't want to contaminate the area so we'll need to keep them well away from the hole."

We retrieved the dogs and climbed up the slope and were astonished as to what lay below us.

"Well I guess we know what happened to Arthur's quad don't we? Do you recognize it as his? I suppose the trailer lying in the creek is what they used to haul the bloody rug up here in."

"I am pretty sure it's Arthur's. You said "they" Jesse; do you think there is more than one person involved in this?"

"It's beginning to look like that Hon. Damn it; I need to see the coroner's and medical examiner's reports." Jess cursed.

"Why, it's not going to prove anything is it?"

"It could certainly prove your innocence. All we have now is an estimated time of death guessed at by the local constabulary and doctor. I need to know if there was only one entrance wound because if there was more this could very well be a crime of passion."

"If you are insinuating that Richie had something to do with Arthur's death you are barking up the wrong tree and **I** didn't kill him, so that leaves no one!" I was adamant.

"We can't leave any stone unturned Lace. I'm not accusing Richie, but it wouldn't be the first time a lover's quarrel has escalated into violence."

"Well, I didn't kill you did I? Lord knows that I wanted to." I hoped I had made my point. "When you meet Richie, you will know he couldn't do such a thing."

"You are probably right and I hope for your sake you are. Were you really that angry with me Lace? Did you want to do me bodily harm?"

He was teasing, but I wasn't. "Angry is not the word I would use to describe how I felt. I think I went a little crazy, and sometimes even now, I look at you I want to punish you for what you did to me." I turned away from him and started up the hill with Trixie in tow. Jess and Mickey caught up to me. I didn't want to but I started crying. Jess took me in his arms.

After a long silence he said. "We will never be at a loss for conversation because you are never going to let yesterday go, and you'll keep finding new ways to bring the past into our day no matter what a great time we are having, won't you? I'll keep dealing with it because the alternative would be for me to leave, and that is not going to happen because I love you. So go ahead hit me, abuse me, make me feel guilty…I can take it. If I only have the nights with you when you portray your sweetness and your true feelings for me, I think I'll survive."

I did hit him and he let me beat on him for a while until the dogs started attacking us both. I looked into his eyes and stroked his face.

"Sorry; I think the cavalry is here." I took his hand and we strolled back down to where Timothy and Ms. Moore and half a dozen other policemen were surveying the burial hole. I walked over to Timothy. "I suppose you are curious as to what that mud-covered piece of carpet has to do with Arthur's demise? Well, it's not mud; it's blood, and it is the entrance mat from the carriage house that was missing when I discovered Arthur's body. The boot tray is still missing, but perhaps you will find it over the next knoll where you will also find Arthur's overturned quad." I said unemotionally. I took Mickey's leash from Jess. "I'll be in the jeep with the dogs if anyone needs me."

I heard Timothy ask if I was all right, and Jesse's excuse for me before I shut the jeep door.

"I think she's almost reached the breaking point. Half the time she doesn't even realize what she is saying. I'm certain that she didn't mean to be so abrupt with you."

"You don't have to apologize for her Jess; she has every reason to be stressed. Not only did she find Arthur's body, but she has to endure this long wait to be absolved of any culpability even though she has never been formally charged. I'm sure she has been expecting a knock on the door and to be taken into custody at any time. I think the evidence will prove that she is innocent, and I hope it will be forthcoming by the end of the day. Thank God that she has you. Take her home and look after her. I'll stop by the house after we wrap up here."

Jesse parked on the back lawn. "You go in and rest Honey. I'll tend to the dogs and then I want to take the hose to the jeep and turn some sprinklers on okay?"

I attempted a smile and dragged my body out of the jeep. Jesse ran ahead of me and unlocked the door. I thanked him and smiled. He kissed me and I didn't resist. I watched for a few minutes while he sprayed the dogs and hosed off the jeep. I went in the house and sat down on the kitchen steps to wait for him. He came in fifteen minutes later.

"Do you want to talk Lacey?"

"I always want to talk to you Jesse, but no, I don't need to talk. I just couldn't get any further."

He scrambled up to me. "Well, that's what I am here for. Timothy told me to look after you and that's what I am going to do." He helped me to stand up.

"Do you think I need looking after Jess?"

He laughed. "Normally, no, little Miss Feisty, but today you are going to surrender and let me take charge. I'll run a bath for you and while you are soaking, I'll make you some breakfast."

"Oh Jesse, I fear I will sink in the tub and I don't have the strength to shower. I just want to crawl into bed and pull the covers over me, but I think I might be able to eat."

"Okey dokey, do you want me to help you undress?"

"Who will make breakfast then?" I teased.

He threw me a nightgown and left smiling. "Are you still going to be awake when I return?"

I assured him I would be as I was starving. I apologized for my outburst earlier.

He blew me a kiss from the doorway.

Jess

I put on a fresh pot of coffee and readied the pan for the eggs. I hoped poached was still her favourite. The house needed music. I turned the radio on and sang along to the song that I recognized from another lifetime ago. I couldn't remember ever being this happy. There was just one flaw in the ointment and that was Marsha. I wondered how long I could put off telling her about Lacey. I cursed to myself and put her away for another day. I found a small vase and popped in one of the daisies from the bouquet I had bought. A thought occurred to me; why were there no sympathy arrangements or cards anywhere? I'd ask Lace later.

She was sitting up anticipating my arrival. A small tear slid down her cheek. "Oh Jesse, you remembered I like poached eggs and that daisies are my favourite."

She took a sip of orange juice and asked where her coffee and my breakfast were.

"Do you really think you need the caffeine Honey? And, some things, one never forgets. I'll eat when I know you are resting. Do you want your music on? I found a station on the radio that plays songs from the sixties and seventies. It's very refreshing to hear music that makes sense."

"I'll skip the music for now. Have you heard our song yet?"

I said I hadn't and hoped she wouldn't pursue the subject any further as I hadn't a clue as to what our song had been. I took the tray from her and kissed her. She said she'd see me in an hour or two. I cleaned up the kitchen and poured a cup of coffee and retreated into the den to complete my notes on what I knew so far about Arthur's death. Mostly everything was from Lacey's account of her discovering his body. Hopefully, I would have the answers by tomorrow when I would have access to the coroner's findings. I had just shut the computer down when I heard the dogs barking enthusiastically and ran out to quiet them. I encountered Timothy playing ball with them inside their pen.

"Sorry Jess, I needed a diversion. I didn't expect them to be so noisy."

I laughed. "It doesn't take much to get them excited. Let's go inside as Lacey is sleeping."

"God, I hope we didn't wake her."

"We'll soon see." I grabbed two cokes out of the fridge and led Timothy out to the sun porch listening to any sign of movement from upstairs. Satisfied that she was still asleep I sat down and let Timothy describe the findings up Sugarloaf.

"First, I should inform you that there weren't any prints on the outside of the doggie door, besides the dogs, of course. The inside is another matter, but Mellie is sure that they will turn out to be the families'."

"Who is Mellie?" I asked.

"Sorry, Melanie Moore…she told me to call her Mellie."

"Oh, she did, did she?" I said jokingly.

Timothy blushed ever so slightly. "Yeah, she did."

I asked if they were done with the carriage house yet.

"They are wrapping up but don't take Lacey there until tomorrow afternoon. The carpet hasn't been removed yet. We've got a cleaning crew coming into tomorrow morning to remove it and clean the floor. I don't think that Lacey needs to be subjected to that again."

"Thanks Tim, send me the bill."

"That's not for you to worry about right now Jess. Now, about our findings from the pit…there was nothing buried underneath the rug and we did dig down until we hit bedrock. It's damn heavy and not just from the dirt. Lacey couldn't possibly have lifted it. It looks like it is blood soaked, but until it's tested it's just speculation. Anyhow, there is still a crew up the hill searching for God knows what. I don't mind telling you that it is very hard for me to be objective. Lacey is like a second mother to me even though I would only see her for a week or two every year when her and James would come to Kings Crossing in the summer, and periodically at Christmas. She and my Mom have remained friends and Mom even visited her in New York or whatever that suburb is where she lived. I always suspected that something was up with her and Arthur because they didn't live together. Mom said it was because Lacey didn't want to live in the city, but Arthur had to because of his work in the theater. There is more to it than that though isn't there Jess? No, no explanation needed…none of my business anyway."

"Lacey and Arthur did not have the typical marriage. She did love him…it just wasn't the love between a man and a woman.

I can't say anything more right now as that part is up to Lace and James. Tell me Timothy, has James ever discussed his father with you?"

"I know Arthur was not his biological father. I don't know if he knew who was as he never said anything to me. I think he went on a fact finding mission a few years back because when he got back here he was different. I think he must have found something out."

"When was that and where did he go?"

"Don't know Jess…is it important?" Timothy was most curious as to my questions.

I leaned across the table. "Come on Tim, you're a cop so surely you have had your suspicions about me and Lacey? She's way more than just a client, and I am damn more than just her lawyer friend. Have your parents not mentioned that we were sweethearts back in the seventies? Have they never told you that they suspect that I am James's father?"

Timothy did not register shock. "No Sir, they have not. I knew about you from Uncle Sam, but just that you were all school friends. I may have seen pictures of you and Lacey in their albums or yearbooks, but I had no idea that you two had a thing for each other."

I smiled wide and shamelessly. "I don't know why I feel I need to confide in you, but I don't mind telling you that Lacey and I definitely have "a thing" for each other. Actually, it's a lot more than that…we have found ourselves madly in love with each other again. What do you say about that and would it surprise you if I told you that James is indeed my son?"

Timothy nodded his head. "No, it would not. My only question is, does James know?"

"Lacey has never told him, and I am still not sure she ever would have if I hadn't come to Kings Crossing. Nobody else knew for sure except maybe Arthur. I have to confess Timothy that I am more than a little apprehensive about our first meeting." I passed the pictures of James to Timothy. "She gave me these the other day, and I am not ashamed to say that they brought tears to my eyes. He resembles me doesn't he?"

"Yes, he does. When I first met you the other night, I knew you and James had to be related. It did cross my mind that you may very well be his father, but it was none of my business and so I didn't say anything. I think I can assure you that once all the facts are known James will be only too happy to have you as his father."

"Thanks for the vote of confidence Tim. However, there is one thing I will not tolerate, and that is blaming his mother for keeping my identity from him. I will come clean about everything and then it will be up to him to accept me or not."

"Jess, I have only known you for two days, but I know you are an honourable and compassionate man. James will see that too, and Lacey's happiness will speak volumes."

"One can only hope. Now what other information do you have for me of Arthur's misfortune?"

"There are no new findings besides the discovery of the buried carpet that I am aware of, and that is in the hands of the crime lab as we speak. Clara Brankco, Hilda's companion, was kind enough to come down to headquarters for fingerprinting which will no doubt account for half the prints taken from the bedroom. The majority will be Hilda's and maybe Arthur's and Lacey's, and yours are only on the inside door knob right? Did you know that Lacey's prints are on file with the data base?"

I nodded in affirmation. "I do Tim. She told me of her arrest in New York for possession of marijuana. Do you know about her daughter-in-law's health problems?"

"Yes, and that and has no bearing on this case. James informed me of his mother's run-in with the law last year. I believe that she received a slap on the wrist and a hefty fine."

"She didn't go into great detail with me, but I know that she would do it again in a heartbeat."

Timothy laughed as he got up to take his leave. "I think you are right Jess. Tomorrow is the day that you should be privy to the coroner's report and anything else of relevance to the case. None of us at headquarters believe that Lacey is guilty of anything."

I shook his hand and walked with him to the door. "Thanks Tim; I appreciate it greatly."

No sooner had I closed the door when I heard Lacey on the stairs. She was dressed in a knee length blue white daisy patterned dress. "Hey, sleeping beauty, I was wondering if I was going to have to come up there and bestow a kiss upon those ruby lips to awaken you."

"I wouldn't have minded that. How long was I asleep?" She asked yawning.

"Not all that long; two hours maybe. I hope Timothy and I didn't wake you?"

She turned the radio on. "What did Timmy have to say? More bad news I suppose…by the way, did you by any chance remember "our song?""

"Fifty Ways to Leave Your Lover" came barrelling over the air waves. Lacey smirked.

I pulled my chair up next to hers. "I have to be honest with you Honey; I don't remember us having a song so to say."

She patted my hand. "That's because we didn't. I was just foolin' with you. We did like music though, and we did like to dance. Tell me Jess, do you and Marsha dance a lot?"

"That would be a resounding "NO." I honestly can't remember when I last danced…oh yeah; it was at Leigh's grad. How about you Lace?"

"It would have been at James's and Blyth's wedding. Do you think we can try it now?"

I pulled her up into my arms. "I think so, but I'm a little rusty."

The radio obliged us with Terry Jacks "Seasons in the Sun" and Paul Anka's, "You're Having My Baby." The blare of the telephone rudely interrupted us.

I danced Lacey over and freed one hand to answer it. "Tudor House, you've got Jess Jameson."

"Hey Jess old buddy, how the hell are you?"

"Tim Newman, I would know that voice anywhere! Timothy said that you and Laura were thinking of dropping by for a visit?"

"Laura has seen Lacey briefly at Sam's, but I haven't had the pleasure. If it's a good time, we would like to drop by and pay our condolences?"

"I'll ask her Tim; she just stepped out of the room…hold on." I put the phone in the rest.

"What's that all about; I'm right here." Lacey declared.

"I want to clear it with you before I invite them over. Are you up for a little visit?"

"I thought we had plans already." She pouted.

"We do Hon, but it's not even noon yet; we have lots of time."

"All right; but just for a little while. I can tell that you are anxious to see one of your old cronies." She let go of my hand. "Tell them to come over right away."

I told Tim that we were free until one o'clock. He said they were on their way.

Laura presented Lacey with an enormous bouquet of freshly cut flowers. "I know the house is probably overflowing, but I needed to bring something special to a very dear friend." They hugged and Lacey told her that she had the florists put a hold on deliveries until the service.

"Most of them would mean nothing to me, but these do. They are beautiful; thank-you."

She acknowledged Tim with a hug and a quick kiss to the cheek. "Jess, if you will take these and put them on the piano in the living room and show our guests in, I will bring the tea."

I wondered why we were going to the formal living room, but did as I was told. I was just about to go and see what was taking her so long when she appeared in the doorway with her hands empty. I asked her if she needed help with the tray. She didn't answer, but came over and sat down beside me. The only way she could have gotten any closer would be if she had sat on my lap. I smiled at her and asked her again what had happened to the ice tea. She giggled and started to get up. I stopped her and told her I would get it. She thanked me and sat back and told Laura again how much she appreciated the flowers. When I returned she thanked me again. I knew something was up with her by the look in her eyes. I passed everyone a glass of tea and squeezed in next to her. She took my free hand. Well, I thought to myself, so much for keeping our relationship under wraps.

"I heard you ask Jesse if this was the first time that we had seen each other in a while…it's the first time in almost twenty four years." She smiled at me. "We find that we still have feelings for each other… very intense feelings. The truth is that I never stopped loving him, and I have not been able to find love with anyone else. Oh, you must be thinking that I am some sort of a harlot for jumping into bed with Jesse when Arthur isn't even cold in the ground yet. Well…"

Laura interrupted her. "We think no such thing Lacey. We always thought that you and Arthur married for something other than love."

"You're right Laura because we did. Arthur wanted to give his mother a grandchild and I needed a father for the child that I was carrying. Wait, that isn't right, I needed a name for him since the real father wasn't available." Lacey started to cry. "That's not what I want to say…"

"Honey," I said putting my arm around her. "look at me; it's okay." I pulled her close to me and addressed Tim and Laura. "I am crazy about this little lady and I knew that I still loved her the second I saw her." I squeezed her tightly. "I think what Lacey was trying to tell you is that she and Arthur did not have a traditional marriage; it was a marriage of convenience. This is not for public knowledge though many people suspect it… Arthur has always been gay. He proposed that they should marry as it would solve two problems; Hilda would have her grandchild and Lacey would have a legitimate name for her son. I think that you both have had suspicions that James is my son, and I am pleased to say that yes, he is."

Laura and Tim both nodded and Tim asked if we had told James yet.

Lacey sat up perfectly composed. "No, we are going to tell him when he arrives on Tuesday. I think as soon as he sees Jesse, he will know. They resemble each other don't you think? I need you to know that Jesse had no idea that he had a son; he only found out the other day. I kept it from him all these years because I couldn't forgive him for what he had done to me. Oh, my God Jesse, I just realized that this was my way of punishing you. Can you ever forgive me?"

"Honey, we have already discussed this." I didn't want to air our dirty laundry any further. "I don't harbour any ill feelings toward Lacey. She did what she felt she had to do. I take full responsibility for her actions as I hurt her very deeply back then. But, this is today, and we are going to go forward. I want to spend the rest of my life with her…I could never go back to the life I lived before." I kissed her and she beamed.

"Are you still married then Jess?" Laura asked.

"Yes I am, in name only. I hope to end it legally as soon as this mess is all cleared up."

Tim asked if it was going to be a problem or had I already discussed divorce with my wife.

"No, the subject has never come up. I suppose I would have gone on living in a meaningless and loveless marriage if I'd never set foot back in Kings Crossing again but I did, and I've found my heart and my soul mate again."

Lacey's eyes met mine and the connection sent a warm feeling up and down my body.

I directed my question to Tim and Laura. "You two are still in love, aren't you?"

Laura answered for the both of them. "Yes, we are. I can't imagine my life without Tim."

"I can't imagine my life without her either. Remember how we always talked about us and Sam and CC all growing old together? It's none of our business why you split up…something to do with a lot of bullshit I think."

Lacey laughed, but it wasn't a joyful laugh. "Yeah, you're right Tim…a lot of B.S. and a little blonde vixen named Mavis." She scowled at me. "Or should I say… two blonde vixens."

I knew she was vexed, but she apologized immediately, and said she was only joking. "I'm almost over that part. Let's just say Jesse had some wild oats to sow."

"I'll say this until my dying breath; nothing happened with Mavis and me. I don't think Lace really believes me, but she has forgiven me for everything else I did back then, or at least she says she has." It was more of a question than a statement.

"We've forgiven each other Sweetheart." She reached across the table to Tim and Laura. "Nobody else knows about us except Sam and CC for now. We need to tell James first. It will mean a lot to us if you can give us your blessings."

They both placed their hands over hers. Laura said with a little tear falling down her face. "Oh, we do Lacey! We can see how happy you are together." She got up and hugged us both.

"I need to clear one thing up." I said. "I told Timothy, but it wasn't any great surprise to him that I am James's father, and he said anyone with eyes could tell that Lace and I were in love."

Lacey wasn't at all alarmed that I had discussed our relationship with Timothy. "Jesse doesn't want to tell his wife about us over the phone, and then he also has to tell his two daughters. We may be in for a rough ride, but we are going to be together no matter what."

I agreed. "I have been living a ho-hum existence for so long that I wasn't even aware that I was unhappy or that I had a desperate need for love. I have felt more needed and loved in the past few days with Lace than I have in my twenty years of married life. I don't care if we argue every day, or face insurmountable odds because at least I know I'm alive with her."

Lacey was crying again and she blubbered. "See, why I love him so much?"

"I think I can speak for the both of us…thank-you for confiding in us. We are so happy that you two have found your way back to each other, and we will help you anyway we can won't we Tim?" Laura said.

"Yes, you have our support. Now, we are going to let you get on with your day and we will see you at the May Day festivities tomorrow. Good luck with the pole and kids Lacey!"

We said our good-byes at the door. Lacey turned the radio back on and stacked the glasses in the dishwasher.

"Honey," I said casually, "I sure hope I never have to put you on the witness stand."

She turned and stared at me. "What do you mean by that?"

"I thought that we had agreed to play it cool and not reveal too much about our relationship but you kind of went overboard with the details didn't you? I don't suppose that you can hide the truth about us from anyone can you?"

"The truth; you think I told them the **truth**? Did I tell them you broke my heart into a thousand pieces or that you turned me into a whore?" She snapped.

"What? What the hell did you just say?" I demanded.

"You heard me." She slammed the dishwasher shut and headed for the staircase.

"Don't you dare go up those steps Lacey Leigh Monroe!" I shouted.

She kept walking.

"If you have any respect for me at all or have any hope for us you won't take another step!" I was so dumbfounded by her remark that I was shaking. To my astonishment, she stopped. I stormed up the stairs and stopped one step above her.

"Sit down and tell me what you meant by that outrageous remark!" I was fuming.

She glared at me contemptuously. Her eyes had turned a steely grey colour. She scared me. I realized that she may be feeling threatened by me and I moved down to her level.

"Sit down, please Lace."

She did, and without making eye contact with me spoke with very little emotion. "I told you that I had boyfriends."

"Yes, you did. You just never told me how these men came into your life. Did you pick them up in bars or off the street, or did you work for an escort service?" I didn't mean to accuse her of anything, but she had opened up the door for speculation.

"NO, NO, and NO! Is that what you think of me? Do you think I was a prostitute?"

"Hey, you're the one who brought up the "whore" word…I just want to know how I fit into your lewd description of yourself."

"I will have you know Mister that all the men I dated were respectful and gentle. I can name them all for you…"

I interrupted her. "I don't need to know their names."

"Well, I'm going to tell you so you don't go on considering me a "lady of the evening.""

"Lacey, I never said that…"

"Shut up Jess, I'm not finished. There was Weston and Floyd; they were both business men and had lost their wives. They both had children in my cares. They are the two that wanted me to move in with them. Then there was Bobby who was a construction worker, and Christian who was an architect. I met them through friends. They are the ones that wanted to marry me. There was one more; his name was Taylor, and I almost eloped with him."

We had both calmed down, but I still didn't have the answer that I wanted. "Why didn't you?"

"Two things; James didn't like him and I was still legally married to Arthur."

"Were you in love with him?"

"He was exciting and he made me forget you for a while, but no, I was not in love with him. I was not ever "in" love with any of them. I knew they would only take 'no' for an answer for so long… after all, they were normal red blooded men. It was agonizing for me to take the next step. I could never relax and afterwards I felt ashamed and dirty. I couldn't keep up the premise anymore and that is why I couldn't make any of the relations work out. That's what you turned me into Jesse. I was an unfeeling woman who couldn't enjoy the most fundamental aspect of a relationship. Sex was shameful for me because there was no love on my part. That's what you did to me Jesse. I'm sorry I said what I did. I don't seem to be able to control my emotions around you. I think I am taking twenty four years of frustration out on you."

I reached out for her. "Come here Baby. I'm so sorry that I was the reason that kept you from loving anyone." She came into my arms, and I was happy to see that her eyes were a beautiful lavender again. "You scare me you know. Your mood goes from calm to erratic in a split second. After all this affair with Arthur is over I want you to make an appointment with a doctor for a complete check-up. Will you do that for me Lace?"

"I will do anything for you Jesse. What do you think is the matter with me…do you think I'm going crazy."

I managed a small laugh. "No, I don't think you're going crazy, but you are irrational at times for reasons that I can't understand. One minute you're in seventh heaven, and the next you are off on some bizarre tirade. You almost had me walking out the door after your last outburst."

"I told you didn't I? I told you not to tell Marsha about us because I would drive you away, and I almost have, haven't I? What's to stop you from really going the next time? You were ready to leave the other day before I told you about James. Am I going to drive you away? Am I going to become so insufferable that you won't make a stand and fight to keep me?"

"You can kick me to the curb, but I am still not going back to Marsha. Do you know that never once in all the years that we were married did we ever argue? That means there was never any making up. Wouldn't you agree that this is the best part of arguing? You exasperate me to no end, but then you come into my arms and I know that I will do it all over again because I know we'll always end up like this. I was sure that you were in love with me, but that little story just sealed the deal for me. Yes Darling, I will fight to keep you in my life until the end of time."

"If you can't take it anymore Jesse and you really do leave, what will you do then?"

I squeezed her and said. "Well, I'll take an ad out in the local papers."

She asked me what it would say and I gave her my answer.

"Lonely man in his early forties seeks a woman of similar age. She must love to be kissed and held and not be afraid to portray her feelings. She must like to stay up all night talking and making love. She doesn't need to know how to cook or keep house or have a job. She must be feisty and slightly argumentative and

unpredictable. She must be willing to make a permanent commitment. She must have dimples and a scattering of freckles across her pretty face and one last thing… she must have lavender eyes."

She giggled. "Good luck with that, but I can do you one better."

"I'm listening."

"My ad would read: **"Young grandmother desperately searching for a swashbuckling gentleman who can sweep her off her feet and mend her broken heart. He must be tall and strong and ruggedly handsome. He must be intelligent and compassionate. He must be willing to fight for her at all costs. He must be able to love passionately and be able to forgive her for past mistakes and meet her on the stairs for heated discussions. He should know his way around the kitchen and love children and dogs. And, oh yeah, he must be able to melt her frozen interior and turn her desolate life around with just one kiss."**

"I hope I am already all those things to you Lace. I don't think I'm the daring swashbuckling type, but I will certainly give it a try. One thing is for certain though and that is that my ad has already been answered; my lady is sitting right next to me on the very steps where we meet every day. If she will kiss me, she will see that she has already turned **my** life upside down."

She whispered as she kissed me. "Is that a good thing Jesse?"

"It's a very good thing my darling. I would rather be hanging upside down with you wondering what is coming next then living life on the straight and boring ever again."

"I love you Jesse." She said cheerily.

"I love you too Lace. Now what say we take that little trip to Seventh Crossing? Are you okay with visiting with C.C. and Sam while I have my little chit-chat with Hank?"

"I am because I certainly don't want to come with you to the Bernard house."

"Good. How about you make out a shopping list while you are at CC's? We'll need to stock the pantry with 'kid-stuff. It's been a long time since my girls were little so I am sure there are hundreds of new items out there. What do Harrison and Leah like?"

"They would probably eat tacos every night if they were allowed. Other than that, anything that isn't green or mushy."

I laughed. "So things haven't changed in that department. Have you thought about what you would like for dinner?"

"I have that all under control Jesse so don't you go worrying about that."

"This ought to be interesting." I kidded.

"I do know how to cook Jesse." She smiled provocatively.

"I'm sure you do my dear… especially in the bedroom."

She ran out the door laughing.

Lacey was right; Seventh Crossing was not how I remembered it at all. The path that we used to walk down was now a concrete parking lot. A family of four were dining at one of the picnic tables that sat looking down at the bridge. The huge rocks that we once sat upon were gone. A protective metal fence had been erected along the cliff. I wondered if the train whistle would still sound the same as it made its way across the wooden structure. I doubted it. I took Lacey's hand. "Come on Honey, let's go. The magic that we knew back then may be gone for us here, but it will live on in our hearts forever and we'll continue making many more magic memories."

I knocked heavily on the barn-like door of the Bernard residence while observing the sad state of affairs that the so-called yard was in. A raspy voice yelled that the door was open. I pushed my way into a cluttered and dirty kitchen. An unkempt woman was sitting in a wheelchair watching television. She acknowledged my presence without taking her eyes off the TV.

"Are you another one of them salesmen or Jehovy Witness people?"

"No, Mrs. Bernard, I am not. I would like to speak with Hank if he is home."

"The name is Hanks. Just because that loony changed his name don't mean that I changed mine. As far as I know he is here.... HANK!" She yelled. "Get down here, someone to see you."

She turned her chair to face me. "Do I know you?"

"I don't know Mrs. Hanks; I have been away from Kings Crossing for a long time. My name is Jess Jameson. I doubt that you would remember my family."

"Oh, I know the name all right. You're the lawyer fella come here to try and keep that woman from going to jail for murdering poor Arthur. Such a shame and with his mother dead too…talk is she may have done them both in." She cackled.

I was about to defend Lacey when Hank came barrelling down the stairs.

"What are you bellowin about Ma?"

"You got company is all. Before you start gabbing so that I can't hear my shows help me into my big chair."

Hank glared at me as he wheeled his mother out of the room. He returned in a minute cursing under his breath. "What the hell are you doing here Jameson?"

"It's just a friendly visit Hank. I'm sure you know that I am here to help Lacey if I can and I am wondering if you can tell me anything more about the day Arthur died."

"I don't know a thing. I saw her come in the taxi and I saw her pull the knife out of him. That's all I know."

"I was hoping that maybe you saw someone suspicious hanging around the grounds or something. Anything at all would help in Lacey's defense. You know she is innocent don't you? She thinks of you as a friend and I hope you think of her the same way."

"You should go back where you come from you smarty-pants lawyer man! You can't help Lacey. You had your chance, you and rich boy Arthur, you both had your chance with her and you both ran out on her. Well, it's my turn now. I'm going to look after her so you can just get on your high horse and get out of town before you do anymore damage! I'm the only one who can save her so get out before it's too late!"

He pushed past me, opened the door and suggested I leave or he would gladly kick my ass out. I took it as a threat and left of my own volition wondering if he had become completely unhinged. He was at least five inches shorter than me, but probably outweighed me by forty pounds. He still wore the same thick horn-rimmed glasses; I was pretty sure he was half blind. I could probably take him in a fist fight, but to be perfectly honest, I didn't want his grimy hands touching me. His hair was just as I remembered it, long, scraggly and slicked back with boot grease. The scruffy stubble on his face didn't help his appearance any. I shuddered at the thought of him with Lacey. I wanted to tell him to stay away from her and that I had better never catch him sniffing around Tudor House, but I held my tongue. It wouldn't do any good to ire him anymore than I already had. I was pretty sure though that he was all talk and no action.

Back at Sam's I reiterated his bizarre behaviour to everyone. Lacey wasn't at all disturbed and laughed it off. She said that she hadn't been aware of his feelings for her and that I had better treat her right or that she might just take him up on his offer.

I didn't think it was funny at all. "I wanted to knock his block off, but he wasn't worth it, and besides, I haven't been in a brawl since tenth grade and I'm not too sure how I would fare."

Lacey put her arms around me and said to CC and Sam. "See what I mean guys; he really is my hero. He's willing to fight for my honour even though it isn't necessary. Hank is still a confused and disillusioned little boy and couldn't possibly do any harm."

I wasn't so sure but let it go. CC collected the white dress from the closet that Lacey would be wearing for the May Day events, and the two of them walked to the car. Sam held me back.

"Jess, I sure as hell hope that you're as serious as Lacey is about your relationship. I know it's a dilemma for you as you're still married, but God Jess, this woman is head over heels in love with you. I can't even begin to comprehend what would happen to her if you were to leave her again. I hope to God that you won't make the same mistake twice."

"Sam ole buddy, you're worrying for nothing. I don't have a problem with asking Marsha for a divorce. I am already divorced from her in my heart anyway. Thinking that I would run out on Lace is ludicrous. We have only been together for three days and I know already that I could not go back to living the mediocre existence I had before. Sometimes I do feel like strangling her when she goes off on one of her tirades and I'm afraid that she is going to kick me out. Earlier today she was completely off the charts, and I was ready to walk out the door. I'm not going to cave in to her moods though Sam; I just have to be patient and hope that I can quell her insecurities. I have found that she calms down when I am assertive. If that's the role I have to play then I'm all right with it. I'll do anything to keep her happy and in my life. Have I extinguished your fears ole man?"

"Yeah, yeah, I was pretty sure anyhow, but I don't know what you are talking about when you say that Lacey has tantrums?"

"I could be the cause or it could be something medical. Anyhow, it is cause for concern and she has agreed to see a doctor next week."

We stopped at Poppy's drive-thru to pick up Lacey's 'dinner'. "There had better be fried chicken in there young lady." I said. There was. We sat on the living room floor and ate "her" scrumptious meal along with a few light beers.

She smiled at me provocatively and said that we'd head over to Canterbury right after dinner.

"I was hoping to spend a quiet evening here with you and get to bed at a decent hour. Timothy asked me to keep you away from the house until tomorrow afternoon."

"Why?"

"Because a cleaning crew is coming in tomorrow morning, and Tim didn't want you to be upset with the mess they had left, and the yellow tape is probably still up."

"Screw the tape! A little disorder will be nothing compared with the bloodbath I witnessed last week. Please say you'll come with me Jesse as I really don't want to go alone. I really need to get that tape; it's been driving me crazy. I just can't put my finger on that tune but I know it means something."

I had been expecting her to tell me to suit myself and that she was going with or without me. Maybe things were looking up. "Of course I will go with you Sweetheart. I'm sorry; I had no idea that you were fretting so much about that music."

"It's what is keeping me awake at night. It plays over and over in my head…this macabre tune drums on and on tediously, and then just before it reaches its crescendo, it stops."

"That's probably because you shut off the stereo, don't you think? I thought I was the one keeping you up at night?" I tried to sound wounded.

"Maybe, anyhow I know it has some significance and I hope I can figure it out."

CHAPTER 5

Disruptions

The path to Canterbury, more commonly referred to as 'the carriage house', was almost obliterated by the tall grass. Lacey knew exactly where it was and commented that she had better phone the yard maintenance crew before the memorial. Good, one last job for me. Close knit Lombardy poplars lined the overgrown greenway making it almost impossible to see Canterbury from Tudor House. The footpath needed a good weeding also. Instead of ducking under the police tape, Lacey cut it with a pair of scissors that she pulled out of her pocket.

Stamping on the fallen ribbon over and over she uttered. "That's what I think of you!"

I was very amused by her rantings. She handed me the keys. I unlocked the door and followed her into the den. She didn't hesitate and went right to the stereo cabinet and pulled opened a drawer. She ruffled through it and triumphantly extracted the cartridge. She was all smiles and I hoped for her sake that she would be able to recognize what was on it and that it would give her some peace in this disturbing unsolved mystery. We quickly went through the rest of the house and discarded all the decaying bouquets that had been delivered after Hilda's passing. We went home totally unaware of tomorrow's prognostication.

May 24th 8:00 a.m.

I awoke the next morning and reached for Lacey. Of course she was gone. I made a quick bathroom stop deciding to shower later as the aroma of freshly brewed coffee was too much to ignore. I found Lacey sitting half way down the back stairs. She handed me a cup of steaming coffee as I sat down along side of her.

"Thanks Babe; how long have you been waiting for me?" I asked.

"Twenty-four years." She replied.

I really didn't want to have 'the conversation' with her again. I smiled sombrely. She laid her head on my shoulder.

"Would you miss me if I went away Jesse?" Her voice was low and sad.

"Are you going somewhere?" Her question had caught me off guard.

"Maybe…I just want to know if you will miss me."

"Honey, I would miss you if you were only gone a few hours. I can't imagine not waking up and having coffee with you every morning… not to mention our rendezvous on the stairs. I don't even want to think about not having you in bed with me every night. Yes, my darling, I would miss you very much. You are so much a part of me now that the thought of you going someplace without me is inconceivable. How much time are we talking about anyhow?"

"I'm not going anywhere Jesse…I just wanted to know if you would miss me."

"Good. I know that someday you are going to have to return to New York to settle your affairs there just as I will have to at the coast, but I'm hoping we'll do all that together."

"Are you saying that you see us living here in Kings Crossing?"

"Well, I can't see myself living anywhere near "the big apple" and I don't think you want to move to metropolitan Vancouver, and I want to spend the rest of my life with you, so 'here' is okay by me. What do you think?"

She smiled approvingly at me. "I'm happy here Jesse because I'm with you."

I kissed her. "Good; now what can I fix you for breakfast?"

"Oh, I can't even think about eating. There are so many butterflies in my stomach that I am afraid if I feed them they will start into fluttering uncontrollably!"

I laughed. "I think a light meal is what you need, butterflies and all. A bowl of cereal and fruit should supress them into dormancy. Come on, I promise you it'll help."

Reluctantly, she agreed. We descended the stairs hand and hand.

"After breakfast I need to finish cleaning out Hilda's room before Clara and her daughter arrive with the moving van. I think I will keep her costume jewellery for Leah to play dress-up with."

"Moving van, are you getting rid of the furniture?" I asked puzzled.

"I gave it all to Clara's daughter, Shelly. She's a single mother and can really use it. I wanted us to have a brand new bedroom suite."

"Are we moving down stairs?"

"You know why Jesse." She said matter of factually and winked at me.

Yeah, I knew why. "I have been with you practically every hour of the past three days, so how in hell did you manage to go shopping for furniture?"

"I phoned Mr. Newman who owns Newman's Department Store when I was at Sam's yesterday. I apologized for disturbing him at home on a Sunday and asked him if he still had the cherry wood bedroom suite in his display window. He said that he did. I told him I wanted to purchase it form him for forty percent off the asking price because it had been in his window for over a year and that should warrant a discount. I told him I needed it delivered by Tuesday morning at the latest. I compromised at thirty per cent off; it will be here Tuesday at nine a.m."

I told her I was proud of her bargaining ability and that I could use her expertise in the courtroom. She said that she hoped I would never have to bargain for her freedom. With those solemn words we cleaned up our dishes and started the task of de-junking Hilda's old room. Lacey informed me that Shelly and Clara were also going to clean the room along with the rest of the house before James and family arrived. I didn't mind cooking the occasional meal, but I was glad the cleaning was being looked after. I asked her if she had been listening to the tape again. She said only once.

"It's just like last night Jesse…I close my eyes and listen to it, but nothing comes to me. The music is in my head, just mulling around in there, not making any sense. I know it from somewhere, and I know it's important. Why can't I recall it? I can hum the tune to songs from the fifties; I know the words and the name of the songs, but this one keeps evading me."

I had listened to the tape with her last night. It was a macabre recording. It was something one would play on Halloween for the trick or treaters. I told Lacey that it reminded me of some morbid theatrical overture. She said I might be on to something and that she would think about it when she had more time. Right now she needed to get ready for the parade. She delicately hinted that we should shower in separate bathrooms.

It was 10:40 a.m. the next time I saw her. CC was picking her up at 11 as I had my meeting with Darryl Hanson, the family lawyer at precisely the same time. I watched her come down the stairs. I whistled and she smiled radiantly at me.

"You're beautiful Lace. I only wish you were coming down those stairs dressed for me on our wedding day." I playfully looked around. "Is there a preacher in the house?"

"Don't you dare make me cry Jesse Jameson!"

I held her as close as she would let me. "I wouldn't dream of it."

The phone rang; it was CC saying she was leaving. Lacey told me to get going as I didn't want to be late for my meeting with Mr. Hanson. I said I wasn't leaving until CC arrived. She ushered me to the door saying I was a worry wart and that nothing was going to happen to her in five minutes. Reluctantly, I agreed to go. "Don't get dirty, and have fun! Hopefully I will catch the tail-end of the parade."

She blew me a kiss and I heard her lock the door. I yelled at the dogs to keep their ears and eyes open. I drove three blocks before I saw CC's little orange car coming down the road. I turned off unto Dickens Drive and parked in front of a small office building. Ten minutes later I was seated in the lawyer's office.

At 11:15, my phone rang. I apologized and answered. It was CC, and she was in panic mode.

"CC, slow down, I can't understand a word you are saying. Put Lacey on the phone.

"That's what I am trying to tell you Jess…Lacey isn't here. My car broke down and Sam had to come and get me and when we got here she was gone, the door was open and the dogs were going crazy, but she's not here Jess." CC was almost incoherent because she was blubbering and gasping for breath. I got the picture; Lacey wasn't where she was supposed to be.

"I'm on my way." I closed my cell phone and apologized to Mr. Hanson telling him that there was some sort of crisis at Tudor House that involved Lacey. He told me to run along and look after her. I was going to look after her all right…this time I fully intended to reprimand her for scaring the living daylights out of her best friend. Who was I kidding? I was worried sick myself. I didn't even bother to fasten my seat belt, and for the first time I knew what the saying "flying like a bat out of hell" really meant. My feet hit the ground running as soon as I slammed the gearshift into park. The back door was open and

CC was still sobbing hysterically. Sam was trying his hardest to calm her down.

She saw me and sunk to the floor. "I'm so sorry Jess, I'm so sorry."

I went over to her and with Sam's help we pulled her up. "Look at me CC; I'm sure you have nothing to be sorry about. Now, how about you two tell me exactly what happened."

In between sobs she filled me in. "Two seconds after I saw you my car conked out. It just died. I called Lacey and told her what had happened and that Sam was on his way to pick me up. She told me not to worry and that we had lots of time. You tell him the rest Sam."

"When we got here, maybe ten minutes later, the door was open and like CC told you on the phone, the dogs were running around in their pen and barking up a storm. Her purse and cell phone were lying on the table. All her credit cards and identities are in it and several hundred dollars. While CC searched the house I thought I'd run down to the carriage house thinking she may have ventured down there. I let the dogs out thinking they would come with me, but instead they ran into the house and up the stairs. They stopped at Arthur's old bedroom and started to bay and scratch at the door. We finally got their leashes on just before you arrived. We had a hell of a time getting them back in the pen. Their leashes are still on."

Sam had never made it to the carriage house. I asked him to check it out while I dealt with the dogs. CC asked me what I wanted her to do. I thought it was a good idea for her to go with Sam as I didn't want to deal with her histrionics at the moment.

The dogs were only too eager to be let back into the house. They didn't even give me time to get a hold of their leashes before they went bounding up the stairs. I followed them and found them pawing at the door of Arthur's room and whining. I opened the door and they immediately ran to the far wall and started clawing at it. It was then that I knew where Lacey was. I called out her name.

"Are you in there Lace? Do you need me to come and get you?"

No answer. I got the dogs to calm down and sat and waited for Sam and CC. She wasn't at Canterbury House. I told them she was in Neverland. They thought I'd lost my mind.

"Look guys, I don't have time to explain right now. We've already lost half an hour of what might be valuable time. I'll just tell you that there is a secret room behind this wall and by the way the dogs are carrying on I'm sure Lacey is in there somewhere, and why, I don't know."

"Good enough for me Jess, how do we get in there?" Sam asked.

"Good question. When Lacey took me through it the other night these theatre seats weren't here; there was an old bench instead. That's how I know the wall was activated. Shall we give it a go?" I knelt down hoping to find a lever or knob or some sort.

"I'm coming too." CC declared.

"You can't come CC; you have a parade and the dance recital and you'll have to do the May pole for Lacey. You need to get going." I know it sounded like an order.

"I want to wait and see if Lacey is in there…she may need me Jess."

"Honey, Jess is right. You need to get to the school; the kids are counting on you. I'll contact you as soon as we have any news." Sam put his arm around his wife and walked her to the door.

"You can do this, I know you can."

"This was all for Lacey; it was to take her mind off finding Arthur…"

We heard her crying all the way down the stairs.

Sam sat in one of the seats with Trixie on his lap and I had Mickey on mine. I had found several decorative buttons on the side of the chair that might be the controller. I started pushing and pulling and one worked as Neverland was before us. The dogs were up and running towards the cave-like wall the second we landed. Sam was too flabbergasted to say anything…he just stood and threw up his arms and said, **"WHAT?"**

I quickly checked the pirate ship as that was the only place big enough for a person to hide in. Of course Lace wasn't in it. "I'll explain on the way Sam. We need to try and keep up with the dogs." We could hear their yelping getting further away.

All the lights were on in the tunnel and the big red door was open. The dogs were pawing at the ground at the bottom of the steps. We descended and each grabbed a dog. There was a large indentation in the dirt which they had already disturbed. It was hard to tell what had made it. The dogs were eager to carry on and they tugged on their leashes until we followed them. The light that radiated from the low wattage light bulbs was not adequate enough to make out how many footprints we were following. We skirted around them as best we could to try and preserve any crucial evidence. For all I knew, these prints may have been here for a very long time, but somehow I doubted it. At one point it appeared as though someone was being dragged. My heart was beating so loudly that I'm sure Sam could hear it. We came to the junction. The dogs wanted nothing to do with the left fork and so we carried on until we came to a rickety ladder. At the top was a half-opened circular cap that I assumed would come out in the garden. The dogs struggled to pull their bodies through it. We let go of their leashes and they managed to squeeze through.. Sam and I managed to pry the lid open fully. We emerged under the arbour where we found one of Lacey's white sandals and what looked like a piece of her white dress hanging from a bramble bush. Linwood Road that led up to Sugarloaf Mountain was only two hundred feet away. The dogs were sitting there waiting for us. They were whining. I pulled my cell phone out of my pocket and called Timothy.

We sank into the deep grass next to the dogs to wait for help to arrive. "Do you think the dogs need water Sam? If I hadn't been so preoccupied with finding Lacey, I would have grabbed a couple bottles of water…it's been so long since I've owned a dog. The girls always wanted one, especially Leigh, but Marsha wouldn't hear of it. Lacey would have got them a puppy farm. Sam, suppose if I never get her back? Who would do such a thing? It's my fault you know. I should never have left her." Trixie laid her head on my lap and Mickey nuzzled under my arm. I patted both of them and took a little comfort in doing so.

"Jess, let's not assume the worst here. Maybe there is a logical explanation for all of this…"

"You don't believe that any more than I do Sam. The same person who killed Arthur has got Lacey. It's as simple as that. Damn it, damn it all to hell! It's that crazy Bernard Hanks or Hank Bernard…whatever the hell his name is." I got to my feet. "You wait here for Timothy; I'm going to head down to his mother's house…"

Sam grabbed me by my shirt. "Hold on Jess; the cops will be here soon. Let them find him. You don't want to do anything you'll be sorry for later. You're too emotional; you can't go after him half-cocked… you know that Jess."

"I need to confront that son-of-a-bitch myself Sam. If it was CC, you'd already be long gone."

"Yeah maybe, but that's because I don't know the law and you do. Think about it Jess…what evidence do you have that suggests it's him?"

"Are you forgetting that he said that he was going to look after Lacey because both Arthur and I had failed to do so? It's him Sam, I know it!"

"If you're right Jess, this will be over as soon as he is found because where could he have taken her…he doesn't even drive. They couldn't have gotten very far in thirty minutes."

"Maybe he has an accomplice."

"Really Jess; who could that possibly be…his mother?"

"I wouldn't put it past the two of them. The ole biddy even suggested that Lacey did Hilda in. Sam, how did I screw up my life so badly?"

"What the hell are you talking about? Do you mean with Lacey?"

"Yeah, with and without her; the time between 1975 and now."

"Well, you worked hard at getting an education and you became the lawyer you always wanted to be. You made it work Jess, just as you did when we were kids. You always stood up for the under-dog, and you always fought for what you thought was right. So the marriage didn't pan out, but you have two great daughters and now you have Lacey, so what more do you want?"

"I settled Sam; I fucking settled. Why did I think I had to tie the knot when I was only twenty three? Did I take the easy way out and let Marsha pay my way? Lacey and Arthur made a bargain with each other and in a way I did the same thing with Marsha. She wanted to get married and have children and I accommodated her. Don't get me wrong, I love Leigh and Hilary and I would do almost anything for them. I say "almost anything", but I won't give up Lacey…not even for them. I'd still be in that stale marriage if it wasn't for your phone call."

"When did things start to go sour for you and Marsha, Jess? You must have loved her once?"

"We never had a passionate relationship; there were never any fireworks in the bedroom but it seemed to work. Somewhere along the line that part of our marriage disintegrated, and we did nothing about it. Marsha is not an overly affectionate person. When the girls needed a shoulder to cry on, they came to me. I guess I took my cue from her because I did nothing to correct the situation, and I didn't even know I was love starved. That all changed the day I set foot in Kings Crossing. One look at Lacey and I knew I wanted her. Every part of me was crying out for her, but there was this little problem…she wanted nothing to do with me, or so I thought. Thank God I persevered and took all her admonishment. I can't tell you the last time Marsha and I had sex…Christmas of 1995 maybe."

Sam laughed.

"I'm not kidding Sam. Now, all Lacey and I have to do is look at each other and well… you get the picture. She is so loving and giving of herself. I honest to God don't know how I lived without her. I've got twenty-four years to make up for with her, and I damn well better have the chance to do so! We have only been together three days, but we have spent every possible minute together. It's less than two hours since I last saw her, but it already feels like an eternity. I should be watching her dance around the May Pole…" I couldn't get any more words out.

"We're going to get her back Jess; we're gonna get her back."

His words were meant to reassure me, but they fell on doubting ears.

The dogs sat up and started to whine. A few seconds later we heard the whirring of the police sirens. Sam and I darted to the middle of the road to divert the cars away from the tread marks that we felt were from the get-a-way vehicle. Three squad cars came to a screeching halt beside us. I recognized Sergeant Lewis in the lead car with several other officers. Timothy and Mellie were in the second vehicle and Constable Jones and another officer brought up the rear. Sergeant Lewis extended his hand towards me.

"Mr. Jameson, I don't mind telling you that I am very disturbed by this latest incident. We have all but ruled out Mrs. King as a person of interest in Mr. King's homicide, but now, she has disappeared. Sir, before I proceed with an immediate closure of the Hiway and issue a bulletin, is there any possibility that Mrs. King may have left on her own accord? What evidence do you have to support otherwise?"

I introduced him to Sam and together we related the events that had led us here. He was most interested in the dogs leading us to the secret room and our findings. He ordered a road block and asked if I would escort Mellie and Timothy back through the passageway. I reiterated the conversation I had with Hank the other day and highly suggested that he was the one who had taken Lacey.

"You could me right Mr. Jameson, and if it is so, we will have him in custody post haste."

He ordered Constable Jones and his partner to proceed to the Hanks home. He said that if they were denied access to the house and grounds then he would have a search warrant issued immediately. He would return to headquarters and expected a report from them in twenty minutes. If Mr. Bernard, alias Hanks, was not at the residence they were to keep it under surveillance until dismissed. He suggested that Mellie might call her team back to assist her after she had surveyed the alleged crime scene.

"Corporal Newman, you are to continue on as the lead in this investigation." He turned to me.

"Sir, please know that we are, and will continue to investigate Mr. King's murder, and now the disappearance of his wife, as our number one priorities. I am still hopeful that Mrs. King's absence is just a misunderstanding. The coroner's report and our findings are at your disposal, and perhaps you might offer some insight into our assessments. I don't mean to rush you as I know your priority is finding your client, but as soon as possible Sir."

"I am most interested in the reports Sergeant, but at the moment my only concern is for Lacey. Nothing else is of any importance to me at this time."

He looked at me and I was positive he wanted to ask me a question regarding my relationship with Lacey. I would have told him the truth if he had of asked. Instead he said, "I will leave you on that note then and hope we will have something positive to report to you soon."

He shook my hand again. I set off with Timothy and Mellie to retrace our steps through the cellar. Sam took the dogs home through the garden as we didn't need them disturbing any more evidence. It was 1:25 P.M. when I had Mellie and Timothy sit on the bench that would take them into Arthur's bedroom. I had given them a brief explanation of how Neverland came to be. I followed behind them and escorted them into the kitchen where I immediately checked the house phone messages. There was only one, and it was from Clara Branko. I did not call her back. I put on a pot of coffee while Mellie put in a request for her team to join her at Tudor House. The dogs were barking up a storm again and I went out to try and keep them quiet.

Sergeant Lewis called at 2 P.M. Constable Jones had not met with any resistance at the Hank's residence. A thorough search of the house and grounds, including out-buildings had been executed, but there was no evidence that Mrs. Lacey King had ever been there. Mrs. Hank's car was in the driveway and appeared as though it hadn't been moved in quite some time as the dust on it had not been disturbed. Hank was at the United Church where he went every day to do odd chores. Sergeant Lewis had told them to discreetly keep watch over the residence and he would dispatch another unit to the church. Sam arrived back with CC. I asked her if she would go shopping with me as I had to be prepared for when James and his family arrived tomorrow. She realized that I needed a distraction and agreed. We left Sam manning the house phone. Mellie was in the cellar again.

With CC's expertise we finished our grocery run in less than half an hour. She was a little surprised that I had a list compiled in my head. I told her that Lacey and I had already discussed what the children liked and that we had menus all planned. We had no idea how many people would be coming and going and so we bought enough cold cuts and fixings and pastries to last for a few days just in case Lace didn't make it back home today.

Word had spread fast in Kings Crossing. I was a little amazed at how many people we met in the grocery store inquired about Lacey. Of course most of them didn't know me, but they knew of CC's and Lacey's friendship. The girl at the check-out was the same one that had been on when Lace and I had shopped the other day. She reached across the counter and touched my hand and said how sorry she was and the whole town would be praying for Lacey's safe return. I thanked her and rushed CC out the door before we had to endure another sympathizer.

Clara Brankco had called again; Sam told her what he knew and assured her that someone would call her the moment we had any news. I made some remark that made it sound like she was responsible for Lacey being left alone. CC asked me what I was talking about and I told her about the furniture thing and the house cleaning. Because Clara' daughters' children were in the May Day festivities, they couldn't do the cleaning today. They would have still been at the house if it wasn't for that.

"Well, if anyone is at fault, it is me once again because I am the one who talked Lacey into helping me with the May pole event!" CC cried.

I put my arms around her. "Don't cry Cees; I'm sorry. I shouldn't be blaming anyone but myself. No one else is responsible for my failure to keep her safe."

"Oh Jess, you big boob, you couldn't possibly be with her twenty-four hours a day! Have you ever thought that this "someone" would have gotten to her sooner or later? How he knew that my car was going to break down, or that you would have an appointment is a mystery in itself."

"We should have the answer regarding the car any minute now, right Sam?"

"Yup, the mechanic promised he'd get to it right after the festivities and so it should be forthcoming any minute now. I wish the two of you would quit blaming yourselves…"

"Sure Sam; what do you say Cees?" I said hugging her.

She snivelled. "No one has called me that in a very long time. Thanks for making me feel young again Jess."

"Hell, we are all still young, and we have a lot of living to do and the four of us are going to do just that…just as soon as we get Lacey back."

"Amen to that." Sam said as he opened the screen door to let Timothy in.

He shook my hand. I asked him if he had any news.

"Nothing very promising Jess I'm afraid. The Reverend was tracked down at the school, but he had no idea where Hank could be. He'd given him the afternoon off to attend the parade and didn't expect to see him until the next day. Hank has not shown up at home or at the school."

Timothy left assuring us that it was only a matter of time before Hank showed up, and that a bulletin had been issued to all the surrounding towns regarding Lacey's disappearance. He also suggested that her disappearance might be completely isolated from Arthur's murder and that a ransom note may be forthcoming. I didn't believe that for a minute. It was 4 P.M.

At 6:45, Constable Jones arrived at the back door. A cruiser had spotted Hank several kilometers from his house. They had alerted headquarters and he had been picked up and taken in for questioning. Corporal Newman was conducting the interview and would be contacting as soon as the interrogation was complete. He had nothing further to tell us. I wanted to jump in the car and go to the station and confront Hank myself, but Sam and self-restraint held me back. We took turns pacing the kitchen. What could be taking so long? Finally, at 8:15, Timothy showed up. The news was not promising.

Hank had been apprehended near Claymore Marsh; he was dishevelled, cut and bleeding. His accounting for his whereabouts of the day is as follows: He started the day as usual, biking to the church. He worked until 10 A.M. He wanted to get a good seat for the parade and so he took a short-cut through the woods to Main. He said he often took this route when doing errands for the Reverend. The last thing he remembered was hitting a rut and losing control of his bike. He must have lost consciousness because he remembered nothing else until an hour or so ago. He had awakened to find his bike on top of him. He had no idea how long he had been at the bottom of the ravine. He had made his way to the top and was heading for home when he was picked up by the police cruiser. I did not believe his story even though the evidence supported it. His bicycle had been recovered from the ravine. It was a total wreck. His dried blood had been found at the scene on a large boulder. The hillside showed that "someone" had clawed his way to the top. The scene had been cordoned off and a further inspection would be conducted at first light the next morning. He had been asked if he had seen Lacey that day. He stated that he had not seen her since the day he found her standing over Arthur's body.

There was nothing to tie him to Lacey or her disappearance. After a trip to the emergency room it was deemed that he had only superficial wounds and had been escorted home. The house would continue to be under surveillance.

"Sorry guys, there wasn't any evidence to warrant an arrest. He still remains as a person of interest and his actions will be highly scrutinized. I'm going to try and get a little shut-eye, but I will be back here before midnight. Constable Jones is on duty all night and so if anything should arise, please feel free to call him. Are you all right with that?"

We were. I saw him to the door and told him there was no need for him to return tonight and that he needed to get his rest.

He laughed feebly. "Thanks Jess, but I doubt that I will even be able to fall asleep. I have never been involved with a case so personal before and it weighs heavy with me that we don't have any viable evidence yet. I so want this to be resolved before James arrives tomorrow."

"Me too Timothy, me too."

I borrowed Sam's cell phone to make a call. Mine had to remain open for when Lacey called. I went into the living room and punched in a number. She answered on the second ring.

"Hi Honey, I hope I am not disturbing you."

"Of course not Daddy…what's wrong? You never call this late…oh, has something happened with the case you are working on?"

"Yes, something has definitely happened. Is your sister there Leigh?"

"No, and as usual, I have no idea where she is or when she'll be back."

"Good, I'm not ready for her condemnation at the moment."

"Why would you say that? You're scaring me Daddy…"

"No need to be scared Honey. I have something to tell you and I don't think you are going to be too happy with what I have to say, but at least I know you will hear me out and hopefully, you won't hate me too much."

"I could never hate you Daddy. I fail to see why you would even think that I could."

"It's about Lacey; Lacey and me."

"She's the old friend that you went to help, right?"

"Lacey's not just an old friend…we were high school sweethearts. We planned on being married one day." I heard the intake of breath at the other end of the phone. "I've fallen back in love with her and she says she has never stopped loving me. I didn't expect this to happen Leigh, but it has and she has awakened something in me that has been dead for a long, long time. I can never go back to your mother or to the life I had. Except for you and Hilary, that part of me is gone. I don't expect you to understand right away, but I hope in time you will be able to accept my decision to be with the woman I love."

She was definitely upset. "How long has this been going on? Surely, you didn't fall in love with her the minute you saw her?"

"As a matter of fact, it happened just that way. She fought me at first because I had hurt her so badly many years ago, but she couldn't deny her feelings for me and we have been together ever since… until eight hours ago." I choked back the tears.

"I hate to even ask, but what happened eight hours ago?" She snapped.

"Lacey was kidnapped." That was all I could get out.

Leigh gasped. "Did you say kidnapped? And, her husband was murdered? What den of debauchery have you got yourself into Daddy? I think you had just better forget what you think you feel for this woman and get back home. Do you hear me?"

I would have laughed at her reference to decadence if the situation hadn't been so serious. "I'm not coming "home" as you call it. You know perfectly well that your mother and I are only going through the motions. We haven't shared so much as even a kiss in months… hell, it's more like years."

"I don't need to know that Dad." Leigh said emphatically.

"Well like it or not, it's the truth. Your mother and I share a house and an occasional meal, that's all. Obviously, neither of us cared enough to make any changes, and we never talked about it. I guess we are pretty good actors because neither you nor Hilary have noticed the distance between us growing. I haven't seen Lacey in twenty four years. She did marry Arthur King and they have been living in New York State all these years.

However, their marriage was a fraud. Arthur is gay and Lacey knew it when she married him. She did so because she had to get out of town as she was pregnant, and Arthur offered to give her child a name. The wheels are turning in your head aren't they Leigh? You're right; she was pregnant with my child. For twenty four years she has kept it from me, but I have forgiven her just as she has me. You have a brother Leigh; he has a wife and two children and tomorrow he will be here. He doesn't know about me, and I am scared to death to meet him. He thinks I am just his mother's lawyer and I promised him that I would keep her safe…"

"I don't mean to burst your bubble Dad, but how do you know for sure that she is telling you the truth about being her son's father? Is there proof?"

"The only proof I need is that Lacey told me so. She would not lie about such an important thing. I know this is a lot for you to absorb all at once, and don't think for one moment that it is easy for me to cry my heart out to you…"

"Oh Daddy, I wish I was there with you. There is much more to this story then you are able to tell me right now so I will tell you what I am going to do okay? I have some loose ends to see to here and then I am going to come to Kings Crossing. I want to be there for you and I want to meet my new family." She was crying.

"I need you with me too Leigh. I don't want you driving this far alone though so will you please take the bus or fly? Do you have enough money? It's my job to tell your mother and Hilary…I just can't do it right now."

"I understand Daddy, and I won't say a word. But, is there a possibility that this is only an infatuation and that you have just been caught up in everything that is happening? Maybe when it is all resolved you will realize that it was all a mistake…"

"Sorry Honey, that isn't going to happen. If this an infatuation then I'm going all the way with it, but I can assure you that we are crazy in love with each other. I haven't felt this invigorated since I was a teenager, but Lacey is missing and I am scared to death for her safety. I don't know how I am going to make it if…"

"You will Daddy; you need to stay strong and positive that she will be found. I hate to think that you are there in a strange town and all alone."

I laughed a little. "Honey, this is hardly a strange town. Are you forgetting that I spent the first nineteen years of my life here? And, my best friends, CC and Sam are in the next room and Timothy will be here later."

She asked who Timothy was. "He is the son of another couple we used to hang around with. In fact, his mother Laura, is Sam's sister. He's an R.C.M.P. officer and has the lead in Arthur's murder and now Lacey's disappearance. James and he are best friends."

"Now, I have to ask who James is."

"Sorry, I realize that I am talking about people you don't know; James is my son's name. Lacey named him after me."

"His name is James and he has a wife and two children… where did you say he lives?"

"I don't think I said, somewhere…sorry, Sam is calling me; I have to go in case there is some news about Lacey. Phone me as soon as you know when and how you are coming. Please don't worry about me. I love you honey."

"Daddy, I have so many questions, but I guess they will have to wait. I love you too Daddy and I will say a prayer for Lacey."

"Thank you Honey, I knew I wasn't making a mistake when I called you."

I closed the phone. I felt as though one millstone had been lifted from my weary body.

CC and Sam were watching the local television station. They were running a tape of an interview with Sergeant

Lewis regarding the investigation of Arthur's murder and the subsequent mysterious vanishing of Lacey. It was nothing we didn't already know.

I squeezed in between CC and Sam on the sofa and put an arm around their shoulders.

"I just told my daughter that she needed worry about me because I was with my best friends. That term has been foreign to me for a long time. I'm afraid I lost more than Lacey when I moved away from here. I'm sorry I let our friendship slide. I don't think I could get through any of this without you. I love you guys."

"We love you too Jess." CC said through her sobs.

"Thanks Buddy, you made my wife cry again." Sam smacked me on the knee.

CC picked something up off the coffee table and passed it to me. "I found this in Lacey's wallet."

It was a worn photo of me and Lacey. I turned it over. Lacey had written on it.

"The best day of my life! June 11th"74. Jesse and me forever."

"I remember this day; it was her seventeenth birthday. I gave her that locket that she is wearing. I don't think she ever took it off…I wonder what happened to it."

"I'm impressed old man; I can't even remember what I bought CC for Christmas last year." Sam confessed.

"Well, seeing the photo of her with the locket brought it all back. It was a very special time."

I told them to go home and get some shut-eye. They insisted on staying until Timothy retuned.

We sat and reminisced for the next few hours downing two pots of coffee.

Timothy arrived. It was now Tuesday and Lacey had been missing for 13 hours. There was still no news. None of the other precincts had anything to report; Lacey had not been seen anywhere. Hank Bernard's house was still under surveillance as he was the only person of interest at this point in time. Timothy had brought me a copy of the coroner's report on Arthur. It was very detailed. I read through it quickly and then reread the summation over several times more carefully.

Autopsy report: Conducted May 19, 1999
Time: 21 hundred hours
Place: Kamloops, British Columbia
Subject: Arthur Clinton King
White male, 46 years old
Weight: 76.2 kilograms
Height: 173 centimeters
I received the body of said Arthur Clinton King at 2030 HOURS, 8:30 p.m. 05/19/99
He had been transported by ambulance from Kings Crossing. He had been pronounced deceased by Dr. John Simpson at 1730 hundred hours; 5:30 P.M. 05/19/99
Clothing was removed and handled over to my assistant, Marlena Denton for analysis.
Upon initial examination of the body, I found no remarkable birth-markings. No tattoos.
Scarring from an appendectomy was noted.
Scrapings from under the fingernails were taken.
X-rays to the body show no broken bones. No bruising to genital area.
Heavy bruising to the upper arms and wrists was noted.
Blood, urine, samples extracted
Stomach contents examined
Liver and body temperature ascertained
No abnormalities to heart or lungs. Tissue samples of all organs extracted.

Eyes and head: unremarkable.

May 24, 1999 Conclusion:

No drugs, alcohol or poisons were found in Mr. King's blood.

There is nothing to suggest that strangulation or asphyxia occurred.

Cause of death: Massive haemorrhage class 4, 40% loss of blood; 2.25 litres

Mr. King would have required immediate replacement of blood and aggressive resuscitation to prevent death. Seven knife wounds to the torso and abdominal areas were significant in the loss of blood and trauma to the body. The final blow to the heart cavity was conducted with such force that immediate cessation of life was immediate.

Mr. King's death was not the result of suicide; but one of manslaughter.

Time of death: 13:30-15:30 hundred hours, Tuesday, MAY 18, 1999

No liver or body temperature was available from the crime scene as Dr. Simpson did not want to contaminate the wounds that encompassed the body. In agreement with the temperature at the scene and my findings, I am confident that the Time of Death {T.O.D.} is accurate. I will also note at this time that the blood and tissue samples along with the organic materials related to this autopsy, that being of Arthur King, have been handed over to the R.C.M.P. crime lab for further testing and analysis.

The body will be released to the family upon instruction.

It is at this time that I offer up my summation.

It is my belief that this horrendous crime was one of passion and utmost personal animosity. The

knife wounds were meant not to incapacitate, but to mortally wound. Due to the severity of the bruising and indentations on the arms and wrists, and the intensity of the lacerations, I am of the mind that there was more than one assailant. Further discovery and examinations of the evidence will no doubt conclude that this will hold true and that the unidentified blood will point to the assassin (s). There are no defense injuries so to speak which leaves me to the conclusion that Mr. King knew his attackers(s) and was caught completely off guard by the assault. This is my unbiased finding and is based strictly on the findings of the autopsy and my gut.
Dr. Jacob C. Lawson, Chief Coroner and Medical Examiner for the District of Cariboo

Dr. J. C. Lawson

I folded the report up and placed it in the envelope. "This pretty much exonerates Lacey of any involvement in Arthur's death wouldn't you say Tim? There is no way she could have been there at that time. I never thought for one minute that she did the deed anyway. There is no reason for Lacey to ever see this Tim. If she asks, I will give her the bare details. She does not need to relive this traumatic event over again, and I am sure if she was to read these findings…well, let's just say it is beneficial to all if she doesn't."

"Right you are Jess. With the evidence found up Sugarloaf and this report, the department is in full agreement that more than one person was involved."

"Is it usual for this Dr. Lawson to offer up his own personal opinion?"

"I don't know Jess, but he may have been an acquaintance of the family and so took a personal interest in the case while still remaining professionally objective. If one reads between the lines, it does sound as though he was disturbed by the brutality of the crime."

"I didn't mean to imply otherwise Tim. Now tell me if you truly believe Hank's alibi for the time of Lacey's disappearance?"

He said he had no choice but to go with the evidence. I was still not convinced.

Tuesday, May 25th

Damn it, Lacey was gone again! Doesn't that girl ever sleep in? The aroma of freshly brewed coffee and bacon cooking enticed me to sit up. What was I doing in the den? Jesus, Joseph, and Mary! The full realization of why I was waking up in the den suddenly dawned on me…Lacey wasn't just absent from bed… she was GONE! I bolted into the kitchen and found CC standing with her back to me at the stove. She turned when she heard me.

"I'm sorry if I woke you Jess." She apologized and poured me a cup of coffee.

"When did I fall asleep? Is Lacey home?"

"Honey, we would have awakened you if she was. I'm sorry to say there is no news."

"That's good isn't it Cees? They always say that no news is good news, don't they?"

She tried to smile. "Yes."

"Where's Sam?"

"He took the dogs for a walk, oh, here he is now."

Sam came in breathing hard. "Damn, those dogs are energetic!"

"Thanks for doing my job. Where did they drag you to?"

"Where didn't they is a better question." He laughed. "Glad you got a little sleep my friend."

"I have no idea how long I slept. The last thing I remember was discussing the coroner's report with Timothy. When did you two get here?" I glanced at the clock and saw that it was 7:30.

"Half an hour or so ago. Timothy was going to check in at headquarters and then head home for a few hours." Sam said.

"You know, you guys don't have to babysit me. You should go home and check in with your own family for a while."

"You are family Jess. Shall we all sit down and have something to eat?"

"Thanks CC; it's going to be a long day so I guess I should fortify myself."

Clara Branko and her daughter Shelly arrived with freshly baked bread and two dozen cinnamon rolls that made my mouth water. I asked Clara what time she had to get up to have accomplished so much already.

"I don't need much sleep anymore…three or four hours is all and then the aches settle in, so I just get up and get on with the day. I wanted to make these buns for Mr. James as they have always been a favourite of his. Now don't yous worry about a thing; Shelly and me will see to the moving van and the new furniture, and we'll get the cleaning done and all the beds made up fresh. You got other things to worry about."

I thanked them and reminded them that there would be two children running amuck in the house and not to go to great extremes with their scrub brushes. Clara said that those two "youngins" were very well behaved and never made a mess. CC agreed. I hoped I would get to know my grandchildren as well as everyone else already did.

I made a mental note of the things I needed to do before James and Blythe and the kids arrived. The first thing was to call Leigh from Sam's phone before they left. She did not answer and so I left her a message directing her to phone Sam and relay her travel plans to him as I had to leave my phone open for Lacey. I left CC and Sam cleaning up the kitchen while I went to retrieve the car-seat from the attic. The entrance to the "spiral staircase", as Lacey had called it, was behind a large oak door next to the upstairs covered veranda. It was locked. I hadn't anticipated that and retreated back down the stairs hoping that the key along with a dozen other ones would be on the huge brass ring that hung on the coat rack by the front door. After several attempts I found the right key and entered into a small vestibule that housed three more doors. Two of them were imitation pocket doors and didn't open at all. The third opened straightaway unto the winding flight of steps. I wound my way upwards wondering why this ornate set of narrow oak stairs had been erected. The handrail was most definitely mahogany. The walls were papered in exquisite Elizabethan or Victorian patterns or some other historic period of which I knew nothing about. Had someone once lived up here? My curiosity was only piqued more when at the top I came upon elaborately carved French doors. Two smaller doors were to the right and left. I turned the glass knobs of the French doors simultaneously and they opened into a room furnished from another century. I realized that this spacious spherical shaped room had to be in the tower that was a distinct feature from outside. Antique dressers and cabinets complete with china lined the rounded walls. Candles in tall brass holders, vases and other bric-a-brac sat on the fancy tablecloths that covered two dining room tables. A wood-burning fireplace with a cast-iron grate, andirons, and a carved mantel stood against a brick wall. Several old fashioned light fixtures hung from the highly decorated ceiling. Amidst the colourful sofas and chairs awkwardly sat a blue claw-footed bath-tub. It was so out of place that I laughed at its intrusion to an otherwise regal room. I meandered my way across the pine floors that were spread with heirloom rugs to the south wall. Here, under an elaborate stained-glass window was a marvellous old-fashioned sleigh bed completely decked out in luxurious linens. I couldn't resist…I laid down and peered out the glass dome. I fantasized that Lacey was lying next to me holding my hand. As we gazed out upon the starry sky I asked her if she would spend the rest of her life with me. Just as she was about to answer me a large black bird landed on the projecting weathervane. It was a raven and it was laughing at me.

I arose from my dream-like trance and tried to locate the car seat. It didn't appear as if it would even belong in this accumulation of treasured furnishings. I retraced my steps backwards and took an objective survey…nothing caught my eye. There was nothing here from the twentieth century that I could see. I was about to leave when that annoying raven crashed into a small porthole on the side of the rotunda. I waved him away and he flew off scolding me in his own peculiar language. "I must be losing it." I said out loud if I actually believed that a bird was talking to me. I decided to try one of the outside doors. I chose the right one and sitting waiting for me upon an upturned ugly ceramic gothic gargoyle was the baby seat. I soon realized that this little room held recent discarded acquisitions. I grabbed what I had come for, locked up, and promised to return to the dome room with Lacey.

CC was still in the kitchen cleaning up. I sat down opposite Sam and asked if Leigh had called. I knew Lacey hadn't as he would have come running for me if she had. Leigh had not called either. I asked them if they had ever been in the rotunda.

"Until this past week I haven't even set foot in this house since the eighth grade." Sam grinned at me. "So, the answer is no, I have never been in the dome, but have wondered what's in it."

"Me neither Jess. Why were you here in the eighth grade? Was that when Arthur's father died?"

"No, that was several years earlier. Have I never told you about our essay project?" Sam asked.

CC shook her head. "Remind me to tell you all about it later Hon. What does the room look like Jess? Is it just a big round bubble?"

"I think someone might be living there." I said bluntly.

Sam looked at me questionably. "You're kidding…what makes you say that?"

"It's too clean; there's not a speck of dust anywhere. There are no dust covers on any of the furnishings and everything is spotless. One of the tables is set with dinnerware for two. The floors look as if they have been recently vacuumed. I wonder if Clara or Shelly are keeping it that way?"

CC volunteered to go and find the women. They were just as mystified as I was. Shelly only started helping her mother a month ago and had only been to the house three times and hadn't even been upstairs until today. Clara said she was only in the so called "attic" twice. The first time was three or four years ago when Hilda had sent her up with an arm full of knick-knacks that she no longer wanted. The other time was a year ago when Hilda asked her to bring down the commode from the bathroom.

"Wait a minute Clara…are you saying that there is a bathroom in the dome? Where is it?" I asked. "I certainly didn't see one. But then I wasn't looking for one neither."

"It's in the small room outside the dome."

"It must be behind the left door; I only went in the right."

"Yes, that is right Jess." Clara said.

I remarked that I was surprised that there was no dust on the furnishings in the rotunda and that nothing was covered.

"Well Mr. Jess, everything was covered in drop cloths when I was in there and I certainly didn't remove any. I was only up there for a minute but surely I would have noticed."

"There are no cloths covering anything now Clara, and the bed is made up as if it is being slept in. There are no dust bunnies anywhere. The small room where I found the car seat for Leah is also neat and tidy. And now you tell me there is a bathroom up there…is it in working order?"

"I couldn't tell you Jess. Do you really believe someone is living up there? How would one get in and out without being detected? They would have to go for food and surely that bell above the door would have alerted you and Miss Lacey."

"What bell Clara?" I asked probingly.

"If you didn't see or hear it then it must have been dismantled. You may be right Jess…maybe someone has indeed been living there." Clara answered hesitantly.

"Or at least someone has been up there. Is there another way in and out of the dome?"

"That I do not know, but perhaps James will know. There is no one left anymore except him, and Lacey, of course. I'm sure she would know, don't you think? In all the years that I have known Hilda, she never mentioned any secrets about the house. I guess I am not very curious because I never did any exploring. Oh, I know the history of the house and the family as it is common knowledge and is written up in the town's archives. Sorry I can't answer any of your questions Jess." Clara said she had better get back to work as the new furniture would be arriving any minute. She asked me if I had any preference as to the arrangement of the furniture.

"Thank you for the consideration Clara, but this is not a decision for me to make; I am but a guest in this house. If Lacey doesn't like the layout we can always change it. She does like to lie in bed and look out the window so perhaps keep that in mind. One more question Hilda; what can you tell me about Ainsley?"

"Not very much Jess."

"Who else would know the lay-out of the house? Do you think that she heard about Hilda's and Arthur's death and is back to claim the family's riches?"

"I have no opinion as I did not know Ainsley and Hilda did not confide anything to me. The only time she was mentioned was on my initial tour of Tudor House and Canterbury. Hilda pointed out Ainsleys's bedrooms. Apparently, she preferred to sleep at Canterbury. I believe that had something to do with her expulsion from the family. Hilda's words were, and I quote as they have stuck with me, and they were said with great animosity. "Ainsley is long gone from this family. There is no absolution for her and the disgrace she brought upon us. We will not speak of her again." And, we never did. It was none of my business and to this day, I have only a small inkling to the reason Ainsley was disowned. I am sure there are plenty of people who know the whole story… including my own daughter." Clara looked directly at Shelly.

We all stared at Shelly who had been silent up until now. "We moved to Kings Crossing when I was fourteen so I never knew Ainsley as she had already left town. Arthur was a year younger than me and ran in different circles, so I really didn't know him. He was the talk of the town when he and Lacey ran off together…but that was good talk, not at all like the ugly gossip about Ainsley. This is all hearsay you understand, and it was a long time ago. Apparently, she was running some sordid business from the carriage house and her mother caught her in the act and cast her out. The talk had pretty well died down by the time I arrived. It is a long time since I have heard her name mentioned and it is as though she never existed."

I asked Shelly how old Ainsley was at the time and did she remember what year it was. She said that the year was 1965 and Ainsley would have been sixteen. Sam, CC and I would have only been eight or nine and it wouldn't have made much of an impression on us at that age if we had heard about it. What could a young girl have done that was so disgraceful that her own mother banished her? I asked Shelly if she knew the exact nature of Ainsleys's "business".

She blushed. "I believe she was entertaining men."

"Oh, that's sad." CC let out a long sigh. "She was so young."

I thanked the ladies for there in-put and waited until they had left before turning to CC.

"You think sixteen is too young to have sex Cees?"

"No, and you know that is not what I meant Jess. It's too young to be engaging in it for money, and not love, and too young to be thrown out on the street!"

I got up and put my arm around her. "I know what you meant. I think we need more information before we can put a label on Ainsley, and perhaps Lacey can set us straight.

Speaking of her…I think I have been distracted enough and I best get back to looking for her. First, I am going to call Sergeant Lewis and find out if his men searched the dome. Then I'm going to examine every inch of Canterbury and all the out buildings once again. Then it will be time to get started on dinner preparations…you two will be here, right? I need every ounce of support I can muster. And then, I will settle in to go crazy with worry once more."

Sam passed me his phone and CC hugged me. "You know we'll be here Jess. Timothy has offered to pick James and family up from the airport. I think that's a good idea, don't you?" She didn't wait for an answer. "She's going to come home to us Jess; she just has to."

I called Sergeant Lewis at his personal number. No, there were no leads. Hank had left for work at the rectory at 8:15 and had returned an hour later. He had boldly walked up to the squad car that the surveillance team were sitting in and said. "I'm back; too sore from the accident to work. How about you get the hell off my property and quit spying on me?" He was informed that they were on city property and don't give them any reason to arrest him. He gave them the finger and he hadn't left the property again. I asked the Sergeant if both front and back doors were being watched and he said "Yes." I wasn't sure I believed him. He said he would get back to me on the business of the dome and relayed his condolences again. I assumed he thought Lacey was dead.

I sent my friends home saying Clara was perfectly capable of manning the phones. They said they'd be back in a couple of hours. I collected the dogs. They were more than eager to do a grid search of the property again. I upturned every rug and moved every piece of furniture at the carriage house looking for a sealed wall or trap door. I found nothing and the dogs showed no unusual interest. The out buildings revealed nothing either and I returned to Tudor House vowing to do it all over again tomorrow. I fully intended on confronting Hank again regardless of being warned to stay away from him. It would have to wait as I had to deal with James first.

CHAPTER 6

Confrontations

I thought the day would drag on, but it passed reasonably quickly. After Clara and Shelly had left, I wandered down to Hilda's old bedroom, which Lacey had told me would be mine and hers as long as the kids were here. I wanted to check out the new furniture. It was as Lacey had described to me; a rich cherry wood color. The ladies had placed the queen-sized bed exactly as I had suggested. I sat on the edge of it and looked out the window. I would not sleep here without Lacey; there was nothing of her here. At least the bed upstairs was full of her essence.

Dinner was in the oven and the dining room table was set. I chose Lacey's favourite blue and white "Old Mill" dinnerware. Sam and CC arrived and we sat and waited for my son to arrive.

I had rehearsed my speech over a hundred times. I knew exactly what I was going to say to James. We all heard the car door shut and hurried footsteps on the sidewalk. The screen door opened and all my carefully selected words went down the drain. He took two steps across the floor and nodded to CC and Sam, and without hesitation he turned his attention to me.

"You promised me you'd look after her." He blurted with malice.

Those were the first words my son said to me. I had five seconds to access him. He was a few inches taller than me and definitely more muscular. His hair was dark brown, the color mine used to be. His eyes were also brown, like mine and a million others'. Did I think he looked like me? Yes, and it wasn't just wishful thinking. How had Sam and CC and Timothy and his parents not seen the similarities? Maybe they had but had decided that it wasn't there place to confront Lacey or expose the truth to James. It didn't matter anymore as here we were face to face, father and son.

"I'm sorry James, I dropped the ball there, and believe me, there is no one sorrier than I am."

CC intervened. "It is not Jess's fault, it's mine. I wasn't here when I was supposed to be."

Sam reached out his hand to James. "Until Lacey is found, they will go on blaming themselves. The truth is no one is to blame except the deranged culprit who manifested her abduction."

"Dad, why did you shut the door on me?" It was my grandson, Harrison.

"Sorry Son, I didn't mean to. What's keeping your mother?"

Harrison didn't answer but walked over to me. "Do I know you? Are you Gramma Lacey's friend? Is she home now?"

"Sorry Harrison, your Gramma isn't here right now. My name is Jess and she asked me to take care of you until she gets home." We shook hands.

"Mother said that Uncle Arthur had to go to heaven and that you are my new uncle now."

"I would be most honoured if you would call me Uncle Jess."

"A little help here please James!" Blythe was struggling with the little girl in her arms while holding the screen door open for Timothy who was packing two large suitcases. James apologized and rescued Leah from her. CC hugged Blythe and proceeded to introduce her to me.

"I don't need an introduction CC… this could be no one but Jess. I'm Blythe, James's wife. Everyone calls me Bly, and I am absolutely delighted to meet you!"

There was no hand shaking, just her warm arms embracing me. I returned the gesture. "Lacey told me I would love you the minute I saw you and she was right. And, who is this little Goldilocks hiding behind you."

"That's not Goldilocks, that's my sister Leah!" Harrison declared. "Come on Leah, say hello to Uncle Jess."

Bly laughed and tried to coax her daughter out from behind her skirt. Gradually, Leah dropped her mother's skirt half-way and peered out at me. I had lowered myself to her level. Peeking out at me was a little blond dimpled cherub with the eyes the color of the precious stone…amethyst. Astounded, I looked up at her mother.

I whispered. "Is this my granddaughter Blythe? Is this my granddaughter?"

She smiled. "Yes Jess, she is. And Harry is your grandson."

James had not spoken again and I was pretty sure he was not going to be as accepting of me as his wife was. I had the distinct feeling that she had known about me for some time; but how?

"Do you know Leah that you and your grandmother have almost the same name?"

"No, they don't!" Harry announced emphatically. "Our grandmother's name is Lacey!"

"Yes, but Leigh is her middle name. Do you have a second name Harrison?" I asked.

"My whole name is Harrison James Monroe!" He said proudly.

Monroe? Why wasn't his last name King? I'd ask Blythe later. Leah was not going to come out from behind her mother's skirt and so I stood up and faced James.

"Dinner is in the oven and ready whenever you all are. Your rooms were newly made up this morning so if you would like to freshen up before hand, there is plenty of time. This is your house and so I will take my cue from you. If you will excuse me, it's time for me to exercise the dogs." They needn't know that I'd already had them out for their run twenty minutes ago.

"Can I come too Uncle Jess? They like me to run with them don't they Mom?" Harry begged.

"Me too Uncle Jesse." Leah had come out of hiding.

"NO, you're too little!" Harry asserted.

A tear formed in the corner of Leah's eye and she pouted. "Am not."

Yes, she was definitely Lacey's granddaughter. I lifted her up and sat her on the kitchen table. "She doesn't look too little to me Harry…what do you say Mom, Dad…can she come? I'll keep her safe."

I don't think James knew what to say, but Bly laughed and said. "Of course she can go. The flight was very long so the fresh air will do her good. Try not to get dirty okay Sweetheart?"

That stung as those were the last words I had said to Lacey.

"I won't Mommy."

"Okay then, let's go." I leaned down and told my granddaughter to jump on my back.

She giggled. "Let's go horsey Uncle Jesse."

Harry stated that my name was Jess and not Jesse and I told him that it was okay if she called me Jesse because her grandmother did. James opened the screen door for us and told his daughter to duck her head and hold on tight. I took off in a slight gallop and she squealed in delight. I helped Harry with the lock on the dogs' gate and they bounded out. I told Harry not to let them jump on him and to speak to them in a firm voice. Leah and I followed behind the trio at a much slower pace. They led us down the hill to Canterbury and up to the sheds, and through the overgrown garden path and around Tudor house. Fifteen minutes later I collapsed on the bench at the picnic table.

"That's enough for me Harry; bring the dogs here so that Leah can pet them." I unwound her arms from around my neck.

"They played me out too Uncle Jesse. Sit and be nice because my sister is just a little girl."

"Am not." Leah piped up. I held Trixie and Mickey while she caressed them. I looked up and saw James watching us from the bay window in the living room.

Dinner was on the table and after Blythe did a quick scrub of the children's hands we all sat down. James had taken the seat at the far end of the table; Leah sat between him and Bly. CC directed me to take the chair next to her at the head of the table. I didn't feel comfortable sitting there. Harry sat to the left of me.

"You shouldn't have gone to so much trouble CC. Everything looks delicious." Bly said smiling in my direction.

"Oh, all I did was toss a few vegetables together for the salad, Clara Branko made the bread. The real chef here is Jess." CC made sure everyone knew that the main dinner was my doing.

"How did you know that tacos were my favourite Uncle Jesse?" Harry asked.

"A little birdie told me." I winked at him.

"Yeah, my Gramma, right?"

"Please join me in a little prayer." Bly requested.

We joined hands and bowed our heads.

"Thank-you Lord for this meal that we are about to partake of and thank-you for delivering me and my family safely here. And though, we are here under dismal circumstances, we know you can turn the tide and bring joy back into our lives by bringing our beloved Lacey home to us. Please protect her and keep her safe. Please here this prayer Dear Lord, I beg of you."

We all chorused "Amen."

"Thank-you Blythe. Will you all please excuse me for a few minutes?" I pushed my chair away and attempted a weak smile when Harrison asked me where I was going. I tousled his hair and said that I'd be right back. No one else objected.

I didn't know where I was going myself…yes, I did. I climbed half way up the back stairs and sat down with my head in my hands. "Please Lord; Bly's plea goes double for me. We just found each other again…I don't care what you do to me, but bring her back to her family."

I heard footsteps on the stairs and knew that it was James who plopped down beside me. I had just met him but I already knew the smell of him. Without looking up I spoke.

"This is where your mother waits for me. This is where we laugh and argue and made plans." I reached into my blazer pocket and handed him the pictures. "It was on the other staircase where she forgave me, and in doing so, she forgave herself. I'm not ashamed to say I cried like a baby. It was then that she told me about you and gave me these. My heart broke for all the yesterdays we had missed." I knew I was close to losing it but I continued. "We only had three days together, but you need to know that they were the best days of my life and I won't settle for anything less than spending the rest of my life with her. I love her and she loves me." I passed him the picture of Lace and me that CC had found in Lacey's purse.

"I've seen this picture before." James said casually.

I wanted to ask him where he had seen it but didn't. I had an uncanny feeling again that he had known about me for some time…but how?

"Come on you two," Bly called up to us. "dinner is getting cold and Harry's getting antsy."

"We better get going. I'm sorry we had to meet this way James." I said.

"I know you love her, and by the way, this isn't the first time that we've met."

What the hell did he mean by that? I took my seat back at the table and cast a curious glance in his direction. CC passed me the lasagne saying she would warm it up if it was too cold.

"No need Cees, I'll pass on it as I am going to get my boy here to show me how to build the perfect taco. How about it Harry?"

"I sure will Uncle Jesse. I'm pretty good at it aren't I Mom?"

"Yes Dear, you are." Bly smiled.

"Yeah, but how do you keep the shell from breaking up?" I asked.

"I haven't figured that one out yet Uncle Jesse."

We all laughed and carried on with dinner. I brought out the cherry custard ice cream and asked if anyone wanted any. Harry asked how I knew that it was his and his father's favourite.

"What a coincidence; it just happens to be my favourite too."

As soon as the table was cleared Bly ushered the kids upstairs for their baths. Harry protested.

"Do you really want to do this Harrison?" James asked authoritatively.

Harry bowed his head. "No, but I want to go with Uncle Jesse to walk the dogs again."

"They are all done walking for today Harry, but we'll do it again tomorrow okay?" I promised.

"Sounds like a plan to me." James said. "How about you say goodnight to everyone and do as your mother tells you?"

"Yes." Harry said sheepishly. He hugged CC and Sam and then he turned to me. "Do you think my Gramma will be here when I wake up Uncle Jesse?"

"I am hoping that she will be Son. Will you say an extra big prayer for her and tell her how much we all miss her?" I reached out and shook his hand and sent him up the stairs. "James, when you are done helping Blythe I think we need to talk."

He acknowledged me with a nod. I thanked my dear friends for all their help and went into the den to wait for James. Half an hour later he took a chair opposite me.

"Where do you want to start?" He asked me.

"I think you know perfectly well where we are starting. What was that remark you made about us meeting before?" I was already sounding like a father demanding an answer from his child.

"It's just as I said; today is not the first time that we have met." His eyes did not leave mine.

"I leaned back. "The floor is all yours."

"A few years back I came looking for you. I was actually in your house."

He left the statement dangling in the air. "Excuse me; did I hear you right…you were in my home? I think I would remember meeting you."

"Well, I didn't introduce myself as James Monroe! I told you I was applying for a scholarship and that part of my dissertation was to include interviews with professional individuals and their families and how their professions impacted their lives. You invited me into your home and said you would be pleased to answer any questions that I had. You…"

"Stop right there! I remember the young man who came to my door; he was quite young, I'd say about seventeen. He had papers that proved who he was and that what he was doing was legitimate. He also had a school identity card and picture. That picture was not you. Do you want to explain yourself?"

"Hey, I'm from New York. A person can get anything for a price. So the photo was doctored a little, but it was me. If you remember, I never took my cap off citing that I was embarrassed by the hair-cut I had just gotten."

"Oh, I remember all right, but that was six years ago, am I right? Are you telling me that you deliberately deceived me by not telling me who you really were, and that you have known that I was your father for six years?"

"Actually, it was seven years ago. I had just had my sixteenth birthday that year and as usual we all came here to visit with Grandma Hilda. Mom and Arthur only stayed for a week and I begged to stay on for the rest of the summer. Timothy's parents said I could stay with them whenever I wanted. The year before when Timothy was showing me some old photos of his mom and dad we came upon one of Mom and you. I asked Laura who the fellow was with my Mom. She just said that it was an old friend. I asked what his name was and she hesitated, but finally said Jess. She said she couldn't remember the last name, but I didn't believe her for one minute. She said that you had moved away a long time ago. Well, I already knew what your name was because Mom had the exact same picture and it is the one you showed me earlier. From there I went to CC's and caught her canning cherries. I told her that I needed Laura and Tim's address as I wanted to send them a thank-you card when I got back home thanking them for their hospitality in letting me stay with them. She said that she wasn't sure of their postal box number and told me to get her address book from the telephone desk. I did, and I snooped. Sure enough there was a listing for a Jess with the last name Jameson. I wrote it down because I already had my suspicions as to who you were. Then I made a side trip to Vancouver. That's it; it's as simple as that."

"I think you have missed a few steps here James. Why did you have suspicions and why didn't you confront your mom with what you thought you knew…or did you?"

I had to know if Lacey knew that James had found out about me.

"No, I never spoke of it to her. She must have had her reasons for keeping me from knowing who my real father was and so I respected that. What happened Jess? What happened between you and my mother that was so horrible that she kept your identity a secret and let me go on believing that my father was a sailor that she knew for only one night, and that she never heard from him again? What did you do to her Jess?"

"Perhaps I will tell you one day what broke us up, but tonight is not the time to go there. When did you put your plan into motion to look for me? Had you ever doubted your mother's story before? When did you find out that Arthur was not your father and why the name change?"

James laughed. "One question at a time counsellor; I will answer you, but then you must do me the same courtesy. Does that sound fair to you?"

I got up and crossed the room and stopped at the door. "It's going to be a very long night so why don't you go into the living room and make yourself comfortable? I'm going to put a pot of coffee on and maybe you want to check on Blythe while it's perking?"

I heard him say under his breath. "Yes Sir." I chuckled as I saw him salute me in the mirror.

8:30 P.M. Tuesday May 25th

I set the coffee to perking and stepped outside into the cool evening air. The dogs were whining and so I let them out of the pen. They nuzzled me and I bent down. "I know, I know fellas; first Hilda leaves you and then Arthur, and now Lace has disappeared." I threw a couple of Frisbees for them and sat down until they returned. Trixie placed her head in my lap and looked at me sadly from her puppy-dog eyes. An overwhelming feeling of hopelessness encompassed me. I sunk to the ground and sobbing, buried my head in her shiny black mane. Mickey burrowed his head under my arm and knocked us over. I let them nibble on me for a few minutes until I gained my composure. I brushed us all off and he three of us ambled into the house. James was waiting for me in the living room and I wondered if he had been watching me and the dogs from the bay window again. They both sat down at my feet.

"They're lonesome." I said. "Now where were we?"

"Are you lonesome too Jess?" My son asked wistfully.

"Very much so. Lacey and I have only been together for three days, but we were barely apart. It seems like a lifetime has passed since she's been gone. I'm done waiting for the cops to find her and tomorrow I take matters into my own hands, and I promise you I will get results!"

"What can you do that a whole police-force can't?"

"Ask the right questions of the right people and I don't care how much force it takes."

"You have a suspect in mind don't you? Who is it? Surely you have voiced your suspicions to the authorities and what are they doing about it? What are we doing sitting around here instead of acting on your suspicions?"

"I do respect the law and I am giving them every opportunity to do their job, but so far they have come up with nothing. I have been in the business of interrogating people for a very long time and I'm pretty good at getting results. Tomorrow they are taking the surveillance team off the Bernard house and I will have my say with Hank."

"Are you suggesting that weird Hank killed Arthur and kidnapped Mom…for what reasons?"

"He wants your mother for himself. He said that Arthur and I had our chance with her and we blew it. He has her all right, but he is not the one who killed Arthur."

"Now you are not making any sense at all." James looked at me dubiously.

I opened my briefcase and passed him the autopsy report. "Read this, and you too will conclude that more than one person was involved in Arthur's death, and that it was perpetrated with great malice. Hank had no reason for such hatred but someone else did. He, she, or they hated Arthur so much that they plotted his demise and waited for the perfect opportunity that would also implicate your mother?"

"You're barking up the wrong tree Jess; Arthur had no enemies and certainly Mom doesn't."

"Oh, come on James, you don't strike me as being naïve. Surely Arthur had competitors and rivals; the theatre can't be one big harmonious family. He must have ruffled a few feathers in his day, and what about Richie…was there not conflict there?"

James made an attempt at laughter. "If you're looking at Richie as a suspect I will tell you that you are sorely mistaken. I never once saw them in any kind of disagreement, professionally or personally. I would stake my life on it…Richie had nothing to do with Arthur's death."

"Lacey said the same thing, but I will reserve judgement until I have analysed him myself."

James laid the papers down. "Is this all there is? I thought there would be more."

"That's all there is until the crime lab submits its' analysis. Here are my notes and the police report from what was discovered up Sugarloaf." I watched for his reaction as he read intently.

"I see what you mean about there being more than one suspect. But, why would they bother to get rid of that piece of the carpet when I understand that the rest of it was saturated with blood?"

"Exactly…it doesn't make any sense does it? Do you want to know what I think?" I didn't wait for him to answer me. "The "so-called" plan went awry. Did something or someone interfere with them? Did Arthur put up more of a fight then they had planned? I know the coroner's report states that there are no defensive wounds so to speak of but there was bruising and lacerations which to me suggests that he was bound and held by one assailant while the other did the stabbing. The question is: did Arthur wound one or both of them? The blood found on the unearthed carpet does not belong to him or Lacey…so whose is it? Then there is the macabre tape that was playing on the stereo when Lacey discovered the body. She believes it was left for her and if she could only figure out what it is, she will have an answer as to who murdered Arthur. She has listened to it over and over, but she always comes up empty."

"Do you have the tape? I would like to hear it, and I also want the gruesome details of what my Mother walked in on. You, being a lawyer pried it out of her didn't you?"

"I didn't have to pry James, but yes, it was pertinent that she tell me everything. Are you sure that you want me to retell her nightmare?"

He nodded and I recounted her testament verbatim as every word was etched in my mind.

He sat perfectly still and listened silently. I saw him cringe several times, but I carried on keeping my recital professional. I cleared my throat and stood up when I had finished.

"I need a few minutes." I called the dogs and took them to their room.

When I returned I found James gazing into space looking very distraught. I placed my hand on his shoulder. "It disturbs me to picture what your mother encountered. She sat and relayed the whole thing to me as if it had happened to someone else. She was calm and focussed throughout which brings me to the question; what do you make of your mother's sudden mood shifts?"

"We became concerned a few months back, but then Bly became sick and…"

"All right then. She is aware of it too, and we will deal with it when she gets home. Now, I would like to go back to where we left off…the months leading up to your plan to find me."

"Then we will have to go back a lot further than that."

"I'm listening."

"I don't know how much Mom has told you so stop me if you have heard any of this already. We lived with Arthur until I was four. He and Richie had bought a large Brownstone a year or so before. Mom and I lived on the main floor and they lived on the second. They had separate bedrooms and I never knew there was anything between them except friendship and their professional partnership until I was much older…if you are wondering. Anyhow, Mom didn't want to live in the city anymore and Arthur bought us a house in Pyra which is only a twenty minute subway ride away from the Brownstone. He also was instrumental in helping Mom open up the day care centers. She must have told you all of this?"

"Not really, but I am curious as to why you never called Arthur, Dad?"

"Because he wasn't my father and Mom made sure I knew that as soon as I was old enough to understand. He was always Uncle Arthur, and then one day I just started calling him Arthur."

"Did you wonder what happened to your real father?"

"Of course I did, and I asked Mom several times when I was young. She never went into any great details and I could see that my asking upset her and so I never asked again until I was ten. A friend of mine from school had found out that he was adopted and I began to think that I was also. I remember going to Mom and demanding that she show me my birth certificate. She was very upset that I doubted that she was my mother, but she produced the certificate. Arthur was listed as my father. I did not understand and it was then that she explained things to me. He claimed fatherhood so that I would legally have all his benefits and a name…"

I interrupted him. "And yet, you took your Mother's maiden name…why?"

"I was getting to that. Mom told me that day that I had every right to be curious about my biological father, but that he had gone away before I was even born. I asked her if that meant that he was dead, and she said: "I'm afraid that he left me a long time ago." She said that it was just her and me. She asked me if I was all right with that and I said that I was. She was very sad, but she did promise me that she would talk to me about the matter again when I was older and that I was luckier than most kids because I had "two fathers", and they would always be in my life. So that was that and I let it go until a few years later when I overheard Richie ask Arthur if he was ever going to tell me about my real father. Arthur said that it was better that I didn't know. That only made me curious; had my father been a horrid person? Maybe he was a criminal. I started snooping through all of Mom's stuff, but I found nothing. I thought that I would question Gram and Gramps the next time I saw them. Mom's sister and husband were always off on some quest to save the world so I couldn't go to them for answers. I would just have to bide my time until I got back to Kings Crossing. Quite by accident I came upon that picture of you and Mom. She was cleaning out her wallet and a bunch of papers were lying on the floor. I passed them to her for sorting and I noticed that one was a photograph of her. I had seen very few pictures of her when she was a teenager so it was quite a surprise."

James eyes met mine for a few seconds and then he carried on. "I asked who was in the picture with her and she said that he had once been her very best friend."

He paused; I'm sure for effect and to see my reaction. After assessing my discomfort he said.

"I turned the picture over and read: Jesse and me. This is the best day of my life."

I got to my feet and walked over to the liquor cabinet and poured myself a stiff drink. I held up the glass asking James if he wanted one. He declined. I sat back down and motioned for him to continue.

His voice was calm yet cold. "I asked her what Jesse's last name was and she laughed and said: "Would you believe James?" I then asked her if she had named me after him and she had smiled and said: "Yes, I think I did, and it's time that we changed our last name. What do you think about being James Monroe?" I didn't let her off the hook quite that easy though. I asked her if she was still in touch with you and she said that you had left Kings Crossing a long time ago and that she had no idea where you were. I was sure she was keeping something pertinent from me, but we never spoke of that day again, but I didn't forget. When she held the photo of you and her to her breast, I seen a longing in them that I had never seen before or have ever seen again. Yeah, you're wondering how would a teenage boy recognize longing aren't you? Well, her eyes were moist and sad and yet there was serenity in them. She put the picture away and in doing so, she filed you away also. I did not know that she still carried the photo with her. And that's it, that's all she wrote."

"That's hardly the whole story James. You left out the part about how you felt when you found me. You met my daughters and sat and talked with us. Are you going to tell me that you went on your merry way and never gave me another thought? Why in God's name didn't you tell me who you were?"

"I was brought up better than that. For Christ's sake, you had a wife and children! Did you think that I was going to blurt it out in front of Hilary and Vivian?"

"So you remember their names?"

"Of course I do…after all, they are my half-sisters and I keep in touch with Vivian."

"What…what did you say?" I stammered.

"You heard me right. How do you think I've kept track of you? I knew you were here because Vivian told me that you were in Kings Crossing helping out an old friend. It didn't take a rocket scientist to figure out that it was my mother. I knew you were with here before I even talked to you on the phone. Remember, I asked you to keep her safe?"

"Thanks James, I needed to be reminded of that. So, you have kept an eye on me; what else do you know and think about me?"

"Just that Vivian worships you and you and your wife live a very boring life. My question to you is what are your intentions towards my mother? Do you plan on keeping her on the side? Is she willing to share you? I only have your word that she loves you…are you sure she does?"

"I told you I am not going back to Marsha. Twice I have fallen in love with your mother at first sight. When you see us together, you will see how she loves me. We need each other James."

"Marsha, is that your wife's name? When do you plan on explaining your relationship with my Mother to her or will your philandering be nothing new to her? And, what about the girls: have you thought how this affair will impact their lives?"

"I see that you have not understood anything I have said to you. I will explain it to you one more time. I am in love with your mother and this is not some cheap affair we are having. I will tell Marsha when I am damn good and ready. For your information, I have never cheated on her before and I do not classify what Lacey and I share as an affair; it is so much more and we will be married as soon as I procure a divorce. There has been nothing between Marsha and I for years; we are just roommates and the parents of our children. I have no idea how Hilary will react. I've already discussed my intentions to divorce Marsha with Leigh and she knows about Lacey. In fact, she is coming to be with me in the next few days. She is going to be all right with us because she knows I haven't been happy. My concern is how she's going to react to knowing that her brother is someone she already knows."

"I don't think it is going to come as any great shock to her because she knows you are here and she knows that I am here also. I gave her a call saying that I was coming to Kings Crossing as my Mother was in a bit of trouble and that over the next few days all our lives were going to take a 180 degree turn. I could tell by her reaction that she had put two and two together as she knows my Mother's name is Lacey. Why do you call her Leigh?"

"It's her middle name and I like it; Vivian sounds so old. I suppose I better get used to calling her that so not to confuse Leah. How long has Blythe known about me?"

"You picked up on that did you? I promised myself that I would keep that information to myself after I met you until I figured out how to deal with it. I planned on discussing it with Mom someday, but I met Bly on my way home and everything changed. I was on my way to the subway and there she was… this waif of a girl sitting at a bus-stop crying her eyes out in the pouring rain. She was homeless as her legal guardian had died and knowing full well that she was going to be placed in a foster home, she fled. The few meagre belongings and two hundred dollars that she had escaped with had been relieved from her by a street thief. That's how I found her and I took her home with me. Two years later we were married and Harry was born. It was then that I told her about you and we decided to keep it our secret. Time went by and I put you further and further out of my mind."

There was so much more to the story of James and Blythe and I wanted to hear it all, but James was struggling with fatigue and so I told him to go upstairs to try and get some sleep. He declined and said that he would stay up with me. I told him to suit himself but I was going to close my eyes and that we could take up where we left off tomorrow. I remember getting up once and covering him with a blanket and nothing more until the shrill blaring of the house phone startled me awake. I caught it on the second ring.

CHAPTER 7

Seventh Crossing

Jess

"Lace, is that you Honey?" I beseeched.

"Jesse, can you come and get me"

"I can Honey. Can you tell me where you are?"

"I don't know, it's dark and I'm cold and it's so loud and I hurt. I'm scared Jesse."

"I'm coming Baby, but you have to give me some clue as to where you are? Can you do that? Is someone there with you?" James was beside me asking if it was his mother.

"He's asleep. I think I'm at our bridge Jesse because…"

"How the hell did you get my phone…give it to me!"

"Lace… Lacey?" I heard her crying just as the phone went dead.

"That God damn little piss-ant! I knew it was him!" I bellowed as I dropped the phone and ran into the kitchen. I grabbed a jacket off the coat rack and my keys.

"Jess, is she all right? Where is she?" James pleaded.

"She's at our bridge. Phone Timothy and tell him to meet me at the Seventh Crossing Bridge and to bring a squadron with him! I'll wring that little bastard's neck if he's harmed one hair on her head!" My hand was on the door knob.

"What's going on…is it Lacey?" Blythe was questioning from the top of the stairs.

"I'm going with Jess" James said as he instructed her to call Timothy.

"Come on then." I ordered throwing two jackets at him. "She said she's cold."

"How do you know where she is, what did she say?"

"She said she's at "our" bridge and I heard the thundering of the train coming down the tracks. The last thing I heard before he grabbed the phone from her was the shrill sounding of the whistle as it entered the tunnel." I turned the key in the ignition. "Buckle up and hold on Son as this isn't going to be a pleasure ride!"

"But Jess, there are other bridges; how do you know which one it is?"

"The Seventh Crossing is the only one that is covered and every morning and every afternoon the train arrives and the engineer sounds the whistle at precisely 4:10. No other whistle sounds like it does. It was always "our" bridge and nothing has changed in twenty four years."

"How did she sound? I mean, do you think…?" James was struggling to find the right words.

"She's been held by a mad man for two days so I don't have any idea of what he has done to her, but whatever it is, we will see her through it. She's alive and that's all that's important."

The minute the tires left the pavement I realized that I should have brought the jeep. I cursed as we bounced in and out of the ruts.

"It has been twenty four years since I've been here so how about trusting me that I am trying to get us to Lacey as fast as I can? We are five or ten minutes ahead of the police so we better have a plan for what we are going to do once we get to the bridge. If he has her locked up inside of the maintenance shed we are going to have to be very resourceful in how we draw him out."

"Do you think he's armed? He's got to be thinking that someone is coming for her after he caught her with the phone. Do you think he has an escape plan?"

"I have no idea what goes on in that deranged mind of his so nothing will surprise me. Do I think he has a gun? Yeah maybe, if his father was a hunter then there would probably still be guns in the house. I don't have any idea how he even got Lacey here. As far as I know he doesn't even drive and his mother's car hasn't left the drive-way in a very long time."

"Could he possibly have an accomplice?"

"I doubt it. We are getting close…Jesus Christ!"

The headlights outlined two shadowy figures on the berm not thirty feet in front of us. Hank was holding on to Lacey with one arm while his other shielded his eyes from the glare of the lights. I slammed on the brakes. James had his hand on the doorknob but I stopped him from opening the door.

"Let's let him think that there is only one of us. I want you to climb out the back door on my side at the same time as I get out. I need you to make your way up and around and come up behind him while I am distracting him. Can you do that James?" I passed him a flashlight. "I don't think he can see five feet in front of him and the high beam is blinding him."

"Let's go." James was over the seat and simultaneously we opened the doors. I stepped out into the light.

"What are you doing there Hank?" I called trying to distract him and sound unemotional.

"Who the hell are you? Get out of here; you have no business being here!" He yelled.

"It's Jess Jameson Hank; how about letting Lacey go? You haven't hurt her have you?"

He released his hold on her and she slipped to the ground. She didn't move.

I panicked and started to move towards her but stopped when I saw that Hank had picked up a rifle and was aiming it in my direction.

"What have you done to Lacey Hank? Let me come and get her; she hasn't done anything to you. Just let me get her to safety and then you can do whatever you want to me. I'll help you get away before the cops get here. You know they are coming… what'd you say Hank?"

He had both hands on the gun and I was pretty sure he knew how to use it. I caught a glimpse of James flying through the air and I fell to the ground but not before I felt a bolt of electricity surge through my left arm. I strained to right myself.

"Is she all right James?" I cried. "Please tell me she's alive!"

James was cradling her in his arms. "She's unresponsive; she's breathing, but it's laboured."

I heard the howling of sirens behind me. James was cursing; he had his foot on Hank's back.

"I thought I told you to stay down you son of a bitch!"

Two officers appeared out of nowhere and relieved James of his prisoner. He picked Lacey up.

"Bring her to me James, bring her to me." I cried.

I felt strong arms helping me to my feet. "Jeeze Jess, you've been shot!" It was Timothy.

"Never mind me, get Lace; James says she's barely breathing. I need to see her Tim."

I leaned against the car as they tried to place her in my arms. I couldn't support her without their help. She looked lifeless and she had an ungodly smell. "Christ, he's chloroformed her! Where's that little bastard Timothy, let me at him!"

"He's already in custody Jess. You can see him tomorrow. Right now you need to go to the hospital with Lacey; let them take her Jess."

Reluctantly, I relinquished her to the paramedics. I watched them place her on a stretcher and load her into the ambulance. Timothy told the attendants that I was going with them as I needed to be treated for a gun-shot wound. He said he and

James would follow us. They helped me into the van and asked me if I wanted to lie down. I declined and told them that Lacey needed me. They administered oxygen to her and did a quick assessment and relayed the information to the hospital. I didn't have to tell them that she was cold as they had already piled blankets on her. I sat beside her and held her hand. It was like holding a block of ice.

"Why hasn't she wakened? Isn't chloroform short lived; shouldn't it have worn off by now?"

"Sir, it would only be conjecture to offer an opinion without further testing, but she may have been subjected to more than just chloroform." The one called Denny said.

"You think she's been drugged?" I questioned.

"We'll be at the hospital in a few minutes and the doctor will have a better idea of that."

I held her as best I could stroking her muddy face and matted hair. How could she have gotten so filthy in such a short time? I kept talking to her telling her that she was safe and that I loved her. She never moved a muscle.

The siren was turned on the second that we hit the pavement and minutes later we pulled into the ambulance bay. "We're here Lace; you're going to be all right." I said it for her sake, but I wasn't sure that she would be.

A nurse brought me a wheelchair. I protested saying that I needed to go with Lacey. I surrendered when she promised me that I would be more comfortable sitting in it next to her. By the time she wheeled me into the exam room Lacey was already hooked up to an I.V. and blood pressure machine. I was told the doctor would be arriving momentarily. I reminded myself that this was a small town hospital and that doctors were not stationed at the hospital twenty four hours a day. One nurse, her name was Aubrey, wanted to help me remove my jacket so that she could assess my injury. I declined not wanting to let go of

Lacey's hand. A large round faced gentleman parted the curtains and in a robust voice asked the attending nurses if this was indeed the damsel who had disappeared from the Tudor House?

I answered him. "Yes Sir, it is Lacey Monroe."

He walked over to the head of the bed and opened her eyes and closely examined them. "Is it not Lacey King then?"

"She goes by Monroe; they are one and the same."

"And, who are you?" He asked never taking his eyes off Lacey.

I answered him flatly. "Jess Jameson."

"Ah, the lawyer." He was now checking her for head trauma.

"Lawyer is at the bottom of the list of who I am to Lacey." I stated.

"I see; has she no next of kin?"

"That would be me." James said as he came to stand next to me. Ignoring the doctor he asked me how she was.

"She hasn't regained consciousness yet. Perhaps the good doctor can shed some light on why she hasn't?" I directed my question towards him.

He looked at us from over his bi-focal glasses. Without interrupting his examination he reached across Lacey's unmoving body and extended his hand first to me and then James. "Dr. Macey at your service gentlemen."

James told him that he was Lacey's son and what could he tell us of her condition. He didn't answer immediately but asked the nurses to remove Ms. Monroe's dress so that he could properly assess her. I told them to go ahead and cut the dress off if necessary but that there was a zipper in the back. The nurse named Holly smiled at me. Dr. Macey continued his evaluation of Lacey while the nurses worked at removing her clothes. He threw back the warming blanket.

"What do we have here?" He said as her feet were uncovered and then her legs.

"Good God!" James exclaimed. "What's happened to her?"

I put my hand on James's arm to comfort him even though I was sickened by Lacey's swollen, cut, and badly bruised leg. The damage stemmed from her ankle all the way up to her hip. "I think she may have fallen down the stairs when she was abducted James. How bad is it Doc?"

"Yes, I do believe the lass has had one horrific tumble. The bruising suggests that it is at least two days old. There is no apparent fracture, but we will do x-rays to be sure. She will heal, but it is going to be a week or so before she will be able to walk." He put his hand on the wheelchair I was sitting in. "I'm afraid she will be confined to one of these for the time being. Will that pose a problem for her or you?"

What a silly question; we had Lacey back; there were no problems. "There are enough of us to see that she stays off her feet. I think we are more concerned with her unconsciousness. Is it possible that she has been drugged with something more potent and sinister than chloroform?" James backed me out of the way so that the doctor could finish his examination.

"Quite possibly Mr. Jameson; the blood tests will verify that." He removed the oxygen mask from Lacey and lightly placed his hand over her mouth and then smelled his hand. He nodded.

"Very good, she is coming along. All her vitals are improving; she's on the comeback boys."

Timothy appeared at the curtain asking how Lacey was doing and asking the doctor if he would drop by the station after he was finished here.

"Sure, why not; after all, it is on my way home and I suspect that it's not really a request? Am I to assume that I am to verify the condition of someone in custody that may be associated with my patient here?" Dr. Macey asked.

Timothy did not deny or confirm the question. He thanked the doctor and turned to me. "I'm going to need that jacket Jess."

"I thought you might; is there any hurry?"

Before he could answer Dr. Macey asked Holly to accompany me into the next cubicle and help remove my jacket so he could assess my injury. I said I wasn't leaving Lacey.

"Well Mr. Jameson, you are not going to be much use to Ms. Monroe if you get infection in that arm now are you? Am I wrong in assuming that the hole in your jacket was made by a projectile; perhaps a bullet?"

James agreed with the doctor. "You really need to have your arm looked at Jess. Mom's not going anywhere and neither am I."

"Okay, but hold her hand and keep talking to her. I don't want her to feel alone."

"Damn it, I was sure the bullet would be here!" Timothy exclaimed after he and Holly managed to get me out of the jacket. There was no sign of the slug in it.

"Were you hoping it was still lodged in my arm?" I asked him jokingly.

"Of course not!" He retorted.

Holly commented that the leather coat probably kept the bullet from doing serious damage.

"Yeah, thanks for the save Arthur." I mumbled.

Timothy asked what Arthur had to do with anything and I told him that it was Arthur's jacket. Dr. Macey came in and agreed that the wound was only superficial and a cleansing and several stitches were all that it required. He suggested that I keep my arm in a sling for a few days. Holly had the tray all ready for the procedure when we were interrupted by Lacey's screams. I was out of the chair in a flash. I found James and the other nurse attempting to restrain her. She was fighting them and calling my name over and over. The nurse stepped back as soon as she saw me. I reached for Lacey and cradled her in my arms.

"I'm here Lace, look at me Honey, it's me."

She clung to me sobbing. "Oh Jesse, is it really you? He said he was going to kill you!"

"Well, he didn't did he? Look at me Baby…thank God you've come back to us." I forgot about the pain in my arm as I smothered her with kisses.

"I'm so sorry Jesse that I didn't listen to you…I shouldn't have opened the door." She sniffled.

"It's all right Honey; hey, have you even said hello to your son?" I nodded towards James.

Lacey turned her head. "Oh James, you're here? Is it Tuesday already?"

"Hi Mom; we are all here and it is actually Wednesday." He said kissing her on the cheek.

"What…Wednesday?" Tears were running down her face. She looked at me and then James and back at me again. "Does he know?"

James answered her. "Yes I know Mom; there's nothing to worry about."

"I so wanted to be there when you two met…I'm sorry." Lacey sobbed.

"It's all good Sweetheart." I said kissing her. "In fact, James saved my life back at the bridge, and this isn't the first time that he and I have met."

"What…what are you saying?"

"Perhaps this is not the best time to get into this Jess." James suggested.

"Twenty four years ago I kept things from your mother and seven years ago you chose to do the same thing. I've come clean and now it's your turn."

"Someone please tell me what is going on?" Lacey begged of us.

"Well, you…I should say "we," have a very resourceful son. Seven years ago he came to visit me at the coast…"

"Wait, wait, wait…what are you saying? You knew all this time that James was your son?"

"No, Mom, I never told him who I was."

It was then that Lacey noticed my bleeding arm. "Oh God Jesse, what happened to you? Was it Hank…did he do that?"

I assured her that it was just a scratch and that I would have it bandaged while James told her his story. I winked at her. "Cut the boy some slack Hon. James, you have the con."

Ten minutes later I returned with Dr. Macey. A few stitches, a sling, a tetanus shot and a mild pain killer and I felt human again. I was happy to see that Lacey and James were both smiling and holding hands.

"We're good then?" I asked.

Lacey nodded and questioned the doctor about my injury.

"My dear lady, your friend is perfectly fine and the sling is just a reminder to him not to use his arm for a few days. Now, you are another matter. Although your stats have been constantly improving, I still want to do a full blood panel work-up and as soon as the lab tech arrives we will do so. Ah, here she is. Will you gentlemen please excuse us for a few minutes?"

James and I wandered down to the waiting room. "So, how did it go with your mother?"

"Well, she cried of course and asked me over and over if I could ever forgive her. I told her there was nothing to forgive her for and I fully understood why she had never told me about you. She wanted to know if you had told me the whole story of what broke the two of you up and why she had married Arthur. I asked her if she loved you and she said "yes". I told her that was all I needed to know and we left it at that. Her only concern seems to be is that I like you and accept you as my father and her boyfriend."

I laughed. "Boyfriend, she actually referred to me as her boyfriend?"

"Yes, she did. What is so funny about that?"

"Well Son, we are way past the boyfriend/girlfriend stage, but how did you answer her?"

"I told her for a lawyer, you were all right and that Harry and Leah already loved you."

"The sentiments are definitely mutual. You and Blythe have done an amazing job raising them and it couldn't have been easy with her being ill for the past few years. I haven't had much time to get to know you, but I applaud you for your devotion and conviction for succeeding in a teenage marriage. It's obvious that you made better decisions than I did when I was your age."

"You and I do have one thing in common…we both fell in love at first sight. I was just as young as you were and maybe someday you will explain what went wrong between you and Mom. It's pretty obvious that whatever you two had two decades ago never completely died. She has been an amazing mother not just to me, but also Bly. When I brought her home that cold rainy day she never once asked me what the hell I thought I was doing. She just took her under her wing and loved her. She has supported us in everything we have done and when our lives were interrupted with Bly's illness she insisted we move back in with her. I couldn't have managed without her. As it is, I had to drop out of college and take odd jobs to help pay the bills, not that I needed to as Arthur made sure we never wanted for anything. I know he has provided for me in his will, but I need to stand on my own two feet. Thankfully Mom is back safe and sound, but she has been through so much in the last week and in all honesty, I am afraid that she wouldn't be able to handle it if…" James didn't finish his sentence leaving me to think that he was worried that I wasn't going to hang around.

"You can put that notion of yours away for good as I am not going anywhere. My life is with Lacey, no matter where it takes us or what obstacles we face. Marsha may not be willing to give me a divorce, but I can assure you Son that it will not stop us from being together." I got up and cleared my throat. "Might I add that you and your family are an added incentive? I can only hope that someday you will be able to think of me as your father, but I know I am going to have to earn that title."

I asked James to excuse me as I needed to see about acquiring a private room for Lacey as it appeared she was going to be here for a while and she may as well be comfortable. He said that he should come with me and see if her insurance policy was valid in Canada. I told him that was my department as after all it was because of my negligence that she had been abducted and held captive and injured.

He put his hand on my shoulder. "I need to apologize for my outburst the other day in accusing you of not protecting Mom. It was quite a shock when Timothy told me that she was missing and I needed to take it out on someone and who better than the man who promised me he would keep her safe. Thankfully Bly was there to counteract my combatant behaviour. There is one other thing…seven years ago you took me at my word that I was doing research and invited me into your home. I knew then that you were a kind and caring man and father by the relationship you had with Hilary and Vivian. That's why I decided to keep in touch with Vivian because someday I wanted to be able to come to you and tell you that I was your son. It wasn't the right time then and I just couldn't do it because the girls were so young and even though I was only sixteen; my upbringing wouldn't let me ambush you that way. Besides, I was scared to death you wouldn't have accepted me."

"You do not owe me an apology James. To be perfectly honest, I was expecting a hell of a lot more admonishing and yes, I was glad that Bly came in and took over. But, no matter how much CC wants to take the blame, it was me and only me. I knew there was a killer out there and I should never have left her alone. You know, it is easy for me to say that I would have taken you at your word that you were my son, but we will never know will me? If you had of told me that your mother was Lacey Monroe…well, I can tell you without a doubt that would have sent me into a tail-spin. She should have told me about you and I should have questioned her perplexing decision to marry Arthur and tracked her down. CC and Sam should have told me their suspicions a long time ago, but none of that happened and so we aren't going to lay blame or speculate on what might have been. I hate to say it, but Arthur's death has brought us all together. We can grieve his passing but can rejoice in our newly found blessings. I offered my hand to my son. "It may be a little late or maybe a little too early, depending on how you look at it, but I would be overjoyed if someday you find it in your heart to accept me as your father and honoured if you would take the Jameson name as your own."

Instead of taking my hand James embraced me. All he said was. "It's done."

We were both too emotional to say anything else and were saved by the good doctor saying that Lacey was waiting anxiously for us. I sent James on ahead and went to see about a room for her. When I re-joined them, I found them all laughing. I asked what was so funny.

"These angels are trying to make me presentable, but I fear it is impossible. Holly says my hair is a rat's nest and Aubrey says no matter how hard she scrubs she can't get my feet clean."

I walked around the bed to where Lacey's dress lay in shambles on the floor. "What was the last thing I said to you on Monday Lace?"

She smiled. "That you loved me?"

I chuckled and held the dress up for her to see. "That too, but didn't I tell you not to get dirty?"

She gasped. "Is that my May Day dress…the one CC bought for me? Oh dear, it's ruined; what will she say?"

"I don't think she will care Honey; she will just be so thankful that you're alive. As soon as you can walk I will take you out and buy you a hundred dresses, okay?"

"Well, I do like dresses…just a minute, what do you mean, "when I can walk?"

"Doctor Macey wants you to stay off your feet for four or five days, maybe longer depending on how fast you heal. Didn't he tell you that?"

"Well, he said my ankle and leg were bruised and that I must have taken quite a fall. He said I may have some discomfort for a few days, but no, I don't think he told me that I couldn't walk."

"Yeah, he did Mom." James told her. "How did you fall, do you remember?"

"I didn't fall. I threw myself down the stairs hoping that Hank would leave me if I was injured. He didn't, and that was when he told me he'd kill you Jesse if I tried anything stupid again."

I kissed her. "Thanks for sacrificing yourself for me, but I wish you hadn't. The bastard sure knew how to pull your strings and it's a damn good thing he's behind bars or I would be."

"What are you saying Jesse?"

James saved me from uttering a death threat in front of the nurses. "I don't think he meant anything Mom, just that it is a damn good place for him."

Lacey waited until the nurses had left the room. "I don't think you meant that at all, did you Jesse? Promise me you won't go after Hank if he gets out on bail?"

"I promise. I think I will have my hands full looking after you. Now, what do you say we send James home for a much needed sleep?"

"Yes James, you must be exhausted, flying from Virginia to New York and then here, and you need to be with Bly when the children wake up." She looked at me. "And you too Jesse, you should go back to the house and rest."

"Yup, I will just as soon as I can take you with me."

"The doctor said he wants me here until at least noon tomorrow so there is no need for you to sit with me; I'm safe here you know."

Only after Holly and Aubrey returned informing Lacey that they were moving her to a more comfortable room did James agree to leave. Of course I had to promise that I would never leave his mother's side…as if I was going to.

The nurses transferred Lace into a respectable size bed in a nice private room. They checked her saline solution in her I.V. bag and charted her statistics. They told us that they would not be disturbing us for several hours. I closed the door behind them and closed the blinds.

"Are you comfortable Missy?" I asked Lace. "Is there any room for me?"

"Are you going to sleep with me Jesse?" She said smiling broadly and patting the bed.

"I didn't rent this make-shift honeymoon room so that I could sit in that dreadful looking chair while my sweetheart slept in comfort. But, no I am not going to 'sleep' with you so to say; I just need to hold you. Is that okay with you?"

"Oh yes Jesse, I'm so cold without your arms around me."

"Sorry Honey, you're going to have to settle for one arm as I seem to have a wounded wing."

She laughed and managed to move herself into the middle of the bed. She parted the blankets for me, but I declined the invitation. "Not a good idea; I'll just lie on top of the quilt."

She pouted a little. "Suit yourself, but I'm not going to attack you, you know?"

"History wouldn't agree with you." She smacked me playfully.

Awkwardly, I was able to get my right arm around her and she cuddled into my chest. She placed her hand on my impaired arm. "Does it hurt?"

"No, nothing hurts anymore." I kissed the top of her head. We were both silent for a few minutes and then she started asking questions about my first encounter with James.

"What would you have done if he had told you that he was your son right there on your doorstep? What would you have said? Would you have wondered which one of your dozen girlfriends was his mother?"

"I can't rightfully say what I would have done. I suppose I would have needed proof, like a paternity test. And, for your information, I did not have unprotected sex with dozens of girls."

"I won't ask you how many because I really don't want to know. I know the names of all of the men I had relations with… can you say the same?" Lacey questioned.

I sighed. "I don't know why you want to talk about this right now, but I will indulge your curiosity. I didn't have any long lasting relationships; I didn't have girlfriends, so to say, after you. There was nothing serious until Marsha which I now know was a mistake. She seemed to need me and I suppose I needed someone to settle me down. I don't regret marrying her for she gave me Leigh and Hilary. What I do regret is that you needed me too and my bloated ego wouldn't let me keep trying to correct the wrong that I did you. I believe I have told you all this before. Are you satisfied now?" I was feeling slightly uncomfortable, but that turned to humiliation when she asked the next question.

"When do you want to do the paternity testing with James?"

I knew she was serious. I felt the muscles in my body tense up for a second. I appreciated that she was still coping with the murder and the kidnapping, but now she had her doubts about whether I believed that James was truly my son. I needed to nip this in the bud.

"I'm going to pretend you just didn't say that."

She lifted her head off my chest and said. "Why?"

"Well, despite the obvious and that is that he looks like me, the time frame is right, but most of all because you told me that he is my son."

She started to cry. "I'm sorry I asked you all those questions Jesse."

"I love you Lace and you can ask me anything. I promise I will always answer truthfully."

"I love you too Jesse and I want you to know that I wasn't molested. I asked Holly to do a rape kit on me and she said there was no sign of forced…"

I stopped her. "Oh sweetheart," I hugged her tightly. "that must have been so hard for you to ask. For your sake, I am very happy that he didn't touch you, but in no way would it have changed my feelings for you."

"I know that Jesse. You've dealt with rape cases haven't you?"

"Yes I have and they are the most disturbing and emotionally draining of any cases that I have taken to trial. Now, can we please talk about something more cheerful?"

"Yes, as soon as you reassure me that Bly is all right. James says she is doing fine, but I know he doesn't want to worry me…what do you think?"

"Of course I didn't know Blythe before so I have no idea of how she looked, but one would never know that there is anything wrong with her."

"The last time I saw her was only a month ago, but she was pale and gaunt. She was so fatigued that she could barely stay up for fifteen minutes and she was in a great deal of pain. She had lost weight and her beautiful golden hair had lost its sheen. We didn't know if she had Lupus or M.S. or cancer. We were all so terrified. Although Fibromyalgia and R.A. have many debilitating complications, they can be managed I'm hoping."

"You will be pleasantly surprised then when you see her and that will be in a few short hours."

"I'm going to take your word that she is all right. James said that she is on some strong medication while waiting for the R.A. meds to kick in. I'm wondering why her doctor in New York didn't start her on the drugs right away."

"From what I understand, he was a general practitioner, and very young. He was the one who originally diagnosed her with fibromyalgia as she didn't test positive to the Rheumatoid factor or other symptoms like swollen joints or morning stiffness. But, she was fatigued, lost weight and ran low grade fevers. These whole body symptoms are also signs of other diseases such as Lyme disease, gout, and lupus. Her doctor was wise to insist she see a Rheumatologist. She was very lucky to have been selected to the trials that were being conducted in Virginia Beach. A small percentage of patients never test positive to the R.A. factor, but within two years, 80% do and Bly now does. Her x-rays show some thinning of the joint linings. As far as she knows there is no history in her family and the doctors said that and her age, and attitude are all positive signs that they caught it in time and the medications will work for her."

"Her own body is attacking her, right?"

"Yes, it is an auto-immune disease that causes the body to make antibodies against healthy joint tissue. But, because she also has Fibromyalgia, not only does she have joint problems, but muscle pain also. She said that four hours after she had taken her first dose of prednisone, she was almost pain free, and that was the first time in almost two years."

"I worry though as prednisone is a corticosteroid and it can have severe side effects."

"Don't worry Hon; she will be on it only until the Hydroxychlorquine, better known as Plaquenil kicks in which could be up to three months. She is to keep taking the Elavil that is supposed to help with her sleep disturbances, and hopefully, she will not have to graduate to adding Methotrexate. But, I know from experience that it and Plaquenil are often taken together; one thing at a time though."

"Experience…I was only gone for two days, how do you know so much about these drugs?"

"Clients my dear, clients. I have helped many people receive disability benefits that were denied to them by their insurance companies because of health problems. I have been down this road a few times before. It has never been so personal before, but Bly is my daughter-in-law and I already love her. Have I eased your mind a little?"

"Yes, you have; thank-you. Now, you should try and get some sleep, okay?"

"In a minute; I have a question for you…when were you last in the rotunda?"

"You mean the dome room at Tudor House…maybe two years ago, why?"

"How did the room seem to you? Was it neat and clean; were the dust covers on the furniture?"

"Yes, I think so, but I really don't remember. Why are you asking?"

"When I was looking for the car seat for Leah I visited the dome and was amazed at how clean the room was. I asked Clara if she had been keeping it up and she said no. I have a hunch that Ainsley is here and has been living there. Do you think that's a possibility?"

"I have absolutely no idea."

"Think about it Lace. Don't you think that although Ainsley had been disowned by her mother that she wouldn't come home for her mother's and brother's memorials? Perhaps she thinks that there might even be an inheritance of sorts for her, or maybe Hilda had even willed one of the houses to her."

"That is doubtful, but in my mind, she is certainly entitled to something. Arthur never talked about his sister, but I did know that he had flown up to Calgary Alberta to see her many years ago. I did not know the circumstances of the visit as he did not discuss it with me. I believed that Richie might know and perhaps we could ask him when he arrives on Thursday."

We left it at that and I encouraged her to try and get some sleep. She said she would if I would too. I said I would. She snuggled close to me and I was comforted by the slow, constant rhythm of her breathing. I put my hand on heart and she put hers on mine. We whispered "I love you" and drifted off to sleep.

CHAPTER 8

Aftermath

Lacey

I tried to put the events of the last two days out of my mind, but I couldn't. I was going to have to give my statement to the police later in the day and maybe then I would be able to get some rest. Just a few hours ago I was a hostage to a deranged man who had vowed to kill Jesse if I did not co-operate with him. He was taking me away from Kings Crossing. I fought him, but he was too strong for me and he managed to subdue me with some foul smelling substance on a cloth. The doctor had told me that it was chloroform. I still had a slight headache, but I was lying next to the man I had been in love with all my life and never thought I'd ever see again, so I could endure anything. I guess I did manage to fall asleep because the next thing I heard was James.

"Well, this is certainly a sight I never thought I'd ever see… my mother in bed with my father in a hospital bed."

Jesse was already awake. "Shh, let's not wake the sleeping beauty."

"Too late, I'm already up, but I'm not too sure I can move."

Jesse untangled us and gradually managed to right himself. With James's help they sat me up and swung my legs over the side of the bed. I winced in pain. Jesse said he was afraid of that and sent James out to find a nurse.

I was given a pain killer in an overly large needle and was told to let it work before I attempted to get dressed. I was too impatient and the minute the nurse was out the door I begged Jesse to help me. Blythe had sent underclothes and my red caftan and some slippers with James. I refused the bra which brought an amused smile to Jesse's face. "I'm only going home you know." I said.

Of course it was too painful to walk and so I had to use a wheelchair. Dr. Macey met us at the nurse's station and requested that he examine both me and Jesse. He sent us home with pain pills and told us not to hesitate to contact him or the hospital if we needed anything more.

With great difficulty my two supermen managed to get me in and out of the car. Harry and Leah and Blythe were waiting for us outside Tudor. I broke into tears at the sight of them.

"I know you want to hug your grandmother but let's get into the house first and then you can hug and kiss her all you want, okay?" James said holding the children at bay.

He retrieved the wheelchair from the trunk and he and Jesse manoeuvred me into it. Harry asked James if he could help to push me promising he'd be careful. Bly walked on one side of me and Jesse and Leah on the other side holding my hands. I was deposited on the chesterfield in the family room and the kids wasted no time claiming their seats next to me. Jesse managed to talk Leah into sitting on his knee. Harry asked a thousand questions and we answered them all. I explained that I had fallen and had bruises from my ankle up to my thigh and that the doctor wanted me to stay off my feet for a few days. We embellished slightly on the truth about Jesse's arm being in a sling saying that he had to have a few stitches for a small wound that he got while playing with the dogs. Harry said he'd look after both of us. Then he asked me why I had never told him about Uncle Jesse before. I hugged him and asked him and Leah if they would like to hear a story…of course they did.

James interjected. "Mom, do you really want to do this now?"

"Yes, I do." I answered smiling. "Why don't you sit in this big ole wheelchair Harry so I can see you? Good." I placed his hands in mine. "You know how you have always asked me why James doesn't have a father and why you and Leah have a grandmother but not a grandfather?"

He nodded that he did.

"Well, you do now. Jesse is your grandfather." I paused. "What do you think about that?"

Poor Harry, he was confused. "But I thought he was my uncle… Mom told me so." He looked inquiringly at Jesse and then Bly. "How can he be my grandfather too?"

"Sorry Honey, that's my fault, but it wasn't my story to tell." Bly said.

"No, it wasn't; it's Jesse and my story and it started a very long time ago when we were both teenagers. We met and we fell in love, you know just like the way your Mom and Dad love each other. From that love is how you and your sister came to be, and that is how your Daddy came to be because Jesse and I loved each other. Jesse is your Daddy's Dad. Do you understand?"

"I don't think so. Why did nobody tell me? Did you know Dad?" Harry asked turning around to look at his dad.

"I'll handle it James." Jesse said. "No, he did not know. Your grandmother and I had a very big argument and I went away and married somebody else and she married your Uncle Arthur."

I interrupted before Jesse could take all the blame. "I was already pregnant…you know what that means don't you Harry? That baby that was in my stomach was your father, but I didn't tell anyone, not even him. I was too angry with him and I married Arthur instead and never told James who his real father was. You knew that Arthur was only his pretend father didn't you?"

"Why didn't you tell anyone Grandma? Why didn't you want Daddy to know?"

"I really don't know why Harry. I am very sorry that I didn't because I hurt a lot of people…"

Bly and James both came and knelt on the floor beside Harry and me.

"Don't cry Grandma. Dad, you're not mad at her are you? I'm not mad at you Grandma."

"No one is Harry. We love her and could never be angry with her." James said. "We are all together now and that is what is important."

Leah asked why I was crying and Blythe told her they were tears of joy. Harry was not through with questions though.

"Did you know Uncle Arthur Jess? Did you come back because he died?

"Yes, I did know Arthur a long time ago and we were friends, but no, I came back because I knew your grandmother was going to be here and I wanted to see her." Jesse put his arm around me and took my hands in his. "I should never have waited so long to find her."

"But she wasn't lost Jess. Did you think she was?"

"I could have and I should have tracked her down, but I didn't. I regret it now because from the first moment I saw her at Sam's and CC's, I knew I still loved her." Jesse kissed me and ruffled Harry's hair. "But, you can be sure that I'm not going to let her get away on me again."

"Aren't grandmas and grandpas supposed to be married? Are you going to get married?" Harry asked looking back and forth at Jesse and me.

"You bet we are Harry, just as soon as possible. What do you say; do you want me for a grandfather?" Jesse asked hopefully.

"Can I call you Grampa or do you want me to call you grandfather?"

"Grampa is just fine." Jesse said shaking hands with his new grandson.

Leah wasn't going to be left out and she shook his hand too though I am sure she had no idea what was going on.

"You have two new Aunties too because Jesse has two daughters. Their names are Leigh and Hilary. I can't wait to meet them and hope they will like us. What do you say Harry?" I asked.

He asked how old they were and where did they live and when could he meet them. Jesse answered his questions and told me not to worry because they would love us all.

"He's right Mom. I can't speak for Hilary, but I can for Vivian. I know that you call her Leigh, Jess, but I think to avoid confusion to Leah here, we had better all call her by her first name. Will you and she be all right with that?" James asked his father.

"Yeah, I will try. Why do you say you can speak for her James?'

"I'm picking her up from the airport in a little while. She is most anxious to meet everyone."

I took a deep breath. I wasn't at all prepared to be introduced to one of Jess's daughters.

Jesse squeezed my hand. "When did you talk to her James, and just what did you tell her?"

"She knows I'm her brother."

"I think it's time for lunch; come and help me kids." Blythe's request was more of an order.

They followed her into the kitchen marching like two little soldiers. James waited until they were out of earshot before asking Jesse if he was out of line by confessing to Vivian.

"She was bound to know sooner or later and you just took the later out of the equation. What was her reaction to finding out that the boy she had met seven years ago was her brother?"

"She'd pretty much figured it out already as I told you last night. She said she always wanted a big brother and that I came with a wife and kids only put the icing on the cake."

"Yup, that's my girl. I'll warn you though that her sister is a horse of a different color and I cannot see her accepting my new family any time soon." Jesse said fervently.

I leaned into him. "I pray that Vivian won't hate me and maybe she will have some influence over Hilary. I feel so guilty that I have uprooted a family…"

"Hey Babe," Jesse stopped me from saying anymore. "I seem to remember that you wanted nothing to do with me and that it was me who convinced you that we belonged together. How many times did you try and send me packing? No Lace, you have nothing to feel guilty for."

"But Jess…"

"Shh, here comes lunch and right on time as I am famished!"

Soon as we had eaten, Jesse managed to get me into the shower. He had placed a plastic lawn chair inside the door for me to sit on. I was able to wash myself with the hand held shower. I was trying to reach down and scrub my feet when he came back to see how I was doing. I said I was finished. He laughed.

"Hardly, my dear; do you call these feet clean?"

"Well, it is the best I could do."

"Then I guess I am going to have to finish the job." He said scrunching down. "The nurses were right; these feet are in terrible shape especially the right foot. Am I scrubbing too hard?"

I had braced myself against his back and I suppose I flinched a little. "No you're not. Thank-you for everything you have been doing for me Jesse."

"It is totally my pleasure I assure you. I'm afraid I am going to have to enlist James's help to get you out of here. Are you all right with that? I'll wrap you up as best I can in your robe."

"You hurt your arm getting me in here didn't you?"

He didn't answer me but told me not to go anywhere while he fetched James. Very funny.

They carried me firemen style to the bed. James asked if I was going to wear a short skirt so I could show off my colourful leg. I shooed him out and managed to have a fifteen minute rest while Jesse showered and shaved. He hadn't let me discuss my kidnapping yet because he said once was enough and that would be when I gave my statement to the police.

CHAPTER 9

The Declaration

I had called CC and asked her if she and Sam could come over. I barely had time to hang up the phone before they appeared at the door. Blythe had phoned them with the news that I had been found as soon as James had called her from the hospital. I already knew that she blamed herself for my abduction so it took a little while to assure her that nothing was her fault. Jesse informed Sergeant Lewis that he wanted CC and Sam present during my testament and he did not object. CC and Jess sat on either side of me each holding a hand. James and Timothy, the Sergeant and a stenographer sat across from us. My declaration was going to be recorded. Blythe had the children corralled upstairs.

Sergeant Lewis stated today's date and that the following was the statement of Lacey Leigh Monroe King to the incidents that took place starting on May the 24th, 1999. I began.

I was waiting for CC Blier to pick me up to attend the May Day festivities. Against his wishes I had insisted that Jess Jameson, my lawyer and friend, {Jesse smiled amorously at me} *should go to his meeting with the King family lawyer as I didn't want him to be late and CC would be here any moment. He didn't like to leave me alone with a killer* on the loose. He had only been gone three or four minutes when the phone rang...I really thought it was him phoning to check up on me. It wasn't; it was CC and she said that her car had broken down and that Sam, her husband, was coming to pick her up and they would be here in five minutes.

Barely a minute later there was a knock on the door. I wondered how they had gotten here so quickly. The dogs were in the house with me and they started barking and pawing at the door which was very unusual for them. I asked who was at the door. "It's Hank, Lacey. My bike has a flat tire. Can I use your phone to call my mom to come and get me?"

I let him in. I tried to silence the dogs but they kept barking. Hank said the dogs scared him and could I put them in their kennel. They had to go out before I left anyhow so I called them to come with me. Mickey would not budge; he just sat and growled at Hank. That should have been my first clue. {Jesse squeezed my hand and said. "It's okay Babe".}

The dogs were most uncooperative but I managed to get them out their doggie door and into the pen. When I returned Hank was waiting for me with a very large knife in his hand. I asked him what he was doing with it and he said he hoped he wouldn't have to use it and to get upstairs and get him into Neverland...do you all know what Neverland is? Good. I told him I didn't know what the heck he was talking about and he pushed me towards the stairs and said that if I valued Jess's life I would do as he told me. That's when I started to panic. I asked him what he had done to Jess and he said, "Nothing yet, and if you want to keep it that way then you had better do as I ask." I could feel the tip of the blade in my back as I opened the door to Arthur's room. He told me to sit on the bench and do my magic and open the wall. I tried to tell him that I didn't know how but that only angered him and he repeated his threats again. I thought that maybe he already had Jess tied up somewhere and so I pushed the lever. He then ordered me to go to the cave and get us out the secret passageway. I knew I had to try and save myself so that I could save Jess. I plotted my next move. I was in front of him on the stairs and when I was near the bottom I flung myself to the cellar floor. Of course that didn't work and I only ended up injuring myself. Hank was unconcerned that I was hurt. He picked me up off the ground and pushed me forward. I told him I couldn't go any further but he prodded me with the knife and so I limped along until we *came to the exit. I could barely manoeuvre the rickety ladder that led to outside. I could not lift the man-hole cover off the portal and I saw my opportunity to escape when he ordered me out of the way. Unfortunately for me he was too fast and he caught me before I even got five feet away. He pushed me up the ladder and through the opening where I fell again. He flung the knife away and picked me up and carried me through the garden to the road where a car was parked.*

"Sorry to interrupt you Ms. Monroe, but we did not find any knife on the trail. Are you sure that he got rid of it?" Sergeant Lewis asked.

"Yes, I am sure; it was right beside the pergola. Shall I continue?"

"Yes, please do, sorry."

I shall describe the car to you as I am sure you are going to want me to. I do not know the make or year and all I can tell you is that it was dark blue and I would say at least twenty years old. The passenger side had a huge dent in the side door and Hank had to yank hard on the handle to force it to open. He pushed me inside and told me that I was driving. I realized that the car was not an automatic and I lied and told him I didn't know how to operate a clutch. He said I had better learn in a hell of a hurry. He made me wear an ugly wig and sunglasses. He pulled a small hand gun out of the glove compartment. I started the car and followed his instructions. We never once went down any street I recognized. We went through back alleys and side roads. Maybe ten minutes later I saw something familiar off in the distance...it was the train bridge. He ordered me to keep driving. About a mile further he told me to stop and take a right; there was no road, just a field of tall grass that soon became a forest. We didn't go very far before he told me to stop. He got out and came around to my side of the car and told me to get out. I did. He wrapped one arm around my neck and with the other he placed a hood over my face. He pulled me along and showed me no mercy for my cries of distress. I tried to count my steps but lost count somewhere after three hundred as I couldn't think of anything else except the pain in my leg. I heard him open a door and then he pushed me inside. He removed the hood and told me to lie down on the sleeping bag and he would give me a drink of water and something for my leg. I willingly accepted an aspirin and the thermos of water and drank it all. I must have fallen asleep because I don't remember Hank leaving.

"Damn him all to hell; he drugged you!" Jesse swore. "Do you want to continue or do you want to take a break Lace?"

I patted his hand and told him I was fine and wanted to get it over with.

When I woke up I tried to open the door; of course it was locked. I was in a little metal building. There was only one tiny window at the top of a wall and one in the roof. They were both open. I called out but no one answered. There were newspapers scattered around and bags of potato chips and jars of liquid that I presumed contained water. My leg still hurt and I had a dreadful headache. I could hear a rumbling off in the distance and it was getting louder and louder. I put my hands over my ears to try and drum out the deafening sound. The thundering click-clacking noise was nerve-wracking. The walls were vibrating from the reverberations.

Then I heard the whistle blow and I knew where I was and what time it was.

"Excuse me again Ms. Monroe; how did you come to that assumption?"

Jesse answered for me. "You have not been in Kings Crossing for very long Sergeant Lewis, so you probably aren't aware that you can pretty much set your clocks to the arrival of the trains. It is a well-known fact that every day and night the south train enters the seventh crossing bridge at precisely 4:10 p.m. and 4:10 a.m. and that is how Lacey knew the time."

I smiled, nodded and asked the Sergeant if he was aware that Jess and I had a previous history.

"Yes, I have been informed of your connections to Mr. Jameson and that James is your son."

"Very well; I shall continue then. Let's see, where was I…oh yes, the train."

Jesse and I had our own special spot up on the ridge where we used to go and watch and listen to the train as it approached the tunnel. Periodically, we would take the trail at the bottom of the ridge to the bridge crossing and even though that was in the seventies, I have never forgotten the sound. It gave me a little ray of hope that I knew where I was. I knew there was no way I could reach the window as it was a good eight feet above me and so I would just have to bide my time. I'm afraid to admit but I was plotting to do whatever I needed to do to escape and that included doing bodily harm to Hank. How I was going to accomplish that was the problem as he was a lot bigger and stronger than me and I had the injured leg to deal with. I waited, reading the papers and eating potato chips, but Hank did not return. I fell asleep contemplating that something had befell him and I would never be found and the tin can I was in would be my tomb.

Jesse was on his feet. "That's enough, stop the tape; this interview is over." He sat back down and pulled me into his arms. CC was crying.

I unwound myself. "You have to quit babying me Jess; I'm all right. I'm sorry if my retelling my captivity upsets you. I shouldn't have said what I did but I cannot recapture those two days without emotion." I looked back and forth at him and CC. "Perhaps it would be best for you and CC if you didn't stay for the rest of the story for I fully intend on finishing."

"I'm not going anywhere Lace and if you are sure that you can continue I promise not to interrupt anymore. Do you see why I didn't want you telling me the ugly details? I didn't want you to have to go through this more than once though I'm pretty sure that you have been reliving it over and over again all day already."

I patted his and CC's hands. "I really am okay." I tried to make light of the whole thing. "Really guys, I was only gone for two days…it's not like I was missing for a year."

"Easy for you to say Mom because you knew you were alive, but we had no idea if you were, or where you were, or who had taken you. I didn't for one minute think that you had given up hope because you are a survivalist! If we hadn't found you there is no doubt in my mind that sooner or later you would have outsmarted that dimwit. I'm just thankful that Jess knew what you were talking about when you called him. How did you manage to get a hold of Hank's phone anyhow?"

"You are absolutely right James. I had too much to live for to give up and I wouldn't have. Does everyone want to stay?" They all said they did. "Very well, I'd like to get it over with."

Sergeant Lewis encouraged me to continue at my own leisure and that I could pause anytime I felt overwhelmed.

"Lacey, wake up; I've brought you something to eat!"

I could hear him but he seemed to be calling me from a distance. I fought through the fog in my head and I asked him what time it was. He told me it was two o'clock. I told him that was impossible because I could see it was dark outside. He said it was two in the morning. I asked him how long I had been sleeping and he said "A long time." His idea of food was some soggy meat on very dry bread. I told him it was garbage and he said it would have to do until we were out of town. I asked him where we were going and he said he hadn't figured it out yet and where would I like to go.

I said. "Home, I want to go home."

He got very angry. "Tudor House is gone! Jess is gone! There is only me and you and the sooner you see that the better off you will be. Now eat up and take these to help you sleep."

All I could think of was that Jesse and Tudor House were gone...had he burned it to the ground? I don't know if I could hide the panic in my voice but I knew I had to get more information out of him. "I just woke up; I don't want to take anything and I am not hungry. Have you done something to Hilda's house and why did you leave me here all alone?"

"I had to get back to work. If I don't work I don't get paid and we are going to need money for gas."

He hadn't answered me about the house. I needed to find a way to get it out of him. "When are we leaving? Maybe I can help you figure out where to go. You know Hank, that car is pretty old; could you get a better one? I have one at Tudor you know or did it go up in flames with the house?"

He seemed confused by my question. "I don't know what you are talking about. If I had of been smarter we could have taken your car, but then it would have been missed and nobody is looking for Reverend Steven's old jalopy. No, this one will do. I have to go now before daylight comes. Tomorrow I get paid and we will leave as soon as it gets dark. You can drive in the dark can't you Lacey?"

I said I could and that I had lots of money and we should go and get it before we left the next day. I told him I was afraid to stay alone so please don't leave me again. He said I was crazy. "The house is crawling with coppers. They are even camped out in my yard. They are not very smart; they think I am in bed. That's why I have to get back while it is still dark. I'll leave you the flashlight. There is nothing to be afraid of as I lock the door and no one has the key but me. Don't worry; I won't leave you like your boyfriend did."

He got up off the floor and I tugged at his pant leg. "Suppose if they catch you Hank? Won't they see you going into the house? What if your mother notices that you are gone?"

"That old biddy...she sleeps like a log. I told you that the cops are stupid; they never even bothered to check the cellar out. It's not only rich people who have secret rooms you know."

"I've been meaning to ask you; how did you know about Arthur's secret room?"

"He felt sorry for me because I didn't have any friends. I ran away from home after my father died and Arthur was the one who found me. I was twelve years old. He took me to his house and told me how he had managed after his father had died and that he would help me to do the same. One day he told me that he had a secret room and he wanted to share it with me if I promised never to tell anyone else. I promised."

"That was a very long time ago Hank and you kept it a secret all this time...I thought you didn't like Arthur?"

"I didn't like him anymore after he took you away from me."

"But now you want to take **me** away from my family. They are going to be sad. Will you let me say goodbye to them?"

By the way he spoke about the police presence at the house I was pretty sure it was still standing. I had to make every effort to find out where Jess was but I didn't want to ire him. He told me there was no one to say goodbye to and so again I was petrified that he had done something to Jess.

"My son and his family are coming Hank; they will be so worried. Please let me send word to them that I am all right."

"After we are gone from here, you can call them. There is no one else who will be missing you. Now I have to go."

Now I knew he had done something to Jess. I could think of nothing but escaping from this mad man.

Jesse cursed under his breath.

"Before you go you are going to have to take me to the bathroom." I said insistently.

He told me there was no bathroom and so I was going to have to hold it.

I had managed to get to my feet and tried to ignore the pain in my leg. "Really...you thought I could go all day without needing a bathroom? You never put much thought *into this plan of yours to keep me hostage did you? Why did you kidnap me anyhow? I thought you liked me...well, you sure have some way of showing it! Now I suggest you take me outside so that I can pee..." I was yelling and he didn't like it.*

He grabbed my arm to steady me. "I didn't kidnap you Lacey; I rescued you from that two-timing bastard. I can't let him hurt you again." He unlocked the door and helped me out.

I felt Jesse stiffen and knew he was reliving what he had done to me so many years ago. I took a deep breath and carried on. We would mend fences again later.

I came to the dismal realization that there was no way I could escape as I could barely stand. I had no choice but to squat on the railroad tracks as I certainly wasn't able to go any further. I sucked in as much of the fresh air as I could because I knew I was going to be locked up again. I pleaded with Hank not to take me back into that little shack. I told him he could take me with him. He said that he couldn't do that until later and that I should just get some rest. He deposited me on the sleeping bag and pulled a prescription bottle out of his pocket and told me to take two pills as they would ease my pain and help me sleep. I asked him if he had gotten the pills from his mother's medicine cabinet. He said he had stolen them from the hospital. I asked him how he had managed to do that and he said that he did odd jobs at nights at the hospital and it was easy to get into the medicine cabinets if one knew how to pick locks. I was stunned that he was admitting his crime to me. He passed me a thermos which he said contained tea. It smelled foul and I refused. He told me to suit myself and threw the flashlight at my feet and left saying he would be back later.

I had no idea what was in the vial and chose to take a couple of the aspirins that he had left me earlier. Fortunately or unfortunately, I chose to drink from one of the bottles of water. I read some more of the papers and attempted to do a crossword puzzle in my head. I felt somewhat comforted by the arrival of the 4 a.m. train. I curled into a ball and listened to its rumbling and the mournful sound of the whistle. I put myself on that train and let it carry me back to happier times.

I stopped talking and leaned back on the sofa. Jesse knew I was exhausted.

"Can we continue another time Sergeant Lewis? I'm worried for Lacey's state of mind and I know she's in pain."

I could see the sadness in Jesse's eyes and I wish I hadn't been so liberal with Hank's accusations. "I'm going to make it Jesse because you are here and all of Hank's threats were just a bunch of malarkey. I'm sorry for what he said about you, and if you can go on then so can I."

"He didn't say anything that wasn't true Lace but you have absolutely nothing to be sorry for. Let's get this over with, okay Babe?" He winked at me and that was all the encouragement I needed. I wanted this day to be over so that I could lie in the arms of my love.

"There isn't much more to tell anyhow as I seemed to sleep most of the time and when I was awake my head was throbbing and I just wanted to go back to sleep again because then I was oblivious as to my dreary surroundings. Here goes…"

I awoke to a terrible thirst and an unusually dry mouth. I crawled to the corner where the jars of water were sitting and drank until I felt like I was going to vomit. I figured it was now afternoon. I could see the sun was high in the sky through the sky-light and it was much warmer. It wasn't long before I heard the train rumbling down the tracks again. How odd that it was the only way I could tell time. I found two half melted chocolate bars and a warm Pepsi in the bag that Hank had left. I devoured everything. I needed to keep my energy up if I expected to escape. I noticed that my ankle and leg were swollen and that there was a gash in my calf. I ripped a piece of my dress and wet it and washed the dry blood off. I read some more and I guess I fell asleep for the next thing I remember was hearing Hank cursing. He shone a light in my eyes and asked me what I was doing.

"What the hell do you think I'm doing? You left me locked in this hot house all day with tepid water and no food and no bathroom… what's wrong with you? I could have died."

"I'm sorry Lacey, but it's okay now. Everything will be okay."

"When, when will everything be okay? I'm hungry and my leg needs attention and I'm tired of lying on a cement floor! I need to go to use the crude facilities so open that door and let me out!"

He told me to quit yelling and that if I didn't drink so much I wouldn't need to go to the bathroom so often. I wished I had something that I could hit him over the head with…and then I remembered the flashlight. I would find a way to use it.

He helped me out onto the tracks again and after I had emptied my bladder I sat down and refused to move. Again he asked me what I thought I was doing. I told him I was not going back into that prison and he said I would if I valued my boyfriend's life.

I screamed at him to quit threatening me because I knew Jess was already dead. He told me to quit screaming because someone might hear me. Then I started to laugh hysterically at how ludicrous his words were. He pulled something out of his pocket which I did not recognize; it looked like a walkie-talkie. He appeared to use it like a telephone.

"Where are you...come on, answer." He became very upset that no one was answering him.

I asked who he was calling because I thought it may very well be a large cellular phone. He said that I would be very interested to know but he had no intention of letting the cat out of the bag just yet. That really confused me because I had thought that he had been acting alone but now I wasn't so sure. Who else would want me out of the way? I asked him who had helped him kill Arthur and dispose of the evidence. He appeared to be perplexed by my question.

"Is that what that shyster told you? He's trying to throw me to the wolves so he can have you all to himself. Did you ever ask him where he was when Arthur was killed? I bet you didn't...anyhow I was with you when you found the body so you know perfectly well that I didn't do it. Now, get up and come inside. I need to get some sleep before we take off."

I was adamant that I wasn't going back in that shed. I started yelling at the top of my voice again hoping that someone would indeed hear me. Hank came up behind me and placed something foul over my mouth and nose. The next thing I remember was hearing Hank snoring. It was pitch black except for a sliver of light coming in the overhead opening. I let my eyes adjust to the glimmer coming from the moon hoping I could locate the flashlight. I did, and beside it was Hank's peculiar looking phone. I dared to believe that it was but wondered if there would be any signal. I knew I had to chance it. I crawled stealthily around Hank until I reached both devices and then I moved as far away from him as I could. I shone the flashlight on the phone and punched in the number at the house. I was so surprised to hear it ringing that I started to cry. Jesse answered calling my name. I managed to tell him where I was just as the 4 a.m. train arrived and Hank grabbed the phone out of my hands. I was so afraid that the noise from the train drowned out my words before Jess heard me say "our bridge." I had renewed hope because Jesse was alive. Hank forced pills on me and covered my face with that cloth. I woke up in the hospital.

Sergeant Lewis leaned across the coffee table that separated us and offered his hand first to me and then to Jesse. "Thank you for your diligence Ms. Monroe. I know reliving that nightmare has not been easy for you. We will have your deposition typed up for you to sign…but not today, no, not today. I now have the unpleasant task of informing you that Hank is not to blame for Mr. King's murder; he has an iron-clad alibi."

Jess was on his feet. "Bullshit! Hank does not have the mental capacity to instigate this plot by himself; no someone else is pulling his strings. That call he tried to make proves it and alibi or no alibi, Hank had a hand in Arthur's murder."

"If you will let me continue Mr. Jameson…"

I tugged at Jesse. "Sit down Honey; let's hear what Sergeant Lewis has to say. I'm pretty sure myself that Hank couldn't have killed Arthur."

Jess sat back down. He looked at me worriedly. "How did he convince you of that? You accused him right to his face remember?"

"Of course I do. He arrived at the carriage house almost simultaneously to me discovering the body, I told you that. He wouldn't have had time to kill Arthur and dispose of the carpeting and return home and clean up. You yourself believe that more than one person was involved Jess. Just who do you think was his accomplice?"

"When we find out who he was calling last night then we will know." He turned to the Sergeant and Timothy. "Now, what is his so-called alibi?"

"Reverend Stevens and Terry Small and Sister Agnes all attest to Hank being at the church from 8 a.m. until 3:30 p.m. on the day in question. At that time he removed his coveralls and changed back into his street clothes. He had been assisting Mr. Small, a local contractor with the painting of the rectory. He was in the company of one of them at all times, and then

Ms. Monroe vouches for him after that.. You may take it upon yourself to question them yourself Mr. Jameson."

Jesse assured him that he would definitely be doing just that. I asked him and James to help me up as I needed to stretch and ice my leg. They helped me to take a few steps and just before they sat me in the wheelchair I noticed several R.C.M.P. officers out the side window. I asked what they were doing out there.

Timothy explained. "There is still a murderer on the loose Lacey and so for the protection of you and your family you and the grounds will be guarded around the clock. It is a necessary precaution. I will be overseeing the operation and will continue to keep you posted. Be advised that they will not hinder any of the family's activities. James, you will need to come up with a reasonable explanation as to why there are policemen in the yard to the children…especially Harrison, as he will be most curious."

We all chuckled for we knew that to be true. "One question Timothy, Sergeant Lewis…why did you not feel the need to put guards on me before my abduction? Never mind, I can answer that myself; you thought I was responsible for Arthur's death didn't you?"

Sergeant Lewis smiled wryly. "Timothy never believed you had anything to do with Mr. King's demise. I didn't know you, so yes, there was doubt. In this business we learn that anyone is capable of murder for one reason or the other; right Mr. Jameson? By the way, are you still entertaining the thought that someone has been living in the rotunda?"

"Well it definitely has not been the utmost thought in my mind for the past few days." Jesse put his hand on my shoulder. "Now that we have our fair lady home I may revisit the dome again and then again, maybe I won't. If there is nothing else, I need to see to Lacey's ice treatment."

"Thank-you, that is all for today; we will not waylay you any longer. Ms. Monroe, you are probably not even aware but you have answered most of our questions as to how Mr. Bernard was able to avoid surveillance. The house is being searched once more as we speak and you can be assured that there are several officers that will be taken to task for dereliction of their duties. Mr. Jameson, I fully understand if you are not comfortable in leaving Ms. Monroe alone. We can accommodate you and Mr. Monroe by returning tomorrow for your statements. One last thing; the mechanic who examined your car Mrs. Blier has no explanation as to why it suddenly stopped. However, he did find that there was a slight crease in the gas line and that it may have momentarily caused a disruption in the gas flow. We are conducting our own investigation."

Jess thanked him and said they would probably take him up on his offer. James went to grab the ice packs and Jesse wheeled me into the bedroom. The new furniture was lovely and the bed had a special treatment of rose petals scattered all over it. I thanked Jesse and he laughed and said he could not take credit for it and it must be the work of our daughter-in-law. He no sooner had me settled when we heard squealing and running footsteps in the hall. James tried to hold them at bay, but they squeezed by him.

"Gramma, Uncle Jesse, save us from the trolls!" Harry cried as he jumped on the bed beside me. Leah struggled to get up by herself.

"Whoa cowboy; don't jiggle your grandmother. Have you forgotten she has a sore leg?" Jesse scolded Harry as he placed Leah next to me.

Blythe appeared in the doorway. "Sorry Mom, they got away from me. James, you either watch the little goblins or go shopping for supper; your choice."

"No one needs to go to the market." I stated. "It's your turn to have a rest Bly; you are not here to cook for us. James has to go and pick Vivian up from the airport so the children can stay with me. Jesse, you can place an order for Poppy's chicken, okay?"

"I don't mind really, it's no trouble." Blythe insisted.

Jesse put his arm around her. "Lacey is right; it's time we pampered you. How would you like one of Uncle Jess's massages, guaranteed to relax you?"

"Are you serious? James will you keep an eye on the children?"

"He doesn't have to as they are going to be right here with me telling stories. I have a lot to catch up on." I said.

"What time do you want me to come back for you Lace?" Jess asked.

"I want to be up when Vivian arrives so in about an hour. Now shoo, all of you… go."

We settled in the family room awaiting the arrival of James with Jess's daughter. I think Jesse was a little nervous for her and me to be meeting. He kept looking at me and smiling as he paced to and fro from the kitchen. Bly sat next to me holding my hand. She was the daughter I never had and I loved her dearly. Leah was coloring at our feet and Harry followed his grandfather from room to room jabbering all the while. We all heard the car in the driveway. Jess was out the door in a flash with Harry right behind him. A few minutes later Vivian walked in on the arms of her father and newly acquired brother who had Harry on his shoulders. I smiled at her and felt a tear roll down my cheek. This beautiful girl could have been my daughter; mine and Jesse's. I had no idea what her mother looked like because Jesse never wanted to talk about her. Vivian had dark brown hair, {the color mine used to be} and it was short and curly like mine. Yes, she could have been my daughter. She was petite. Her eyes sparkled when she bent down to say hello to Leah. Harrison informed her that she was his baby sister.

"Am not, Mama, I not a baby!" Leah blubbered.

Blythe rose to greet Vivian bending over to pick Leah up. "No, you're not a baby Darling; Harry's just teasing." She held her arms out to Vivian. "We are so very pleased to meet you. Welcome to our home and family."

James was beaming as he introduced the two of them though there wasn't any need to. "And, this is the third beautiful woman in my life…my Mother, Lacey."

Vivian held out her hands and I took them in mine. Jesse was smiling lovingly at me. I said with as much sincerity as I could. "I am delighted to meet you and am very glad that you have come to help me keep an eye on your father." I winked at him.

She laughed. "Yes, James has been filling me in on Dad's and your escapades. Thank God that you are both home safe and sound, well reasonably sound. I understand that you injured yourself trying to escape from that mad man. Dad was a nervous wreck when he phoned me."

"I am quite certain that I would not be here today if your dad and James had not found me. My leg is nothing compared to the wound that your father sustained. He is downplaying his injury…maybe you can talk him into putting his arm back in the sling?"

Jesse sat down beside me. "I will just as soon as we get Leigh settled. It's going to take some time for me to get use to calling you Vivian you know?"

"Doesn't matter Dad as the pronouncement of our names is different enough don't you think, but I don't mind if you call me Vivian though because everyone else does. Now, how about you do as Lacey suggests?"

"Yes Jess, do what Mom tells you because we can all see that you are hurting. Bly and I will show Vivian her room." James said sternly.

"I see that I am outnumbered." Jess said jovially.

"It's for your own good Sweetheart, and you need to phone our dinner order in don't you?"

I wondered if I should be calling Jesse pet names in front of his daughter…too late.

I was not very good at manoeuvring my wheel chair around but I helped him set the table. He never once complained at how slow I was. The kids were giving Vivian the grand tour of the estate and the lands. She was full of enthusiasm when they returned from Canterbury.

"I am so going to enjoy my stay here. I can hardly wait to hike up the mountain with the dogs. I can't believe that they like me. I never had a dog." She looked at me. "We tried, but mother wouldn't hear of it…anyhow, it is all so Victorian and I love my room. Lacey, you have a beautiful house and thank-you for making me feel welcome."

"There is no need to thank me as we are all delighted that you are here. This house does not belong to me though. If it belongs to anyone, it will be James and that we will know after the reading of the will. Arthur has a sister, and I hope that there will be some provisions for her, but at this time we just don't know what Hilda wanted."

We sat around the table chatting for an hour after dinner. Timothy had come by to meet the newest addition to the family. We invited him to join us. He kept the conversation lively relating funny stories about James and himself. Vivian was a captive audience interjecting things like "Oh no, you didn't!" every once in a while. A lot of the stories were even new to me. Jesse listened intensely and I am sure he was wishing that he had of known his son in his younger years. I was feeling guilty again and decided that I had better fake tiredness and go to my room. Timothy came around the table and put his arms around me.

"If I didn't already have a loving mother, this lady would win the job hands down. I tried to be the brave one during her disappearance for Jess and James, but it wasn't easy. I was introduced to Jess the first night that he arrived here after the break-in. I knew that Lacey was in good hands with him and although they pretended to be just friends, it didn't wash with me. The eyes don't lie. I can't express how happy I am for her safe return."

He reached out and shook Jesse's hand. "And you Jess…I have such respect for you Sir and the way you have conducted yourself through this whole ordeal. I am honoured to know you and then to find out that you are James's father, well, that's a bonus, and then there is this charming daughter…" He smiled at Vivian and she blushed. "Thank-you all for including me in your family."

"Timothy Newman," I scolded. "you're going to have us all in tears. It is I who owe you a debt of gratitude. Thank-you for everything you have done for us and you will always have a place in our family. We love you. Now, please excuse me everyone as it is time for my cold pack."

Jess wheeled me to the bedroom and helped me get changed and do my nightly routine. He asked me if I was in for the night. It was not even eight o'clock so I said I didn't know. He settled me in bed and placed the ice pack on my ankle telling me that I had been standing too much as it was pretty swollen again. I shrugged. He kissed me and said he's see me later.

As he started for the door I said. "I like her Jesse."

He turned back. "She likes you too Honey." He blew me a kiss.

"I expected her to be blonde."

"Why would you think that?" he asked hesitantly.

"Because your wife is a blonde, so naturally, I thought her daughters would be."

"Well, she isn't anymore and neither are the girls. What's this blonde thing with you anyway?"

I said matter of factually. "You know; Mavis was one and you left me for a blonde bombshell."

"I am not having this senseless conversation with you again Lacey." He started for the door.

"Maybe you should find another bed to sleep in tonight then…"

"And, there she is; the woman who'll never let the past go. Maybe I will take your suggestion and mosey on down to the bar and pick me up a little blonde piece. Is that what you want Lacey? How you can turn a joyous day into a nightmare is becoming a never ending saga and I am growing weary of it all. Have a nice time with your delusional self. Me, I prefer to live in the present and it's entirely your decision whether you want to join me or not. I'm pretty much done convincing you of anything." He turned and left before I could tell him I wasn't serious.

He'd be back.

I tried to get comfortable but I could not. My leg was throbbing and reluctantly I reached over to the night table and downed a pain pill. I lay back on the pillow and scolded myself. What was the matter with me? Why did I always berate Jesse? Was I ever going to leave the past alone? Was it going to take Jesse walking out on me to bring me to my senses? He had forgiven me and he only wanted to live in the present…why couldn't I? I should be so thankful that Hank hadn't fatally shot him. I shivered and fell asleep admonishing myself.

I awoke with sensing that someone was in the room. "Is that you Jesse?"

No one answered. It was dark and I reached over and turned on the lamp on the night stand. It was only 8:40. I had only been asleep for half an hour or perhaps it was 8:40 in the morning. I looked at the clock again; no, it was P.M. I needed to find Jesse. I rolled over and checked to see if the brakes had been set on the wheelchair. Of course they were, Jesse always made sure they were. I swung my feet onto the floor and carefully stood up. I grabbed the arms of the chair and gingerly turned and sat down. The pain was tolerable. I wheeled myself to the dresser and pulled out a large shawl and draped it over my shoulders. I was glad that Jesse had left the door open. I heard voices echoing from the family room. I almost made it there but my shawl fell off and became entangled in the spokes of the wheel. I was just about to call out for help when I heard my name mentioned. It was Vivian speaking.

"Daddy, why are you so quiet? You're worried about Lace aren't you? She says she is good, but do you really think that she has dealt with the events of the last week? I mean, my God, she found the bloody body of her husband and then she was kidnapped…how could she possibly be so composed and act as if it all was just an everyday occurrence? I have only known her for a few hours but I sense she is not as undisturbed as you all might think."

"Honey, believe me, Lacey is anything but calm. Yes, she puts on her smiley face for you all because she takes her hostilities out on me and I let her though sometimes what she says makes no sense at all. Of course I am the catalyst for her emotional outbursts. There are times when I have contemplated making myself scarce but I just can't leave her. I have told her that I am here for the long haul but deep down inside she still doesn't trust me and I am not sure that she will ever truly be able to forgive me, so it's just as much me as it is the kidnapping."

"Oh Daddy, don't say that! I see the way she looks at you and says your name…"

"Vivian is right Jess. I have never seen my mother so happy. I can't explain her sudden mood changes because she wasn't always like this. I may be breaking confidences here when I say that something happened to Mom a few years back and it's obvious that she hasn't been able to deal with it successfully. She doesn't want to talk about it and then Bly got sick and so we put everything else on the back burner. She said that we were all she needed in her life and she put her personal life aside to look after us. She told me that the love she had once hoped for was not in the cards for her any longer. Then Hilda died and Mom came here and so did you. Let us help you weather her stormy moods Jess…please."

I visualized Jesse shrugging his shoulders as he said. "Believe me, I want to hold on Son, and for the time being I am not going anywhere because I can't see myself living without her again. But ultimately, she is the one who is going to make or break us."

So, my sudden changes in temperament had also been a concern to James and Bly. I wonder why they hadn't said anything. I decided I had eavesdropped enough and called for help. James and Timothy came out to find me struggling with the mess I had gotten myself into.

"What have you done Mother?" James said laughing.

He and Timothy attempted to untangle my shawl. Blythe appeared at the door and asked if I was all right.

"Of course I am dear, just a little mobility problem. Where's Jesse?"

I guess he heard me because he came out to see what was going on. He looked at me and raised one eyebrow the way he always did when he was irritated with me. "Looks like you're in good hands." He turned and went back into the family room.

Timothy suggested that they could untangle my shawl easier if I wasn't in the chair and so they picked me up and deposited me next to Blythe. Jesse and Vivian were on the couch across from us. Jesse rose and brought an afghan to me. "Cover yourself woman." He said. "Can I freshen your drink Bly? Club soda for you Lacey?"

I answered "yes" and waited until he sat down again. "Are you upset with me Jesse?"

"No more than usual." He answered.

"Daddy," Vivian pleaded with her father. "be nice."

"It's all right Vivian. I know I annoy the hell out of your father but he also knows I have no control over some of the things I say and do, don't you Jesse?"

He shrugged his shoulders and got up and made himself another drink. Then he set it on the table in front of him. "I guess I don't need any more liquid fortification as I am already primed for another of your tongue-lashings. Go ahead Lace… you may as well air all of our dirty laundry and get twenty four years of hating me out all at the same time. Tell them what you suggested to me earlier." Then he winked at me.

That infuriated me. I gripped the arm of the divan and willed myself up and threw my drink at him. "I'm sorry Vivian; I didn't mean to splatter you." I collapsed back down on the seat.

She was laughing as she wiped her face with the sleeve of her sweater. Jesse asked her why she was laughing. James had just deposited my wheel chair next to me.

"Mother!" He scolded. "And what do you think is so damn funny Viv? My mother and father are sitting here exchanging insults and throwing drinks around and you find it funny?"

Blythe started to giggle also and James flashed her a cautionary look. She ignored him.

Jesse didn't even bother to attempt to dry his face. "Do you all see what I have to put up with **now**?" He grinned.

"You know perfectly well that I didn't mean what I said Jesse, but maybe you did? You can wipe that smirk off your face or I will come over there and wipe it off for you!"

"I'll meet you half way if you're sure you can handle me." He enticed.

"You don't want to mess with me right now Jesse James Jameson."

"I always want to mess with you Lacey Leah Monroe, you know that." His eyes were twinkling and I'm sure mine were too.

Vivian and Bly had mischievous smiles on their faces. James asked again what they found so damn amusing.

"Can't you tell that your parents aren't fighting…they are flirting with each other." Vivian said.

"Really?" James looked back and forth from Jesse to me waiting for one of us to agree.

Finally, Jesse stood up and bowed to Vivian.

"My daughter, ladies and gentlemen…she's not even twenty-one yet, never been in a serious relationship, well, maybe once when she was very young, and yet she knows passion when she sees it." He came over to me and held out his hand. "What do you say Doll, want to flee this popsicle stand with your old man?"

"Yes, I do Jesse, very much. I want everyone to know though that I am well aware that I torment you some times and that there is no rhyme or reason for it. Not that there is any excuse for my behaviour but I am hoping that blood work I had done while I was in the hospital will reveal that I have some sort of chemical imbalance that can be dealt with. I'm sorry, if I upset any of you. Timothy, are you sure you want to be part of this family?"

He laughed. "Oh yeah, I'm sure."

James helped Jess sit me in the wheelchair. "You two are going to be the death of me. Can you just act your age…please?"

"What would be the fun of that James?" I asked.

He walked with us into the hall. "I hope you are looking after my Mother Jess?"

"Exactly what do you mean by that James?"

"I'm not going to wake up one day and find out that I'm going to have a brother or sister am I?"

I broke out in laughter.

"Would that be so bad?" Jesse asked amusedly.

I tried to assure James that I was probably going through menopause and so that it was highly unlikely that I could get pregnant but it was going to be a lot of fun trying. I embarrassed my son and he walked away shaking his head.

"Did you all hear what my Mother just said? Someone tell me what just happened here?"

Vivian laughed. "Is he always this uptight Bly?"

Jesse parked me next to the bed and asked me what I wanted to do next.

I ran my fingers up and down his face. "We should wash your face first; you are very sticky. I'm sorry I threw my club soda at you."

"Sure you are. I really don't think I said anything to warrant that... or did I?"

"It's not so much what you say but what you do. Are you aware that you raise one eyebrow and wink at me? Are you reprimanding me or is it your way of seducing me in front of everyone?"

"Well I'm definitely thinking about it most of the time and if it turns you on..."

"I scare myself Jesse. You said that you are tiring of my antics and accusations and I don't blame you. I am one crazy bitch. How long before I let the past take over our lives?"

"Hey, careful what you're calling my lady! We'll get through this I promise."

I said tearfully. "You should have come looking for me Jesse."

"Yes, I should have, but would you have forgiven me and taken me back? Have you ever thought that if we had stayed together that we might be all used up already? This way we are starting anew and we have years of exploration ahead of us."

I couldn't argue with that, but I wanted to. I wanted to tell him that it was easy for him to say that because he had married and had a life but I hadn't. I scolded myself for that was just plain nonsense as I had led a very fruitful life even if I had not been able to fall in love again. I had James and my day care centers and I was active in the theatre world with my two best friends, Arthur and Richie, and then Bly and the children came along. I had been reasonably happy.

Of course I couldn't sleep. Jesse was snuggled up close to me and asked me what was wrong.

I reached over and turned the lamp on.

"Are you satisfied with me Jesse because I can be whatever you want me to be. I can be a femme fatale, or a naïve teenager, or a little Miss Susie homemaker, or I can dye my hair and become a blonde vixen…what do you want Jesse?"

He nuzzled his chin into my neck and kissed me on my cheek.

"You can be any of those creatures if it pleases you, but me, all I want is for you to be mine."

"I am Jesse, you know I am. I just want to make you happy."

"You do. Now, do you think that you can get some sleep?"

"I have been wondering about you and Marsha."

"Again…what do you want to know now?" He said annoyingly.

"Well Jesse, you are this rugged handsome hunk of a man… there must have been dozens of women who came on to you. Clients maybe…I mean if things weren't exciting for you with Marsha… did you really not look for gratification with someone else?"

Jesse sighed and turned me over to face him. "I'm only this person in your eyes Lace. I'm pretty ordinary and I have told you a hundred times that I was not unfaithful. You still don't believe me though do you?"

"I want to run my hands through that thick mass of hair on your head and I want your soft hands all over me and I want you to smother me with kisses and you are most obliging so why wouldn't I think that other women have wanted the same thing from you?"

"Are you jealous of things that never happened? You are dead set on turning me into this Don Juan aren't you?

"No, but you love me so intensely that I can't believe you have been living the life of a monk."

He laughed. "Honey, the reason I make love to you so intensely is that I love you and I have never needed anyone like I need you. But, you want me to be honest with you, right?"

"Aha, I knew it!"

"Don't be so smug Missy. Okay, so there were several "older" women who were clients who may have come on to me a little, but I am too professional to even consider anything and anyhow, I was not interested. About ten years ago, I won a case against a large corporation and my client, Taylor Clarke, received a very substantial settlement. She was extremely grateful, but it was her mother who wanted to thank me personally and invited me to join her for drinks. There would only be the two of us as Taylor was out celebrating with friends and Mr. Clarke was out of town. I was pretty sure what she had in mind and for some ungodly reason I agreed to follow her home in my own vehicle. On the seat of the car I found a large note from Leigh saying that her concert started at 7 o'clock.

"Please don't be late Daddy." That was all I need to turn around and go home. That's it; that's all there is to my extra-curricular love life. Are you disappointed?"

"Shut up and go to sleep. You're a pretty boring story teller."

"Do you still love me Sweetie even if I am not very exciting?"

"I love you more than I did five minutes ago. There is one more thing though Jesse…did your Mrs. Robinson have blonde hair?

"I think I was way beyond the Mrs. Robinson thing, but no, she was not a blonde. She had flaming red hair; you know the kind that comes in a bottle."

"I dyed my hair red once."

"And, I am sure it was very becoming. Did it not clash with your lavender eyes?"

"Are you ever going to quit asking questions? What has a girl got to do to get some sleep?"

CHAPTER 10

Arrivals

Jess

Lacey's screaming woke me at 2 a.m. I tried to wake her but her thrashing and wailing only became worse. I held on to her wrists so that she couldn't strike me and out of her mouth came the foulest language I had ever heard from her. She was so angry that it was scaring me.

"Get these fucking handcuffs away from me! I swear I will rip you to pieces with my bear hands if you put one fucking hand on me!"

I quickly let go of her wrists and firmly placed my hands on her shoulders and shook her gently and called her name over and over telling her that she was safe.

"It's me Jess, Honey. Can you wake up for me?" I was sure that James was going to burst into the room any second probably thinking that I was killing his mother.

I felt her body go limp and knew that she was awake. I reached over her and turned the lamp on. "Are you okay Lace? Why didn't you tell me that Hank had you in shackles?"

She said solemnly. "It wasn't Hank. I need to get up."

She rolled over and sat on the edge of the bed. Before I could reach out and grab her she stood up and immediately fell flat on her face. I jumped out of bed so fast that I got a head rush. I shook it off and cradled her in my arms.

"Are you hurt Lace? Tell me, did you hit your head? Oh Baby, I'm so sorry."

She was half laughing and half crying. "I'm such a klutz Jesse. I think it would be safer if I just stayed down here for the rest of the night…can you cover me up?"

"No silly, I need to get you up and examine you. I might need to call James."

"Don't you dare! Help me to sit up and I can crawl to my chair and then pull myself up."

I had never felt so helpless in all my life. Lacey was lying spread eagle on the cold bare floor and I couldn't pick her up because of my stupid wounded wing. I told her she didn't have to crawl as I would move her chair.

"I would have crawled all the way down the hall to find you Jesse. The pain in my leg is nothing like the pain I felt in my heart when I thought you'd had enough of my foolishness and took me seriously when I told you not to come back to my bed."

"I don't know what you are talking about Lace…why would you have to crawl to find me? Did you really think I would spend the night somewhere else?"

"Yes. I was certain that I would tip the wheelchair over getting to it and I wouldn't be able to right it and so I would have to crawl and I would have Jesse."

"For your information my dear, I was checking on you every five or ten minutes while you were supposed to be sleeping so I would have found you if you had of fallen. I don't care how secure we have made the house, or that the police are patrolling the yard I needed to keep an eye on you myself."

"Why were you so mean to me then in front of the kids? It wasn't all an act was it?"

"I'm sorry, I didn't mean to be. I guess I wanted to see if you would get down and dirty and accuse me of every rotten thing that I did to you. Maybe I needed to get it all out in the open."

"I think maybe we did. I am going to try really, really hard to be a good girl Jesse."

"You are Lace. Now let's get you back in bed before the sun comes up. I bet you'd like to go outside and have a cigarette wouldn't you?"

"Don't be silly Jess, you know I don't smoke!"

I laughed. "Right…well tomorrow Richie will be here and you can sneak off with him. Try and get some sleep for it'll be dawn before you know it."

Was I ever going to get used to waking up and finding Lacey gone? How she managed to climb out of bed and escape out of the room with her wheelchair without waking me was somewhat disturbing. I never knew I was such a deep sleeper or was it because she had kept me up so late? I quickly dressed and set out to track her down. I didn't have to go very far; her wheelchair was sitting at the bottom of the central staircase. Lacey was not in it but sitting on the third step.

"Are you waiting for a bus?" I asked her smiling.

"No, a train, smart Alec. I wanted to go upstairs and surprise the children but I soon realized that it was not a feat I was up to yet and so I'd just wait for someone to come and rescue me."

"Will I do? I haven't had much experience in rescuing damsels in distress but I'll give it a try."

"You haven't? Well, who saved me from Hank and didn't you also rescue Marsha once?"

I didn't answer her as it would have been pointless. We went into the kitchen and put on a pot of coffee. Lacey said she was hungry and so we started to prepare breakfast for the masses. She said the kids loved pancakes and did I know how to cook them. I told her it wasn't one of my specialties and she said that it was one of hers and she would teach me how if I was up to learning. She beat up the batter while I heated up the griddle and started the bacon cooking. She stood watch over me until I got the hang of when it was the exact time to flip the cakes. We didn't have to wake up anyone as they all arrived at the same time still dressed in their night attire. Harry hugged his grandmother. "You're the best Gramma Lacey!"

"She is isn't she? Eat up everyone and what is on everyone's agenda for the day?" I asked.

Vivian said that Timothy was coming by and they were going to take Harry and Leah to the park and to visit with his parents.

"Just a minute, young lady," I tried to sound stern. "I didn't hear you ask for permission to go out with someone you just met?"

"Oh Daddy," she laughed. "it's not a date and these two rag-a-muffins will be our chaperones!"

"All righty then. What about you and Blythe, James?"

"I'll answer that." Lacey volunteered. "They are going to spend some much needed time alone, right James?" He readily agreed and asked what we were going to do. Lacey said that after I walked the dogs and helped her shower she was going to whop me at a game of chess. I laughed and said it was nice to have my day already planned out. She said I was welcome.

At a quarter to four we left for the airport. I had decided to take the sedan as it was easier to get Lacey in and out of. Timothy rode with us and two officers followed in a cruiser. Lacey was antsy. We couldn't talk her into staying in the car until the plane touched down so there we stood on the hot tarmac for fifteen minutes. Richie was the first to disembark. I knew it was him by Lacey's exuberance. He ran towards her and she was on her feet and flung herself into his arms. I had not formed a mental picture of him in my mind. He was the complete opposite of a recent photo of Arthur that stood on the mantel at the house. Arthur was only of average height and stocky; Richie was svelte and well over six feet tall. He was attired in a light gray leisure suit, pinkish dress shirt and tie. He was clean shaven and when he picked Lacey up, I could see his eyes were a transparent green with grey flecks.

I thought that he kissed my girl a little too long and passionately.

I pushed the chair ahead and grabbed her around the waist and sat her down. She patted my hand and turned and smiled at me. She was about to introduce me to Richie when someone behind him caught her eye.

"What the hell are **they** doing here Richie?" She shrieked.

"Sorry Honey, they followed me." He said apologetically.

A tall woman with long black silky hair stepped forward. At first glance I could see that she was exceptionally beautiful and the way she carried herself and tossed her head I had the feeling that she wanted everyone to acknowledge it. She wore a short loose cobalt blue dress that was almost a perfect match to her eyes. Her hair cascaded out from behind a white floppy hat that matched her three inch heels. A pasty looking man with small piercing grey eyes appeared to be her companion.

I bent down and quietly asked Lace who they were.

She scowled. "They are thespians."

"Darling," the woman cooed, "you don't think we would miss paying our final respects to Arthur now do you?"

There was something very disconcerting with the way she smiled at Lacey. "Aren't you going to introduce us to your friend?"

Lacey ignored her and took Richie's hand. "Richie this is Jess Jameson." She turned around to acknowledge me. Richie and I shook hands.

"These rude uninvited people were once associated professionally with Arthur. This is August Strange and the one and only Miranda Desoto." She said it with such revulsion that I thought she must be foaming at the mouth. But then she turned again to me and smiled.

"Richie, this is my Jess. He is everything to me; friend, lawyer, James's father, and my past and present lover."

Miranda took a step towards me but Lacey held up her hand to halt her. Cattily she said. "You can look, but you cannot touch…understand?"

Miranda threw her head back and laughed wickedly. What had transpired between these two? Had they once fought over the same man? For sure; it wasn't this wimpy August fellow. Lacey had shocked me when she so casually referred to me as her lover and now she was warning this dark beauty to keep her hands off me…or what, I wondered. Richie seemed amused.

"Thank God this woman wasn't a blonde or I would be in big trouble for even looking at her." I said to myself.

Miranda smiled provocatively at me. "It is a pleasure to meet you Mr. Jameson…is it all right if I call him Jess, Lacey dear?"

Lacey ignored her. She introduced Richie to Timothy and said that he would be riding with us.

Miranda did not miss that Lacey had referred to Tim as Corporal Newman and that there were also two other offices standing guard. "Why do we have a police escort Lacey?"

"I'm sure they aren't here for our benefit Miranda." Richie stated.

Timothy explained that they were taking no chances with Ms. Monroe's safety as they had not arrested anyone in connection to Mr. King's murder yet. He added that extra precaution was being taken in light of Lacey's kidnapping.

"What?" Richie exclaimed. "Kidnapping? How come I wasn't informed of this Lacey? Is this why you are really in a wheelchair? What the hell happened?"

"I'll tell you all about it at the house Rich." She patted his hand. "As you can see I am perfectly fine and as for the leg, well, it was of my own doing."

Timothy and I transferred Lacey into the car while everyone else stood by and watched. I closed the door and put the wheelchair and Richie's bags into the trunk. I asked the unwelcome twosome where they were staying. Miranda said they had not made any reservations yet but were hoping that Lacey would invite them for a visit to Tudor House. Yeah, like that was going to happen. I asked them to give me a moment. I got into the driver's seat and trying not to grin too broadly relayed to Lacey what her friend had suggested.

"I'm glad you find this so amusing. She is no friend of mine, nor has she ever been!"

"I kind of gathered that…so, what should we do with them?"

"They are not our responsibility so I don't give a rat's ass where they go!"

"This is not like you at all Lace. How about we bring them back to the house for a quick visit and then we'll send them on their way? What do you say Hon?"

"Do as you want as long as I don't have to entertain them. As usual, you get your way again."

"My way…are you suggesting that I always win with you?"

"Yes, and it's a fact not an assumption."

As usual I let her have the last word. I re-joined the crowd waiting at the back of the car relaying what Lacey had said… partly anyhow. Timothy suggested that Miranda and August could ride in the cruiser to Tudor House. The second we were back in the sedan Richie apologized to Lacey.

"It's not your fault Richie. We both know what a conniving she devil she is, and of course August goes along with anything she wants. They will not be staying at the house though and I trust that you will keep her as far away from me as possible."

"I will Honey, you can count on that." Richie promised.

I was most curious about Lacey's animosity towards Miranda and I was pretty sure she would not hesitate to tell me as soon as we were alone, but I was wrong.

Richie wanted to carry Lacey into the house but she refused saying that she was not an invalid and that I wouldn't like it seeing that I was unable to because of the gunshot wound I had received while rescuing her. She got that right. I wheeled her into the kitchen where the rest of the family were gathered.

"Run for your lives!" She exclaimed. "The enemy has arrived!"

James hugged Richie and asked his mother what was going on. She explained about the unwanted visitors and that I had invited them back to the house for Lord knows what. I tried very hard to keep a straight face and suggested that we should leave the welcoming up to James and Blythe as it was obvious that they knew who Miranda and August were. I said that we would be in the family room. Richie said that we had a lot of explaining to do.

"Yes, yes." Lacey said over her shoulder.

Blythe said she'd make tea.

I deposited her in an easy chair and stood over her. "Are you going to tell me what is going on between you and Miranda, or am I going to have to get the answers somewhere else?"

"It's an old feud Jess, not important and certainly not worth discussing. Will you please bring me a glass of water and maybe a pain pill?"

"I'll let it go for now as I don't want you irritated any more than you already are. I think you need to come clean about a few things though young lady."

"Why would you want to be involved with girlie stuff? Is it going to turn you on?"

"Stop being so impudent; I'm talking about that kiss that Richie bestowed upon you. That is not the kiss of a friend who is supposed to be gay."

"What are you inferring Jess? I don't think I like your tone."

I left to get the water. "You get back here Jesse James!" She yelled.

I met Richie in the hallway. "Everything all right here?" He asked.

"I think maybe it would be a good idea if you took Lacey out on the balcony for a few minutes. Actually, she has been craving nicotine and I think you can help her with that…am I right?"

"I think I can accommodate you. You know she doesn't actually smoke, right"

"Yeah I know. I'll be right back with her pill and then you two can have some alone time."

I found one of her pills in her purse that she had thrown on the table and collected glasses and a pitcher of water and set them down in front of her and told her that I had an errand to run.

"What could you possibly have to do? Do you think it's safe to leave me alone with Richie?"

She said testily.

Richie looked confused. I bent down and kissed her solidly on the lips.

"Whatever are you talking about Darling? I have no problem leaving you alone with your best friend." I turned to Richie. "She's quite a handful; you can't let her out of your sight for one moment. I did and she got herself abducted." I winked at her and I was quite sure that she wanted to throw the pitcher of water at me.

I arrived back at the house forty minutes later and was happy to find Sam's car parked in the driveway. James and Vivian were manning the barbecue on the front patio. I caught a whiff of grilled onions and guessed we were dining on hamburgers. Vivian asked where I had been.

"Just running a little errand; is everyone else in the house?" I asked kissing her on the cheek.

"Actually, they are all out on the sun porch waiting for us. Tell them dinner is on the way."

I stopped at the fridge and grabbed a beer. I was surprised to see Miranda and August sitting at the far end of the table. I bent down and kissed Lacey tenderly on the cheek.

"Darling", she cooed. "you're back. I was afraid you'd miss James's superb burgers!"

Richie was seated on one side of Lacey and CC on the other. CC offered to move but I told her not to and slipped in next to Sam which also put me next to Miranda who was all smiles.

"Jess," she salivated. "Lacey has been most gracious and invited us to dine with you all. It has been years since I have enjoyed a hamburger and am most ravenous."

I bet you are, I thought. I asked where the kids were and Bly said they were in the den watching a Disney feature. "I think I will go and say hello. Anyone need a refill while I'm up?"

Sam said he would join me and collected several orders for drinks. I put my hand on Lacey's shoulder as I passed her. "You okay Hon?"

"I am now that you are back." She smiled looking up at me.

"Va, va, va boom!" Sam exclaimed shaking his hand as soon as we were out of earshot. "That is one hot tamale!"

"I wouldn't let CC hear you say that. How have she and Lacey been getting on?" I asked.

"Well, I sense a little tension there, what's up with that?"

"Don't know Buddy, and Lace isn't talking."

Harry and Leah were too engrossed with the television to pay us much notice. We filled the drink orders and re-joined the dinner crowd. Timothy had arrived and he and Viv set two baskets of oven fries on the table. James passed the burgers and buns and condiments around. I piled the onions on as I watched Lacey do the same thing. How many times had we shared this exact meal when we were teens I wondered?

The conversation was light as everyone was too busy eating. I got up once to get another beer and when I returned CC had changed places with me. She said she had a lot of questions to ask Miranda about her career. I figured that would be good for an hour but she surprised me and said she didn't want to talk about herself. Instead, she wanted to know all about the investigation into Arthur's murder. She directed her questions towards Timothy and he answered as best he could.

She said she found it most distressful that the perpetrator had not been apprehended yet. It was then that Lacey shocked the hell out of me.

"Are you at all squeamish Miranda? If you aren't, then I have a proposal for you to consider."

"And, what would that be Lacey?" Miranda asked curiously.

"Free lodging, but it would mean sleeping where Arthur was murdered…"

"Mother!" James stammered.

"Canterbury has been thoroughly cleaned and there are no lingering odours. They don't even have to go into the study as the bedrooms are upstairs. We will loan them a car so they can have their meals elsewhere. We will be much too busy tomorrow with food drop-offs for the memorials to worry about feeding anyone else. Is there something wrong with that?"

Half the people at the table were watching Miranda's to see her reaction and the other half, including me had our eyes on Lacey. "Honey, don't you think that's a little ghoulish?"

"No," she answered. "but, it's entirely up to them."

Both CC and Blythe told me afterward that when Lacey suggested the manor house that August nudged Miranda and they both thought that he was encouraging her to take the offer; for what reason I could not fathom.

"To answer your question Lacey; no, I am not intimated by gruesome matters though as far as I know, I have never slept in a house where a murder took place. Jess, is it true that the murderer always returns to the scene of the crime? Do you think we would be in any danger there?"

"I am not a criminal lawyer Miss Desoto and have had limited experience with murder scenes. I myself think it is just a fallacy that the perpetrator always returns to his crime. Of course television and the silver screen have romanticized that conception as you would surely know, but perhaps Timothy is the one you should address your concerns to?"

"It's as Jess says. The only reason an offender would need to return to the site of his crime would be if he felt that he had left damaging evidence behind or was trapped into thinking that he had. Just as an arsonist needs to watch his handy work go up in flames, a killer may want to observe the police and their proceedings and even offer a clue as to what he saw. No witness has come forward in Arthur's murder or Lacey's kidnapping. There have been a lot of "looky-loos" as there are at every crime scene, but none that have posed any great suspicion. The two properties are under police surveillance and so I can say with some certainty Ms. Desoto that you and Mr. Strange are most assuredly not in any danger. It is entirely your decision however."

Miranda had already made up her mind. "Thank-you for your input Corporal. If August is agreeable, I think we will take your offer Lacey. I suppose we should make friends with the dogs so that they don't think we are intruders."

Lacey smiled cunningly. "Very well, James, will you be a dear and take them to Canterbury? Perhaps Miranda would feel securer if you let the dogs take a run through the house?"

Timothy offered to accompany James who was not thrilled at all by his mother's proposal. The four of them got up and proceeded to the door. Lacey told them that they were welcome to come back for coffee and cakes after they were settled and then suggested to Richie that they continue their conversation on the front porch.

I hoped it had not been her intention to dismiss us. I apologized to CC and Sam for Lacey's rudeness. They laughed it off saying they had to leave anyway as their grandson was coming over for a sleep-over. Bly left to join the kids in the den and Timothy had to check in at the station after he helped James settle the guests at the manor house so that left Vivian and me. After the clean-up, she linked her arm through mine and asked if she could talk to me.

We made our way to the family room where she automatically went to the bar and poured me a snifter of apricot brandy; my after dinner nightcap. I asked her if something was bothering her.

"Am I a horrible daughter Daddy?" She asked.

"Just the opposite Leigh, a father couldn't ask for a sweeter or more loving daughter. Why would you ask such a silly question?"

"I don't mean to you Daddy; I mean to Mother. Here I am in a house full of laughter and love with you and your friends and my new family and Mother is all alone. She is roaming around in that big house with no one to talk to and nothing to do. I can't help feeling guilty that I am so happy and she isn't."

"Honey, I doubt if your mother is even home. She is probably working or at one of her charity functions or wedding events. I'm afraid that we have not had much to talk about in a long time. She is no longer interested in my cases, though she pretends to be, and I am certainly not one bit interested in wedding plans. You have nothing to feel guilty about; your mother is happy just the way things are."

"But Daddy, she doesn't know how "things" are. She doesn't know about you and Lacey; she doesn't know that you have another family and that I am here and supporting you…what will it do to her when she finds out? Have you talked to her yet?"

"Will you let me worry about that Leigh? None of this is any of your doing and you are in no way responsible for my actions. As soon as Arthur's killer is found and Lacey is safe then I will confess all. Until then I guess I am going to have to bend the truth a little bit. Can you live with that? I left a message for her saying that the case was more than I had envisioned and that I had much to discuss with her but that I would not be coming back until everything was resolved."

"I can, but I'm wondering if you can. You have always been this stalwart honest man that I have looked up to all my life and I have never known you to tell a lie or hurt anyone."

I laughed. "I'm sure I have told my share of little white lies, but I haven't lied to your mother and I won't. I never left home thinking that I was going to fall back in love with my teenage sweetheart. There is no going back for me Leigh; my life is with Lacey wherever it may take us. I do hope that your mother will grant me a divorce and that someday your sister will understand."

"I honestly don't know what mother will do and as for Hilary, well, as long as it doesn't interfere with her life style, she probably won't care one way or the other."

"Is there dissention between you and your sister?"

"She has always been mean to me; I just hid it well I guess. She was always blackmailing me for one thing or the other. Well, that is all over now for I am done with her."

"How can you say that Leigh, I mean you room with her? What has happened?" I was totally surprised with what she said next.

"I'm not going back to Victoria. I can go to college anywhere; it just won't be there. Besides I want to be close to you."

"Oh Honey, I want you close also…I just don't know where that is going to be. Are you assuming that we are all going to stay in Kings Crossing and live in this house?"

"Maybe." She said optimistically.

I pulled her close to me and kissed her on her forehead. "No one knows what tomorrow will bring but I don't think it is going to have the fairy tale ending you want so let's just live in the moment where we are both happy for now. Are you okay with that?"

She said she was. Timothy poked his head in the door and asked if he was intruding. I told him he wasn't and asked if there was anything new to report and he said there wasn't. He told Leigh that it was a beautifully warm evening and would she like to go for a walk. I sent them on their way reminding Leigh that we would discuss the 'school thing' and her sister at another time. I thought I might take a walk myself if the dogs were back. Surely James was done at Canterbury by now. I heard the squeak of Lacey's wheelchair and decided to confront her first. My God, I was looking forward to accosting her!

"Hi Darling," She purred. "what have you been up to?"

Richie wheeled her chair close to me. "Are you two all caught up now?" I asked as I rose to help her unto the sofa beside me. She gave me a little kiss.

"Just as I thought; the pungent smell of tobacco." I teased.

"Well, it's no worse than your stale beer breath!" She retorted.

I smiled. "Sorry, I would have thought that the apricot brandy would have nullified that. Speaking of that, may I offer you a night cap Richie?"

He declined saying that he was bushed and if we didn't mind, he was going to call it a day. "If Miranda and August are coming back for coffee I can stay for support if you like though."

I told him that I didn't know just as we heard the kitchen door slam. Lacey murmured something under her breath which sounded like "I better brace myself for James's wrath."

"How did it go James?" I asked

He stood at the door and addressed his mother. "It's a good thing I love and respect you Mother or else I would have told you in not very gentlemanly terms where you could stick it when you saddled me with that insufferable woman."

"I'm sorry Darling; I don't know what came over me. The idea just came to me and I went for it. Are you terribly angry with me?" Lacey started to get up.

I put my hand on her to stop her. "Don't be too hard on your mother James; we all know she does and says things that she "appears" to have no control over. It's done now and I thank you. Was it really all that bad?"

"I will just warn you Jess…don't ever find yourself alone with that man-eating woman!"

"Damn it! Lacey cursed. "I'll kill her if she laid one of her sluttish hands on you!"

"Let's hope it doesn't come to that Mother. Thanks for wanting to protect my honour but I can assure you that it is still intact. We all know that you two have an ugly history so why she would even consider attending Arthur's service is beyond me. Can you offer any insight Richie?"

"You know just as much as I do James. I take full responsibility for her being here. Arthur's death hit the tabloids of course and Miranda did approach me and asked for the details. I'm afraid I told her when the service was and when I was leaving. Believe me; I was completely bowled over when I met them at the airport especially when I knew that she was recovering from abdominal surgery. So, all of this falls on me and not Lacey."

"We all know that woman can wrangle her way around anything…" Lacey stopped and a peculiar look passed between her and Richie. "Well, almost anything." She continued. "What's with the surgery? Is that why she is wearing that ugly mu-mu?"

"All I know is that August told me that she had surgery, an appendectomy I think, about ten days ago. She has not been forthcoming with any more details."

I sat back. "I noticed her clutching her stomach several times at the supper table. She passed it off saying that she had a very delicate constitution and that she wasn't used to fatty food."

Lacey smirked. "Delicate constitution, my foot! And, what were you doing my dear keeping such a close eye on her?"

"I was seated next to her if you remember correctly. You all keep saying that "we" all know what transpired between you and Miranda…well, I am not part of that "we". I think I have been kept in the dark long enough, so how about cluing me in?"

"Jess, I already told you that it wasn't important enough to warrant an explanation but I can see that you aren't going to settle for that any longer. I stood with Arthur when he wouldn't cast her in a role and she has never forgiven me. That's all Jess, that's all."

"That does not explain your animosity towards her does it? If that's the way you want to play it then you leave me no choice but to accept it, or perhaps Miranda will be more informative." I had called her bluff, now what was she going to say?

She shrugged her shoulders. "Do as you want Jess." She grabbed the arm of the wheelchair and stood up and before anyone could help her she swung herself unto the seat. She took the brake off and turned it around and said she'd walk Richie to the stairs.

I grabbed one of the chairs arms and stopped her. "Just one damn minute Lacey; I am not through with you yet! Excuse us will you boys?"

Richie said he was on his way out and James grinned and said he needed to help Bly with the kids. He wished me good luck. "By the way they'll take a rain check on the coffee and cake.

She's all yours Dad. Have a good night."

Lacey turned around and smiled. "He called you Dad."

"He did, didn't he? Well, that doesn't change anything though does it my love?"

"Why are you so angry with me Jesse? I already apologized for sending James to do my dirty work. Are you mad because I've been smoking with Richie?"

"Yeah that's it Lace; I'm pissed because you've been smoking. If you must know, it was I who suggested Richie take you out on the porch in the first place. So no, your pretence of smoking does not bother me. What does is your rudeness. Are you even aware that you deserted everyone at the dinner table? I'm not talking about me or the girls, but Sam and CC. You didn't even say good night to your best friends."

Lacey hung her head. "I don't even think I was aware of that Jesse; thank-you for telling me. I will apologize to everyone, especially you. Do you think you can forgive me?"

She looked up at me with her puppy dog eyes. "Damn it Lacey, stop playing me! You know you can do anything and I will always forgive you but I won't tolerate you being ill-mannered."

"She brings out the worst in me Jesse. I promise I will be more tolerant. Do you think we can go to the bedroom now?"

"Do you think that everything can be resolved with sex?"

"Are you saying that's all there is between us?"

"Not for me it isn't. I can't imagine my life without you, in or out of the bedroom. I was as close to going crazy as I ever want to be during those two days you were missing." I knelt beside her. She took my face in her hands.

"I know Jess, I know. I love you and I know you love me and you are just trying to help me be a better person. Am I trying your patience?"

"Honey, you are a good person…you just get waylaid at times. None of us are perfect, especially me, and if I am out of line by lecturing you then it is I who needs your forgiveness."

"Silly, you are perfect and I don't deserve you but I'm not letting you go. Can we just go on living here Jesse and be one big happy family?"

"Funny, Vivian said almost the exact same thing. She wants to stay here with her new family. One thing for certain is that you and I are going to be together. Now we can go to the bedroom."

CHAPTER 11

Surprises

I awoke Friday morning to a nibbling on my ear and a warm hand running through the hairs on my chest. "I don't know who you are lady but I would suggest that you vacate the premises before my woman comes back and finds you in her bed with her man." I warned.

She said in a deep sensual voice. "Why, what would she do to me? She wouldn't mind if you played around with somebody else would she?"

I laughed wickedly. "Believe me, she has dibs on the woman scorned theory; I can testify to that. Now, let's have a look at you and see if you are worth her wrath?"

She giggled, "Surprise, it's me!"

"Me who?" I said jokingly.

"Your woman silly; who else would dare to be in bed with you?"

"I'm still not convinced because I never wake up to find her in bed with me. What can you do to prove that you are my Lacey?"

She rolled me over and kissed me passionately. "Will that do?"

I smacked my lips. "I think I need more." She obliged me.

"What do I owe the pleasure to? Have you been up for hours and just crawled back into bed?"

"Nope, I've been here all night. I slept like a baby."

"You didn't even sneak out to the smoking parlour?"

"I'm trying to quit Jesse 'cause you don't like the smell of me when I smoke."

"You do realize that you have to start smoking before you can actually quit, don't you?"

She laid her head on my chest and was unusually quiet. I lifted her chin up and was baffled to see that she was crying. "Hey, what's this all about?"

She sniffled and attempted to wipe her tears away.

I said. "Here, let me do that. Are they tears of happiness or are you sad?"

"I'm not sad Jesse; just the opposite. Do you know how many nights I went to bed praying to God to let me fall asleep with you and to wake up with your arms around me? Just once, I would plead, just once. But He never answered me; He never talked to me. I promised Him that I would do anything… anything." The crying became heart-rending sobs.

"Oh Baby," I said rocking her. "I'm here now and I can promise you that we will always wake up in each other's arms and pretty soon I am going to have two strong arms to hold you."

"You're hurting aren't you Jesse?" She asked between sobs.

She lowered my arm and offered to get the sling. "I'm good Honey; I just can't hold you as tight as I would like to."

She was about to say something when the phone rang. "Now who would have the nerve to be calling at this time in the morning?" She reached for it but I snatched it away from her.

"Tudor House…Jess Jameson here." There was sinister laughing on the other end. I didn't give him the satisfaction by asking who he was. The laughing ceased and he spoke.

"You're in bed with her right now aren't you? How is the little home-wrecking whore?"

I hung up the phone. Lacey asked who it was and I told her "another heckler." She said she thought she heard laughter and wondered if it was the same person as the other day.

"You mean last week don't you?"

"No, I mean last night. Vivian answered the phone and hung up because the person at the other end was laughing menacingly and making lewd suggestions. I guess he thought it was me."

"Why didn't you tell me Lacey?"

"We both decided not to upset you. Please don't be angry at Vivian."

"I'm not angry with either of you but you need to tell me everything. Where was I anyway?"

"I guess it was when you went off to run your errand."

"If I am occupied somewhere else please let James or Richie answer the phone, okay?"

"I will, but I am sure the calls are harmless."

"We don't know anything of the sort; there is still a killer out there remember?"

She promised and then promptly broke her promise as she answered the phone while I was on my way to the bathroom. I turned when she said "Hello…how are you Clara?"

She waved me signalling that it was okay. "It's Clara, Honey."

I sighed and shut the bathroom door. I showered because it didn't really matter what I asked of her as she was going to do whatever she damn well wanted to. When I came out she was sitting on the edge of the bed with her housecoat wrapped around her shoulders. I helped her to stand up as it was clear she had an agenda. She told me she wanted to try and walk to the bathroom holding on to the wheelchair. I walked behind her and asked her why she answered the phone. Her answer was of course logical; she didn't want to wake the kids.

"I knew it wasn't anyone menacing Jesse."

"How could you possibly know that Lacey?"

"I could tell by the ring."

"You know that makes no sense what so ever, don't you?"

"Yes, I'm not psychic. Anyhow, Clara has made us breakfast croissants and wants to drop off all the goodies that people have been delivering to her house for the services tomorrow. She is wondering if she will have a problem getting through the gates. I told her that we would make sure the sentinels would admit her."

"I'll get you into the shower and then I will alert them."

"Are you going to leave me alone? Terrible things happen to people when they are showering you know." She teased.

"This is not the Bates Motel Lacey but I could wake Richie and get him to supervise you."

"Don't you even think about it!"

"Why, I'm sure he has seen you naked before?" I sat her on the chair in the shower.

"Why would you say such a thing Jesse? Of course he hasn't!"

I kissed her and turned the water on ordering her to stay there until I got back. She promised.

Clara and I unloaded the truck while Lacey contemplated where to put everything. We invited Clara to stay for breakfast but she said she had already eaten and had to get to her cleaning job. Lacey dug through the cupboards and came up with a large aluminum pot. She grabbed a metal mixing spoon and proceeded to the bottom of the stairs. She banged on the pot and yelled.

"Breakfast is ready! Come as you are and make it snappy!"

I could only smile at her antics. "I hope no one sleeps in their birthday suit."

"I hope so too, and just to be clear…no man has ever seen me naked except you and maybe a doctor or two."

"I find that very hard to believe." I said dubiously.

"Believe it or not, it's the truth." She retorted.

James was the first to come down the stairs and was soon followed by everyone else. Vivian was astonished to see the kitchen table and counters overflowing with casseroles and goodies.

"This is how they do it in a small town; the whole town participates. I'm going to need all your help to store it all safely. We might require more coolers." Lacey explained.

I told her I would call Sam and see what he could come up with. She asked me to remind him to bring his patio tables and chairs. That was going to be Richie's, James's and my job; rounding up, cleaning and setting up all the outdoor furniture for the memorial luncheon.

After we had finished Clara's delicious breakfast Lacey asked if anyone wanted to volunteer to take what was left over to the "guests" at Canterbury.

"That's very considerate of you Honey." I said thinking that she had lost some of her hostility towards Miranda.

"I'm not always a bitch you know." She almost snapped at me.

"Mother", James chided. "can't you accept a compliment without a put-down?"

"Apparently not; sorry Jess." She looked away from me quickly.

"I'll go." Vivian volunteered. "I'll run upstairs and get dressed quickly. Can I take the dogs?"

"Of course you can and thanks. I'll make up a nice tray… will you help me Jesse?" Lacey smiled at me and I thought that was her way of apologizing for snapping at me.

The day went by very quickly and we had everything organized by two in the afternoon. I suggested that Lace take a little rest and for once she didn't argue with me. Bly and Leah were also resting. Vivian and Harrison chose to accompany me on my shopping trip as I needed to purchase a dress shirt and hopefully, a suitable jacket. I had not planned ahead when I had packed. James and Richie were left to hold down the fort which meant keeping an eye on Lacey.

Three hours later we were getting ready to sit down to a meal of crockpot dinners, homemade breads and freshly made salads when Timothy called. We had not heard from him or anyone else at the precinct all day and so it was reasonable to think that nothing new had transpired. I was wrong. He was bringing us a surprise visitor and Hank was talking.

"I think I will put a movie in the V.C.R. for the kids before Timothy arrives." Blythe picked Leah up and told Harrison to follow.

He didn't budge from his chair next to me.

"You heard your mother Harry; do I need to escort you?" James asked him sternly.

"But Dad we haven't given Gramma her present yet." Harry looked at me. "Aren't we going to Grampa Jesse?"

"You two bought me a present?" Lacey exclaimed. "I just love surprise presents; whatever could it be?" She leaned close to me. "Where are you hiding it Grampa Jesse?"

"You will never guess what it is Gramma." Harry giggled.

"Is it bigger than a breadbox?" Lacey asked Harry teasingly.

He turned to Vivian and whispered. "It's not is it Auntie?"

She answered that it was not.

"Ah ha, so you are in on the secret are you Vivian, and what about you James, and Bly too?"

James said he had no idea what was going on and Bly concurred. I sat back in my chair and decided to let Lace play twenty questions with Harry.

"Okay, so it is smaller than a breadbox…hmm, can I wear it?"

"Yup." Harry nodded.

"Is it red?"

"Nope."

"Let's see… I can wear it, but it is not red, so it must be yellow?"

"Nope." Harry giggled again. "She'll never guess will she Grampa?"

"I don't know." I said. "She's pretty smart you know."

"I know," Lacey exclaimed. "it's a dress! Now, let's see, what color would it be?"

Harry almost fell off his chair he was laughing so hard. "It must be a really small dress if it can fit in Grampa's pocket."

"Umm, it's in your pocket is it Jesse?" Lacey reached over and put her hand in my pants pocket and not finding anything tried the shirt pocket. "Let me see the other ones."

"You don't think I would carry such a valuable thing in my pockets, do you Hon?" I kidded.

"Just how valuable is it?"

"I'll let you be the judge of that. What do you think Vivian… should I ask her?"

"Well, the cat's almost out of the bag Dad, so you may as well go for it."

"Aunt Vivian, we don't have a cat." Harry said matter of factually.

We all laughed a little and James explained what it meant to let the cat out of the bag.

"What do you want to ask me Jesse? Do I have to answer before I get my present?" Lacey batted her big purple eyes at me.

I reached behind me and opened a drawer on the sideboard and extracted the little box. Harry jumped up and stood between Lace and me.

"Open it Gramma, open it!" He said excitedly.

I took both her hands in mine. Tears were already forming in her eyes. Everyone was dead silent. "Just a minute Son, she needs to hear me out first. I should have given you this twenty four years ago. You already know that I want to marry you more than anything else in this world and by God it will happen someday. I am asking you officially now with our children as our witnesses…will you accept this ring as my promise of eternal love?" I opened the box. Our eyes locked. Against my better judgement I sank to the floor in front of her.

She was laughing and crying all at the same time. "It is the most beautiful thing I have ever seen in my life! Where would you have gotten such a perfect stone? Oh, it's an amethyst!" "Its beauty only comes in second to your eyes Honey. It is your very own dream stone and it is supposed to help with insomnia, protect you and quell your fears…not that you have any." I got to my feet and pulled her into my arms. "What do you say Lace?"

"Say? There is nothing to say but yes, yes, yes! Yes to whatever lies ahead for us Jesse. Look everyone it's an amethyst, and you all know how I love amethysts!"

Blythe was crying and Leah started though she probably didn't know why. James brought her over to see Lacey.

"Look Sweetie, look what your grandfather gave me. It's a ring and it is the same color as our eyes. Do you like it?"

"Can I have one too Uncle Jesse?"

"You bet you can Sweetie. I'll see what I can find for you." I promised.

James hugged his mother and shook my hand. "Is it official then…my mother and father are engaged?"

"I think we are engaged to be engaged. We were already that before this amazing rock weren't we Jesse? Are you sure you still want me after all my rantings and ravings?" Lacey asked.

"That is part of your charm my dear." I assured her.

"You couldn't have chosen a more fitting gem for the rarest gem of all ole boy. This deserves a toast but first I need to hug my best friend…you don't mind do you Jess?"

"Richie, you can hug her as often as you like as long as you always give her back to me."

"It was Arthur's and my deepest wish that Lacey find someone who was worthy of her love. I'm sorry he is not here to witness this. I may have had my doubts at first Jess but I believe that you are the only man for the job."

"Hey," Lacey grumbled. "what's that supposed to mean?"

"Oh, I think you know perfectly well what that means my dear. Now give me a kiss and let's crack open the champagne."

"We don't have any champagne Richie." Lacey laughed.

"Really…what's this then?" Richie reached into the sideboard and produced an ice bucket that held a large bottle of the bubbly.

"Did you know about this Richie? Did you tell him Jesse?" Lacey asked smiling.

I winked at her. "I had to get his approval."

"Suppose if he had of said 'no'?"

"You of all people should know that I don't take no for an answer." I pulled her onto my lap and kissed her. "I love you Lace."

She buried her head in my chest and told me this was now the best day of her life.

James passed a tall glass to everyone just as Timothy appeared in the doorway.

"Looks like a celebration…what's going on here?" he asked.

"We are going to have a wedding Uncle Tim! My Gramma and Grampa are going to get married!" Harry announced.

"Is it official then?"

"It's as official as it can legally be Timothy." He was still in his uniform so I figured he was still on duty but I asked if he could have a glass of champagne to celebrate with us.

"Sorry, I will have to take a rain check on that. I have someone I want you all to meet." He reached out his hand to someone waiting in the wings. A woman stepped forward.

Lacey sprung up so fast that I barely had time to hold on to her. Her hands were in the air.

"Oh Ainsley, you have come! I was so hoping you would. Welcome, welcome to our family."

Ainsley fought to hold back tears as she took Lacey's hands. "Lacey, I would have known you anywhere. You are just as Arthur described you so many years ago."

I held on to Lacey as she hugged her. "Come, meet my family…oh, it is yours too. This gentlemen holding on to me so tightly is Jess Jameson and this is James, our son; it's a long story of which I will tell you later."

She introduced Ainsley to everyone else explaining who they all were to her. She came to Vivian. "And this beautiful young lady is Jess's daughter and James's sister. We are so happy that she has come to be with us and now, you are here; our family is complete. Come and sit next to me and share a glass of cheer. You may think that we shouldn't be celebrating the night before your mother's and brother's memorials…"

Ainsley put her hand over Lacey's. "You need not apologize for Corporal Newman has filled me in on everything. I have been in the Crossing for a while so I am already pretty informed."

The lawyer in me took over. "How long have you been here Ainsley?"

She looked at Timothy and he nodded to her. "I arrived the day after Arthur was murdered. I know what you are going to ask me Mr. Jameson and the answer is yes. Yes, I was here at the house and it was I who was staying in the dome room. Corporal Newman has already told me that you had your suspicions. I wanted to go to Canterbury but it was under police surveillance so I couldn't."

"How long were you here and weren't you worried that the dome would be searched? Why were you in hiding?" I asked hoping she would answer me truthfully.

"I don't know; I just didn't want anyone to know I was here. I suppose I was scared that I would be accused of Arthur's murder so I needed time to figure out what I was going to do. I double bolted the attic door from inside and removed the warning bell.

I know the police were here at least once but they never made it past the second floor."

Timothy shook his head. "Yeah, another blunder. Anyhow, no harm, no foul."

"I'm curious Ainsley, how did you gain entrance into the house without being noticed? How long did you stay in the attic and how did you come to hear of your brother's demise? I have been led to believe that you have no ties left to the family or town… am I correct?"

Lacey put her hand over mine. "You will have to forgive Jess, Ainsley. He's a lawyer you know and wants to know everything all at once; isn't that right Honey?"

"I stand reprimanded. Yes, please forgive me but I am most curious about the circumstances leading up to you arriving here tonight."

"First," Ainsley cleared her throat. "I want you all to know that I had nothing to do with my brother's death. We have not seen each other for almost twenty years and that was after I sent word to him through the family attorney asking him to contact me. He did and I asked for his help as I couldn't go on living the way I was. His came immediately to Calgary where I had been residing if one could even call it that. He moved me to Edmonton, got me into a clinic for my addictions. Eventually, I was able to move to a half-way house. Two years later Arthur bought me my own little house. I now board several people at a time who need help just as I once did. My brother saved my life. I did not come back here for my mother; I came for Arthur and I want to help in any way I can to bring his murderer to justice." She turned her attention to me. "Now, Mr. Jameson, I would be pleased to answer your questions."

"Thank you Ainsley. First, I want it made known that you are not on the witness stand and I am sorry if I made you feel that way. I take it that you know about Lacey's kidnapping…

Timothy would not have you brought here if he thought she was in any danger from you. I myself was once a resident of Kings Crossing and have not been back for many years. I did know Arthur back in the seventies but I do not remember you."

She laughed. "Lucky for you as I was not a very nice person."

"That has no bearing on the here and now and I for one am glad that you have finally decided to make an appearance. I am curious though, where have you been staying?"

"With my one and only friend here; his name is Clifford Roper. He called me after my mother's passing and again after Arthur's death. I did not tell him or Mr. Hanson that I was coming. It was only after you and Lacey took up residence here did I seek sanctuary from him. He has been trying to convince me to make myself known for a week now. Today, it was now or never and he called Corporal Newman and here I am. Of course, the police couldn't just take my word for it that I had nothing to do with Arthur's murder so I have been questioned already and I guess I passed. It's all right Mr. Jameson, I was asked if I would like a lawyer and I declined. Corporal Newman said he knew someone who would represent me if it wasn't a conflict of interest to his other client. I assume he meant you, Mr. Jameson, and you are his client aren't you Lacey?"

Timothy smiled. "We weren't hard on her Jess and everything she told us checks out."

"I'm sure it does. Just a couple more questions if you don't mind Ainsley?"

"I don't, and perhaps I can answer without you having to ask. You want to know how I managed to gain access to the house when it was being watched. I came at night through the garden passage into the cellar. I had hoped that the code to the door had not been changed and luckily it hadn't. I knew about Arthur's secret room but I never took much interest in it as it was more a boy thing. I stayed until you both got here. I happened to be peeking out the porthole on the west side of the house when I saw you drive up. I thought you were probably a reporter or a copper. Then Lacey came up the drive and you followed her. I was pretty sure who she was. I crept down the stairs and unlocked the attic door and opened it a crack. I heard the backdoor open and muffled voices. I shut the door quickly and relocked it when I heard you come up the stairs. You tried the door but were satisfied when Lacey told you it was always locked and she wasn't even sure where the key was. I didn't know who you were at the time but I had a feeling that you were the one in command. I didn't find out who you were until Clifford found out that a lawyer friend of Lacey's was staying at the house with her. Anyhow, I decided that night that I had better vacate the premises. I want you to know that I did not spy on the two of you but when I was leaving that night through Arthur's room again I heard the two of your voices wafting up the vent from the first floor. I heard Lacey talking about finding Arthur."

"Oh how awful for you Ainsley! I'm sorry you had to hear that." Lacey apologized.

"I could barely make out your words so it was nothing for me compared to what it was like for you. It must have been appalling."

"I think perhaps these little ears have heard enough and Leah has fallen asleep in my arms so if you will please excuse us, Bly and I will take these two babes upstairs." James said. "I'm glad you came Ainsley; we'll talk more later."

"Thank-you James, I feel like I already know you as Arthur always talked about you in his letters. He was very proud of you."

James smiled and told her that he owed his life to Arthur as well. I wondered if Lacey had told him that for a short time she had considered abortion or was there another reason entirely. Whatever it was I owed Arthur a debt of gratitude that I could never repay. Lace sensed that his words had hit home with me and she put her hand on mine and then spoke directly to Ainsley.

"I have a feeling that you already know about James, Jess and me?"

"I do and I am happy that James has come to know his father and it appears as though the two of you are rekindling your feelings for each other."

"Yes, you are very perceptive. It didn't work out for Jess and me before but we are trying to correct our past mistakes. He never knew he had a son until last week and that is entirely my fault. Arthur always wanted me to come clean about James's parentage but I didn't. How ironic that his death would bring Jess and me together. It's a cruel twist of fate I'm afraid."

"It is but I know my brother was happy with the life he chose and the family that you gave him Lacey and his life with you Richie. He told me that you had a big hand in his decision to visit me and help me put my life back together. I thank you for that Sir."

"There is no need to thank me Ainsley. I am going to miss Arthur until the day I die. I will carry on with his ventures and continue supporting all his enterprises for a while. It's not going to be easy as he was the driving force behind our operations and I have the feeling that Lacey will not be returning to the theatre life anytime soon." Richie left the words hang out there in the air.

What had he meant about Lace and the theatre?

"Honey, are you involved in Arthur's and Richie's business more than you let on?"

"Richie is too modest. He's the one behind all that goes on in front of and behind the curtains. Arthur was the creator, but Richie made everything happen. I have only seen them in a heated disagreement once. Richie relented and yielded to Arthur." She smiled knowingly at Richie.

"True, but aren't you leaving one important fact out my dear? It was you who pointed out and not too delicately, I might add, that I was wrong. Well, that is all water under the bridge now but to answer your question Jess, Lacey is not just an observer and dispute settler, she has a very active part in our enterprises and we have always valued her input. You weren't keeping this a secret were you now? Sorry, if I let the cat out of the bag."

"I think that poor cat has had a busy day." Lacey tried to make light of Richie's disclosure.

I decided to take it up with her when we were alone. I went back to questioning Ainsley.

"How did you manage to survive in the dome for three days? Did you bring provisions with you? And, did you know that the house was broken into on Friday?"

"I only had a small suitcase with me and I came here directly from the bus. I was hoping that there would be enough food in the house to tide me over until I decided what I was going to do. There were canned and packaged goods and fresh milk and produce in the fridge. The hot plate was still in the storage room in the attic and I even found an old cooler. The power had not been disconnected and the water still flowed in the bathroom. I was quite comfortable Mr. Jameson. I was long gone by the time the break-in occurred. I hear they have found the culprit."

"Well, that is news to me. Timothy, did you neglect in telling us that little detail."

"That was next on my agenda Jess. Earlier today a woman appeared at the station with a lad of eleven in tow. She overheard him bragging to his friends about the loot that he had made off with at Tudor House. He was planning on selling his stuff to the local pawn shop. He admitted that he had been watching the house for weeks. He was just about to make his move after he heard Hilda had died but Arthur showed up and so he put it off until that Friday. He knew that the dogs were gone and that the police only had guards at the carriage house. His prints match those found in Hilda's bedroom and inside the doggie door. He was hoping to find Hilda's stash of weed but had to settle for jewellery as he was interrupted in his search. He admits he screwed up because he didn't know that the house was occupied. He said that something spooked him and it was then that he broke the window to make a quick getaway. I suppose that is what woke you and Lacey. I have asked Ainsley if perhaps it was she that alarmed him but she says she arrived at Mr. Roper's house around nine thirty and the break-in happened after midnight so I suppose it was just the creaking of the old house that saved all of Hilda's valuables from being stolen. We have recovered several antique brooches and bracelets from his house and the pawn shop is being investigated as we speak. Lacey, perhaps you can aid us in a description of what is all missing?"

"I cannot Timothy. I would have already informed you if I had of known what was missing but I do not. Perhaps Clara Brankco could help or what about you Ainsley?"

"I'm sorry but I have absolutely no idea. When I was very young Mother found me playing dress-up in her room. I remember having many bangles around my neck and on my arms. She scolded me quite harshly and told me I was never to enter her room again. It might have been paste but she took it all from me and locked it all up in her safe. I never saw any of it again unless she was wearing it. For my birthday that year she gave me a little chest filled with colourful trinkets. I believe I was five years old."

"There was no jewellery in the safe Ainsley; in fact there was nothing of interest at all in there. There were a few cheap things that we found in the bedroom and I put them away for Leah. But now, Timothy says that antique pieces were found among the stolen pieces so I just don't know what happened to the rest of it unless she sold it." Lacey suggested.

"Oh no, I cannot see her doing that. She treasured everything that Father ever gave her. He was always presenting her with expensive jewellery especially when he came home from a trip. He even brought Arthur and me presents. He was quite young when he died you know and I didn't think Mother would ever recover."

I thought that this might be the best opportunity I would have to find out why Ainsley chose to spend her nights at Canterbury. I would have to approach the subject delicately or Lacey would indeed have me sleeping in another bed…probably with the dogs.

"How old were you when your father passed away Ainsley?"

"I was sixteen and Arthur would have been eleven. Mother blamed herself for the longest time. It was about ten at night when I heard her screaing. I ran out into the hallway and tried to get in their room but the door was locked. She was crying hysterically and I didn't know what to do so I called Clifford as he was a family friend and Dad always told him to keep an eye on us when he was out of town. He came right up and called the police and they broke the door down. The doctors told us there was nothing anyone could have done as he had died instantly of a massive heart attack."

"Oh, how horrible Ainsley; you were both so young. Arthur never spoke about it to me, but I understood that he was very close to his father." Lacey squeezed Ainsley's hand.

"I suppose I was too young to have known the details back then, not that it would have made a difference. No child should have to witness that. I cannot even begin to comprehend what you all went through and though it is many years later I would like to offer my sympathies. As I said before, I did not know you then and if I had of, I probably wouldn't have understood anyhow."

"Thank-you Mr. Jameson, but it is not necessary."

"First thing; you must stop calling me Mister…I am Jess all right?"

"Yes, you have all been so kind but I think it is time that I get back to Clifford as he is going to require my help in getting ready for bed?"

Lacey asked if Mr. Roper was ill.

"He had a surgery many years ago to correct a back problem. It was unsuccessful and he has been confined to a wheelchair ever since. He has a live-in nurse/housekeeper. We sent her away on a much needed vacation as I am perfectly able to care for him. She will be back tomorrow. May I come in the morning and help you with anything that needs attending to."

"We would like you to come and stay with us Ainsley. Do you think you would want to?"

"Yes Lacey, I would very much. I will see you all early tomorrow then."

Timothy said he would have Constable Jones take her back to Clifford's. She turned at the door and said. "If we have time before the service I will show you where Mother's safe is. Till then…goodnight."

"We've already opened the safe Ainsley and as I said there wasn't anything in it." Lacey reminded her.

"Oh no, I don't mean the house safe; Mother had one of her very own. We will probably need a locksmith or a safecracker as I do not know the combination but I am sure it still exists." Ainsley smiled as she waved goodbye.

"Well, isn't she the cagey one?" I said to Lacey.

"Something is fishy here Jess."

"What do you mean?"

"Do you remember my Mother's saying… that 'something was rotten in Denmark'? Yeah, well I definitely smell a not so pleasant story here that involves this Clifford character."

"I think you are right Hon and we'll talk about it later in private after Timothy has filled us in on the Hank story. By the way, do your parents know about what happened down here? How come they are not here supporting you and where is that sister of yours?"

"Connie would be here if things got worse for me and Daddy just had a surgery, nothing too serious, but I told them not to come just yet."

"And when are you going to tell them about us?"

"Oh Sweetheart, they already know. I phoned them when I was at Sam's when you went to confront Hank. Mama said: "Well then everything is going to be all right isn't it? Jess won't let you down again will he?"

I didn't have time to respond as Timothy reappeared and plopped himself down next to Lacey.

"What a day; thank goodness it is almost over. Where is everyone?"

I poured him a glass of champagne as I figured his shift must be over. "That depends on who you are asking about; James and Bly are upstairs putting the kids to bed and I have no idea where Vivian has disappeared to."

"What are the other two down at the carriage house up to?"

"I don't know and I care even less. Why don't you go and find everyone Jess so that we can hear what Timothy has to say?" Lacey suggested.

No sooner were the words out of her mouth and the three of them magically appeared. Timothy pulled out a notepad and started relaying Hank's story.

"Hank is being escorted to Vancouver for psychiatry assessment as we speak. He has been thoroughly examined here by several doctors and they all agree that his physical health has not been compromised by his or our actions. His mental state is another thing. They are not willing to make an evaluation as mental health is not their area of medical expertise. He has been uncooperative about revealing any circumstances leading up to Lacey's kidnapping; that was until today. Out of the blue he started talking to one of the guards who alerted Sergeant Lewis."

Timothy consulted his notes and relayed what Hank had stated.

"I had to get Lacey out of town or else they was going to put her in jail. He had it coming you know as he was not a good husband to her and then that lawyer came thinking he could save her. After calling you a few choice names Jess, he said that no one could save her but him and so he planned it all out."

We asked him how long it took him to come up with the idea of kidnapping you, Lacey.

"I didn't kidnap her. I told it was for her own good and she agreed."

Lacey sniggered.

Timothy continued in Hank's own words. "Soon as I seen Jess I knew I had to get her away from him. He was mean to her before so I knew he would hurt her again."

Lacey squeezed my hand and her eyes told me not to take his words to heart. It wasn't easy for me knowing that I was the catalyst that put his sick plan in motion. I told Timothy to continue.

"I knew I could get a car from the old garage at the church. No one knew where the key was but me. I knew it ran because I had started it lots of times before."

"Just a minute Timothy," James interrupted. "how come no one was aware of that? Wasn't that garage inspected? Wouldn't the priest know that the car was missing?"

"Unfortunately, the garage was only inspected from the outside. Reverend Stevens did tell the officers that there were old cars in the run-down garage but none of them were in running condition. He did not know where the keys were but told them they could break the door down if they deemed it necessary. By their account they were able to see inside through several dirty windows and did indeed find an old vehicle. Somehow they missed the fact that there was supposed to be more than one. Anyhow, the driveway is composed of rocks and they found nothing undisturbed. Again, shoddy detective work. One can only guess if that information would have helped in the search for Lacey. We were already checking every vehicle in the three districts so there wasn't much more that could have been done. So, there he was adamant that Lacey went with him of her own free will and that they had planned her "escape" last fall. We asked him where he was planning on taking her and he replied "Wouldn't you like to know?" We asked who he was trying to call on his phone and he denied that he even had a phone. Sergeant Lewis stayed on him until he finally cracked and said. "Dakota, I was trying to call Dakota." He did not know his last name. After half an hour of interrogation he became quite hostile and said. "If you damn well have to know then you can ask Reverend Stevens."

"He clammed up and wanted to go back to his cell. We then called the Reverend down and he supplied us with information about Dakota. He was a transient who showed up on the church steps last summer. His full name was Dakota Danser. He was in need of a bed and board for a few nights and was willing to work for it. Reverend Stevens says he was a gifted carpenter and made many renovations that the church had been in need of. At first Hank resented that someone else was honing in on his territory but Dakota had this way of gaining people's trust and soon the two of them were working side by side. Hank was staying late into the evening just so he could spend more time with Dakota. It all came to an end in late September when Dakota decided it was time to mosey on. He left in the middle of the night with nothing more than what he had arrived with. Hank took it very badly and would wait on the steps every day for him to return. Dakota has not been heard of since. The Reverend says he has no idea why Hank would say that he was phoning Dakota as he certainly didn't own that kind of phone."

Tim shrugged his shoulders. "That's about it I'm afraid. We have put calls out to other precincts to see if they have had any dealings with a drifter fitting Dakota's description. Lacey, just out of curiosity, did you meet up with Hank last autumn when you were here?"

"I did run into him at the church. Hilda had wanted to meet with Reverend Stevens in private, probably to discuss her last wishes as that is about the time her health really started to decline. I left her alone with him and wandered off through the gardens. Hank was weeding and a man was mowing the lawns. Hank told me that the man was his new friend and that they were going to travel the road together. I forgot about it until you mentioned it Timothy. I did not get to meet the man in question but he was very tall and slim. His hair and beard were red as fire. Does that fit the Reverend's description?"

Timothy said it did indeed. He was interrupted by his phone ringing. We sat quietly waiting for him to finish his conversation. He didn't say much but kept nodding his head and saying "Very good." He hung up and told us that it had been Constable Levi on the phone. Inquiries had gone out to all the officers asking if any of them had seen this Dakota chap; Constable Levi had. He had met the man when he was dropping his son off at Sunday school. He had found Dakota to be a quiet, friendly person and did not think that he posed a threat to anyone. Reverend Stevens had nothing but high praise for the man. The Corporal says somebody's time frame is off because he knows for a fact that Dakota did not leave town until sometime after October fourteenth. That date was his son's tenth birthday and Levi had hired Dakota to assist with the set-up for the party. No one else remembers seeing the man but then several officers are out of town at the moment. I can't see that when he left town factors into Lacey's kidnapping. If he was still here then maybe he did help Hank, but that is unconfirmed at this time. I'll ask you again Lacey if you know where your guests are?"

"I do not consider them guests Timothy. Jess lent them his car and so I guess they are out on the town. Hopefully, they will not show up tonight, but then I do not know what that woman has up her sleeve. I think there is an ulterior motive for her showing up here."

"What would that be Lacey? I thought you believed that she came just to annoy you?" I asked.

"I think perhaps Richie can answer that question better than I can." Lacey smiled at him. "What do you say Rich? Why are Miranda and August here; no one else from the theatre world is and I thought you weren't going to publicly announce the date of the service."

Richie pulled his chair up next to Lacey and put his hand over hers. "I told you that they followed me here and that is precisely what happened. The announcement of Arthur's death had made all the tabloids. Of course they had a field day with it." Richie produced a clipping from his wallet. "I carry this around with me just to remind myself how idiotic and biased the press can be." He read the article.

"Arthur King, playwright, producer, entrepreneur and the gay partner of fellow magnate Richard Stevens, was found brutally murdered in the small hamlet of Kings Crossing which is located in the far north of Canada. It is unclear at this time why he was there. It has been verified that Mr. King's wife, Lacey King, whom is also a partner and prominent figure in the "off-off Broadway" scene was found standing over the body with the murder weapon in her hand. She is in police custody in an undisclosed detention centre. Rumour has it that there was much tension and jealousy between the three partners. Mr. Stevens has refused all interviews at the moment. His whereabouts for the time of the murder has been brought into question. Uncertainty runs high as to what role he played in the demise of Mr. King. A ménage a trois indeed!"

Lacey broke out laughing. "Oh Richie, that is priceless! I don't know whether I should be flattered or insulted. But you were only questioned that once right?"

"Yeah, apparently it was only you the authorities were interested in. Anyhow, no mention of the service here was leaked. My secretary Betty, released a statement to the press stating that there would be a celebration of Arthur's life to take place at the Treatre in late June. I suppose that Miranda could have gotten wind of the memorial here if she contacted the local newspaper, but I suspect it was from my lips alone that she learned of it. You and I were on the phone discussing the date and time when she barged into my office. Betty had stepped out for a few minutes and had not secured the door. Do you remember the day that I ended our conversation rather abruptly…well, she is the reason why. I did not know how much she had heard but it came abundantly clear when we came face to face at the airport. In all honesty Lacey, I don't think she came just to spite you. Perhaps it is her way of forgiving you and Arthur."

"You are too kind Richie. She will go to her grave hating me. I hope I am alive to bury her."

"It's high time someone told me what's going on. These two don't seem willing to share so what say you enlighten me regarding this vendetta James?" I ordered.

"Oh Jesse, there is no vendetta. It's all in the past and has no bearing on today."

"Of course it doesn't Lace and that is why you keep saying that Miranda has an ulterior motive for being here. Anyhow, I was talking to James."

"All I know is that Arthur and Mom disagreed about a role Miranda wanted and she was not happy and said they conspired against her. I honestly thought she had broken all ties with them and then she shows up here like all is forgiven. I doubt there is much more to it than that Jess."

"See Sweetheart, there is nothing to worry about." Lacey smiled but I was not convinced.

CHAPTER 12

Finalities

Jess

We said our goodbyes to Hilda and Arthur in intersecting tributes Saturday, May 29th with Reverend Stevens officiating. The church was filled to capacity. Those who had been turned away lined up on the lawns and heard what they could through the open doors. Security had been doubled and the majority of the guests had been approved with a nod of the head by scrutinizers like CC, Sam, Laura, Tim and many other family friends. I had brought in my own security team from Vancouver. They were former military personnel. I had selected these four as I had used their services before. I had hired them for the week ahead as I had been informed that the R.C.M.P might be pulling their detail off Lacey and the properties Monday morning. If that did happen then we would have to come to a decision one way or the other if we still believed that her life was still in jeopardy, so I needed to be prepared.

Lacey sat in the front pew flanked by Richie and James. Blythe, Harry, Ainsley, Clara Brankco and CC and Sam and two officers occupied the rest of the seats in the row. I was to sit in the row directly behind Lacey with Leah, Vivian and Timothy and his parents, Miranda and August. I had my hands on Lacey's shoulders as Reverend Stevens entered the room.

"I need you Jesse, I need you!" She cried turning around and reaching for me.

I was on my feet in a flash. Richie moved over so I could take his place next to her. She didn't say a word just crumpled into my arms. The congregation was silent. I gave her a few minutes to compose herself and then asked her if we could carry on and she said "yes". I nodded to the minister. I don't think I heard too much of what he said as I was too concerned about Lacey. She had been cheerful, even joking this morning as she gave everyone their final instructions for the luncheon. I had asked her what my job was to be and she had said that it was to wait on her hand and foot. She had held up valiantly through all the ordeals of the past week and a half and now the finality of the horrible ordeal had finally sent her crashing.

After the final hymn was sung Reverend Stevens reminded everyone of the luncheon at noon at Tudor House and asked everyone if they would respect the family's privacy until then. James, Richie and I supported Lacey as we exited out the rear door and scrambled into one of the security cars. She was still holding on to me for dear life. When we reached the grounds I offered to carry her inside.

"I will have my throne if you don't mind. And, who do you think you are…Superman?"

"I'll be whoever you want me to be, you know that."

She caressed my face. "Thanks Jesse, I don't know what came over me back there in the church. I just suddenly felt so cold and alone like I was back in that tin shed and I needed to feel your warmth. Did I make a spectacle?"

I laughed and held my thumb and index finger out. "Little bit, but what the hell are funerals for if not a little drama? I was more than glad to offer you sanctuary. Are you okay now?"

"I am and I hope someone recorded the ceremony because I didn't hear one word of it."

I told her I was sure someone did but in actuality, I hadn't a clue. She complained that she was too hot in the dark blue suit that she was wearing and so I wheeled her into the bedroom and helped her change into a pale blue cotton dress. We met Miranda, {who had dressed the part, long black dress, veil and hat and of course, sunglasses to hide her tear ridden eyes} awaiting us in the kitchen "August and I did damage control so no need to worry about the gossip. You did put on quite a show though didn't you Lacey? Arthur would have cast you for the part of the grieving widow."

I came to Lacey's defense. "That was completely uncalled for Miranda. You can't even begin to imagine what Lacey has been through. I believe you owe her an apology."

Lacey laughed. "I really don't give a damn what anyone thinks about me but I know it wasn't for my benefit was it Miranda? You saw it as a chance to put yourself in the limelight and the mourners as your audience. You view the whole world as your stage don't you? By the way Jess, Miranda does not apologize nor does she accept an apology. Can we please go outside and get some air? I think most people will be directed into the garden patio so let's go there. Too-da-loo Miranda; give my regards to Broadway."

I couldn't help smiling; those two really had the monopoly on cattiness.

I would estimate that two hundred or more showed up for the luncheon. I was introduced to so many people that my head was spinning. Approximately fifty had names that I remembered from my youth. Lacey held up for an hour and a half. I was in the process of helping her into her wheelchair when CC appeared and starting making peculiar faces at me and gesturing with her hands. I couldn't make heads or tails out of her antics.

"Do I look like I understand sign language CC? What do you want to say girl?"

Lacey had her arms around my neck and mine were around her waist. I lowered her into the chair and she asked CC what was going on.

"So much for me trying to be discreet…Marsha is here Jess and she's asking for you."

"What? You have to be friggin kidding me!" I lashed out as if it was CC's fault.

"Don't kill the messenger Jesse. Go and talk to her; it's time. CC, will you find James so he can help me into the house please." Lacey patted my hand as I leaned down to kiss her. "Be gentle Darling; I love you."

I found Marsha sitting at the picnic table in the front yard. As usual, she was prim and proper in a tweed pantsuit that I thought was a little too warm for the day. I sat down on the opposite side of the bench.

"What are you doing here Marsha?" I asked rather aggressively.

"Seeing Mohamed wouldn't come to the mountain, I came to him to find out what the hell is going on. Would you care to explain, and who is that little buxom filly I saw you kissing?"

Without hesitation I answered. "Her name is Lacey and I've fallen in love with her again."

"What, what did you say?" Marsha gasped.

I couldn't have been anymore callous. "I'm sorry you had to see that Marsha, I had no idea that you were watching. On the other hand, I have nothing to hide. I never dreamed that you would show up here, but seeing that you are, you have saved me the trouble of coming back and telling you of my plans."

"What do you mean coming back…are you saying that you are staying here?"

"Perhaps and perhaps not; that is up in the air right now. But let me make one thing perfectly clear…wherever I am I will be with Lacey."

"What on earth are you talking about? What are you not telling me? Who is this Lacey person anyhow…oh God, please tell me you are not having an illicit affair with her?"

I interrupted her. "I'm telling you now. Did you not hear the word "again" Marsha? I have been in love with her before just as she was with me. We were teenage sweethearts and had every intention of marrying. I'm afraid I made a big mistake back then and I let her go, but that is not going to happen this time. Look, none of this is your fault, but you have to agree that our marriage has soured and besides passing in the hall on the way to our separate bedrooms, there is nothing between us that is worth saving."

"I do not have to agree to any such thing! It was your decision to move out of our bedroom, not mine. How long has this thing been going on for? Have you been unfaithful to me for years?"

"Marsha, I was never unfaithful nor did I even think about it. Apparently, I was content to live in a loveless marriage until I stepped foot in Kings Crossing and saw Lacey. I can't go back to the life I had. Lacey is my life now and I am crazy in love with her."

"You're crazy all right! Just how stupid do you think I am? What kind of a woman takes up with another woman's husband when hers isn't even cold in the ground?"

"I don't think you are stupid Marsha. I will give you the bare facts and you can think of me what you want because I am not coming back to you." I felt a tugging on my sleeve.

"Grampa Jesse, Daddy wants to know if you know where the tool box is."

Marsha gasped. "What did he call you?"

I ignored her question. "Why does he need the tool box Harry?"

"Gramma fell down in the bathroom and the door is locked and Daddy needs to open it. Can you get her out Grampa?"

I picked him up and said. "You betcha; let's go rescue Gramma." I turned back to Marsha "Yes, you heard right; Harrison is my grandson. I will send Vivian out to keep you company until I get back."

"Vivian? What is she doing here?"

"If you ask her nicely I'm sure that she will tell you."

I found James standing at the bathroom door with Bly and Vivian discussing how to remove the door. "What do you think Jess, take the hinges off?"

"Vivian, your mother is out in the front; please go and keep her company."

"What, why is she here? Do I have to?" Viv was not pleased but she huffed and left.

"I see you found the toolbox; hand me the hammer please." I called through the door. "Are you all right Lace?"

She said she was. I asked her where she was exactly and she replied that she was on the floor wedged between the toilet and the wall. I told her to stay there.

"Very funny." She retorted.

"Cover your eyes just in case any wood goes flying." I ordered as I tapped lightly on the flimsy panels of the old door. Satisfied that a good whack would shatter the one closest to the doorknob I gave it a heavy wallop with the hammer and sure enough it splintered. I reached through it and undid the lock and opened the door. "What are you doing down there Lace?" I asked.

"Waiting for you." She replied.

"I thought as much. Are you hurt?"

"I don't think so. I guess the brakes weren't on and when I went to get in the chair it took off and I fell and it kind of landed on me. I managed to get it off me but couldn't seem to push it far enough away to have any room to right myself."

James and I managed to get her up without too much difficulty. She swore she wasn't hurt and told me she was sorry

I had been interrupted because of her stupidity and that I had better get back to Marsha.

"I think I have told you at least a dozen times that I am not going back to her."

"You know what I mean Jess."

"Yeah, I do. Do you think you can stay out of trouble until I get back?"

She promised she would.

Vivian was only too glad to be relieved of sitting with her mother. She asked me if Lacey was okay and then she said that Marsha wanted her to go home with her.

"I insist she comes home with me. She has no business being here in this house of ill repute, murder and mayhem. Have you lost all sense of morality Jess? How could you invite your own daughter to sleep under the same roof as you and your whore? There is no arguing the point; she is coming home with me!" Marsha stood up signifying that she was done and she was taking Vivian with her.

"Sit down Marsha, we are not done here!" I had enough of her name calling. I am not a violent man but at that moment, I wanted to slap the mother of my children "Vivian, do you want to go home with your mother?"

"You know I don't Daddy."

"Very well; you are nineteen and so I think you can make up your own mind. Now run along; your mother and I have unfinished business. Keep an eye on Lace for me will you?"

Marsha was still standing. "This is unacceptable Jess! How dare you order your daughter to keep an eye on your trashy lover?"

"Daddy is not ordering me to do anything. For your information I am here because I want to be. And Mother, Lacey is more of a lady than you are portraying right now and it's a pleasure to know her. No murder was committed in this house and my brother would not take kindly to you calling his mother such vulgar names! Have a safe trip home Mother."

"You get back here Vivian, right this minute! Are you going to let her talk to me like that Jess? Brother, grandson, what is going on here?"

"She didn't say anything derogatory about you Marsha; you are the one doing the name calling. You could not be any further from the truth regarding Lacey. It was I who pursued her; she did not encourage me in any way. She fought me and tried to get me to go back to you but eventually she confessed that she had never stopped loving me. The truth is that she only married Arthur to give her baby a name and he wanted to give his mother a grandchild. Their marriage was a sham as he was gay and always had been, but he helped make a life for her and her son James. I will be eternally grateful to him as he was more a man than I was and due to my ignorance and stupidity I missed the first twenty four years of my son's life. I have two grandchildren, Harry and his sister Leah; she is three. I love our daughters and I do not regret the time we had together but my life with you is over and I want you to give me a divorce."

"You think I am going to give you a divorce just like that? Well think again because it is not going to happen. Last week I had a home, a husband and two daughters and now I have nothing. Do you really think that I will make it easy for you? You are very naïve Jess. She says you have a son and grandchildren… have you taken steps to prove that she hasn't been pulling the wool over your eyes? Have you already taken a paternity test?"

I shook my head. "There will be no testing; James is my son."

"Just because you want something to be true doesn't make it so."

I pulled the pictures out of my pocket and handed them to her. Reluctantly she looked at them.

"This doesn't prove anything. Anyone can write whatever they want on the back of a photo."

I handed her the last one. "This is James when he was twenty-one."

Her demeanour did not change. She laid the photos on the table in front of her. "So, she has a picture of you when you were that age…it still doesn't prove anything."

"I was long gone from the Crossing by then. James is my son and the girls have a brother.

They have met him before. Leigh has been in contact with him for a six or seven years; she just didn't know he was her brother."

"What in tarnation are you talking about?"

I told her the story. She did not blink one eyelash.

"This is a story for the tabloids isn't it? 'Prominent lawyer's seedy past is revealed. His sleazy lover who is the prime suspect in her homosexual husband's murder deems he is the father of her bastard child. He has taken up with his former mistress and illegitimate son in the murder house. Wife and daughters left to fend for themselves."

I stood up. "Say what you want about me Marsha but don't you ever call Lacey or James vulgar names ever again! For the girl's sake, do not drag this through the mud. If you can't, then you had better get yourself a good lawyer. We are done here; it's time for you to leave."

Harry was tugging at my sleeve again. "Grampa, do you know where the hospital is."

"Of course I do; what's up?"

"Daddy and Uncle Richie took Gramma there and they wouldn't take me with them."

I did not look back at Marsha as she yelled. "I will never grant you a divorce Jess…**never!**"

We had parked our vehicles at Canterbury to make room for the guest's cars at Tudor House.

Harry and I set off down the path. He asked me what a divorce was.

"Do you remember when I told you that I was married to your Aunt Vivian's mother? Well, I can't be married to two women at the same time and so I have to get a paper from the courts saying I am no longer married to her and then I can marry your grandmother. Do you understand?"

"Kind off, but she said she wouldn't give you a divorce Grampa?" Harry sounded confused.

"She will; you let me worry about that. Now let's go see how badly your grandmother is hurt."

I retrieved the spare key I kept taped under the front fender of my car as I had not wanted to go through the house for my main keys. Harry thought that was a good hiding place and asked me if I had anything else under there. At the hospital we found James and Richie sitting in the waiting room. I asked them where Lacey was.

James jumped up. "She didn't want to disturb you Jess; don't be mad at her."

"I'm not, but you should have told me; where is she?"

"Third curtain down in emerge." Richie volunteered.

I took Harry's hand. "Let's go find your grandmother."

I pushed open the doors not bothering to ask permission to enter the ward. I opened the curtain to find Dr. Macey standing over Lacey. Harry ran to her bedside.

"Gramma, Gramma, are you all right? Daddy wouldn't let me come but Grampa brought me."

She assured him that she was just fine and looked at me pleadingly. "I'm sorry Jesse but I…"

"I know; it's okay. How bad is it Doc?"

"She has a new wound to contend with now but it is like before; she will heal. We've cleaned the cut and applied a light dressing. I debated whether to close the incision with a few stitches but decided against it. She will be ready to go as soon as I am sure the pain medication is taking affect but I do I want to see her back here tomorrow."

Harry gave her a kiss. "I love you Gramma."

"I love you too Honey and I am sorry if I worried you. Are you angry with me Jesse?"

I smiled half-heartedly at her. "A little, but as long as you are okay, that is all that matters. Come along Harry, let your grandmother rest. We'll see you back at the house Lacey."

I heard her say to the doctor as I closed the curtain, "I've done it again, I've alienated the man I love. What is the matter with me Doctor?" Her voice was woeful.

I gave James and Richie an update and James and said that I was taking Harry for a little ride if he had no objections. He said he didn't and hoped that I wasn't too angry with him. I told him I wasn't but that he best not keep anything regarding his mother from me ever again.

Lacey

I was home a full hour before Jesse showed up. He found Vivian and me in a tearful embrace in the family room.

"What's this all about?" He questioned.

"Oh Daddy, you're back." Vivian said getting up and hugging her father. "Just girl stuff, that's all. I think I will go and find James and Richie as they are walking the dogs. Where is Harry?"

"He ran off to catch up to them. Shut the door will you Honey?"

Jesse sat on the arm of a chair across from me looking at me. "You're still angry with me aren't you? You know why I didn't tell you don't you? I really thought I would be home before you even knew I was missing."

"How did that work out for you?" His voice told me he was more hurt than angry.

"Not very well. Are you going to stay way over there? I could really use a hug…"

"Me too." He said. He came and knelt on the floor at my feet and put his arms around me. I kissed the top of his head and told him to come and lie down on the couch and put his head in my lap. He did. I reached down and kissed him on the lips. "How did it go with Marsha? You don't have to tell me if it is too stressful to talk about it right now."

"It's not stressful at all. I told her like it is. I had no trouble telling her that we love each other and that we are going to be together. She had a few choice names for you like "buxom little husband killer". Vivian and I both set her straight on that. I told her I wanted a divorce and that she should get a lawyer. She pretty much said that hell would freeze over before that happened."

"Oh Jesse, I am sorry. What on earth possessed her to come here anyhow?"

"She just wanted to know what was going on. Well, now she knows. I didn't break it to her very gently… in fact I was down-right cruel and she told me so. I don't believe a divorce will be forthcoming Lace. Are you prepared to spend the rest of your days living in sin with me?"

"How can it be sin when we love each other so? A piece of paper isn't going to make any difference in the way I feel about you. Are we clear on that? I am sorry that Marsha won't let you go because I know you want to marry me. I am sure she loves you in her own way and I know all too well what it is like to lose you so I am sure she is hurting. I hope she will be all right driving home."

"You shouldn't worry about her. Let's just put it aside for now. How about you tell me what you and Vivian were crying about?"

"She told me about the boy she was in love with several years ago and that you were the only one who comforted her when he broke up with her. She said you understood because you had lost a love once too and that one never forgets their first love. She said that she now knows that the girl you were talking about was me. Is she right?"

"I think you know the answer to that Lace. You need to be patient with me as this is an all-consuming love that I have for you. I need to know where you are at all times. If you feel that I am smothering you, well, you are just going to have to deal with it because that's the way it is!"

"Oh Jesse, I love you so!" I cried.

He sat up and took me in his arms. "So it is okay then …I can be possessive and demanding and you'll be all right with that?"

"I'd agree to anything you ask of me Jesse because I couldn't bear to lose you."

"Hey, hey, hey," He said. "I don't want you to be my slave, well love slave maybe. I don't want you to change from the feisty, hot-tempered woman that you are as that's the woman I fell in love with all over again. Until this assassin is found and behind bars I am going to be ever vigilant and concerned for you, do you understand?"

"I do, but you know he may never be found. The police have no new leads and it might just be that this assailant has committed the perfect crime. The more I think about it, the more I think it was just some random assault and that murder was not the intension at all. Perhaps it was only a robbery that went terribly wrong and it has nothing to do with me at all. Isn't that a possibility?"

"I'll grant you that it is a possibility, but not a very probable one. I see where you are going with the robbery thing seeing that this house was broke into right under our noses. But, you are not thinking that this young thief is responsible for Arthur's murder, are you?"

"Well, maybe not him…"

"No, I still believe this act was plotted in advance; the evidence supports my theory. The motive and perpetrators have yet to present themselves, but believe me, sooner or later, they will show their hand."

"You sound sure Jesse…is this from experience?"

"I'm not sure of anything; its more wishful thinking. I might just have to take you on a long vacation if this isn't resolved soon."

"That's fine with me Jesse, but you do know that if someone was indeed out to get me they could no matter where I was?"

"Not where I am taking you."

We were interrupted by a rap on the door. James asked if we were interested in having dinner.

Jesse told him to come in. "Yeah, I could probably eat. What about you Lace?"

"I'm going to stay right where I am as I am quite comfortable here." I replied.

"I'll fix you a couple plates then; a little bit of everything Mom?" James asked.

"I'm just having desserts; a piece of that decadent chocolate cake with a small scoop of ice cream and a slice of coconut cream pie and a big glass of milk please."

James smiled and addressed his father. "And you Sir, what would you like?"

"I'll have what your mother is having thank-you."

James left shaking his head. Jesse assembled two T.V. trays for us. I asked him where he and Harrison went when they left the hospital. He told me that he took him to the Creamery for an ice cream cone and then they went for a ride to our spot above the Seventh Crossing Bridge. He said he told Harry the story about us. Harry told him that he had been there before with me and that I had cried so he thought I didn't like it there. I was on the verge of tears when James came back with our orders and two side dishes of horrible green bean casserole.

Jesse rolled his eyes and made a repulsive face. "I see our son has a morbid sense of humour."

I laughed. "Believe me Jess; he hates the thing as much as we do. Be gone with you waiter and take that green gunk with you! Send the kids in when they have finished their dinner please. I haven't spent any time with them at all today."

Five minutes later Harrison and Leah came bounding in. They sat between us and helped us finish our meal of sweets. Leah climbed up on my lap and laid her head on my breast.

"I want one of these Jesse." I purred.

"One of what Lace?" He asked hesitantly.

"Dr. Macey gave me the results of the blood work he did last week. I am not in menopause and he said that he can see no reason why I can't conceive."

Jesse looked a little distraught. "Honey, would you really want to have a child that is younger than your grandchildren? We have these two perfect children and they are enough for me. We can borrow them anytime and then give them back when they tire us out. To be perfectly frank Lace, I cannot see myself raising another child? Can you honestly say that you have the stamina to go down that road? Babies don't stay that way for long; they evolve into toddlers and then little people, youths, and then teenagers. They require twenty four hour supervision so that leaves no quality time for you and me. I don't want to be a sixty year old man enrolling his child in college. James and Bly will probably not have any more children but we have Vivian and Hillary…there will be more babies Honey."

I hugged Leah. "I know Jesse, I know. It's just that I never got to raise James with you and Vivian should have been our daughter; she should have been **my** daughter." A little tear escaped from my eye.

"She already loves you Lace. I know it is not the same but we can't change things so can we just be satisfied with what we have? What do you say, are you up to a little ride around the yard before Mr. Hanson arrives for the reading of the wills? We can talk about this again later okay?"

"There is no need Jesse. I have already made the decision to have the little surgery that will enable me from becoming pregnant. I was merely fantasising."

"We are definitely going to talk later as you don't get to make that decision on your own. I'm a candidate too you know."

I didn't tell him that I had already booked an appointment.

Graham Hanson arrived at 7 P.M. He had approached me after the memorial service wanting to know if I could assemble the beneficiaries of Hilda's and Arthur's policies for this evening. He had apologized for the necessity of having to do so on this sad occasion but due to a family health crisis he had to leave town immediately and had no time line as to his return. I assured him that there would be no problem. Ainsley and Richie would be leaving town soon so it would be good to get it over and done with.

Vivian was the only one not involved and so she volunteered to keep the children occupied until their bedtime. James and Jesse had somehow found time to dismantle a wall in Arthur's room so that access to Neverland remained open. The door to the cellar had been locked and barred. Minutes before Mr. Hanson arrived, Vivian came down stairs dressed as Wendy with Harry donning Peter Pan clothes and Leah was Tinkerbelle, of course. Viv said if anyone needed her she would be in Neverland. I think she was hoping that Timothy would show up.

The first order of business was Arthur's insurance policies. I knew that he and Richie had taken large policies out on each other; more so for the business I thought. What I did not know was that Arthur had also made me and James beneficiaries to the sum of one million dollars. I clutched the arms of my chair and pulled myself up.

"I object!" I stammered.

Jesse sat me down. "This is not a courtroom Lace; you don't get to object."

"But," I protested. "I don't want the money!"

Mr. Haney chuckled. "Well, this is a first for me as I have never had anyone refuse money. You may do whatever you wish with your capital Lacey, just as soon as it is legally yours. For the time being it is being held in escrow for you until you meet the conditions demanded by the insurance company, that being until you have been cleared of Arthur's murder."

"Really, I didn't realize I was still a suspect." I shrugged my shoulders. "I don't care anyhow."

"Mom, do you think that Richie and I want the money? We'd gladly give it all away if it would bring Arthur back." James said.

"Did you know about the policy James?" I asked.

"No, not really. Arthur always hinted that I would be looked after but I never gave it much thought. I mean, he was healthy and had no addictions so who would have thought…" He let his words drift off as he was obviously becoming emotional. Blythe comforted him.

"Well, Richie, did you know?" I demanded.

He grinned widely. "Yes, I knew Lacey. You two were a team even before I came into the picture. You brought us all together, not just in business but as a family. We were both better human beings because of your love and acceptance. No amount of money can ever repay that."

Now I was ready to break into tears. "Just tell me that you haven't made me a beneficiary of your policy too?"

"So what if I have?" he winked at me.

"Well, none of you are benefactors in my policy because I don't have one!" I stated emphatically. I don't know why but everyone found that amusing. "Please carry on Mr. Hanson."

"I'm sure proof of your innocence will be forthcoming any day Lacey so we will deal with it then. I would like to start with Hilda's will first. Most of us know that she was a little bit eccentric and so I am reading this exactly as she wrote it and dictated to my secretary and myself. There were no adjustments made.

"I, Hilda Ann Jones King am of sound mind but not so of limb, make amendments to my last will and testimony on this day of our Lord, September 14th, 1998 in the presence of my attorney, Graham Hanson and his secretary, Ms. Jennifer Adams.

I am the soul legatee of the properties listed: 10 acres {more or less} depending on who is doing the measuring. My husband, God rest his soul, Clive Mitchell King, is on record stating that the properties are 10.2 acres exactly. The surveyor has the properties listed as 9.42 acres. For our purposes, we will go with 10 acres...agreed? Thank-you. This acreage was the first legally documented lots in the town site of Kings Crossing, formerly known as Cross Roads. Therefore they are listed as lots one {1} and two {2}. The property known as Canterbury or the Carriage House built in 1860 or thereabouts, occupies lot 1. Tudor

House, having been built many years later, is on lot 2.

It was my husband's wish that the lands and buildings not be divided and that they remain forever in the family. I will honour his wishes to the best of my abilities.

Upon my death which I feel is only too imminent, Arthur Clinton King, son of Clive and Hilda King is to inherit said lands and dwellings. If for some ungodly reason, he is to precede me in death, the properties will pass on to his son, James Arthur Monroe King.

Though dwindling rapidly, there remains a monetary supplement for the upkeep of said properties that passes on to the inheritor. The Royal Bank in Kamloops is the guardian of these monies.

Now, for my personal possessions and capital: To my estranged daughter, Ainsley Marie King, I bequeath one hundred thousand dollars {100,000} and whatever interest has accumulated over these many years that the money has been kept in trust for her.

We all heard a loud gasp escape from Ainsley. James put his arm around her. "See Auntie, Gramma never forgot you."

Mr. Hanson cleared his throat before he spoke. "No one knew this but Arthur and I, but I kept tabs on you for your mother. Her way of asking about you after you made contact with your brother was, "Is all well?" I would merely answer "Yes." She would nod and say. "Good."

He took a sip of his coffee and continued with the reading of Hilda's will.

To my daughter-in-law, Lacey Monroe King, I leave the contents of my personal safe. Within it are my treasured keepsakes that Clive presented me with over the years that we were married and perhaps a dozen bonds...the exact amount or their value I do not know as I have been unable to access the safe and its contents for some years now. I have never had any of the jewels appraised as there value was never of any importance to me, but in today's market, I am sure they will fetch a fair price. I have the contents of the safe insured for two million dollars. Lacey and my grandchildren have been a very bright light in my life and I trust that she will see that some of the monies received from their sale will go towards the children's schooling. I am particularly fond of my grandson's wife Blythe, and she is to have whatever she fancies from my jewels. Otherwise, Lacey may do whatever she wants with the stash. There is one provision however. When Ainsley was a very young girl, I found her in my bedroom playing with some of my jewellery that I had left lying around. I scolded her and told her that she was never to enter my room again. As I recall, she was particularly fond of a red necklace and bracelet set. It is my wish that she be given this set now that consists of a necklace, bracelet, earrings, brooch and ring. It is kept together in a black pouch that is marked thus: Blood red ruby, 10th anniversary gift

from Clive. Also, Ainsley is to have whatever furnishings, nick-knacks, etc. that she wants from Canterbury and the dome room.

The whereabouts of the safe is as follows: It is behind a hidden door to the left of the bay window in my former upstairs bedroom. A portrait of our children conceals the trigger to open the door. The combination is 1947.

This is all I have to bequeath. I will go to my maker knowing that I have done my best to preserve the King legacy. Live long and enjoy your inheritance my children.

Hilda King September 14, 1998

Ainsley was crying and kept saying over and over that she should have tried to make amends with her mother. There wasn't anything we could say that would ease her distress. Mr. Hanson gave us time to try and console Ainsley and then asked us if we would like a few more minutes to absorb and discuss Hilda's will before he commenced with Arthur's. I remarked that I was surprized that she had the contents of the safe insured for such an astronomical sum and at the moment had no further questions for him.

"Very well then, let's get on with Arthur's will. I have not made this known to any of you before but he phoned me prior to his coming to Kings Crossing. He had the feeling that he would not make it home in time before Hilda passed away and indeed, he didn't. He had asked me if I had his will handy. He wanted to know if he had named James as sole benefactor to all the properties and monies listed in Hilda's will. I told him that was right. He said he wanted to amend it to name you, Lacey, as co-benefactor with James. I told him there was no problem. He asked if I could have it ready for his signature when he arrived and I assured him that I could."

I interrupted. "Why would he have done that? We had discussed it and had agreed that James would be the sole benefactor..."

"Mom," James said teasingly. "I don't mind sharing with you."

"That's not it James... I mean why did he feel he had to have Mr. Hanson change it immediately?" The question was meant for the notary.

"I asked him the same question Lacey. He jokingly said that planes crash every day and that he had been derelict in keeping up with his policies and he just needed to know that everything was in order."

"So, it wasn't just me then?" Richie's voice was strained.

I asked him what he meant.

"I thought that he was way too irritable before he left. I asked him what he was so worried about and he said he didn't like leaving me all alone with the new production. I saw right through that and pressed him for another explanation. He finally yielded and said that he had a sickening feeling that things were not going to go well in Kings Crossing. I reminded him that his mother had not been well for a long time, but he said that wasn't it, but he couldn't explain the uneasiness he felt. He started to say something about a curious visit and then abruptly stopped and started to laugh and explained it all on the flying jitters. I had never known him to be skittish of flying ever before; have you Lacey?"

"You think whoever visited him was responsible for his irritability... oh, my God, do you think he foresaw his own death?" I half whispered.

Jesse took my hand. "Don't get yourself worked up Lace. I'm sure Richie didn't mean to insinuate anything of the sort and you told me that Arthur was very upbeat the last time you talked to him didn't you?"

"No, I didn't mean to suggest any such thing Lacey. Arthur never believed in premonitions. I talked to him only hours before his death and there was no indication in his voice that anything was wrong. There is this one thing though…I've gone over that conversation a thousand times in my mind and sometimes I swear I hear a doorbell ring while we are talking. He never said that someone was at the door, but I have agonised over and over again wondering if the killer was indeed waiting to be let in." Richie looked right at me and I could see that he was very distraught. I stood up and Jesse, very astutely helped me shuffle my way over to Richie. I put my arms around him and asked him why he had never mentioned that before and he answered that he hadn't wanted to upset me and it was probably his imagination running amok.

"I think we need to talk about this okay? You may be suppressing a clue that may very well point to Arthur's killer… what do you say?"

He nodded in agreement. I thanked Mr. Hanson for coming and said I would be praying for his family. Jess, Ainsley and James walked him to the door. Bly left to check in on Viv and the kids.

That left Richie and me alone to talk. He went over the days leading up to Arthur's arrival in the Crossing but could not offer any more of an explanation as to why he thought Arthur had been acting strange. He said that he had pressed Arthur for information as to who his mysterious visitor had been but Arthur had laughed and said that there was nothing mysterious about the visitor at all and to forget that he had mentioned it. I suggested that he might have to think about hypnosis in case he was subconsciously suppressing information that might lead to a suspect in Arthur's slaying. He agreed and would certainly consider it.

Everyone arrived back in the living room at the same time. James and Ainsley were carrying a large chest. They set it down in front of me. I told them to open it. The contents were pretty much as I had expected…necklaces and earrings and rings in gold and emerald and diamonds and many other precious stones. Each set was in its own little black velvet bag.

"Have at it girls," I said. "I am not the least bit interested in anything for myself. It has been a very long day and so if you will all excuse me, I am retiring for the night."

"I'm with you Honey. See you all tomorrow." Jesse said as he helped me into my chair. We had a big group hug and left them sorting out the contents of the chest.

Richie walked with us to the bedroom door and kissed me. "Look after her Jess."

"You never have to worry about that Rich, but you need to let us help you get through this too."

"Believe me, you are Jess. Just knowing that Lacey is safe and loved is all that matters."

I cried myself to sleep in Jesse's arms.

CHAPTER 13

The Final Performance Exit-Stage Left

Jesse and I arrived back at Tudor House with a clean bill of health. Doctor Macey said that I was healing very nicely. Jess's stitches had all dissolved as expected and he would probably have full use of his arm in a week or so. The doctor asked us if we had had a chance to discuss our "family situation" yet.

"Jess won." I said. "He convinced me that we don't need any more children and I hate to admit it, but he is right. We have everything we need and he will be coming in to see you soon. He won in that department."

"Very wise decision Jess; I will set up an appointment for you."

"So that is it?" I said to Jesse on the way home. "You'll have the procedure and there will never be any chance that we will have another child?"

"I thought that we had made the decision together…have you changed your mind again?"

"Maybe." I answered.

We walked into the living room and found Miranda prancing around as if it was her stage and in her mind I was sure she thought it was. She held out her arms to me and Jesse.

"Oh, there you are you two! I was just putting on my acting face for your family. I have ordered dinner for you from a nice restaurant we found up town…just my little way of thanking you for your hospitality." She smiled sweetly.

"That is very kind of you Miranda, but totally unnecessary." I smiled back.

"You're welcome. Ainsley and Vivian were asking questions about my acting career. They wanted to know what my favourite role was, how many times had I worked with Arthur and Richie and if I always the leading lady. I told them I had been in their productions four times. That's right isn't it Lacey? I think they may have opened up a kettle full of rotting fish." She laughed. "What do you think?"

Jesse looked at me curiously as he walked out to answer the doorbell. He returned with CC and Sam. "Good," I thought, "reinforcements." I was hoping that Miranda was not going to play the role of the wounded victim over again, but of course I was wrong.

Sam and CC took a seat next to Timothy and James on the sofa. Bly, Viv and Ainsley were squeezed in beside one another on one of the loveseats. Harry and Leah were playing on the floor behind the other unoccupied loveseat. August was sitting in an armchair as was I. Richie was just standing in the doorway. Jesse sat down on the arm of my chair. He had a smug look on his face.

"Aha, and the cats are coming out to play again… am I to presume?" He whispered to me.

I cursed him in a hushed voice and told him to be quiet.

The girls had made iced tea and served it to us all with some of the left-over goodies.

Miranda continued as though she hadn't been interrupted. "To answer your question Vivian, I have had the leading role in four productions at the Treatre on Concorde."

Richie and Arthur owned three theaters. The Treatre was the main one where most of their plays were performed and was located in metropolitan New York. The other two were lesser playhouses, one in Manhattan and one in Sherbrook and were usually rented out to small companies. Schools and charitable organizations were among the groups that they subsidized.

Although I had a small percentage in the company I was not overly active in the everyday operations. I preferred to think of myself as a "sounding block" for their ideas. I often proof read the scripts but had very limited input into the actual theatrical productions. Arthur also came to me from time to time if he was uncertain about whom to cast in a certain role. I could only offer my opinion on actors whom I was familiar with. He was very big on gambling on unknowns and I usually agreed with him. Richie preferred to take a secondary seat in the interviews leading up to the auditions but was always in attendance for the final decisions. The three of us had only had one major disagreement for a leading role and I very much feared that Miranda was about to cast me as the villain to her losing that award winning role. It was all water under the bridge as far as I was concerned but I knew that she still held me responsible. If I knew her at all, and I did, she was about to chastise me once again and this time in front of Jesse and my friends as Ainsley had just asked her the leading question.

"Did Arthur and Richie call you when they had what they considered a perfect role for you?"

"Oh no, my dear; it very seldom works like that. There are always dozens of actors chomping at the bit for even a little part. It was to one's advantage if they had already made a reputation for themselves with the producers…sometimes. We, as actors read many scripts and discard most of them as rubbish. But then, along comes the role you were destined for and even though you had proven yourself many times before there is always the dreaded audition. Arthur would never hire anyone on their laurels…oh no, you had to prove yourself every time and just because you knew you were perfect for the role didn't mean a thing, did it Lacey?"

Miranda's amiable smile had faded into one of contempt as she glared at me. I sat back in the armchair and muttered to Jesse. "And, here we go; prepare yourself for a monotonous soliloquy."

He squeezed my hand.

Miranda nodded to Richie. "I never held you responsible for my losing the "Lucy" Richie. It was **their** doing."

August stood up and suggested to her that it was time to leave.

"You know Miranda; you can't lose something that was never yours in the first place. It's way past time for you to let it go, and now you need to take your leave and get the hell out of our lives!" Richie said coolly.

"I'll never let it go. You know I would have been brilliant as Savannah and the "Lucy" would have been mine. I will never have another chance thanks to Arthur and Lacey."

I barely heard Ainsley ask Blythe what a Lucy was, but Miranda did.

She flung up her arms. "Just the most prestigious tribute voted on by one's peers! It is awarded to an actress in an "Off, Off Broadway" production! That little nobody who won it stole my thunder thanks to your brother and his "so-called wife!"

There was wrath in her voice and I heard the music playing in my head.

"That's enough Miranda!" Richie cautioned her. "Though I didn't agree with Arthur's decision initially, he made the right call. His reasons were all valid. You are not the southern civil war heroine type, your coloring and statue was all wrong for the part. You would have had to gain twenty pounds and spend hours every day being made over, not to mention the countless voice lessons as you couldn't pull off the southern accent. The timeline was a big factor…you know all of this Miranda, so why are you still harping on it?"

"Don't play the innocent bystander in all of this Richie! It's time that you owned up to admitting that the real reason I didn't get the part was because little Miss Lacey wanted the role for herself!"

James jumped in to defend me though there was no need to. "Get off your high horse Miranda! You know damn well that Mom had no aspirations to be on stage. The only time she stepped in was when someone fell ill and couldn't fulfill their commitment."

"I see you have had the wool pulled over your eyes too. Have you forgotten that she was the understudy for the role of Savannah?"

"That's only because you refused it." James stated through clenched teeth.

"I never knew you had such an active role in the theater Lace. Have you actually been on stage?" Jesse asked me a little hesitantly arching his eyebrows.

Miranda answered for me. "Oh, she's been on stage all right; she's just not very good at it. Why don't you tell everyone how that play bombed Lacey?"

I had pretty much had enough of her pettiness." Just a minute, just a damn minute! Where do you get off coming into my house and ranting and raving like a bloody lunatic? I could care less what you think of me but you leave James and Richie out of your accusations and don't you dare ever let Arthur's name escape from your foul mouth ever again!" I fought through the pain racing down my leg as I righted myself to face that spiteful woman.

Jesse grabbed my arm. "What are you doing Honey?"

My eyes met Miranda's and I heard the music playing again. I whispered to Jesse. "Get me the recorder and the tape." He questioned me and I answered. "Yes, now please."

He saw that I was determined to remain standing and asked Richie to support me and left the room saying he would only be a minute. Miranda asked me what I was up to.

"I should have paid more attention to that role you played as a vicious scheming murderess. "The Adulteress" wasn't it, your first and only shot at the silver screen? You tried to duplicate the act in real life didn't you?"

Jesse returned with the recorder and put it on the table in front of me. I asked him to turn it on. As soon as it started playing Richie looked at me curiously. Something clicked for him as it had for me and I was sure he had made the same connection as I had because he collared August who had started baking up towards the door.

"Hey, where are you going buddy? Don't be rude; Lacey isn't through talking yet and I for one want to hear what she has to say. Aren't you curious?"

"No, I don't mean to be rude but we have a plane to catch… come on Miranda, it's time to go."

Miranda and I hadn't taken our eyes off one another. No one knew exactly what was happening but I am sure they knew a show-down was in the works. They were about to find out who was the better player…her, or me. I was pretty sure that I had truth on my side but it was really all a bluff to intimidate her enough to trick her into confessing to Arthur's murder. The big question was how had she pulled it off?

Jesse was supporting me around my waist so that I wouldn't falter. He whispered, "Breathe, honey, breathe."

I exhaled. "So, what was your master plan Miranda? What went wrong? Were you interrupted or did Arthur put up a fight? Did you and your accomplice not have time to plant more evidence implicating me, or did you think that my finding Arthur's body would be enough? How could you… how could you plunge the dagger deep into his heart and watch him die gasping for life?"

A hush came over the room and everyone's eyes were on her expecting her to deny what I had just accused her of. She just stood there in her tailor made chartreuse shirtdress trying to stare me down and then she threw her head back and laughed.

"I think you've been overdosing on your meds Dearie. Kill Arthur…me? Have you run out of suspects and so to save your own bacon, you think you can stand there and accuse me? Well, you have got another thing coming lady because I don't have to be insulted from the likes of you. You're right August, it is time to go. It's been a pleasure people." She said sarcastically. She picked up her bag from off the floor and took one step forward before Timothy halted her.

"Hold on Miranda, I don't think we are finished here yet. Lacey, do you have something more to say; what's with that macabre music for starters? Am I wrong to assume that only the two of you and maybe Richie and August have some bizarre connection to it?"

"That piece of music was composed expressly for her role in "The Adulteress" over three years ago. I am almost positive that it was never released to the public. Who would have bought it anyhow? Ms. Desoto here, exited to that grisly piece of gobbledygook after she had committed two murders; that of her husband and her producer slash lover in that trashy movie. She left the tape playing for me in the den at Canterbury because she knew I would be the one to discover Arthur's body. Sorry Timothy, I kept that piece of information from you because it was mine and mine alone to figure out. One thing escapes me though Miranda; why didn't you burn the house down like you did in the movie or were you planning on setting it on fire with me in it? What went wrong with your plan Miranda?"

She started laughing. "I see your little mind has been working overtime again. I am so sorry I have no more time to listen to your crazy delusions…"

I interrupted her. "I'm afraid you are going to have to postpone your trip back to New York indefinitely. I suspect you will never leave Canada and will spend the rest of your life in one of their fine institutions…oh, you too August." I watched him struggle under Richie's grasp.

"Stop with the theatrics Lacey, this story is even more hair-brained than your last one."

I played my trump card. "You still can't accept that Jorge loved me and not you, can you?"

Her body pulsated as she reached into her handbag and pulled out a gun and pointed it at me.

Jesse sat me down so fast I didn't have time to react. "Stay there and don't move! Who the hell is Jorge?" He turned and faced the crazy woman holding the gun. "You'll have to go through me before you can get to Lacey."

Richie stepped in front of him. "And me, and your pretty boy toy too." He said as he pulled August over to stand in front of him.

Timothy was on his feet. "Lower that weapon Miranda… NOW!"

She turned and pointed the gun at him. "I don't think so and you are in no position to me giving me orders. Now sit down and be a good little policeman for I have no problem sinking a bullet into one of Canada's finest RCMP officers! Actually, I probably have enough ammunition for the whole lot of you… "She threatened waving the gun around the room. "Now do I have everybody's attention? No one else here needs to get hurt do they Lacey?"

"Give it up Miranda, the gig is up. Those three sturdy men will be on you like white on rice the second you fire." Richie nodded to Timothy, James and Sam. "You won't get a second shot."

I tugged at Jesse's shirt. "Let me up, it's me she wants; please Jesse."

"Shut up Lacey and don't move a muscle." He ordered.

"People, people, people…what is wrong with you all? Has she got you all fooled just like she did Jorge? She promised him the moon and where is he now…in an asylum rotting away. I feel for you the most Jess as she is going to trample all over your heart and then sit back and laugh. She's the black widow always on the prowl for her next victim. I'll be doing you all a favour by putting a bullet in her black heart. Move out of the way, all of you… NOW!"

"I'll take my chances with her Miranda. You don't get to take that choice out of my hands. I've already taken one bullet for her and I'll gladly take a dozen more but I promise you one thing…with my dying breath I'll choke the life out of you and send you straight to hell!"

Tears stung my eyes as I kept tugging at him. "Please Jesse, please…"

"Jess is right about one thing and that is that you are going straight to hell and if I can help send you there I won't hesitate." Richie hissed. "Lacey is the exact opposite of you; sweet and caring and lovable. She puts everyone's happiness before hers. If it wasn't for her, you'd already be dead. That's it, isn't it Miranda? It's not only that she vetoed you from getting the role as Savannah, it's because Jorge left you for her. Luckily for you, that she discovered his psychopathic tendencies before he put his plan into motion to kill you. Well, that doesn't matter anymore because you have thrown your life away all for revenge. I hope they have the electric chair in Canada because I want a front row seat watching you fry."

"That's a lie Richie; he was never going to kill me! He was momentarily distracted by that she wolf." Miranda hissed. "He would never hurt a fly let alone me. He was coming back to me but she couldn't bear that he had rejected her and so she made the whole story up and set him up."

"Yeah sure; Lacey beat herself black and blue, half strangled herself and then handcuffed herself to the bed. If we hadn't found her…God, you disgust me." Richie started walking towards her still holding August as a shield.

Jesse turned and looked at me. There was a tear in his eye. "Oh Lacey, tell me it's not so?"

"Not now Jesse, not now." I needed to see what Richie was doing. "Please Jesse, let me up, I need to stop Richie before he gets himself killed!"

"I told you to sit still and I mean it…I'll sit on you if I have to!"

He moved to one side so that I could see Richie advancing towards Miranda. She had backed up a couple of feet.

"Don't make me shoot you Richie; I have no bone to pick with you. Please get out of the way."

"You know I will gladly die for her… She is all that I have left since you took Arthur away from me. Tell me Miranda, how it felt when you drove the dagger into his body; were you enraptured or did you have one moment of remorse? What were you thinking as you watched the blood spill from his body? Did you look into his eyes and watch the light fade out of them? What were his last words Miranda? I hope he got the last word as he cursed you to a life of darkness and misfortune. Death for you would be too easy."

"Richie, Richie, listen to me, just listen to me. How could I have killed Arthur…I have never even set foot in this little hamlet before this week. Do you really think that I am that heartless? Just because Lacey says I did it doesn't make it so. Where is the evidence? No, this is a fallacy created from the mind of a very deluded woman."

"Why are you holding a gun then Miranda?"

It was then that Leah started to cry and ran from behind the couch into her mother's arms.

Miranda waved the gun around again. "Keep your sniffling little brat quiet Blythe or I'll do it for you. Where is the other one…Harry, where are you?"

Jesse started to move as we became aware that Harry was standing not five feet behind her. He was winding up his toy helicopter. We all heard the whirr. Miranda turned, but it was too late…the plane hit her in the small of her back and she screamed and was thrown off balance. Timothy, James and Sam tackled her to the floor. The gun lay at their feet.

"Get Harry, get Harry!" I cried.

CC got to him first and brought him to Bly. "Am I in trouble for hurting that lady Mom?"

We all laughed. "Get over here Buddy." Jesse reached out for his grandson. "He's not in any trouble is he Mom? You're our hero Harrison; you saved us from that bad woman. What made you aim the heli at her anyway? That was really quick thinking Son."

"She called my sister a brat and she called my grandmother a really bad name."

Timothy sent Sam to collect the officers standing guard outside. Richie had a choke hold on August. James held Miranda as Timothy slapped his handcuffs on her. To get her out of the room they had to come pretty close to me and I took another chance.

"I need to look her in the eyes Jess, please help me to stand." He nodded and pulled me up. I took two steps in her direction and ripped open her shirtdress. She squealed. Before anyone could question me I explained. "Appendectomy, I think not! That bandage is too small to be covering up major surgery isn't it Miranda? That's where Arthur stabbed you with his silver letter opener isn't it? I knew something was missing from his office but up until this minute I couldn't place what it was. Where is it, where did you bury it…is it in the bottom of the pit?"

I turned my head just as she spat at me.

"I wouldn't try that again if I was you lady!" James warned her.

I told Timothy that the unidentified blood that was found on the carpet would no doubt be a match to hers. He nodded and told me that we would be talking more about that tape but for now he would have to confiscate it. I said I wanted nothing more to do with it. I detected a certain degree of teasing in his voice when he asked me if I was keeping any more crucial evidence from the police. I told him I would have to think on that for a while. Jesse assured him that I wasn't. He left with the two prisoners but was back again within two minutes.

"August is singing like a songbird. He says he'll tell us everything if we give him a deal. Sorry that I have to ask you this Jess but we're going to need a lawyer present to make it all legal. Do you think you would be up to sitting in on his deposition?"

I said loudly and forcefully that no damn way was Jesse going to be August's lawyer.

"And, there is no damn way that I would take him on as a client either honey. I'll only be present to make sure everything is legal. We wouldn't want his confession to be thrown out because he didn't have representation. We don't even know at this point how much he was actively involved in the plot and the actual deed or even if he was."

"OH," he was involved all right! I'll bet he even had a hand in the actual stabbing. But, you go Jesse, but on one condition… we get to hear everything he had to say when you get back."

"I can't promise you that Lace, you know that."

"If you are not going to represent him then how can it be client confidentiality?"

Timothy took my hand. "Lacey, I promise you that by the end of the interrogation you will have answers…maybe not all of them, but enough, okay?"

Jesse pulled me up into his arms. "I could have lost you today Lace. Why did you have to confront her the way you did? Why didn't you tell Timothy of your suspicions and let him handle it?"

"It had to happen the way it did Jesse, it just did. I wasn't sure of anything… not even when I saw her reaction to the chilling music. I just had to attack her, I just had to."

"I know Baby, I know." He scooted me over and sat me down between Vivian and Ainsley. "I trust that you two will keep her from doing anything rash."

"Jesse!" I protested.

He blew me a kiss as he followed Timothy out. "I love you too. James, I think your mother deserves a drink; it isn't every day that someone solves a crime, especially one that absolves her of murder."

Richie was on his feet. "You're not leaving without me. I think I have the right to be there when August is questioned."

"You really don't Rich," Timothy said. "but, come along, we'll see what we can do."

"So," I moaned. "I guess the rest of us will just sit here and drink and twiddle our thumbs."

"Lacey, are you going to tell us about this Jorge character and what he did to you?" CC asked.

"It is a sordid tale and I will tell it once and only once, and that's when Jesse gets backs."

"Mom, are you sure you want to go through that again?" James asked as he passed me a drink.

"It was a black time in my life and I thought that I had dealt with it but perhaps I haven't entirely. Jesse will not be satisfied until he knows what happened and having you all here will give me the courage to do so." I quickly changed the subject and asked James what he had made me to drink.

"It's your favourite, bartender's root beer and it is very weak. It's been hours since you took one of your pain meds isn't it?"

"Yes, thank-you; I will sip it very slowly. Have you and Bly had a chance to discuss where you are going to live?"

"There is nothing for us in New York Mom. I have the distinct feeling that you will be staying right here in the Crossing and there is plenty of room for us all right here at Tudor House."

"Well, you are right about that but Jesse and I have not made any decisions yet as to where we will be living. I can guarantee you though that it will not be very far away if I have my say."

"I know Daddy wants to be close to his new family Lacey and I do too. Bly and James have told me I have a home here as long as I want." Vivian smiled at her brother.

"I think your father wants you to finish your schooling Honey." I reminded her.

"Timothy tells me that there is a perfectly good college in Kamloops and who knows, maybe James and I will be attending it together."

"Aha, Timothy, I should have known." I teased.

Vivian blushed ever so slightly as she admitted that he was an added incentive to her staying.

"There is just one thing left to discuss then James…what are we going to do about Canterbury?"

"As far as I am concerned I'd like to see it burn to the ground." James admitted.

"We are in agreement then. I would like to see it lying in a heap of ashes also but because it is a heritage building I think we will have it torn down. Town's people will be welcomed to take a piece of the first house built here home as a souvenir. Would you be okay with that Ainsley?"

"I think that is a wonderful idea Lacey. It is a grand old house and I once loved it but that was many, many years ago. My brother's life was taken so cruelly there that I want to take an axe to it myself and I will rejoice when the last brick has fallen."

"Amen." I said.

Two hours later Jesse returned. He sunk into the arm chair next to me looking thoroughly exhausted. I asked him where Richie was. He said he was "collecting himself" which I took to mean that he was having a cigarette. I asked him if Richie had been allowed to sit in on the deposition and he said "no." Sergeant Lewis had been informed of the happenings at Tudor House and made certain that everything was conducted legally. Richie could watch from outside the interrogation room but he couldn't be privy as to what was being said. He was allowed to present us with a list of questions to ask August however and they did prove to be invaluable.

Vivian vacated her seat next to me and offered it to Richie when he joined us a few minutes later. I took hold of his hand and wondered how much Jesse had already told him. He smiled half-heartily at me. I knew the anguish he must be feeling as he told Jesse to get on with it.

"Okay," Jesse started to chronicle August's testimonial. "here's what I can tell you all. August says he first became aware of Miranda's fixation on getting revenge on Arthur and you Lacey, about a year ago. Apparently she had started plotting something sinister for the two of you right after the role of Savannah won awards. However, she didn't follow through with anything because she met this fellow Jorge and fell in love with him." He looked at me and a painful frown crossed his face. I said nothing and told him to continue.

"It sounds as though she was so enamoured with him that she had no time or desire to continue on with her plans of punishing you and Arthur. Do you remember when she brought him to the Treatre Lacey? She wanted to tell you that she and Jorge were going to be married and were moving to Los Angeles to pursue their acting careers. Apparently she wanted to tell you that she held no hard feelings towards any of you…do you remember that Lacey?"

I nodded but wondered why his voice sounded accusing.

"August said he was not present but she had told him later that you appeared jealous of her happiness and made eyes at Jorge?"

Jesse formed it as a question? "Why are you making this about me Jess…I thought we were here to hear how the two of them murdered Arthur not to picture me as the scarlet woman?"

"I'm sorry. I guess I want you to deny that you were out to steal Miranda's fiancée …"

The room was very quiet. James moved in my direction. "Jess, what the hell…?"

I was seething and tears stung my eyes. "I see you can't wait to hear about my relationship with Jorge so you are suggesting that I am the real reason that Arthur is dead! It doesn't matter that he tried to kill me. I will not sit here and listen to any more of this garbage from you Jesse James Jameson!"

I started to get up but Richie stopped me. "Jess is just trying to contradict August's suggestion that you wanted Jorge for yourself. I know it is not so, but he wasn't there…"

I couldn't look at Jesse. "He's blaming me for something I had no control over." I sobbed. I buried my head in Richie's chest. Then I felt him move and strong arms pulling me away.

"Come here, come to me Baby."

I fought him. "Get away from me, don't touch me. I hate you right now! Marsha was right; you are a cruel son of a bitch!"

He held on to me so tightly that I couldn't move. His lips were on my forehead. He whispered.

"I'm sorry, I'm sorry. Please don't hate me; hate the lawyer in me, but not me…please. I don't give a damn if you were interested in this Jorge Honey; I am just trying to get to the facts. August's word doesn't mean a damn thing if we can't corroborate his story. Can you tell me what happened to make this man try to kill you?"

I struggled to breathe and he released his hold on me a little.

"I'll tell you the whole sordid mess if you quit berating Lacey, Jess." Richie volunteered.

"I'm sorry if you all think that's what I was doing. Lacey keeps everything bottled up inside of her and the only way to draw anything out is to anger her. I knew she was keeping something from me the night she woke up screaming for someone to let go of her hands. I figured that it was Hank who had restrained her but she said it wasn't and clammed up and we never spoke of it again. So yes please Richie, enlighten me as I don't believe Lacey is going to."

I told him through clenched teeth that I was going to tell him everything but that he had cruelly taken that opportunity away from me by accusing me of stealing Miranda's fiancé. I asked him to let me up so that I could go and be with my family. He told me he didn't want to.

"Well then, you are no different than Jorge because you are holding me against my will."

He relinquished his hold on me and went and stood by the window overlooking the town.

"Lacey had no romantic feelings for Jorge. She thought he was a bore and as far as I knew never even thought of him as even a friend. Unfortunately, that was not the same for Jorge. He was infatuated with her. He would come to the Treatre hoping she would be there. If she wasn't he would ask us where he could find her. We always said that we didn't know but he would hang around hoping she would show up. He invited her out with him and Miranda on dates. She usually declined but sometimes joined them at Miranda's insistence. I'm sure she was testing the two of them. This went on for several months and then he broke off the engagement to Miranda and she did go a little crazy. She came to Arthur and me accusing Lacey of unspeakable things. She was in a rage and we were fearful of what she might do and we talked Lacey into going to visit her parents in Nova Scotia until the whole thing blew over. It was pretty naïve of us to even think that Miranda would ever stop blaming Lacey. Unfortunately, no one knew that Jorge was unstable and that it was him we should have been worried about. I just thank our lucky stars that it was the day we were to drive Lacey to the airport that he showed his true self…"

I had composed myself somewhat and reached out to Richie. "It's all right; I can take it from here. I want you all to know that this man is my saviour, him and Arthur."

Jesse turned to face me but I did not acknowledge him.

"I had just finished hauling the last of my suitcases to the living room when there was a knock at the door. I yelled that it was open. Jorge walked in with a big grin on his face."

"Don't you know that it is unsafe to keep your doors unlocked even in the suburbs? One never knows what crazies are out there? How are you my darling?" He asked.

"I was more than a little surprised to see him as I had no idea that he knew where I lived. I found out later that Miranda had told him. She said that he had come to her and told her that he wanted her back but he needed to tell me that it wasn't going to work for us and he needed to tell me face to face. She suggested he do just that. I have no idea how she knew my address."

Richie said he suspected that she had followed me when she was stalking Arthur and me.

"What…she was stalking us? Never mind, it doesn't matter anymore."

"It could in the case against her motive for killing Arthur." Jesse said.

I ignored him. "Jorge tried to kiss me. I asked him what he thought he was doing and he said kissing the woman he loved and that we should take it into the bedroom. I panicked a little. I offered to make me and him a drink thinking that I could hold him off until Arthur and Richie showed up. He said that he didn't need any aphrodisiac and that I was all he needed. Then he said that we had one little problem though and that was Miranda. He said that she threatened to kill me and so we had better get rid of her first and so we had better get busy and come up with a fool proof way to do so. Stalling for time I asked him what he had in mind. He said we should talk about it in the bedroom and I told him that now was not the time for romance and that's when he lost it. He produced a switchblade from inside his jacket pocket and jabbed it at me."

Jesse started towards me. I glared at him and he stopped and sat down next to Vivian. His eyes were begging me for something but I didn't know what. I looked away.

"Jorge pushed me in the direction of my bedroom and told me to lie down on the bed. "You thought I came here to kill Lacey for you didn't you Miranda…ha, ha, ha, the jokes on you. I lied, it's her I want and I can't trust you and so guess what…you're it!"

"He put his knee on my chest holding me down while he pulled a pair of handcuffs out of his pants pocket and forced them on me. I tried telling him that I was Lacey and not Miranda but he just laughed. "Lacey and I have been planning on doing this for a very long time and she will be here soon to help me finish the job."

"He yanked the top sheet off the bed and ripped it into pieces and bound my legs and arms to the bedposts and lewdly suggested we have a bit of fun first. He started peeling the buttons on my blouse open with the knife and that's when I screamed over and over as loud as I could until he hit me full force in the mouth, then on the rest of my face. He held the knife to my throat and said. "I see you like it rough…well, I am here to oblige you." He laughed like a hyena.

Vivian was crying and clinging to her father.

Bly was on her feet, tears streaming down her face. James tried to restrain her but she brushed him off and directed her animosity towards Jess. "Do you have any idea what you have done? She was going to play down the whole ordeal but no, you had to incite her into reliving it in living color all over again by suggesting she was in love with that monster. I am so disappointed with you right now that I can't even look at you! You are not the man I thought you were. Come on Mom, you don't have to do this anymore."

"It's done my darling, it's over now. Let me finish for I am all right." I hugged Bly. I continued. "He was just about to bear my breasts when Arthur yelled from the front door asking where I was. Jorge held his hand over my mouth. "We're in the bedroom, why don t you come and join us?""

I bit his hand and yelled at Arthur to call the police.

Jorge hit me hard and said that now he was going to have to kill Arthur too. He got off me and met Arthur at the bedroom door holding a much bigger knife on him. I have no idea where it came from. He directed Arthur over to the side of the bed and told him to lie down next to me. He said something highly suggestive as he pushed Arthur on top of me. It was then that I heard glass breaking and Richie came crashing through the French doors and coldcocked him. My life was saved that day by two very best friends and I'll love them forever."

Now it was time for me to address Jess. "Are you satisfied or do you want to hear more details about my attempted rape? And, for the record, I never had any feelings, romantic or otherwise for that despicable man. You can get on with August's confession now." I turned away from him and asked James to pour me a glass of water.

Jesse beat him to it. He handed it to me and asked if he could have a few minutes alone with me. I said I had nothing to say to him.

"Well, I have a lot to say to you. Please Lace, give me five minutes." He begged.

"I thought you only wanted a couple." I was not yielding but everyone took my words as such and vacated the room.

Bly asked me if I was sure. I nodded for her sake though I was still far too angry with Jess to be alone with him. It wasn't his questions about me and Jorge that upset me so much, it was the accusing voice in which he had delivered them. I had once loved him and so I guess I had better listen to his reasoning. Just a minute…did I just say, "once loved him?"

"May I sit next to you Lace?"

"My name is Lacey and no one calls me Lace. Someone I used to love who called me that but he is gone and I don't think he is ever coming back."

"He's still here Lace and he always will be. You have to know that I would take back what I said if only I could but Darling, believe me, I was not accusing you of anything. I realized the second I spoke that you were going to take it the wrong way and you did. It wouldn't have mattered to me if you did have feelings for Jorge. You told me about your other beaus so why didn't you tell me about him?"

Now he had really angered me. I pushed him away. "What part of **"He was not my boyfriend do you not understand?** He meant nothing to me so why would I even mention his name. It was a very unpleasant time in my life…I just wanted to forget it. But you want to know all the gory details and so I will tell you."

"I've heard enough Lace; I don't need or want to know anymore."

"You opened up the door and so you are going to listen whether you like it or not and then you are going to go to our room and you are going to pack up your belongings and get the hell out of my life and my house!"

"Lace…"

I ignored the pleading in his voice. "My battered face was plastered all over the tabloids. Don't ask me how they got the police photos for I do not know nor do I care. I was humiliated on the witness stand because I am a woman and maybe I was asking for everything I got…" I couldn't hold back the tears any longer and I did not resist Jesse's arms. He cried with me and rocked me until my sobs subsided. "It was my family that got me through it. The trial was worse than the attempted rape. My lawyer said that there should never have been a trial and the jury agreed. That son of a bitch is now locked away in a maximum security insane asylum. Apparently, I was not his first victim. I am done now Jesse, I don't want to talk about it anymore."

"I will never ask you to Darling. Please say you will forgive me for I can't go on if you don't. You once asked me if I would fight to keep you and the answer is yes, I will fight tooth and nail for you. I know I hurt you but you must let me make it up to you. Please Darling, please don't ask me to leave."

He put his head on my breast. I could feel his heart beating a mile a minute and just like that day on the stairs I forgave him. I forgave him because deep inside I knew he hadn't intended to hurt me and because it was also my fault. I shouldn't have acted so vehemently. James poked his head in the door and asked if we were all right. I beckoned them in. Vivian entered first and ran straight to me, tears still escaping down her cheeks. I sat her between Jesse and me and we each took one of her hands.

"I was so afraid that you were going to throw Daddy out." She said sniffling.

I tried to make light of it. "I did, but he won't go."

There was a faint attempt of laughter by everyone. I apologized for going all postal and promised to behave myself. Jesse said it was him that needed to apologize.

"I know you all love this woman and objected to the way I was questioning her. I was not very tactful, but believe me it was not my intention to hurt or accuse her. I was very insensitive to her feelings. I wasn't there and I should have known better. My God, you all know how much I love her…"

"Daddy, sometimes I hate the lawyer in you." Vivian interrupted her father.

"Me too Honey, me too." He said. "And what about you Bly, do you hate me too?"

James had his arm around his wife and answered for her. "It's not in her nature to hate anyone Jess but you upset the woman who is the mother she never had, so no, she doesn't hate you but she came mighty close to renouncing you and I might add, so did I."

"I could not bear to have that happen. Please tell me what I have to do to get back in your good graces. I can't promise you that your mother and I won't have disagreements now and then but I can promise you that I will always love her and do my best to take care of her."

"We know Jess, we know. No hard feelings okay?" James got up and shook his dad's hand. Bly just nodded.

"What about you Richie?" Jesse asked warily.

"Well, I was about to take her and run off with her but I guess I will just sit back and wait for you to make another blunder. You're skating on thin ice my friend."

"Thanks for the warning ole man." Jesse said wryly. Then he told Vivian that there wasn't going to be anymore crying today. He moved closer to me and took my hand. "I want this freaking day to be over with. Shall we get on with Miranda's and August's plot to commit what they thought was going to be the perfect crime? They made the age old mistake…they returned to the scene of the crime. Why; did they think they left crucial evidence behind, the tape, for example or did they simply come back to gloat? Lacey, are you up to it or do you want to leave it for another day?"

"No, and I think we are all in agreement; let's get on with it and don't spare any details!"

Jesse asked Vivian to change places with me so he could be close to me. He took my hand.

"I'll be as brief as possible. August pretty much talked non-stop. He wanted us to know that none of what happened was his fault…it was all Miranda. He thought she just wanted to play a prank on Lacey and Arthur and never dreamt that it would escalate into murder. He says she conned him and because he loved her he went along with her plan. Yes, she wanted to get back at Lacey and Arthur for denying her, as she put it, "the role of a lifetime", but when she met Jorge she abandoned that idea but wanted them {Lacey and Arthur} to know that she held no grudge against them. She often invited them to join her and Jorge for dinner until she realized that Lacey was after her man…his words Honey, not mine." Jesse apologized. I told him I knew and to continue.

"When Jorge broke off their engagement she knew it was because of Lacey and once again she sought retaliation but this time it was much more sinister and "murder" crossed her lips. Then that thing happened with Lacey and Jorge and she had to let it go as Jorge was in jail and there was going to be a trial. She testified in his behalf but he was deemed mentally unstable and sent to the Lothom Psychiatric Institution. Every time she came back from visiting him her hatred for Lacey intensified and she set the plan in motion to murder Arthur and frame Lacey. He pretended to go along with her plot but never thought she would go through with it. There was no way she could get away with killing Arthur as everyone knew there was bad blood between them and she could very well be their number one suspect. He told her that and she said no one would suspect "us" because it was going to take place in some little hick town that Arthur once lived in. She said he was always going back there. He had no idea it was way up here in Canada. But first she had a lot of fences to mend and she had to get back in Lacey's and Arthur's good graces. That didn't go over too well but she said she had laid the ground work and it was time to set the plan in motion. Sergeant Lewis asked him when all of this plotting took place and he answered right away saying that it was in the spring of last year. He knew that because at the end of June they were on a plane to Vancouver British Columbia and were here in this town on July first."

He was asked how he could be so sure of the date and why did they go to Vancouver.

"Because we arrived here and it was a holiday…something like Founder's day…yeah, that's it; it was Founder's Day because we came to Canterbury."

At that Jesse said he had to interrupt and asked if August was telling them that this was not their first visit to Kings Crossing or to Canterbury.

"That's what I said. We rented a car in Vancouver and drove here and found out that it was that holiday and that people opened up their old homes to the public. It fit right into Miranda's plans…in fact, she was downright ecstatic. She was a little disappointed that Tudor House was not available for viewing because Mrs. King was under the weather. However, she had given her permission for people to walk the grounds and take photographs and that is where we met this woman who knew all about the Kings. Miranda somehow signalled her out and this woman agreed to send the local weekly paper to her and keep her informed of Mrs. King's health. He wasn't sure of her name but thought it might be Maude. He described her as an older unkempt woman who needed the assistance of a walker to get around. Timothy and I knew at once that it was Mrs. Hanks."

"So," James interjected. "they had already cased Canterbury and the yards? I wonder who was in charge of the people running amuck in the house."

"I don't know for sure Son but I imagine it was someone close to Hilda like Clara Brankco."

"Well wouldn't she have recognised them when she saw them last week?" James asked.

"We asked August that same question and he laughed and said that we didn't know crap about actors did we. I assume he meant that they wore disguises."

"Yeah, I guess you're right. Sorry for interrupting Jess."

"Don't be and if anyone else wants something clarified or wants to ask a question please don't hesitate to do so. Okay then, back to the story according to August. Apparently, Miranda paid Maude a thousand dollars cash on the spot and promised her more if she kept it between the two of them and came forth with more information. August said that he knew of only one phone call and that was when this Maude woman called to let Miranda know that Hilda was in the hospital. It was then that Miranda went to see Arthur. She told him that she wanted a part in his next play and he told her he had no time to discuss anything with her as his mother was on her death bed and he was off to Kings Crossing that night. So off they went to Vancouver again, rented another car and drove here the next day. August says he just accompanied her but had nothing to do with the actual execution and so he is no way responsible for Arthur's death."

"Really Jess, he said that? He knew about the plan from the get-go and is just as culpable as her. He is even stupider than I thought if he thinks he is going to be spared from going to prison just because he didn't pull the trigger, you know what I mean…What kind of a deal is he trying to broker anyhow?" I wanted to know.

"That I cannot tell you, but believe me when I tell you that he won't be getting off Scott-free."

"There are still too many unanswered questions. How did they know that Arthur would be at Canterbury? How did they know that I was arriving that very day? They must have been covered in blood…" My voice was breaking as the nightmare of that day was on me again.

Jesse pulled me close to him as he was the only one who really knew what I had walked into on the darkest day of my life.

Richie stammered. "I am to blame there Lacey. Remember I told you that Miranda had come to my office at the Treatre barging in past my secretary pretending to be concerned for Arthur because he had told her that his mother was very ill. It was the day after he had left. She asked me why you didn't go with him and I told her that it was none of her business but you'd probably be going tomorrow. I'm sure it was then that she decided to set her plan in motion and was on the first available flight to Vancouver so that's on me."

I tried to tell him that she would have found out one way or the other but he was having none of it and continued to admonish himself for letting that she devil wheedle my plans out of him. He said he was positive now that she was the unidentified visitor who had unnerved Arthur.

None of us said anything for a few minutes. It was like we were all preparing ourselves for the final revelation…how August and Miranda maliciously ended Arthur's life. I had been there already so I knew I could handle it but I wasn't at all sure if Richie could. He told Jess to end it and don't leave anything out. Jesse looked at me for confirmation and I nodded and whispered for him to be gentle.

"They knew Arthur was at Canterbury because Miranda phoned here and there was no answer so she dialled Canterbury… this was from a phone booth. Arthur answered and she hung up and they drove over there immediately. I will try and remember August's exact words."

"We didn't drive right up to the door because Miranda didn't want Arthur to hear us coming. There was an all-terrain vehicle blocking the road anyway. She rang the doorbell. Arthur called out that it was open and to come in. To say that he was totally surprised to see Miranda and I would be an understatement. He came out of the den carrying a letter opener; I did not like the looks of it. We stayed on the carpet runner at the door. He asked us what the hell we were doing there and Miranda said that we were on a little fishing trip and wanted to stop in and say hello. He laughed at that and said: "You expect me to believe that?" She said: "No, but would you believe this?" And then she stabbed him. He said: "What the…?" and staggered a little and she let him have it again. I looked away but not before he jabbed her with the letter opener. She grabbed her stomach and yelled at me to help. I told her I couldn't but she kept yelling and saying I was in this up to my eyeballs so if I didn't want to get caught I had better make it snappy. She told me to grab his arms. I did and she stabbed him again and he reeled and staggered off down the hall. She yelled at me to follow him and make sure he was dead and then to bring her some towels from the bathroom…we had made sure we knew where it was when we came for the open house. She was bleeding profusely and made me take the "tape" from her movie and put it on the stereo and to make sure I hit the button so it would play continually over and over. I checked Arthur again; he was most definitely a goner."

Richie covered his mouth and ran from the room. James went after him.

"I don't like this role as chronicler." Jesse said flatly and got up and walked over to the window.

James returned a few minutes later without Richie. He just shook his head.

Jesse turned. "So they loaded up the rug with her blood all over it and loaded it into the quad. August drove it up Sugarloaf and attempted to bury it and dumped the quad into the ravine. She picked him up in the car. They drove somewhere, cleaned up and changed clothes. They threw their bloody clothes and gloves into the garbage bags they had brought and dumped them somewhere in the Fraser canyon and drove back to Vancouver. Miranda saw a doctor at a clinic and he gave her antibiotics and didn't ask any questions. That's it; I'm done."

He opened the French doors and walked outside and down the front steps.

James asked Blythe and Vivian if they would help me get ready for bed and then he went after his father. Ainsley offered to do the clean-up. I thanked her and the girls and I went looking for Richie. We did not find him but the dogs were gone and so I figured he must be off with them.

After I had washed and changed into a nightgown I sat down with my daughter-in-law and my new daughter on the bed and we all had a good cry. I didn't think I would ever stop but I told them that I had to get it over and done with before Jesse came back because he was going to need me but then perhaps he was done with me because I had been so horrid to him.

"Oh Mom, you never have to worry about that! I think he just needs a few minutes to collect himself. It was very hard on him to have to relay the nauseating details to us. I am so sorry that I attacked him…"

"Honey, you were just coming to my defense. He knows it was all in the heat of the moment."

"Lacey is right Bly; Daddy is a very forgiving man. And I know he loves you." Vivian told her.

"I can vouch for that; he has forgiven me so many times already that it is becoming a ritual."

"I think that maybe you had a lot to forgive Daddy for too, didn't you Lacey?"

"We are still finding our way with each other. It's not easy for me as I have always been my own keeper and so having someone other than James and Bly love me and care for me is almost foreign to me. I was never able to fall in love or be loved by anyone after your father and I am afraid I am failing miserably at this commitment that I have made to him. He is very patient with me but how much contrariness can one man tolerate? I do love him with all my being and I couldn't imagine life without him ever again." Of course I started to cry all over again and that is how Jesse found us.

"How come every time I leave you girls alone I come back and find you in tears?"

"Oh Daddy, you big boob, you know girls cry a lot especially when there is a man involved?"

"I hope I am not the man anyone is crying over." Jesse said looking at me sadly.

I managed a little smile and sniffled and asked him if he had seen Richie. He said they had caught up to him on the hill and that James was still with him. He came back to see how we were faring and met Ainsley coming down the stairs saying that Leah needed her mother. He said he would leave me and Viv to our girl talk and started to leave but Bly corralled him and said that he was also needed by a certain someone. She nodded in my direction and told Jess that she was sorry and that she loved him and called Vivian away with her. Jesse hugged the two of them and said something I couldn't hear but I imagine he said. "I love you too."

I had crawled under the blankets thinking that he would crawl in beside me but instead he lay down on top of it and put his head on my chest.

"I am so ashamed of myself Lacey and I won't blame you if you don't want me in your bed ever again or want anything more to do with me." He lamented.

I cradled him in my arms. "You have nothing to be ashamed about my Darling. It was a horrendous day and things were said and feelings were hurt, but it's over now, it's all over."

He asked me if I forgave him then and I laughed and said. "To love is to forgive…always."

June 3rd

Jesse and I were leaving Kings Crossing tomorrow on a trip across country. He and Harrison had gone on one of their secretive missions yesterday. We were all out in the front yard when they arrived back at Tudor House a few hours later in a huge motorhome. Harry informed me that it was called a coach. Okay then. They stood there at the door grinning from ear to ear.

"Look what we got for you Gramma!" Harry said.

"Oh, you got this for me did you? You don't really think I can drive this big rig do you?"

"No, but Grampa can and he's taking you on a trip."

"Really…and just where is he taking me pray tell." I asked playing along.

Jesse reached for my hand and helped me up the steps and James gave me a boost from behind.

"I thought we would give Ainsley a ride home and then take a jaunt across Canada to see your parents with a little side trip to Montana." Jesse said watching me closely for my reaction.

"Sounds wonderful, but why would we be going to Montana?"

"You know perfectly well why Lace."

"I've told you a dozen times Jesse that it doesn't matter anymore. I don't need to hear what Mavis might and might not confess to."

"But I do Honey."

"All righty then, it will be done." I knew then that his peace of mind was more important than any hard feelings I was still harbouring towards Mavis.

A few things had come to light over the past few days. Maude Hanks was indeed the guilty party who had relayed information to Miranda. She also knew about the underground tunnel that Hank had used to get in and out of the house without being detected by the surveillance team. Apparently her husband, fearing a nuclear war in the early fifties wanted an escape route in case of an invasion by the Russians. He had plans to build a bunker but they never materialized. Her explanation for not informing the police about its existence was that she simply forgot.

In a roundabout way we had asked Ainsley about Hilda's connection to Clifford Roper. She laughed when we told her that we thought he and Hilda may have had an affair. She assured us that they did not and that her mother never had eyes for any man but her father. She could not speak for him though as he seemed to "have to be out of town a lot." She then surprised us and said that Clifford had been her boyfriend. Even though he was much older than her they had planned on one day being together but his wife became very ill and he could not, would not, leave her, so that was that. She had renewed her friendship with him a few years ago.

We had received a phone call from Mr. Hanson about the improving progress that his nephew was making. His real reason for calling was to tell Jess and James that Arthur had left letters for them and he was sorry that he had forgotten to mention it. James picked them up immediately.

The letters, curious enough were only dated May 16th. It appeared as though Arthur had penned them just before his fatal trip to the Crossing. He told each one of them the truth about each other. He apologized saying that he had kept the truth from them long enough and he needed to right the wrong because it appeared as though I was never going to own up to. He prayed that I would forgive him and that things would all work out. We would never know why he had decided to make the truth known. His death was all so senseless.

On a lighter note, Arthur asked Jesse if he remembered the essay he had him and his friends write for their initiation. Jesse laughed when he read that Arthur had resurrected them and was planning on bringing them to the stage. The play would definitely be a comedy and he would need sign-offs from all those who had participated in the project and could Jess help him track down all those involved. I told him that I knew where that manuscript was and would ask Richie if he would see that Arthur's vision was fulfilled.

Richie had returned to New York. We talked every day and would visit him on our return trip home. Our plans were to go there after visiting my parents in Nova Scotia. I already had a buyer for my day care centers and so there was just the house to deal with.

We had already contracted Canterbury out for demolition. If Miranda had managed to set fire to the house there would have been no need to do so but then I guess I wouldn't be her either. Even though August says he had no idea if it was her plan to incinerate the house with me in it, I believe it was her intention to do so, but Arthur and the letter opener may have saved my life. August says he never saw it again. Do I believe him or is it somewhere up Sugarloaf with the boot tray? Their trial is scheduled to begin in September. Unfortunately, all my family and friends will be called to testify. I am not looking forward to being in court again.

Vivian found us all in the family room and came and squeezed in between Jesse and me as she was accustomed to doing lately. "I'm going to stay home tonight with you; Timothy and I can go to the movies any old night but this is our last night together for a while so I want to spend it with you."

"We'll miss you all too but you'll be so busy with the kids and Timothy and getting to know your big brother that the time will just fly." I assured her.

Jesse and I planned on building a new house where Canterbury once stood. It would be our tribute to Arthur. James was very pleased with my decision and couldn't ask for anything better than having his parents live next door. Timothy arrived and we talked Vivian into keeping her plans as we were going to be busy packing.

"By the way," Timothy said. "Hank's alleged phone has not been recovered yet. The river is still too high for the divers and so it will be a month or so before it can be searched." He turned to me. "Lacey, no such phone exists as you described it and there is not one registered in Hank's name. He has no account with the phone company and only the house phone is billed to Mrs. Hanks."

"What's with this "alleged" thing Tim?" Jesse asked. "Lacey called me and I talked to her. James can vouch for that."

"There is no record of a phone call to this number on that morning nor is there one to your cell Jess." He directed his questioning towards James and Bly. "Did either one of you hear the phone ring that morning?"

James said that something woke him up but he didn't actually hear the phone ring but it must have as Jess was talking to someone. Blythe said she couldn't be sure.

"Well, I definitely called Jesse on the house phone as I couldn't remember his cell number."

"And, I definitely talked to her. How else would I have known where she was?"

"I think Timothy is suggesting that perhaps we had a telepathic experience …" I suggested.

"Nothing would surprise me about the two of you but you didn't hear that from me."

I asked Tim what the name of the movie was they were seeing.

He paused, chuckled and said: "Practical Magic."